The Knights Reborn

The Fourth Book in the
Crusades Series

James Batchelor

Pendant Publishing
Salt Lake City

The Knights Reborn

A Pendant Book
First Pendant Publishing Edition, December 2024
Salt Lake City, Utah

Library of Congress Control Number: 2024920066

ISBN: 978-0-9840044-8-5

This is a work of fiction. Names, characters, places, and incidents either are the product of the author's imagination or are used fictitiously, and any resemblance to actual persons, living or dead, events, or locales is entirely coincidental.

For Rachel
And all those we lost too soon
May your memory remind us to never miss an
Opportunity to love deeply, express it frequently, and
Accept every moment with gratitude for the gift that it is.

Books in
The Crusades Series

Prologue

England: Outside Dawning Castle

Anthony set down his spade in the darkness and surveyed the long, shallow trench stretching across no man's land between Dawning Castle and the enemy encampment. "This is never going to fool anyone!" one of the peasant-soldiers whispered behind him, echoing his own doubts. "They will see it in even the faintest of light."

Anthony climbed out of the trench where thirty men were still working to remove the dirt and spread it inconspicuously along the ground. He stepped back and attempted to view the field as if he did not know the ditch was there. The long channel formed an inky black line in the darkness, but that was the problem: It was too dark and too long to simply be dismissed as a natural feature of the landscape. And if there was any light at all, the enemy could not fail to notice it.

He glanced over his shoulder at the Braddock camp. The flurry of activity around the three remaining siege towers was beginning to die down. The soldiers appeared to be retiring, likely to get a few hours of sleep before dawn and the inevitable attack that would come with it. But that also meant that the enemy's attention would be turning back toward the castle, and the likelihood of someone seeing the team's movement out in no man's land or of hearing an errant scrape of a spade or muttered exclamation was increasing by the moment. This idea had been a desperate longshot anyway. If it did not work, they were none the worse for the attempt. But if Anthony and his force were captured or killed in this endeavor, that could have grave consequences for the battle to come.

Anthony turned back to the trench and forced himself to focus on the problem at hand. The trench was a device that was easily defeated if the enemy knew it was there. Their only hope of success was in the enemy's ignorance of it. They needed to conceal it, but how? Some thatching or burlap might do the trick, even some tree branches could potentially work; but he had none of that at hand and certainly not in the amounts required to cover a pit this size.

He looked over the field, but the only thing out here besides the yellowed grasses that had been largely churned into mud by the repeated tread of thousands of men, beasts, and machines, were the bodies of the enemy soldiers that had been abandoned after their last failed attack. Hundreds and hundreds of bodies …

"Hurry, men!" He whispered suddenly. "Follow me!"

Less than an hour later, Anthony led his men back into the gates of the castle, dirty and exhausted but unharmed and undetected, so far as they knew. He was just congratulating the men on a job well done when Freya, the young runner girl, raced up to him. She had evidently been waiting for him.

"Lord Anthony! Lady Dawning requires your attention at once."

Anthony hesitated. "I must see to the preparations on the battlements. There is little time before dawn."

"She said it was urgent." Seeing that Anthony was still undecided, Freya lowered her voice so as not to be overheard and added, "Lady Evelyn is dead."

Anthony stared at her in disbelief, but it was clear the girl was in earnest. "Take me at once!"

One

eil inhaled sharply and cringed at the pain that lanced through his body.

"Be still," a soft, female voice ordered.

"Ellen!" Neil croaked in relief, emotion choking off sound. "You are here! Where is Kathryn? Bring me my daughter." His stomach was on fire for some reason, but he did not care about that; it did not matter now. The nightmare had ended, and he could begin to make things right again. "Why is it so dark?"

Neil wanted to see his wife's face again, to touch her again after so long, but she made no move to come any closer. She was obviously still angry with him. "Ellen, please forgive me," he choked on the unfamiliar taste of emotion, and his voice broke. "Forgive me for beating you while in my passion. I shall never lay a finger on you in anger again! I swear to you!"

He tried to sit up. The pain was intense, but he was not going to give up. He finally had his chance to make amends, and he would take it. "I will never again breathe a word in anger to you, I swear! Only please, bring my daughter to me and let me hold my family again!"

"Sir Neil, be still," Ellen said in the same firm but quiet voice that was almost a whisper.

"Please, come to me," he pleaded, reaching for her. "Let me know that I am forgiven."

"Neil," she said firmly, though not with any anger, "I am not your wife. Ellen is ... fled; she will not return."

Like the sun burning off the morning dew, the mists of confusion over Neil's mind vanished and with them the exquisite joy he had reveled in only a moment before. His tears of loving gratitude turned to tears of despair. He let out a great cry of anguish at the realization that his family was still gone. It was like losing them all over again.

"Lie back and be still," the woman commanded in a hard voice. "Your bleeding has only recently subsided, and you cannot afford to lose anymore blood."

Neil did as he was told and draped the arm that had been extended to his wife over his eyes to try to block out this new reality that only a moment before had looked like new hope. He had no idea where he was or how he had gotten here, and truthfully, at that moment, he did not care.

"I was not sure if you would awake at all," the woman said after some minutes.

Neil uncovered his eyes and squinted at her. Something about her soft alto voice tickled the back of Neil's mind. Had he heard it before? Her long hair hung in tangled locks in front of her face, which prevented him from making out any of her features.

He looked past her at the dimly lit room for the first time. He did not recognize it. The space was large, about twenty feet long and half as wide. It was furnished lavishly, though it seemed to be in disarray, as if it had been overturned in a brawl. The gray light of early morning peeked around a shuttered window, providing the only source of light apart from a small fire in a hearth at the far end of the room. There was a lamp on a sideboard, but it was not lit. Neil was lying on the single bed in the room.

"How long?" he croaked tersely, not trusting his voice not to betray the crushing disappointment he was still feeling.

"Three days," she said, reaching over and pouring a very small amount of wine into a cup. "Drink this slowly." She held the cup to his lips while she gently cradled his head at a slight angle to keep him from choking. Even that motion hurt his stomach, but he did not complain.

"More," he croaked, but the woman shook her head, her tangled hair waving in the darkness.

"Until we know how that will affect you, I dare not give you more."

"Dawning Castle?"

"It ... will not be long now," she said in a neutral voice.

That was strange, Neil thought. He would expect a Braddock servant to be happy at the prospect of the fall of Dawning Castle and a Dawning captive to be upset by it. But she seemed to be neither. Who was this woman? She was no battle physician. But if she were not a Dawning, why was she helping him? He stopped short of asking her directly and instead said, "Where am I?" His voice was returning to normal.

"Leon's guest house," she answered simply. "It has been fortified to prevent escape."

Neil's brow furrowed at the familiar name. Who of the Braddocks would not only know the young, social-climbing noble from Dawning Court by name but also know that Neil would recognize him by name. "Soldiers brought you here unconscious."

"Why?"

"They did not explain," she said curtly. "But I assume they must have wanted information from you because they have returned each day to see if you were awake ... or dead. I'm under orders to notify the guards if you do come around."

"So? Why not inform them?"

"I am no Braddock lackey!" she hissed suddenly, and Neil's confusion deepened.

"Why do you help me?"

She busied herself with assembling the items beside his bed that she had been using to tend to him and did not respond.

Neil became aware of an unpleasant odor that seemed to be emanating from her. "Will you make a light?"

"No!" she said with too much force. Then, as if recognizing her faux pas, tried to change the subject. "How did you get here?"

Neil stopped at that. What *did* he remember? It took a moment for the fog over his memory to start to lift. He hesitated to tell this woman anything, but could it really matter? It was hardly critical information. "A group of our men went out to destroy the dam that yo—that the Braddocks were erecting to flood the foundation of the west wall." He remembered finding the dam crews already dead, but he still could not make sense of that so omitted that detail. He also left out being attacked by William. "We reloaded the wanes with the stones from the dam. Sir Timothy," he didn't know if she knew who that was but didn't care, "and I drove the wanes into the woods and were disabling them when we were discovered by the Braddock knights and chased back to the castle."

"Is that where you received your injury?"

"This? No. I got this defending the battlements," Neil said simply, realizing but not caring that that was probably creating more questions than it answered. "But this is the reason that I was unable to climb the rope back up the battlements. So I left Timothy climbing to safety, and I led the Braddock knights as far away as I could before the loss of blood caught me up. I lost consciousness believing I would wake up in the afterlife."

"Perhaps you have," she said quietly, "but if this is the afterlife, I assure you that it is not heaven."

"I am still not clear why I have been kept alive," Neil said, ignoring her remark and prying for more information.

"I do not know what they have planned for you. Perhaps they want information about the castle's defenses."

Just then, the sound of wood sliding against wood on the outside of the door reached them. "They must have heard us!" she whispered. "Pretend you are still unconscious."

With no time to ask any questions, Neil did as instructed, letting himself relax and half-closing his eyes. The woman remained in her seat, face half turned from the door and eyes fixed on the floor.

The heavy wooden door swung inward. The silhouette of a large, bulky man filled the space. "How is he?" the man asked, stepping into the room.

The woman glanced up and then did a double take. It was evidently not the person she was expecting. Neil cracked his eyelids just enough to get a look at the man, and then he, too, almost sat up in surprise. There before him stood Thomas Dawning.

Neil immediately wished for a weapon, though he knew it would not have mattered. Even if he had had something to fight with, in his condition he would be lucky if he could even stand under his own power, to say nothing of fighting a healthy knight.

"Is he awake?"

"He—he ..." the woman stammered and then trailed off.

While Neil knew that he could not fight Thomas, neither could he just lie there pretending to be unconscious. So, whether out of anger or curiosity he wasn't sure, he opened his eyes and answered on her behalf: "I am awake, Thomas."

"That is well. Are you able to travel?"

Neil opened his mouth, ready to give a caustic retort, but then stopped, surprised. Not only did the question confuse him but Thomas almost sounded concerned. "I ... what?"

Thomas turned to the woman. "Can he travel?"

"I doubt he can ride," the woman replied laconically.

"But can he travel? In a carriage perhaps? With you looking after him?"

"What is this?" Neil demanded, forcing himself to sit up despite the pain.

"We have been betrayed!"

"We?" Neil shot back.

"The Saracens have double-crossed me. Aden and his army do not know that they are about to be destroyed. Collin Braddock is in pursuit and will wipe them out."

Neil shook his head, his confusion overwhelming his distrust. "What is your game, Thomas?"

Thomas ignored the question. "You must ride out and meet Aden. Warn him that Collin is descending upon him with all the might of the Braddock army. Convince him that his only chance against Collin's superior force is to dig in before Collin reaches him."

"I see," Neil said, finally understanding. "You expect me to convince Aden to dig in against Collin to allow you time to take the castle and secure the battlements for yourself."

"It is fine that you do not trust my motives," Thomas snapped, "but Sir Aden is the castle's last hope. Deny it if you can!"

"I will not be a pawn in your schemes," Neil said, lying back again in a show of indifference.

Thomas looked as though he would burst out in anger, but when he spoke his voice was calm. "And what have you to lose by putting my assertion to the test? If you remain here, even should you escape this cell, you are of no use to the castle in your condition; yet you might save them all if you warn Aden in time! All you need do is have him dispatch scouts rearward to verify what I have said. If I am lying, you have lost nothing and gained your freedom, and Aden may simply proceed to Dawning Castle as he originally intended. But if what I say is true, Aden's only hope of survival will come in the form of your warning!"

Neil considered that. He knew Thomas well enough to know that this must all be part of some elaborate plan. The trouble was that he could not find the flaw in Thomas' logic. "Am I supposed to believe that you are simply going to allow me to walk out of here?"

"The camp is lining up to attack the castle now. No one is paying any attention to this house for the moment. If you slip away now, you may go unnoticed. But you must go now, you and the woman!"

Neil did a double take at that. Was she a prisoner too? He shook his head in confusion. He really did not understand what was happening, but one thing was certain: If Thomas had simply wanted to kill them, he would not need to go to all this trouble. He could have just walked in and crushed their skulls with his mace. They could not have stopped him.

Thomas stepped over and half-helped, half-hoisted Neil up. "There is a carriage hitched up in the courtyard, but you must hurry!"

The woman hesitated. She, too, was obviously mistrustful, but after evidently doing the same mental calculation as Neil, she placed a blanket over Neil's shoulders and slid beneath his arm to support him while Thomas moved to the door to check the passage.

He glanced up and down the corridor and turned back to them. "I sent the guards on an errand, but you do not have long. With all hands at the frontline, the road out of Dawning Court should be clear. But that, too, will change when the battle is joined. You must hurry."

The two followed Thomas' lead to the front door. Neil was not at all sure what to expect when they stepped out into the early morning chill, but true to his word, the courtyard was deserted save for a single old, open-topped carriage hitched to a two-horse team that must have been left behind when the nobility had fled.

The courtyard was on the wrong side of the house to see the camp and the front line, but just as the house blocked their view, it shielded them as well. The woman helped Neil hobble over to the carriage, but he still could not catch a glimpse of her face as her greasy, tangled hair hung in long strands between them as though she were deliberately concealing her identity.

Neil was just stepping onto the carriage when a deep gravelly voice boomed behind them, and his blood froze. "Thomas!"

Amir was entering the courtyard and walking toward them carrying William's long, curved sword in his hand.

"Go!" Thomas hissed at them. "I will cover your escape." He turned to face the giant, pulling his mace from his hip.

Neil did not understand what was happening, but he had no intention of hanging around to ask for explanations. He pulled himself onto the seat of the carriage as fast as the pain would allow him, and the woman leapt up beside him.

"I know about your treachery, Amir!" Thomas said. "I heard you at the hostel conspiring with the Mayfields."

"Pity you will not live long enough to use that information," the giant replied smugly.

"Drive, drive!" Neil said to the woman, who snatched up the reins and shook the leather straps to start the horses into a run.

Even as he watched, Thomas and Amir charged each other, and their weapons rang out in a great clash of steel.

"Should we not wait to see who wins?" the woman asked as they exited the gate of the manor-house and the fence cut off their view of the combatants.

"With any luck, they will kill each other," Neil muttered, settling back into his seat and bracing one arm across his stomach. "But the victor is of no consequence to us at the moment. We must get clear of this place...." He trailed off in shock as the wind blew the woman's hair back from her face. "Salena?"

Once the carriage was out of site, Thomas and Amir stepped back from each other. Thomas was grinning from ear to ear. "Did I not promise you that I would find a reliable witness to warn Aden of his impending doom?"

Amir managed a smile of his own. "I must confess, I doubted you. But Aden cannot help but believe the word of a trusted knight of Dawning Court. Deviousness seems to run in the family," Amir said with a smile that held little humor.

"Just as murder and betrayal run in your blood," Thomas returned the cold smile. "Which reminds me, should you not be lining up for the attack? Are you not leading a tower squad?"

"I will be where I am needed," Amir said without concern. "And where will you be during the battle? Sipping wine in your drawing room?"

Thomas chortled. "The castle falls today. Where else would I be but at the front line? Do not forget that Aden digging in against Collin should reduce Collin's force significantly, but we cannot depend on more time. We must take the battlements and destroy Hans' army before Collin arrives, or we will have a fight on our hands for which we are not prepared."

Two

**The Kingdom of France, near Avignon
Ten days earlier**

Henry nearly collapsed in relief as he gazed upon the familiar crest that hung over the heavy wooden gate—three circles set inside three rectangles stacked vertically—the house of Ambroise.

Behind him, the Ambroise lands descended rolling, green hills to where they leveled out just before a bend in the bank of the Adour River. Two shallow-bottomed river boats were tied to a dock, evidently waiting to be loaded with cargo as their empty hulls bobbed up and down on the current. It was a picturesque scene—the kind of place Henry had hoped to bring Mary. The kind of place they could begin their new life together. The kind of place where he would be free from all the painful ties to Dawning Court and all the old wounds that came with it. But he could not think about that now, lest there be no more Dawning Court at all. His family and home were likely under attack at this very moment, and Henry's last chance for redemption was tied inextricably to the salvation of his family. And this minor noble in the south of France was the last hope for both. Henry was exhausted, filthy, penniless, half-starved, and destitute in every conceivable way. But he had made it to this last bastion of hope. He reached up a hand, heavy with fatigue, trembling with deprivation, and pulled the bell rope. He was not at all certain what reception he might receive, arriving uninvited and unannounced, full of desperate hopes; but he had used every remaining resource at his disposal to get to this point, so there was no turning back now.

While making his escape from the Nizari prison-camp, he had pilfered a cloak and a small amount of money from the guards he was forced to dispatch during his escape. That money had bought him passage to the mainland and some much-needed food but had run out days before. Since then, he had been forced to steal what he needed to make his way across the kingdom of France, plucking food from farmers' fields, even pilfering the old plow horse upon which he now sat—although he had promised himself at the time he took it that he would repay the farmer once he was able. The clothes on his back were his, but they were crusted with filth and hung in tatters, a casualty of the prison camp and of many nights spent sleeping on the ground.

Henry's head hung low. He had never imagined himself in such a depraved condition as this. Before now he would have not thought it possible, but it seemed the more effort he expended to prove himself, the deeper he descended into ignominy. As bad as everything had seemed to him when he had first returned from the Crusades in shame as the sole survivor from the army he had led to destruction, that now seemed a peaceful period of reflection by comparison. Safe, free from responsibility, what had he been contending with then? Memories? Dreams? Jealousies?

No—he corrected himself—not jealousy but unrequited love. Even now, the thought of Leah and her probable fate caused a pang in his heart. "I told you over and over," he said bitterly to her memory, "William was a foolish choice. I suppose you see that all too clearly now, though." *Of*

*course, is Mary any better off for having chosen me? Will she
not suffer the same fate as Leah at the hands of the Moors?*

So consumed was he with these thoughts that he did not
notice a small panel in the gate being drawn back and a pair
of soft, brown eyes peering out at him. "Oui?" said a female
voice after a moment.

Henry's eyes snapped up. "Uh—yes, yes," he said,
stumbling over his words in surprise, "is the master of the
house at home?" *French, you idiot!* "Er—est le maître—" he
groped for the French words, which were slow to his lips,
as he had spoken to almost no one in the week that had
elapsed since escaping the Saracen prison camp. Under the
circumstances, even English would not have rolled off his
tongue naturally, but the French felt positively alien.

Thankfully, the woman put him out of his misery. "What
is it you want?" she cut him off in accented English.

Henry forced himself to sit up a bit taller in the saddle.
"I am Lord Ambroise's relation, and I very much need to
speak to him regarding an urgent matter."

"Lord Ambroise has no kinsmen."

Wonderful, Henry thought bitterly. *How do I explain this
away?* "He does have kinsmen. Me. And I assure you that he
will see me. Please tell him that Henry of Dawning Court is
at his gate and desperately seeks an audience with him."

The eyes pointedly looked Henry up and down, no doubt
noting his shabby appearance and the scrawny, half-dead
horse upon which he sat, before the panel abruptly slid
closed without offering even an inkling of whether she
might return.

Henry, however, had nowhere else to go. He resolved at
once to see Lord Ambroise at all costs. If that required that
he force his way inside, then so be it. But even as he sat
there, he began to wonder how he could muster the
strength in his present condition to force his way into a
child's fort, let alone this fortified estate.

Henry was just starting to look for a way to climb the
wall when the great wooden gate began to open. It did not

open in the center, as he had expected, but was one long piece that hinged on the right side and swung inward to reveal neatly manicured grounds with a small courtyard in front, gardens and vineyards stretching off to Henry's right, and the stable and outbuildings to the left. Though the grounds were not extensive, they were meticulously kept, as was the aging manor house beyond the small courtyard in front of him.

Like the grounds, the house was of modest size when compared with the keeps and manors of many of the nobility, but it was built in several sections up the hillside, which gave it a very stately presence.

The woman from before—at least Henry assumed it was the woman from before—was waiting inside the gate. She was younger than he expected but very pretty, with long blonde hair that hung out from under a red bonnet and ruby red lips to match. Her simple dress was made of a coarse, durable fabric. Her entire appearance was less that of a servant in a noble house than that of a common peasant girl. She had a simple, unadorned beauty combined with an air of natural innocence that struck Henry as very enticing.

"His Lordship will see you," she said in the same soft, accented voice before turning back toward the house.

Henry found his eyes lingering on her shape as she led the way into the house. *I have been away from my wife for too long*, he thought and wrenched his eyes from her.

The entrance hall was fair sized but not what Henry would describe as grand. Nevertheless, ornate and painstakingly-carved woodwork seemed to cover every surface. Directly opposite the main entrance were large, dark walnut double doors carved to look as though they were ancient stone wreathed with ivy.

They were closed, preventing Henry from seeing any deeper into the house. Several passageways led off in different directions, but the girl mounted a steep set of stairs to the right, and Henry followed.

She led the way up to a landing with a balustrade built into the stonework that revealed gorgeous views of the green valleys of Campan. She did not stop here, however, but crossed the landing and ascended another staircase.

Though the staircases were not excessively long, Henry found himself panting as he lifted his leaden legs up stair after stair. The views improved with each new landing, but Henry scarcely even noticed, so focused was he on the task of mounting the stairs in his weakened condition. The weeks of abuse and deprivation he had suffered since being taken captive by the Nizari had exacted more of a toll than he had realized.

He was forced to stop at the top of the third flight of stairs until a wave of exertion-induced-giddiness passed. The girl looked at him curiously. She, of course, was not at all taxed from the effort, and he suddenly felt foolish. "I—" he started to make an excuse but could not come up with anything like an explanation that she could possibly understand—"am rather spent."

She said nothing, only gazed at him with her unreadable, huge brown eyes.

He pushed off the wall and nodded to indicate that he was ready to continue. She proceeded down a corridor toward what Henry took to be the uppermost room in the villa. She opened a door that led into a modestly-sized sitting room that was lavishly decorated with plush divans and sofas, ornate side tables and chairs, and expensive velvet draperies that hung beside a pillared archway that opened to a balcony with an expansive view of the entire countryside. A gentle breeze fluttered the curtains and cooled the room with pleasant, scented aromas from the fields that surrounded the chateau.

In one of the chairs sat a tremendously fat man. His hair was gone, save for a ring of dark hair around the back of his head. His skin was covered with sores, some of which were scabbed, and peeling, some open and oozing. He was dressed in an expensive, salmon-colored silk gown, the size of which made it look more like a tapestry than a garment that a human might wear. Despite the perfectly pleasant feel of the room, the man was sweating profusely. A young woman dressed in a gauzy—almost see-through—white dress was fanning him with a large paper fan, which looked to be gilded in gold, while still another similarly clad woman stood by to wait upon him.

The huge man was just pressing a carved wooden stamp into the cooling wax dripped onto a folded document. Henry could just make out the imprint of the Ambroise crest in the hardening wax. The man then placed the wooden stamp in a small drawer in the table and pushed it closed before looking up.

"Henry Dawning de Angleterre, Maitre Ambroise," the peasant girl presented Henry with a small curtsy. She moved aside for Henry to step completely into the room, where the man regarded him expectantly.

Master Ambroise? The girl had called this wretched creature Ambroise! Henry's heart sank. He did not know this man. He had made a mistake. This was not the bastion of hope he had come searching for. After all he had done—after all that he had sacrificed—he had failed to find the right Ambroise. Henry felt on the verge of tears. He had never even considered that he might be pinning all his hopes for salvation upon the wrong man. He could not hide the despair in his voice when he spoke. "Pardonnez-moi, je dois avoir fait une erreur," Forgive me, I must have made a mistake. He bowed and turned to go, though where he might go, he could not begin to imagine.

"Henry?" The fat noble said in perfect English. "Is that you? You look wretched!"

Henry turned back toward him, and his eyes narrowed at the familiar voice coming out of the unfamiliar face. "Edward?"

With some assistance from the ladies, the fat man climbed up from his seat and stumped over to Henry. He regarded him for a moment, and then put his meaty hands on Henry's shoulders to pull him into a rough embrace.

Henry remained rigid, a mixture of revulsion and disbelief playing on his mind. "Edward?" he ventured again.

"No," the huge man said, pulling back a step to meet Henry's eye, "Edward Dawning is dead. Here I am known as Lord Charles Ambroise." Edward smiled, and the folds of skin on his face tightened enough that Henry could almost recognize the once-familiar face beneath.

"Edward?" Henry repeated incredulously.

"Charles Ambroise," Charles corrected him pointedly.

Henry shook his head to clear it. The brother who had fled Dawning Court almost a decade before had been exceedingly lean, much like Henry himself. It was one more connection that Henry shared with Edward, another way in which he and Edward were different from the rest of the family. It did not seem possible that Edward could have undergone such a dramatic transformation in fewer than ten years.

Henry became aware that Edward—Charles—was awaiting a response, so he said the first thing that came into his exhausted brain. "Are you so ashamed of the name Dawning, then?"

"Are you proud of the name Dawning?" Edward retorted.

Now that they stood eye to eye, Henry could see that Charles was taller than his girth made him appear, nearly as tall as Henry himself. "I am proud of our heritage, though not necessarily what the name has come to represent."

"Ladies, wait in the passage," Edward commanded in perfect French without taking his eyes from Henry's. "Is this what you have come for, Henry?" he demanded once they were alone. "Are you here on Martha's errand?"

"Martha? No, no," Henry wiped his face with his hand, "forgive me, Edw—Lord Ambroise. I have not had a bed or a decent meal in more weeks than I can remember. I fear my manners have utterly abandoned me in my present condition."

Edward visibly relaxed. He waddled over to a sideboard, unstopped a decanter, and poured a generous amount of a red liquid into a cup, which he then handed to Henry before seating himself on a divan. "That wine," he said pointing to the cup in Henry's hand, "is pressed here on my lands. It is some of the finest you will ever taste. Far superior to the ditchwater they pass off as wine in England."

Henry sipped it dutifully. It was strong, and he thirstily drank it down, savoring the feeling of warmth that spread from his belly outward. For the first time since leaving Dawning Court, Henry started to relax. "It is good to see you, brother. It has been far too long."

"Indeed, it has," Edward agreed. "You will stay for a time?"

"Er—as long as I am able. It is an urgent matter which has brought me to you."

"That much I might have guessed." Edward chortled. "You are welcome in my home; however, I must insist that for the duration of your stay, you refer to me only as Charles Ambroise."

"You have completely renounced your heritage, then?"

Edward's disapproving look returned. "You willingly claim a heritage that is built upon bloodshed, warfare, and the backs of the oppressed? From our correspondence, I had understood you to be of a more enlightened mind than that."

Henry quickly backpedaled. "I only mean that I am not so ashamed as to renounce the Dawning name."

"Keeping that name was a choice not available to me when I left England. What did I know but our mother would send Richard or John to hunt me down?"

"It was a blow to the family when you left," Henry said, trying to keep any hint of accusation out of his voice, "but I should not think our mother so mean as that."

"Then you do not know Martha," Edward snapped. The two brothers sized each other up for a moment before Edward's flabby face again broke into a smile. "How rude of me to greet you like this when you are clearly exhausted from your journey. You will wash, rest, and eat, and then I will hear all about what has brought my long-lost brother to me so unexpectedly."

As the tension dissolved, Henry suddenly felt exhaustion settle upon him so heavily that even standing became a chore. He swayed slightly in place.

"Katriane!" Edward called, and the pretty peasant girl who had shown Henry into the house stepped back into the room. "See that Lord Dawning is bathed and fed. And find some suitable clothes for him."

The girl nodded demurely.

Edward winked at Henry. "Katriane will see to your *every* need."

Henry was too exhausted to even react to what he assumed was a salacious joke on Edward's part. He just let himself be led back out of the room without saying a word.

Three

enry awoke late the next morning in a haze. He was ensconced in a cocoon of plush bedding and pillows. *Where am I?* All he was certain of was that this was not his bed at Dawning Court. Lying in the warmth of the goose-down tick and the feather pillows, fading in and out of sleep, images and memories from the past few weeks began to waft across his consciousness. But they were of such striking contrast to how safe and warm he felt, they had to be a dream. He wanted them to be a dream. But the more he insisted that it was a dream, the more firmly those images took hold until they chased sleep from him entirely.

Reluctantly, he sat up and looked around. The room, which he felt as though he were seeing for the first time, was extravagantly furnished with plush velvets and exotic woods that were meticulously carved. No detail was overlooked. The tables were inlaid with gold, and the moldings on the walls and beams supporting the high ceilings were painstakingly crafted to appear as though vines were growing along their lengths. Even the posts of the bed in which he lay continued the theme, being etched to appear as though ivy were growing around them.

Henry tried to think if he had ever been in a room as opulent as this. Dawning Castle was elegantly furnished but a tad austere. Braden had been, after all, a warrior-baron, and his castle reflected that sensibility. Even the accommodations Henry had enjoyed while working for King John had not rivaled the opulence of this room.

He was still trying to take it all in when the door opened, and in sidled the pretty blonde servant girl.

He watched her pad across the carpet on silent, bare feet carrying a platter laden with fruits, cakes, and breads. He noted that her simple, striking beauty had not diminished with refreshed eyes. If anything, she looked even more lovely.

She set the tray on the sideboard without looking his direction and turned back for the door.

"Er ..." Henry started to call out to her. What was her name? Kathryne—Katriane! "Katriane, a moment?"

Katriane froze before turning slowly back to face him. "What is it you desire, Milord?" she asked, not meeting his eyes.

Henry had no idea what to say. He was not entirely sure why he had even called out to her. He slid his legs off the bed and stood, noticing for the first time that he was wearing a dressing gown which he could not remember donning. "Where ... are my clothes?" he asked, holding the sides of the material out to inspect the gown.

"Lord Ambroise ordered them destroyed."

"Yes ... well ... who undress—no, do not tell me; I would rather not know."

"You were quite fatigued, Milord," she explained. "We were unable to rouse you."

Henry flushed at that, which caused a fleeting smile to steal across Katriane's lips that Henry found very fetching.

"Please," he said, gesturing to a small sitting area between the two of them, "bring the food over here."

She did as she was instructed and set the food on a table between a divan and several chairs.

"You will sit?" Henry indicated a chair across from him. "Since you now know more about me than almost anyone," he commented wryly looking down at the dressing gown, "we may as well become properly acquainted."

Katriane took the chair indicated but sat on the very edge of the seat, straight-backed, hands folded tensely in her lap.

Henry sat on the divan facing her. "Do I make you uncomfortable?"

"No, Milord," she said, though she still did not meet his eyes.

"You have nothing to fear from me," Henry told her without knowing why he should feel to say that.

She made no reply.

"Have you been in Edw—er—Lord Ambroise's house long?"

"He took me into his house only this summer past."

"This is your home, then? Your family lives in the village?"

She shook her head. "My family lives in the north."

"Does Lord Ambroise treat you well?"

"Yes, Lord."

"You can speak freely here. Nothing you say will find its way back to Ambroise."

She did not respond to that, so Henry tried again. "How did you come to work for Lord Ambroise?"

Katriane hesitated before replying, "Lord Ambroise provides for my family so long as I am in his house."

"Sacrificing for one's family is something I understand very well," Henry said, beginning to pick at the food she had set on the table. "Even as I sit here in comfort, enjoying your company, my family is in danger. That is what has brought me here. I need Lord Ambroise's help."

"He is a powerful man. I am certain he will be able to assist you."

Henry sighed. "I do hope that is true."

"You are a good man to worry over your family so."

Henry's shoulders slumped. "In truth, much of the danger they find themselves in is my doing." He knew that he should not speak so freely with a servant, as servants were prone to gossip, but it had been days since he had had

28

any real conversation with another human, and he was filled with pent up emotions that he had been unable to voice. Now that he felt safe again, all of those emotions were suddenly spilling out of him. "It is my duty to atone for that—if I am able." She gazed at him, and he thought he saw a hardness behind her soft eyes that did not match the rest of her demeanor. In a leap of intuition, he said, "You know something about the weight of obligation, I think."

She quickly lowered her eyes again.

Henry sighed. It was clear that this girl was not going to engage with him freely. As much as he needed to talk, there was no solace in forcing her to listen to him against her will. "Thank you for the food," he dismissed her.

She nodded and stood. "Lord Ambroise requests your presence for the evening repast. If there is anything you desire before then, you need only ring." She indicated a bell rope hanging by the bed and hurried out of the room as though she were afraid that he might ask for something more.

She is obviously shy, but there has to be more to her behavior than mere timidity, Henry thought. Why keep a servant who was so painfully circumspect that she could not exchange pleasantries with the guests? Yet she hadn't seemed so intimidated when she showed him into the house the previous day. Henry shrugged. Whatever secrets were locked behind those beautiful brown eyes, he would not have time enough to discover them.

That evening, Henry inspected his reflection in the mirror with a sense of satisfaction. His hair was trimmed, his beard shaved, and the new black tunic and grey trousers Edward had provided him fit comfortably. He thought that he almost looked respectable again—a dashing, up-and-coming young noble. But even as he stared with pride at the image before him, he was suddenly hit with a stab of guilt so hard that it was like a physical blow. *Why should I be standing here safe, well-fed, and comfortable, when so many of those who depended upon me are moldering in the ground, and my family and friends, even at this very moment, are likely fighting for their lives?*

For an instant, the weight of it all was almost unbearable. His image in the mirror that had brought him satisfaction only moments before suddenly looked thin, weak, and covered in the blood of a thousand men.

The cold, accusing voice of Patrick's mother—the conscript that Henry had arrogantly sought to mentor only to watch the boy die with the rest of his army—rang in his memory. Now, though, she was not only speaking for herself, but for the mothers and wives of all the men whom Henry had led to the slaughter in not one but two disastrous campaigns! "You took him from me!" her voice sounded exactly as it had a year ago when he had visited her cottage.

"We were overrun," he protested aloud, "there was nothing I could do!"

"You pledged to protect them, and yet here you stand while they all rot."

Henry wanted to run from the accusations. He wanted to hide away from the harsh judgement of a world that did not understand, but where could he run? Even France was not far enough to leave the guilt behind. With some effort, he shook the feeling off. "Enough of this!" he said to his reflection as though it were an unruly soldier. "That is why you are here, is it not? To right these wrongs? And you cannot do that as a whimpering child. You are a leader of men—a general! Like Richard and Braden!" He straightened his tunic and ignored the voice that whispered that his failures proved the very opposite; he was not like Richard or Braden at all, and that was the problem.

A knock came at the door, and he started so violently that he almost leapt into the air.

"Very poised," he mocked his reflection sarcastically, then sighed and turned toward the door. "Yes?"

Katriane stepped silently into the room. "Lord Ambroise requests your presence in the dining hall."

"Of course. You will show me?" He followed her from the room feeling tremendously inadequate, which only increased his anxiety about this meeting. "Tell me, Katriane," he said, trying to sound casual but hoping to hide how nervous he was suddenly feeling, "is Lord Ambroise disposed to grant largess to those in his favor?"

Katriane took so long to answer that Henry was beginning to think she had not heard him. He was about to repeat the question when she finally said, "Lord Ambroise is a most generous man."

Henry gave her a sidelong glance. She was obviously being diplomatic, but what else could he expect? No servant would be so daft as to speak ill of their master to one of his own kin. Nevertheless, if she truly viewed Ambroise as charitable, why be so guarded with her answer? Yet surely the dire circumstances would make it impossible for Edward to withhold his help. After all, the very survival of Dawning Court was at stake. Surely that would move even his estranged brother to act.

And it appeared as though Charles could certainly afford it. The same signs of opulence that he had seen in his own room were present in every corner of the chateau. Every bit of trim, every piece of furniture was not just elaborate but almost gaudy in its lavishness. Gold leaf, silks, and rich velvets were incorporated into the décor and furnishings everywhere. No piece of wood was left unadorned, no stone left bare.

"Lord Ambroise is clearly doing very well for himself," Henry remarked absently, but he realized at that moment that what he was seeing was more than that. This was not merely refinement on display but pure excess. That struck

31

Henry as incongruent with the boy he remembered. Edward had never shown any particular interest in wealth except as it could be used to woo women.

Katriane led the way to the main entrance hall where Henry had first entered the chateau. She crossed to the dark, walnut double doors that were opposite the main entrance, pulled one open, and stood aside to allow Henry to pass through. Henry tried to catch her eye as he walked by, but as usual, they were downcast.

Beyond the doors lay a grand banquet hall. It was similar in design to the Great Hall of Dawning Castle, only smaller and much more elegant. Several long tables were at one side of the room, which left a large, open floor for mingling or dancing. The walls were covered with tapestries, and thick velvet draperies hung throughout the room. They were tied back now but could be drawn to divide the room into many smaller sections. Henry thought that an interesting feature he had not seen before, but its purpose he could not fathom.

At the head of the center table sat Lord Ambroise. He was draped in an expensive purple robe, which must have required yards of fabric to fashion in his size. Beside him stood another young woman gently fanning him. He was again sweating despite the pleasant temperature.

The table in front of him was made from a thick slab of mahogany that had been polished to a high gloss. It was inlaid with some design that Henry could not make out for the piles of food that covered it. There was enough to feed at least ten men, and anything that was eaten was immediately replenished by the small army of female courtiers who cycled in and out to ensure that Amboise's every need was attended to.

Upon seeing Henry, Charles brightened over his enormous paunch but did not stir from where he leaned on the oversized arm of a chaise, while his great sausage fingers peeled the meat off a roasted game bird. "Henry!

Join me. You have recovered yourself? You certainly slept long enough."

"I am well-rested," Henry agreed as he seated himself in the chair on Charles' left. "I am much indebted to you for your hospitality. Are we expecting others?" he asked, looking over the spread before them.

A shadow fell over Charles' brow. "Alas, it is only you and me this evening. But we will enjoy company soon enough. Eat now, and tell me what brings Henry Dawning to my gate unannounced, unescorted, and in as wretched a condition as I have ever seen a young lord. Were you waylaid on the highway?" As he spoke, Charles tore off another strip of meat, stuffed it in his mouth, and washed it down with a swallow from his wine goblet.

Henry flushed. "Waylaid ..." he said slowly. "I was indeed waylaid. Ambushed.... There is much to tell, but I would hear of you first. Tell me what has occupied you for these past ten years?"

Ambroise ignored Henry's attempt to change the subject. "You must tell me how you found me," he said in a tone that Henry thought revealed something beyond idle curiosity.

"Your letters," Henry explained as he let himself be served by a young, dark-haired woman who looked to be about Katriane's age—late teens or early twenties. "Though you signed them as Edward, you affixed the Ambroise seal to them. I merely asked about in Campan where I sent them and soon learned of your estate. I trust I did not overstep my bounds."

"Does the family know of my whereabouts?"

Henry shook his head and tentatively tore into a warm loaf of bread. "If they do, they did not learn of it from me."

"You did not inform them of your destination before setting off?"

"I did not know myself that I would come here until I was already underway.... They do not seek you," Henry assured him after a moment, "the family. They do not seek retribution."

Charles stared at him, his eyes intense. "They nurse no grudge against me? If Martha knew my whereabouts, she would not send Richard to seek redress?"

"Martha and Richard have much more to occupy their minds just now, I assure you."

Charles only grunted noncommittally and picked up his cup again. "So tell me, what has transpired since your last letter? Is matrimony all you hoped it would be?"

"Marriage is ... different than I had envisaged," Henry said delicately.

Charles chuckled into his wine. "I accept no blame for that. I endeavored to turn you from this course, did I not? Man is not meant to be saddled with a single woman. Invariably, his eye begins to wander, and she becomes possessive and demanding. The only surprise in it is that anyone is surprised by it."

Henry controlled his indignation only with great effort. "I do not think that describes my situation at all. Mary is the finest of women."

"You are content in matrimonial bliss, then? Your eye does not wander longingly over a serving girl or maid?" Henry felt his face flush and tried to hide it by digging into the food in front of him. "It is nothing to be ashamed of, Henry. It is only natural. Denying ourselves of these desires—pretending that we do not feel them—that is the only unnatural bit in it."

"Yes, well, admiring beauty is very different than attempting to possess it," he said and tried to change the subject. "You seem to be very prosperous, Lord Ambroise."

Charles grinned. "Trade is quite good."

"And what do you trade in? Spirits?" Henry asked, recalling the vineyards that surrounded the chateau.

"We do press wine here," Charles said, pointing a fat finger at Henry's as yet untouched cup. "That very vintage is from my own stores."

Henry dutifully tasted the contents and started to cough from the strength of it. "It is delicious," he rasped between coughs.

Charles laughed. "Forgive me. I should have warned you. We prepare it strong."

"It would seem so," Henry croaked, wiping his mouth. "Is this how you subsist, then? Are you Lord Ambroise, gentleman merchant now?"

Charles waved the question away. "We may discuss that presently, but it is of Dawning Court that I would hear. What mischief are the brothers about these days?"

"Well," Henry said, considering what to tell him. It seemed too early to unload the entirety of all that had befallen the family since John's death, yet this did seem a natural segue to plead for his assistance. "That is quite a tale indeed and very much related to my reason for appearing unexpectedly at your gates, looking like a half-drowned rat. Are you quite sure you wish to hear of it?"

"One moment." Charles drained his cup, signaled for a refill, and sat back. "Now tell me everything."

Henry shook his head dubiously. "I am not certain you know what you ask, but so be it. My last letter to you some weeks ago informed you of John's demise amidst an attack upon my wedding."

"Moors, was it not?"

"It was," Henry said, his face hardening at the memory. "They slaughtered many innocent people. They humiliated our—the—family and endangered my new bride and her family."

Charles clucked his tongue regretfully. "The Dawnings have made many enemies the world over."

"Enemies or not, this attack was an act of war, but the family refused to respond. 'Twas only Thomas who possessed the will to redress these wrongs."

Henry told Ambroise of the family's refusal to support him and Thomas in their quest to avenge John. He told him of the ambush that had left him a prisoner and Thomas' fate unknown, but likely dead, and how the same massive army that had slaughtered his men was marching upon Dawning Court at that very moment.

Henry finished his tale excited and out of breath. But far from prompting a similar excitement in Charles, as he had expected, his brother did not seem the least bit perturbed by the news. He said nothing, only swirled his wine and sipped it contemplatively.

"So you can see," Henry added awkwardly, "that I must return without delay." He leaned forward over the table for emphasis. "I only came here for aid."

"Return? To what end?"

Henry blinked in surprise. "Why, rescue, of course."

"Henry," Ambroise said in a patronizing tone, "I do not believe that you have thought this through. Why, from what you have told me, it is probable that Dawning Court is no more, or it will be no more by the time you could raise an army and return."

"You do not know that! And even if that be the case, then we must liberate and avenge them."

"Avenge them?" Ambroise chuckled, his belly jiggling over the table. "The Dawnings' enemies are not my enemies and certainly do not merit a declaration of war from me. After all, I have no quarrel with these people. I know nothing about them."

"Know nothing?" Henry rose from his seat. "Have I not just expounded upon their plot against the family—the attack upon my wedding? They slaughtered our people in an unprovoked attack. How can your blood not boil with righteous indignation?"

Ambroise shook his head ruefully, jowls waggling. "While it is true that I know nothing of this group—these Nizari as you have called them—I do know something of the Dawnings. And your claim that these attacks are unprovoked is difficult to support. The Dawnings have been sowing the seeds of their own destruction for generations. Braden, John, Richard, even you, all campaigned upon soil where you did not belong. Now that these Moors are doing the same to you, you cry out at the injustice of it. You demand vengeance. Are not the Dawnings merely reaping what they have sown?"

Henry stared at Ambroise, torn between another indignant explosion and defeat. He finally settled upon defeat and collapsed back into his chair.

"Henry," Ambroise said in a conciliatory tone, "the family has outlived its time. They are barbarians who refuse to adapt to a more civilized way of thinking, and they suffer the same fate as all barbarians. Norman civility has trumped Saxon barbarism."

Henry shook his head bitterly. "I warned mother many times of the folly of allowing our brothers to run unchecked over the world, but she would not hear me."

"But of course. Henry, she is a Saxon by birth and Saxon by character. Her sons bashing in the skulls of other men is how the Saxon barbarians proved themselves noble. It is as ingrained in her as it ever was in Braden or Richard."

"Braden?" Henry shook his head. "I could have used some of Braden's barbarism against those Moors."

Ambroise chuckled.

"You laugh, but Braden was the very model of Norman valor," Henry shot back.

"And *that* is what is so amusing. Henry, what is it that men hope to gain through all their professions of valor and nobility?"

Henry stared at him. "I am not certain that I understand."

"It is a simple question. Being a knight, it is difficult, is it not?"

"It is," Henry conceded.

"So why do it? Why spend your days training to smash away at other men who have trained to do the same to you?"

Henry hesitated. He knew that he could not say that being a great warrior was its own reward because Charles would reject that out of hand, so he said instead, "In order to be the finest men that we can be."

Ambroise shook his head. "It is merely to be better than the next man. When you face an opponent across a jousting fence, you need only be slightly superior to him, is that not so? You are rewarded the same for that as you would be for being twice or thrice as skilled as he."

"I suppose that is so," Henry again conceded.

"Therefore, if the winner is rewarded the same regardless of how superior he is to his vanquished foe, every moment he spends training beyond the merest jot of superiority over his foe is wasted effort, would you not agree?"

Henry was feeling that Charles was leading him into some sort of trap. "I will grant that it is so, provided that one could know exactly the precise skill level of any future opponent."

"Now tell me, why does it matter if you are superior to another in a tournament of sport?"

"Victory, glory, honor," Henry rattled off some standard reasons.

"And, of what material benefit is any of that?"

"The victor is entitled to wealth and ..." Henry trailed off and Charles grinned.

"And what?" he prodded.

"And to a lady's favor," Henry finished reluctantly.

"Ah, there it is. You seek glory in order to get wealth and women, is that not true?"

"I suppose if you lower men's motivations to their basest form, you might say—"

"And you have already conceded that it is wasteful to do one jot more for that than is required. Therefore, if you can simply bypass all such nonsense altogether but still achieve the same aim, would that not be the wisest course of action?" Ambroise leaned forward as far as his paunch pressing on the table would allow. "Henry, look around you! What do you see?"

Henry glanced about at the opulent furnishings, the table laden with food, and the beautiful serving girls that tended them. "I see ..." he hesitated, unsure of how to respond to his brother's assertion that all his long-cherished notions of nobility and valor were nothing more than masks for his basest desires.

"Paradise!" Charles answered for him. "That is what you see! I have all that I could ever desire, and I have never been to the Holy Land. I have never been knighted. I have never even fought in a tournament since I left England. I have acquired all this and never had to risk having my head split open by some brute twice my size."

That stopped Henry. It was his turn to lean in intently. "You have done it, then? You have found some means of achieving a culture founded upon rhetoric and discourse in a world that only values strength and power?"

Charles smiled and raised his cup. "I have knights, nobles, and kings throwing themselves at my feet. Men whom I could never hope to withstand on a battlefield willingly subjugate themselves to me."

Henry's eyes widened at that. "Truly? It is possible? I have long dreamed ..."

"Are you not listening? I have achieved it! Henry, you are sitting in the paradise that I have built without bloodshed. This is the paradise I wrote of in our correspondence. It is not some platonic ideal that will never be realized but a true and living place."

"I ... assumed ..." Henry could not believe what he was hearing. "The more I was scoffed at and ridiculed for believing that such a world could exist, the more I doubted that it could be achieved, not while man is so base. I even came to blows over it," he admitted in embarrassment, remembering his altercation with Thomas.

"Expecting men to be other than they are is why you failed," Ambroise said, reaching over and plucking a bunch of grapes from the table and starting in on them. "That is why all idealists throughout time have always failed."

Henry shook his head. He still could not believe what he was hearing. "You must tell me everything. I need to understand!" He knew that time was still pressing, that the family was still in danger, but if Charles spoke truly, this information was possibly the most valuable thing he would ever learn. Unlike the Norman tradition of honor and valor won in battle, this was an ideal that would not leave him standing on a battlefield, trying to decide if he should run or die alongside his army—*if* Charles had truly achieved what he claimed.

"On the morrow I will show you my lands, and we will talk much."

"But I do not wish to wait," Henry protested. "I would know now."

Just then the doors opened, and a dark-haired soldier, smartly dressed in chainmail armor and a surcoat with the Ambroise crest emblazoned on it, stepped into the room, saluted, and waited to be recognized.

Henry looked back and forth between his brother and the soldier.

"In the morning, Henry. It will keep 'til morning." Ambroise beckoned another girl forward, and she and the woman fanning him pulled his chair back from the table. "Regrettably, I have some pressing business that will not keep."

The serving girls hefted him out of the chair. His once lithe brother waddled toward the door and laid one meaty hand upon Henry's shoulder as he passed. "It is good to see you again."

And with that he was gone, leaving Henry alone, at the central table laden with a feast for ten men, to contemplate the tantalizing mystery of Ambroise's power.

Four

The next morning found Ambroise and Henry trundling along the road in an enclosed carriage. In this confined space Henry became aware of an unpleasant odor emanating from his brother. It was strong enough that Henry found himself repeatedly sticking his nose out the window on the pretext of admiring the scenery in order to catch a breath of fresh air. He did not know if he was being too obvious or if Edward was even aware of the smell, but his brother did not seem to notice.

A mile or so from the gates of the chateau, Charles leaned forward and banged on the front wall of the carriage beside Henry's head with the jewel encrusted hilt of his walking stick, signaling the driver to bring the carriage to a stop.

"This is where my regiment is quartered," Charles explained, pointing out the open window with the collapsible fan he had been using to cool his perpetually sweat-drenched brow. They were stopped before a short wall that enclosed five long boarding houses, all identical to one another, with a small guardhouse built perpendicular to the lanes that ran between the barracks.

A mailed soldier stepped out, walked briskly to the carriage, and saluted smartly. Henry recognized him as the soldier who had interrupted their dinner the previous night.

41

"Sir Henry, this is captain Serge. He is the head of my regiment," Charles had switched to perfect French in the presence of his soldiers without batting an eye. He then turned to the captain. "Anything to report, Captain?"

"No, your Lordship," the young captain said smartly. "All is quiet."

"That is well," Charles said with a satisfied nod and sat back in his seat. "Thank you, Captain. Carry on."

Henry could see they were about to drive on, but he needed a respite from the enclosed carriage. "Ed—er, Lord Ambroise, may I inspect your guard?" he asked, forcing himself into his French with less grace than when Charles had made the transition.

"Feeling the need to flaunt your knighthood over the rank-and-file soldiers, eh?" Charles smirked at him.

"Something like that," Henry said, opening the door and leaping out.

"Very well, do as you must," Charles sighed indulgently, "but you should know that while my men are well trained, they are not knights. You should not expect such discipline from them."

"I merely want to ensure that my brother's fortunes are well looked after," Henry smiled. Though standing at attention, Henry thought he noted the faintest show of surprise on the young captain's face at Henry's mention of being Ambroise's brother. "Captain, have the men fall out for inspection," Henry ordered to cover his mistake.

Serge looked to Ambroise, who grimaced but gave a grudging wave of approval.

Serge hurried back to the main house, flung the door open, and shouted some orders. Moments later, several blasts from a horn sounded from somewhere out of view, and then all was quiet. For several long moments nothing disturbed the stillness; then all at once, the lanes between the houses were in a frenzy. Doors swung wide, and men raced into the streets, throwing mail shirts over their heads and buckling on weapons.

Inside of five minutes, the guard formed up before the front wall, fully outfitted and armed, ready for battle. When the commotion had settled, a thousand men stood in ten rigid companies in the wide-open area beside the main house as they awaited inspection.

Lord Ambroise grudgingly dragged himself from the carriage and stood before the men in a bright silk robe of red with yellow accents. He supported himself on his cane with both hands, and though the sun was not yet high, sweat stood openly on his face, making the open sores on his skin glisten. "Men," he said in French, raising his voice with some effort, "my esteemed guest hails all the way from England. He is a decorated member of their chivalry, and after hearing me boast of the skills of my garrison, he was anxious to see for himself how they stack up to his own. Sir Henry," Charles turned the proceedings over to Henry by withdrawing into the shade of the carriage and fanning himself once more.

Henry clasped his hands behind his back and walked the rows of soldiers, looking them over. He was pleased to see that they were well-groomed and fit. After seeing the way Edward indulged in sybaritic excess, he was concerned that the soldiers may follow that philosophy as well.

Henry halted periodically and directed questions to random men about various aspects of their combat readiness; from others he demanded they present their weapons for inspection to be sure they were well cared for and battle ready. All in all, they did appear to be a well-trained group, even if they did not have the presence of the chivalry. *But yes*, he thought. *I could lead these men into battle.*

He returned to the forefront of the company where Captain Serge stood at attention. The captain was young, probably in his mid-twenties, but he had the weathered face and battle-hardened features of someone who had spent time campaigning.

"Your sword, Captain," Henry said. Serge drew his sword and presented it to Henry hilt first.

Henry inspected the gleaming metal. It was an unremarkable weapon—the kind that blacksmiths all over the world churned out by the thousands—but it was sharp and free of rust, and it glistened with a fresh sheen of oil. "You," Henry said, stabbing his finger at the man closest to Serge, "your weapon." Henry returned Serge's sword to him before accepting the next man's blade. He then stood back a pace with the other soldier's sword held at the ready. "Now, Captain, prove to me Lord Ambroise is in capable hands."

Serge flicked a nervous glance toward Lord Ambroise, but he only yawned, looking positively bored by the proceedings.

Henry stepped forward and lunged at Serge's stomach. Serge parried the blow easily. Henry nodded and swung again. Again, Serge defended. Henry then launched a short, quick combination of strikes at him, which Serge repelled before stepping into Henry's guard and stopping the tip of his sword just short of Henry's own belly.

Henry nodded approvingly, reset, and attacked harder. Once again, Serge kept him at bay. Henry briefly considered really unleashing on the young captain in order to demonstrate why a knight was superior to ordinary soldiers but decided that would serve no purpose other than to stroke his own ego. *Perhaps I am maturing after all*, he congratulated himself. But a voice whispered that it was not maturity at all that stayed his hand but the fear of once again looking the fool. "Well done, Captain," he said, returning the sword to the soldier. "Now tell me, how soon can your men respond to an attack upon Lord Ambroise's estate?"

"The advance guard can respond to a threat at the house within a quarter of an hour."

"And the entire company?"

"They can respond within half an hour."

"Very good," Henry glanced back over his shoulder at Charles, but he was not paying attention; he was half-dozing in the shade. "And how quickly could your entire company be prepared to travel?"

"Locally or abroad?"

"Abroad," he said as quietly as he dared so as not to seem like he was whispering but not wanting his brother to overhear.

Captain Serge paused for a moment, thinking. "Two hours, Sir Henry," he said finally.

"Two hours, is it?" He leaned into Serge, "I suggest you drill on that. The time may soon come that you are called upon to do just that. I want that down to one hour."

"What are you whispering about over there?" Ambroise snapped, suddenly causing Henry to stiffen and step back from Serge.

"My brother is indeed in capable hands," he said loudly enough for Charles to hear. "Well done, Captain Serge." He saluted the group, and the two brothers climbed back into the carriage.

Charles knocked the heavy cane on the carriage wall once more, and with a small jostle, they again started forward.

"I cannot imagine the drudgery of a soldier's life," Charles commented absently as they drove past the lines of men who remained at attention until the carriage was out of sight.

"Why soldiers? Why not knights?" Henry asked.

"Knights? Never!" Charles exclaimed. "A knight expects land and titles. He feels he is the equal of his lord. Soldiers are cheap, easily replaced, and content to live in the barracks."

"They all live here?" Henry was surprised, given the spartan look of the accommodations.

Charles shrugged. "Some have families—you cannot keep them from that—but even that works in my favor, as it settles them down and makes them more dependent upon me. They live with their families in town and stay in the barracks while on duty and believe themselves to be in an ideal situation. Did you not notice the prime condition in which they kept themselves?"

"They do look to be in fighting trim," Henry agreed. "I assumed duty required it of them."

Charles snorted. "They rarely have to fight anything beyond a town drunkard. That is why they keep themselves so fit."

Henry furrowed his brow. "No danger of battle typically results in bored and idle soldiers, not fit and active ones."

"These men would not dare do anything to jeopardize their place in my garrison because this post requires so little of them," he explained. "I am certain they are terrified at this very moment that I have brought in a trained knight to take over."

"Well, they do seem motivated. But tell me, is it wise to station them so far away from the house?"

"It is only about half a league to my gates," Charles replied without distress. "Soldiers have needs, and they are close enough to a city where they can indulge those needs whenever they wish without laying their lusty eyes upon the delicate flowers of my house."

"Is that really such a concern? There are many beautiful women at Dawning Court and many knights, but men and women in civilized society are expected to set boundaries on their passions."

"But they should not have to!" Charles thumped his cane on the floor of the carriage to punctuate his statement. "Why should one human ever deny another the pleasure they can provide to one another?"

"If you really believe that, then why do you care if the soldiers come after the women in your household?"

Charles' flabby face turned up into a smile. "I do not share well with others."

Henry shook his head, trying not to think about the implications of that statement. "What you are referring to, brother, is vice. Vice knows no bounds. Rome and Greece both collapsed in upon themselves after the people became too vice-ridden and corrupt that they could no longer maintain the great civilizations they had built. They became nations devoted to avarice, only looking to satisfy their unquenchable lusts, until there was no one left who was willing to sacrifice their comfort for the greater good. A nation in that state cannot survive."

"Are you not oversimplifying just a bit?" Charles smiled down his nose at Henry.

"My point is that if it is vice that truly motivates your soldiers, they may be temporarily satiated by the ... distractions most readily available, but eventually that will no longer be enough, and the eyes of avarice will turn upon your villa."

"Now you speak of something I understand very well. Were my men left to their indolence, I have no doubt of the certainty of which you speak. Did you not notice what a singular man Captain Serge was?"

Henry nodded. "He has a very trusted position for one so young."

"Serge is an idealist. He keeps his men in check, drills them, rewards and punishes them. He speaks to them of fantasies like honor and valor. If they fall out of line with his ideals, he replaces them with men more like himself."

"So, you use the man of honor to serve your purposes, though you do not subscribe to those values yourself?"

"Oh, do not sound so disapproving. Such has always been the way. What do you think the Church is? It is a class system set up to keep the poor in line through guilt and fear, while those in power are free to indulge at will. Even the very concept of the sale of indulgences proclaims that. Who can afford to indulge? Why, the rich of course!

"Henry, if you will remove the blinders from your eyes that have been placed there through a life of indoctrination by the Church, by your culture of 'valor' and 'nobility,' even by our own family, then you will see that the world around us is a garden of sumptuous delights, ripe for the plucking. We may feast until we are sick, rest, and then feast some more. Men of honor like Captain Serge walk through the same garden, but they have deluded themselves into believing that there is some virtue in restraint—that they are somehow superior to those of us who indulge."

Charles stabbed a fat finger at Henry. "Ah ha! I see that you want to agree with him. So tell me, in what way is he superior to me? I am noble. I am wealthy. I have all that I could ever want, while Captain Serge and his imagined honor serve *me*. He is poor and has nothing of consequence. His noble ideals have earned him a tiny house on a small plot of land, with a plain wife to tend it ... though she is not entirely without enticements," Charles smacked his lips lasciviously. "Meanwhile, I have my pick of the most beautiful creatures in all the land. Nobles and peasants alike—the consorts of kings and warlords—I have tasted them all."

His words stabbed at a deep and abiding fear Henry had long harbored about himself that he was just a naive fool, a dupe in someone else's game. Was he deluding himself that obedience to these strict codes of honor and valor were making him a better man? After all, what reward had he for it?

Of all his brothers, he alone possessed true honor, yet almost all of them had something he deeply desired. Richard had the barony, William had Leah's heart, even Edward evidently had all he could ever want. But were his brothers ever made to suffer the consequences of their weakness? No. It was only Henry, the one who steadfastly refused to yield to his vices, who bore the burden of suffering.

Yet, perhaps his brothers had suffered in their own way, Henry mused. John was dead. Richard had to be rescued, his army and pride left in ruins on the battlefield. And William was an outcast. And Thomas? The reality was that

Thomas was probably dead. A heavy silence hung in the air as the weight of that settled on him. But he was not willing to simply throw all his ideals overboard just yet. "But when will it ever be enough, Edward? Even now, you lust for the peasant wife of your captain of the guard, who—by your own admission—is a plain woman."

"As I said, she is not without her merits," an unconscious smile crossed his face which turned Henry's stomach.

"If you have your pick of the most beautiful women in the land, then there is certainly no end to the plain women available to you. The reason you are attracted to Serge's wife is because you cannot have her. It is her loyalty to her husband which makes her appealing to you. You want her virtue more than you want her body. That is the inevitable result of indulgence. It is insatiable. It desires most that which it cannot have."

Charles snorted. "Do not presume to lecture me on the dangers of indulgence, brother. For all your knightly virtues, of what have you to boast? You have lost your wealth, your position, and your wife, and you have come very close to losing your life. I, on the other hand, have everything I have ever desired because I stopped trying to resist my natural impulses and embraced them."

"Everything you ever wanted except Serge's wife," Henry muttered sourly.

Charles' eyes turned hard, but Henry was not looking at him any longer; he was staring sulkily out the window at the river. *Perhaps I am a naive fool who wasted my life on pretended nobility when I might have been happy by simply indulging.* Was that truly the path to ruin and misery he had always believed it to be, or was that just what he had always been told?

"You still do not understand, do you?"

"Understand what?" Henry mumbled without any real interest.

"I do not speak merely of satisfying my own pleasure—though that is a wonderful benefit. Vice holds power over people far beyond that of the sword."

"Power?" Henry perked up. This was a subject that interested him. "At dinner you alluded to having achieved the perfect society, one that was not built upon power and force but upon higher ideals. Yet have you not just proved otherwise by showing me the force with which you maintain your power?"

Edward chortled. "You believe that small force of men maintains my station? I need to show you something." Edward banged on the wall of the carriage and shouted a command to the driver to return home.

He waved all further questions away until they passed through the gates of his chateau and proceeded down a wide lane at the head of row after row of grapevines. "These," he said at last, "are all mine. Charles Ambroise has one of the finest vineyards in all the realm."

"That is quite an accomplishment," Henry said perfunctorily. "You must be very proud."

"What strikes you about my grounds, Henry?"

Henry glanced out the window but did not see anything particularly noteworthy to comment on. "They are very beautiful."

Charles rolled his eyes. "I know that you see it. Now tell me what strikes you."

"They are ..." Henry scanned them for anything that might be of special interest, but finally said the only thing that came to mind, "not ... large."

Charles leaned back with a satisfied smile on his face. "Exactly. Grounds of this size could not possibly support a man of my stature."

Henry waited for an explanation, but even as he did so, he felt a knot in his stomach. Something about the tone of the conversation told him that he did not want to learn more about his brother's enterprise.

"A fine vineyard is a valuable commodity," Charles continued, "but that is not where I derive my wealth. I am rich because I understand desire! Nobles from all over Europe seek invitations to my feasts in order to sample my most rare vintages. They trade other highly prized objects to get what they want."

"I—I do not understand," Henry stammered, searching his brother's words for some meaning beyond the obvious. "They trade for your wine?"

"Do not be obtuse!" Charles snapped. "You understand perfectly well. Everyone has something they want desperately, something—or someone—they would give most anything to possess. Is that not so?"

Henry wanted to protest, to deny this accusation, but the image of himself sitting on the baron's seat with Leah at his arm sprang unbidden into his mind, stifling whatever protest he might have made.

"Most people will die pining for that thing. Others may conquer entire continents to try to win what they want. But suppose there was someone who could secure for them that prize for which they so desperately yearned? Would you not give everything to possess it?" Charles whispered.

Henry considered that. He had never wanted anything in his life as he had wanted Leah, but he had settled for Mary because Leah would not have him. What would he have given to have it otherwise? Would he have employed an influence peddler to get her had he had access to one? "I ..." he started but did not know how to finish.

Charles leaned forward, a knowing smile on his lips. "Who is she? Clearly she is not your wife."

Henry blushed furiously and clamped his mouth shut to keep from revealing any more.

"And would you not have given anything to possess her?"

Henry could still remember the sleepless nights he had burned for Leah with a fire in his bones that felt as real as any flame. He remembered well the unquenchable desire in him that had led to his foolishly declaring his love to her and asking for her hand before he had left for the Crusades. For years he had cursed himself for that impulsive mistake. But as he remembered the overwhelming feelings that precipitated it, could he say now that there was anything he would not have sacrificed to have her? "I suppose—as an impetuous youth, before I knew my wife—I may have been tempted—but this is all wrong!" he said, waving away the fantasy as though it were a cloud of smoke before his eyes. "I may have given much to have her agree to marry me at the time, but no force in the universe could have made her love me when she did not. Someone like you may have been able to compel a marriage to me, but it would have been a lie. I wanted all of Le—her, not just her body. I wanted her heart and mind, and that you could not deliver."

Charles smiled disdainfully. "You want her to give herself to you, is that it? It is not enough to just take her?"

"Having her body without the willing consent of her heart would rob the moment of its sweetness," Henry muttered. He felt dirty and ashamed of this conversation. He did not like what it assumed of all men, and he did not like what it was making him face in himself. "Men of high character do not speak of things as sacred as the intimacy between a man and wife in this way. I do not wish to discuss this further." But Charles was not so easily dissuaded.

"If you do not believe that a woman cannot be made to give herself to a man simply because she does not love him, then you do not understand the depth of the power I wield. Even 'good' people desperately yearn for something."

Henry clenched his teeth in anger. He refused to consider that Leah had some secret lust hiding beneath her exceedingly good exterior. "I do not accept that. Not everyone is motivated by greed and lust as you suggest."

"I did not say they were, but is there nothing that this young lady of your heart would not have sacrificed everything for?"

William! Henry felt ill, which feeling flashed again into anger. "I will not have you undermine my tenderest feelings and those of the people I care about with this nonsense."

Charles flicked his eyebrows at Henry. "You may refuse to acknowledge it, if you wish, but it is not nonsense, I assure you. Look around you. Everything you see is a testament to the fact that it is not nonsense. You may choose to pretend that your feelings are somehow more noble than mine because they go unrequited, but I have wealth, power, and all the pleasures of life. What has self-denial earned you?"

"Is all that you have built only to support this ..." Henry gestured at the house and grounds at a loss for words, "this harem? Are all your servants merely slaves to your appetites?" Henry felt nauseous to think of the beautiful, innocent-looking Katriane being a sexual servant to Edward. But then it hit him that that look of innocence that he found so irresistible was almost certainly what had attracted his deviant brother's eye as well.

Ambroise smiled at him. "You have it backward, Henry. All I have built is because I have this harem, not the other way round. You seek to castigate me for that because it does not fit in with your moral preconceptions. The central obstacle to your argument is my success. In your world, men and women should eschew such pleasures and only pursue good and wholesome pastimes. Pleasure peddling should only lead to ruin and destruction. But Henry, look around you. I am thriving! My wealth is proof that my understanding of human nature is more accurate than yours. You may rail against it all you like, but I am merely embracing the true motive behind man's behavior. To indulge his lusts is the reason men seek for power. It is the reason a knight becomes a knight, why a peasant would rather be a noble and a noble a king. It is the reason that men seek greatness to begin with."

Henry's brow furrowed. "I did not become a knight to indulge my lusts; I became a knight because I valued honor and nobility."

Charles chortled. "That is only what you tell yourself because we are taught that it is wrong to want to gratify our desires. Therefore, we mask our true lusts in a desire for glory, but that is nonsense. No one wants to spend long years in the training yard only to spend years more battling with other brutes for 'honor.' Think about it. If there were no social, religious, or moral taboos on it, would you confine yourself to one woman, or would there be many?"

Henry did not answer, but his flush gave him away.

"There is no need to be embarrassed about it, Henry," Ambroise reassured him. "No man wants only one woman, though he may want one particular woman above the rest. But once he has that woman, he will want others. We are built to desire them, to crave them, to be drawn to their beauty. What you see here is the natural extension of all quests for power and prestige. If men were willing to admit it to themselves, I am what all men would be, or at least who they would turn to to fulfill those desires. There would be no war, only great festivals in which favors were traded."

"I certainly would not want my wife taking that point of view," Henry said after a moment.

"That is a naive way to look at it, but I understand," Charles winked at him. "I also do not share well, though I find it is sometimes necessary to sacrifice in order to gain more pressing desires."

"But wait," Henry said, shaking his head against the onslaught of doubt that Ambroise was throwing his way. "It is not only physical pleasure that I derive from my wife. There is a deeper bond that we share that sustains me. What you are proposing would strip that from me and reduce our relationship to a hollow, empty shell. It would be no different than visiting a trollop at the local tavern."

"A deeper bond?" Charles leaned forward. "Just imagine that you could have every woman you have ever desired. Imagine that you could pleasure each other at will any time you liked. Imagine a room full of beautiful women. Where would you rather spend your days: fighting with some shrew over how long you spent at the tavern because you 'share a deep bond with her,' or surrounded by beauty and love as it was truly meant to be? Henry, what if I could get her for you—that secret, unrequited desire?"

As much as he tried to ignore it, the idea excited Henry. He had long ago dismissed it as impossible. He was married now, and Leah was beyond reach. But in this world of Charles', none of that mattered. What if he could have Leah? And maybe Evelyn too? He felt dirty for even contemplating the idea, but here was a man who was offering him just that. But surely such refined women would never subject themselves to such debased morality as this. They would never be party to such depravity. But what if they were about to be taken prisoner by the Saracens? What if it was the difference between slavery to the Moors or—suddenly, a memory popped into his mind.

He was sitting back in Murray's seedy tavern in the town square with Thomas, John, and the strumpets they were entertaining. He remembered vividly the revulsion with which he had viewed those women. They had not even seemed to be the same species as Leah. It was not that the women did not have the necessary features to entice a man, or even that they were ugly. That is when he saw the flaw in the illusion Edward was creating, and the mirage evaporated. "But those women whom you want most—the most beautiful women—are beautiful because of their virtue and their purity, and that will always be out of reach for one such as yourself."

Charles grinned wickedly. "I have taken the purity of more than a few of those women."

"But the debauchery of which you speak is not the same thing! What makes them so precious—the creatures for whom we slay dragons—is that they have kept themselves aloof from the filth in which you deal. The desire that the minstrels sing about and the poets espouse is not the crass act of sating your lusts with a beautiful woman; rather that you may win the honor of that virtue being given to you alone, and through it you two will share a sacred bond—the very bond which you have mocked—that can never exist with anyone else. All you did to those once virtuous women is strip them of their beauty. Their virtue was not given to you as the ultimate show of love and respect but traded to you cheaply for something you had that they needed or wanted in that moment."

"Respect?" Charles scoffed. "What is that? All of these vain, self-righteous imaginations of your heart have not been enough for you to earn even your own self-respect, Henry. Where has any of that foolishness gotten you?"

Again Henry went quiet. He was too embarrassed to say anything because he knew that Ambroise was right. Even with all the accolades, accomplishments, and education Henry had achieved, he loathed himself. He was good, but not good enough to win the heart of the woman he had loved his entire life. He was smart, but not smart enough to save his armies from destruction. He was brave, but not brave enough to be immortalized as a hero like his brothers and father.

"We are both contemptible figures in your sight," Charles said, as if reading his thoughts. "Yet I have the luxury of enjoying my life. It is a pity that you cannot say the same."

"Perhaps we should go back to the house now," Henry mumbled sullenly.

"Excellent idea."

They rode in silence back through the vineyard toward the house until something occurred to Henry. "Edward, you are an influence peddler."

Ambroise smiled at the designation. "I suppose that would be one way to put it."

"And from what you have told me, your influence is widespread."

"It is."

"Then certainly there are ways you could help save our family, even if it is not by direct force."

Charles frowned over the jeweled hilt of his cane. "I do not wish to speak of this matter further. There is nothing I can do for the family."

"Nothing you can do, or nothing you will do?"

"It is the same!"

"But surely you could use a favor owed you—I will ev—"

"Enough!" Ambroise brought the cane down sharply to punctuate his statement. "I have no interest in helping the family. I received nothing but abuse at their hands, and I am happy they are meeting their end in this way. It is a just and proper end, and I will not use a single pound of my fortune to prevent it."

Henry was stunned. He too had many bad feelings toward the members of his family for the treatment he had received, but it was his family. He was honor-bound to help them. Where was Edward's honor? Had he truly sacrificed even the last, most basic vestiges of decency?

"What about the money you took from the Dawning treasury that you used to establish yourself here? You stole that from the family, and without it you would have none of this."

"Stole?" Charles sniffed and sat back. "I did no such thing. I merely took that share of the wealth to which I was entitled. My share of the inheritance, if you will. I am, after all, Braden Dawning's son."

Henry stared at him. Edward truly did not seem to feel any remorse or regret for anything he had done in his life. Did that make him enviable, or did that make him a monster?

"So ... the notion of the idyllic society of peace about which we so often corresponded?"

Charles looked up. "Yes?"

"We wrote of a society where war and strength are no longer the currency of realms. I assumed that you were envisioning a society of discourse and oration."

Charles laughed heartily, his paunch continuing to jiggle long after Henry's embarrassment had turned to anger. "Is this all you meant? Your idyllic society is not built upon ideas but on the trading of pleasures of the flesh?"

"Forgive me, Henry," Charles said, regaining his composure, "but the impossibly guileless society you espouse has been the bane of philosophers since Athens. Never once has such a society existed, nor will it ever exist. It disregards too much man's true nature."

"I am beginning to see that," Henry murmured, staring out the window as they returned to the house, "which is why the garrison is required."

Charles touched his nose. "Precisely my point. A man of power will only trade me for what he wants when it is cheaper for him to do so than to just take it by force. The garrison is nothing but a deterrent to make it more cost effective for others to work with me rather than against me.

"But make no mistake about it, Henry. People of power *need* men like me. They have all the comfort and wealth they could ever want. What they need is someone who will allow them to indulge in the vices that they cannot easily obtain in polite society."

"Vices?" Henry asked automatically, even while knowing he did not want to know anymore.

"But of course," Charles leaned forward. "The men and women in one's own court can serve to scratch an itch, but the need grows deeper, more … nuanced as it is indulged, until it cannot socially be maintained. That is where men like me come in."

"I do not even want to think about that," Henry groused.

"Nor should you, brother. It is left to me to understand the deepest, darkest needs of my clientele and see that they are served properly. All you need do is enjoy yourself."

Five

England: Dawning Court
Nine Days later

It was after dawn when Anthony stood upon the south wall watching the Braddock and Moor armies amass around the siege towers. But it was not the monoliths and their promise of death that was most troubling him at that moment; rather, he was trying to banish from his mind all that had happened with Leah, what she had told him of William, and the oath she had extracted from him ... Was he really to kill William Dawning? It was inconceivable that his world could have been completely turned on its head in one hour.

When he had learned from Martha all that had transpired in the chapel, he had immediately gone looking for Leah, expecting to find a grieving, heart-broken woman; he had not expected that her grief would take the form it had. Gone was the sweet and gentle woman he had grown to love; in her place was the same comely face, but it was so contorted with hate that he almost did not recognize it. Instead of tears and despondence, he found his betrothed boiling with rage and bloodlust. Had he been told that she was possessed by a devil, he might have believed it.

Until that moment, Anthony had not believed Leah capable of such base emotions. She had always seemed too good and pure to be subject to such sordid thoughts of rage and retribution. He chastised himself for the doubts he was having about her character in what was undoubtedly the worst night of her life, but she had demanded that he swear an oath to bring William to justice. He was not sure what Leah envisioned when exacting such an oath, but surely she had to know that she had set him on a course that would almost certainly lead to either William's or his own death at the hands of the other. For if she was right about William being a traitor, then he would never submit willingly to Anthony. But if she was wrong....

Anthony shook his head again. Maybe it was all moot anyway. The attack could not but spell the end for the castle, but if it was going to happen, better to get it over with quickly. "Why do they not attack?" he demanded of no one in particular.

"Something must be delaying them."

Timothy stepped up beside him wearing his armor but no helmet because of the bandage he wore around his head. "You should not be up here in your condition," Anthony chided him automatically, though in truth his dismay was more a result of Timothy's part in what had transpired in the Great Hall than any real concern for Timothy's safety.

"If we are to die today, then I will die on my feet."

"Hear! Hear!" Spencer piped up from Anthony's other side.

Anthony did not argue. Instead, he took the opportunity to give instructions to his chief captains. "Since Timothy is here, we will divide up the southern defenses between us. You will remember that during the previous two attacks, we found the portcullis raised and the men stationed at the barbican murdered. Sir Spencer, you will oversee the barbican personally to ensure that there is not a third repetition of that treachery at this most vital hour." Anthony briefly wondered if the saboteurs had been too busy in the chapel to bother with the battlements this time around, but he was not willing to take any chances.

"I will oversee this section of the wall. This is where the previous attacks were concentrated, and I expect that they will be again, so be ready to assist as needed. Sir Timothy, you will be responsible for the southeastern section. Also," Anthony took a deep breath, "our pitch stores are very nearly exhausted. I am reserving what is left for those towers."

"Then what are we to use to defend ourselves?" Timothy demanded.

"I have provided an alternative that may be nearly as effective."

Spencer and Timothy exchanged glances. "What is in the pots?" Spencer asked, nodding toward the pitch pots that were full of a steaming liquid, well on its way to boiling.

"Stew."

Spencer's brow furrowed, and he stepped over to the closest pot to peak over the edge. In the pot was a filthy brown mixture of dirty water, animal and human waste, and apparently anything else that happened to be lying around. Spencer gasped from the smell and quickly withdrew his face, covering his nose against the smell. "Revolting!" He was trying not to gag.

"The cesspool in the yard was overflowing. We've nowhere to put the waste. Why not return it to the people that made it necessary?"

"Innovative," Timothy muttered dubiously. "Is this 'stew' going to be enough to penetrate the heavy shields and armor?"

"Perhaps not," Anthony admitted, "but most of them are not wearing heavy armor, and the leather and gambeson will not be much protection against boiling liquid."

"And even if it is," Spencer added, "the smell will not make their job any easier."

"No pitch, depleted supplies, and no real soldiers," Timothy muttered, looking dubiously down the battered remains of the ramparts.

Anthony followed his gaze, noting the stark changes that had occurred since Timothy was last here. It was not a reassuring sight. Whole sections of the causeway had been destroyed by the enemy catapults and had been patched with planks and ladders to allow continued—if not easy— passage across those sections. Many of the merlons that protected the defending soldiers were damaged or gone.

"Such measures," Timothy nodded to the makeshift barricades of boards, hay, or even broken-down carts dragged into place to cover the missing merlons, "will do little to stop the enemy artillery."

"It will offer some protection from the enemy archers, as well as provide concealment."

"And the army itself?" Timothy asked, referring to the fact that only about every third face was a man of prime fighting age. The others were too young, too old, and in some cases women. "We are using women on the fighting line?" Timothy was incredulous. "The very people whom we as knights are sworn to protect?"

Anthony cringed inwardly at what felt like an indictment. "There is simply no way we could man the defense without them."

Anthony had never been one to over-romanticize the glory of war, but he did believe in the notion of chivalry— the strong shielding the weak and innocent from evil in order that they might remain innocent. Combat was a dirty job that he accepted so that others would not have to be exposed to it. But where were those values now that women and children were on the fighting lines?

"Why did we come back here?" Timothy breathed softly, as though he assumed Anthony was having the same thoughts.

"What else could we have done?" Anthony meant it to sound like a declaration that they had done the right thing but realized that his own doubts made it sound more like an actual question.

"But we knew we could not win!"

"Why should that matter?" The question sounded hollow even in Anthony's own ears. So he said the next with the gravity of the captain of a sinking ship preparing to perish with his crew. "It was never about our survival. The people of Dawning Court were in danger, and we are knights sworn to protect those who cannot protect themselves."

"What foolishness when we knew there was no victory to be had! Neither for them nor for us. Had we not saddled ourselves with the protection of hordes of peasants who could not be saved, then we might have remained free to incite some meaningful opposition! We might have made it to Runnymede and returned here with thousands of soldiers—experienced soldiers—with which to fend off Thomas."

"And what would be the value of those additional thousands if Thomas and his mercenaries held the battlements? Have we not already seen nearly that many of the enemy fall to our farmers? Would we not have found them impregnable when manned by experienced fighting men?"

"Then we would have found some other way! We—"

"Enough!" Anthony cut him off. "I will not debate this point now of all times. We did as our duty demanded, and when we stand before our Maker, we will be able to answer with a clear conscience that we did all that was required of us."

"I see no glory in throwing my life away foolishly," Timothy muttered, though he did look ashamed.

"Somehow," Anthony said, backing away from the wall, "I do not think the choice will be yours."

He could not have said what it was exactly that alerted him. Perhaps it was the slowing of the enemy's activity along the line. Perhaps there was some sound that he was not even aware he was hearing. But moments later boulders pierced the morning mist before crashing into the battlements and courtyard below.

A great roar went up from the enemy line. The black mass of men, still mostly hidden from the long shadows thrown by the rising sun, began to surge and churn, and two of the three siege towers lurched forward in a black line.

Six

The Dawning trumpets began to blare a warning across the ramparts. No one who might have still been asleep could possibly continue to rest now. Timothy and Spencer both broke for their posts. Anthony hurried down the wall, shouting orders as he went. He immediately found the inexperienced third string of farmers-turned-soldiers floundering and uncertain.

"Steady, men!" he called to the quavering soldiers, many of whom had yet to see action. "Stay behind cover!" he roared as some of them began to stand to take aim before the foot soldiers were in range. "Wait for my signal!"

He peeked around a merlon and watched until the enemy had advanced farther than he would have liked. But given the archers' inexperience, he needed to maximize their chances of hitting with their dwindling arrow supplies. "Archers up!" he shouted. The bowmen stood and trained arrows on the black wave of foot soldiers drawing ever closer, as though the darkness itself were rolling toward them. "Draw!" he ordered, waited just a split second, and then, "Release!"

A hundred arrows disappeared into the morning mist. Anthony did not wait to see what effect they had before shouting, "Cover!" Almost before his head was concealed again, the enemy's answering volley streaked over the wall. Most of the men got clear in time, though there was no telling what havoc the enemy arrows were wreaking in the courtyard below.

His archers got off two more volleys before the first of the ladder crews arrived. Anthony sprang into action, rushing along the wall to ensure the battle stations were being restocked, replacement soldiers were stepping in to man the posts of the dead, and the stew was being dumped down the murder holes—the ninety-degree scoops built into the battlements that allowed defenders to drop things onto their attackers but which made it impossible for the enemy to shoot back at them the same way.

Then the tops of the first siege ladders began to appear. He tried to be everywhere at once, as if hoping that by sheer expenditure of energy, he might be able to repel this siege. He helped to push ladders from the wall, dump pitch pots, and even fire ballistae and catapults when the operators were struck down.

Even while frantically repelling the attackers, he watched the approaching towers with a growing sense of dread. Lumbering beasts, they at times seemed to be standing still and other times seemed to be advancing by leaps and bounds. He both wanted them to hurry to his trap before the sun climbed any higher and feared their advance. If all three towers reached the walls, all Anthony's other efforts would be for naught. He simply did not have the manpower to repel all of them at once.

The first distress call came from the barbican, but Anthony did not immediately respond, as he was being pulled in every direction at once.

The horn sounded again, but still Anthony was focused on the ladder he was pushing from the wall where the soldiers climbing it were getting dangerously close.

"Lord Anthony!" A soldier called behind him. A rush of anger surged in Anthony. Couldn't these people do anything without him? The ladder they were pushing fell sideways, and Anthony whirled on the speaker. "What is it?!" he snarled with a venom that shocked even him.

The archer pointed a trembling hand out toward the barbican, where a new armored battering ram on a rolling gantry was being pushed into place in front of the portcullis. It was flanked by rows of fully-armored knights with custom-designed shields. They were ready for the pitch storm that had scuttled their last attempt, but Anthony was not ready for them.

His heart sank a little lower still. When were they going to catch a break? When was Heaven going to move on their behalf? He reluctantly pushed himself into a run toward the barbican and was almost killed.

A boulder as wide across as his shoulders skipped off the causeway a scant five feet in front of him, crashed over the rear of the battlements, and fell down into the courtyard, taking part of the back wall with it.

Anthony froze, staring at the hole the stone had just made. It had come so close that he had felt the wind as it passed by. Had he been one step farther on, he would have been crushed.

He caught himself automatically uttering a prayer of thanks, as he had done a thousand times before, but this time he cut it short. *For what am I expressing gratitude?* Sure, his life was spared, but for what? His circumstances, as well as those of all the people that depended upon him, continued to decline hour by hour. *I would not even be alive now had my doubts not slowed my step. What lesson am I to take from that? Is God really watching over us?* For the first time ever, Anthony could not answer that question.

It was an unsettling realization that left him feeling empty inside. He had always assumed that he was divinely protected so long as he was striving for goodness and honor. And if the worst should happen, at least his soul would be right before God.

Now, however, he was not so certain that God was even paying attention to him—or any of them—at all. Yet God continued to spare William miraculously through all his misadventures, though William apparently served no one but himself.

Perhaps it was his exhaustion or maybe his discouragement, but for the first time, Anthony began to understand the depth of betrayal that Leah must have felt toward William, a man they thought was their friend, a man they thought was fighting for them, but who turned out to be tightening the noose around their neck with every move. Where was God in that? Why were Anthony and this people being punished, but William seemed blessed with divine protection through all that he did? That thought disturbed Anthony even more, but he pushed it aside and continued toward the barbican.

He reached the barbican and was relieved to find it properly manned and the portcullis in place. Spencer and his men were busily employed in dumping whatever they could find down the murder holes onto the ram.

"They are ready for us," Spencer panted as he finished dumping another pot of a boiling, lumpy, brown concoction down the murder holes only to run over and start dropping head-sized boulders from a cart down upon the enemy. "They are ready for us, and this is not working."

Anthony peered over the front of the wall and was unsettled to see that the barrage of stones, arrows, and boiling liquid was having no visible effect upon the ram or the men surrounding it.

The attackers were outfitted in full plate armor, and beside each man operating the ram stood another armed with an oversized iron shield that was obviously built specifically to protect them from this attack.

"Without pitch, I do not know what to do," Spencer said in a voice tinged with panic.

"Pitch would not help us here," Anthony grunted, "unless we could bathe them in it, and we do not have enough for that."

"Well this is not going to stop them," Spencer said as he continued to drop stones down the murder holes. "These are not big enough to penetrate!"

The portcullis shuddered as the ram began to swing into action. Within minutes the iron bands were beginning to bend inward, and some of the pins that joined the metal cross-members together were breaking loose.

"We must open the portcullis," Anthony told Spencer.

"Open it? Are you mad?" Spencer cried, forgetting himself in the emotion of the moment.

"As long as they are in front of the barbican, we cannot have any effect upon them. But trapped inside of it, we can rain down upon them from every side."

Still Spencer hesitated to give up this last line of defense. Once the enemy was inside, all that remained between them and the courtyard was the damaged main gate.

"Damn it, man! The portcullis will fail in moments regardless!"

Spencer took a deep breath and shouted, "Prepare to open the portcullis!"

The soldiers stopped what they were doing and scrambled to take up positions around the barbican. "Prepare the pots! Archers, prepare fire!"

Anthony waited impatiently until they were set, watching the portcullis strain and flex more with each hit of the huge tree trunk. Finally, Spencer gave the order, "Raise the portcullis!"

Two peasant soldiers began to crank the handles on the winch to draw up the iron grating.

Anthony peered over the wall into the kill box of the barbican as the soldiers pushed the ram forward with determined steps, never deviating from their formation. They did not lose a moment before putting the heavy tree trunk back in action against the main gate. Almost at once, Anthony realized he had a problem.

He had assumed that being able to attack the soldiers from every side would mitigate the advantage of the large shields, but he now saw that the large rectangular shields were designed to cover the shield-bearer and the man next to him. They were no more exposed in the barbican than they had been out front.

The defenders' projectiles crashed down on the huge shields and dented the iron skins but had no discernible effect upon the men underneath as they continued to bang the massive ram into the gate.

Spencer, obviously coming to the same conclusion, looked up with wide-eyed anxiety at Anthony, making him appear even younger than he was. "What now?"

Anthony racked his brain. What could they do? They simply did not have enough pitch to use the amount that would be required here, and even if they did, they would never be able to transport it to the barbican and heat it to a boil before the gate fell.

Anthony perked up suddenly. "I have an idea!" he said, snapping his fingers. He cast about for a runner, but for once, Freya was not immediately at hand. He only hesitated a moment, taking one more nervous glance at the soldiers battering the ever-weakening gate before giving orders to those managing the pitch pots. "Bring the pots to a boil, but do not dump them until I return."

Without explaining further, he commanded half a dozen men to follow and descended to the courtyard. Unsurprisingly, they found total pandemonium among the peasants. The shuddering gates and splintering timbers were causing a flurry of panic-induced activity as some of the peasants tried to barricade the gate while others tried to create some semblance of a defensive line to meet the enemy when they did finally break through, and still others tried to push up to the upper ward to get away from the insurgents.

Anthony did not address this, instead directing his steps to the outbuilding that abutted the stables where the supplies were kept.

"Shall we help hold the gate?" one of the soldiers on his heels asked uncertainly, recognizing the obvious need for leadership.

"That is precisely what I mean to do," Anthony replied without breaking stride.

"But the gate—"

"Is holding fast," he cut him off. "The iron bands have not failed; there is still time if you follow my orders!"

They reached the supply depot, threw the large door wide, and ran into the once well-stocked room that was now nearly empty. Anthony crossed the empty space where dozens of barrels of pitch had been stacked only a week before, past the coils of rope, stores of lumber, and lime for brick mortar along with a hundred other miscellaneous supplies, until he came to a dark corner that was piled with unmarked burlap bags that looked to have sat undisturbed for years.

"What is this?" the soldier asked, coming to a stop beside Anthony in the shadows of the barn.

"We are about to find out," Anthony said and dragged a heavy sack over each shoulder. A dull, whiteish powder that stung the eyes wafted up from the disturbed pile. "I only hope that it has not solidified," he muttered.

The soldiers cast sidelong glances at each other. They had no idea what their leader was about, and it did not help that even he seemed uncertain about this plan. But Anthony was already rushing toward the door, so they followed suit, taking the heavy sacks over their shoulders and hurrying back to the wall as quickly as they could manage.

Anthony was panting, and his heart was beating in his ears by the time they mounted the battlements again. But the sight that greeted him when he crested the walls pushed all thoughts of his personal discomfort from his mind. The siege towers advancing toward them were only a hundred yards away. The barbican may be the immediate concern, but within a quarter of an hour, they were going to have three towers breaching the wall. Though the frenzy of activity on the wall had not changed, there was a frantic air of panic now.

Anthony knew the men needed leadership now more than ever, but he could only do one thing at a time, and right now he was working on the most pressing problem. So he ignored the desperate, entreating calls from the peasant soldiers, whose attacks were having no visible effect upon the towers, and hurried down the wall, barely managing to find the energy to bark an encouraging word to the men as he passed.

Without a pause, Anthony stepped to the edge of the barbican, dropped one sack at his feet, and hurled the other one down on top of the men below.

The heavy sack came down on the raised shield of one of the men sheltering his comrades. Since the ram was supporting half of the oversized shield, Anthony aimed for the side where the knight was bearing the brunt of it. He was disappointed that the shield-bearer did not collapse under the weight of the strike, but the sack exploded and sent the off-white powder billowing over all those around him.

Anthony threw the next one down, and Spencer directed the other men to do likewise. Each sack exploded in turn and sent a cloud of white dust across everything it touched.

Spencer gazed over the wall at the enemies they had painted white but had otherwise failed to affect whatsoever. "What is that?"

"Unslaked lime," Anthony answered without explanation. "I hope."

"Unslaked lime," Spencer repeated, nonplussed.

Anthony had come across the sacks while checking their supply levels, but it had not occurred to him what these bags of innocuous-seeming white powder might be or why they would be stored among the siege supplies, until this moment. *Was my sudden realization divine inspiration?* He found himself wondering but pushed the thought aside.

Now was not the time for existential dilemmas. Besides, he didn't even know if that is what it was.

He ran down the wall and took the handles of a barrow full of hay that was kept handy for stoking fires and pushed it over to Spencer. "Help me," he ordered.

Spencer did as instructed, though it was clear he had no idea what the intent was, and the two men hoisted the barrow up and dumped it over the edge of the wall where it rained loose straw down upon the already filthy soldiers, again with no discernible effect.

"Now the stew," Anthony ordered the men manning the pitch pots.

"They are not yet boiling!" someone protested.

"Do as I say!" Anthony barked, and the men obeyed. They pushed the giant cauldrons forward on their heavy wooden spindles until the dark, stinking liquid dumped out and drenched those below.

The soldiers manning the barbican all rushed to the edge to look. As expected, everything around the gate was soaked, but nothing else had changed. In the silence of the stilled defenders, they could clearly hear the boards of the gate crunching beneath the ram strikes.

Spencer deflated. "That was ... underwhelming." He looked to Anthony for an explanation, but Anthony was still staring intently at the battering ram, searching for some sign that he had not just wasted their time dumping cooking flour on the attackers.

"Sir Anthony, we must try something else," Spencer insisted. "The gate is failing more with each new stroke of the ram."

Still Anthony did not look up. This had to work! He just couldn't face one more humiliating defeat.

"There!" Anthony exclaimed suddenly, pointing downward.

All eyes turned to look, but it took Spencer a moment to see what he was pointing at. A thin mist seemed to be forming around the ram. "Why, that is just the disturbed powder ..." Spencer started to dismiss it but realized suddenly that he did not know what it was.

Even as they watched, the light mist coalesced into thick tendrils of white smoke that were rising from anywhere the water mixed with the unslaked lime. Soon it became a thick, noxious cloud, which started the invaders coughing and choking. It did not take long before those receiving the worst of the fumes began to flee the barbican with their lungs and eyes burning. And they were the lucky ones.

Spencer's expression changed from disappointment to surprise to amazement as the unslaked lime burst into flame upon any surface that had enough of the powder mixed with the liquid. The iron-plating of the ram, the ground at the knights' feet, even the armor of one unfortunate man who had taken a particularly heavy dusting, ignited.

In moments the men who had been on the verge of breaking down the gate were fleeing before the white cloud that was filling the barbican.

"That was ..." Spencer struggled for words as he watched the barbican empty below them, "amazing." But Anthony was already gone, racing down the wall to meet the siege towers, leaving Spencer to wonder why they could not do the same thing there.

But then he saw the problem. Even as he watched, the fumes dissipated in the wind, and the flames began to burn themselves out. Anywhere that they could not find a ready source of burnable fuel, they flickered and died. This attack had only been effective within the confined spaces of the barbican where the wind would not dissipate the powder or the fumes. In the open field, it would likely be ineffective.

Seven

$\mathfrak{F}$orward, men! Push!" Hans shouted, frustration creeping into his voice as the two lead towers, rolling side by side, rumbled to a halt in the no man's land between the camp and the castle wall. Amir, who was commanding the third tower with his Moorish troops, had arrived late, and Hans had no intention of waiting for him to get organized. In fact, he hoped his two towers would take the walls before Amir's forces could join the fray, allowing him to exclude the heathens entirely from the Braddock victory.

Hans drew up behind the group of soldiers pushing the towers. The massive structures had been rolling closely together, creating a broad shield for the soldiers to shelter behind as they advanced. The men huddled tightly, eager to remain within the protective shadow, and Hans was no exception. Nevertheless, perched upon his warhorse in full panoply, he felt every inch his proud heritage while he waited for Ranalph to rectify the holdup. Excitement coursed through him; just twelve hours earlier, he had feared imminent defeat, seeing traitors lurking in every face. But now God had smiled upon him, and everything was working in his favor.

Capturing the actual saboteur was an immense relief. But learning that it was none other than William Dawning himself, well that was sweeter than Hans could have imagined. Not only would Hans force William to watch as his home fell, but Hans would have the pleasure of doing what no other man had been able to do—seal William Dawning's fate.

Hans was feeling exultation like he had never known, buoyed by the realization that he was on the brink of proving himself more than just an illegitimate son of a great baron. He was about to show that he belonged among the Braddock men. When the Dawning traitor Salena had appeared at his gates, he had been uncertain about his decision to ally with her—and even more so with the treacherous Thomas. But now, as Hans prepared to dismantle his family's greatest rivals—something his father had not been able to do and even his great brother, Collin, had not undertaken—he felt vindicated. By the time Collin returned, Hans would have won the day, and what could his brother say when Hans had more than doubled the size of the barony?

Snapping out of his daydream, Hans noticed Amir's tower finally moving out of the scaffolding behind him. "What is the delay?" he demanded of Sir Ranalph, who was sheltering between the giant wheels of the towers, which were taller than a man, and carefully peering around the front.

"Clear those bodies out of the way!" Ranalph shouted, pointing at something in the path of the towers that Hans could not see from where he sat.

Irritated, Hans could not understand why Ranalph was wasting time on such a task. It was true that the bodies had not been removed from the field the previous night, as all available labor had been diverted to finish the towers for the assault. But it was the last thing in the world they should be bothering with now.

He nudged his horse into the gap between the towers. "What are you on about? The dead will keep for another few hours!"

From this vantage point, Hans could see that the field was indeed littered with bodies, but it was one particularly long line of bodies, at least twenty yards long, that Ranalph was apparently focusing on. Hans could not imagine how it might have come to be there. Perhaps the bone-collectors had assembled them there for easy retrieval, only to be interrupted by the army's unexpected route. Regardless, this line of corpses posed no threat to the tower; it was only a body or two high, and the massive wheels would easily crush them without a hitch.

"Clear them out!" Ranalph insisted, ignoring Hans, which only fueled his irritation.

"What madness is this!" Hans demanded as a group of eight soldiers rushed forward to comply with Ranalph's order.

The soldiers had scarcely reached the line of bodies when a sudden torrent of arrows rained down from the castle walls, as if every archer had trained their sights on the small group. Five soldiers fell instantly as pincushions for the flurry of arrows. Two of the remaining three hesitated, caught between duty and survival, only to meet the same fate moments later. The last man turned to run back to cover but fell to an arrow between his shoulder blades before he could take three steps.

"You fool!" Hans barked at Ranalph.

Ranalph frowned but remained fixated on the line of bodies. "Shield teams, provide cover! Pikemen, remove the bodies!"

"Hold!" Hans shouted, spinning to face Ranalph. "Are you mad?"

"Those are the bodies of *your* men!" Ranalph shot back. "Would you grind them into the earth like dung?"

"Only a mad man exchanges living men for dead!"

"Does it not strike you as odd," Ranalph persisted, "that the archers should have focused on men clearing bodies rather than those attempting to scale their walls at this very moment?"

"They are bloody farmers!" Hans shouted back. "They will shoot at anything that presents an easy target! And you are making easy targets of my men!"

"Is it not suspicious that so many died in this convenient line?"

"What are you suggesting?" Hans snarled sarcastically, "That the Dawnings placed them in this fashion to trap us?"

"Perhaps," Ranalph replied, though with less conviction than a moment before.

Hans snorted. "Then I urge *you* to investigate."

Ranalph glanced unconsciously at the bodies of the recently fallen soldiers. "That is what I thought," Hans said smugly. "Now shut your mouth and roll over them. I will not be beaten to the wall by the Moors! This is our victory to lose, and your cowardice is not helping!"

Seeing that Ranalph was still hesitating, Hans raised his voice. "Onward, men! Forward!" The towers lurched into motion, and Hans watched with grim satisfaction as the corpse of the man who had run back for cover was crushed under the front wheel of the behemoth like the dried leaves of autumn. It wasn't pleasure he felt but vindication at being proven right yet again over his doubters and detractors, Ranalph foremost among them. Ranalph may be older and more experienced in battle than Hans, but Hans was born to leadership and therefore *endowed* with the gift from on high. No upstart could rival that!

As the towers passed Hans and Ranalph, Hans gloated. "They did not so much as waiver!" But Ranalph pushed forward to stay near the front of the towers as they approached the line of bodies.

Hans smirked at Ranalph's retreating back. *What a fool!*

Just then a great tremor shook the towers, one after another, and both halted abruptly, though it was not immediately evident what was wrong. Confused, Hans glanced up. It could have been a trick of the morning light, but it almost looked as though the tops of the behemoths were wavering high overhead.

In the press of soldiers, Hans could no longer maneuver his horse. So he dismounted and pushed his way up to Ranalph, sheltering close to the wheels as the walls continued to pepper them with arrows and stones.

From this vantage point, he saw the issue immediately. The bodies had indeed collapsed under the weight of the tower, just as he had predicted. But in doing so, the front wheels had sunk into a pit beneath the corpses.

As the towers continued to tip forward, more weight was placed on the bodies, which collapsed even more, causing the rear wheels to lift off the ground. Hans opened his mouth to voice his confusion, but Ranalph darted to the back, shouting and pointing. "The men inside! They are still pushing! Stop them!"

Though the soldiers behind the towers had stopped, those inside remained oblivious and continued to push against the unseen barrier. They gave another heave, and the rear wheels of both siege towers lifted even higher than before as the front wheels settled further down into the ditch.

"Get those men out of there! Get them off the stairs!" he screamed.

Men began to pour out of the rear of the towers and from beneath the now raised back wheels, but as news of the trap spread, panic set in among those at the top waiting to leap onto the walls. They scrambled to descend, further destabilizing the already precarious structures.

"Pull it back down!" Ranalph yelled as the back of the tower continued to rise into the air. But most of the soldiers were retreating, and those who were trying to hold on were forced to let go as the towers tipped dangerously forward.

Ranalph ran back to the front, shoving Hans aside in his haste to find a way to stabilize the structures before it was too late.

In that fleeting moment, with the rear wheels of both towers hovering at head level, Hans grasped the full scope of his mistake: he had led them straight into yet another

Dawning trap, and he had done it over the objection of not only his subordinate but his biggest naysayer! This was a blunder so massive and so glaring that it could not help but ruin his reputation as word spread among the ranks. Instead of being seen as a great leader as he had been imagining minutes before, he would be labeled a fool. He could not have that, especially when his control of his men was already so tenuous.

Ranalph, seeing that the situation was hopeless, turned back to Hans, rage coloring his face. "You half-breed fool!" he bellowed, each word striking Hans like a physical blow.

"Incompetent, worthless, stupid!" Hans flinched, unable to absorb the onslaught, especially now when he was facing his most disastrous failure. This could not be his fault, yet he needed time to think without this oaf screaming in his face. Why wouldn't he shut up?

Hans tried to turn away, but Ranalph grabbed his arm and continued to thunder out his rage. Panic surged in Hans. If this fool didn't quiet down, everyone would hear him, and the blame would fall squarely on Hans' shoulders. He had to silence this man!

Then it happened: the back wheels of both towers lifted even higher, hung momentarily in uncertainty, and then began to inexorably topple forward.

The soldiers scrambled to get clear, leaving Hans and Ranalph alone between the front wheels of both machines. In that moment of clarity, Hans realized that Ranalph was shielded from the view of anyone who happened to be looking on.

In the last instant, Hans acted. He stepped forward, fueled by his doubt, fear, and humiliation, and shoved Ranalph in the chest.

Caught off guard, the force of Hans' push threw Ranalph directly into the path of the collapsing tower just as it crashed down upon him.

Eight

eah was working mechanically. She went through the motions of dressing wounds and setting bones, but she scarcely heard the cries of pain, lost as she was in the despair of her own soul. She couldn't count the number of times she looked up expecting to see Eve at the next table, only to be reminded with a fresh stab of anguish that Eve was not there and would never be there again, which thought was followed closely by a renewed surge of rage toward her murderer.

Leah no longer cared if she survived this siege. She no longer cared about any dream of some future life of happiness; she cared only about seeing William punished before she died. He must be made to pay for all the blood on his hands, for all the misery he had caused!

Leah realized that she was standing before an empty banquet table. Her last patient had been removed without her noticing, and she was clutching the implement in her hand so tightly that her knuckles were turning white.

She turned her eyes up to Edith, her handmaid and friend who had been assisting her and who should have already been escorting the next injured person to the table, but Edith too had not moved. She was weeping silently.

Irritation surged in Leah. If Leah could work through the agony that she was in, what excuse could Edith make?

"What is the delay?" Leah asked, unable to bring herself to address Edith's tears directly. She simply did not have it in her to offer comfort to another person at this moment.

"Forgive me, Lady," Edith said. "I do not mean to interrupt the work," she hastened to wipe her eyes but made no move to call for the next patient.

Leah suspected that Edith was waiting for her to ask further, as she might have done only a day before. But at this moment, she did not care about Edith's sorrow. Why shouldn't she be sad? Everyone else was! "If you are unable to perform your function as my assistant, ask Meredith to step in," Leah ordered, but that only caused Edith's weeping to devolve into quiet sobs. She put her hands over her face to hide them, so she did not see Leah's irritation deepen.

"What is the problem?" Leah asked, not even attempting to hide her impatience.

"Forgive me, Lady," Edith composed herself with obvious effort. "I know this is a terrible time, but you see ..." she seemed to be considering how to proceed, "you see, Najid, my lov—the man who has been courting me—he has yet to appear. I am terribly worried. I fear the worst...." She trailed off into troubled silence, biting her lower lip to keep it from quivering.

Leah stared at her mutely. She had forgotten all about Edith and her lover in the chaos and turmoil of the previous night. She had forgotten entirely that it had been Edith's fear for her missing love that had been the final piece of the puzzle that had enabled Leah to see the whole picture. Edith's revelation was what had clued Leah in that Martha was in danger and that William was involved. That's what had led her and Eve to the chapel where they had managed to protect Martha from William, but only at a terrible cost—a cost that Leah had not been prepared to pay.

Leah now realized that she had not even given Edith a thought since that moment. Her handmaid had been left in her anxiety without so much as a word of explanation. But it was not regret that Leah felt now about leaving her friend in such a state, nor was it embarrassment or even sorrow, as it might have been just twelve hours before; it was anger. This idiot girl was expending tears on a man who had almost certainly been part of the conspiracy that led to Eve's death? Edith herself had likely played a part in the events that led up to that moment, albeit an unwitting part.

Leah only just managed to stifle the irate response that sprang to her lips, but she could not even feign sympathy as she said, "Your serving man is dead."

Edith gasped, her hand coming to her mouth. "He—how do you know?"

"He was part of a conspiracy with William Dawning, and William murdered him."

Edith stared at her in horror, but Leah did not avert her gaze. Part of her felt satisfaction at watching Edith wilt before her. Perhaps now she would begin to understand how naive and stupid she had been. Maybe she would begin to understand that she had put them all in danger. Maybe she would start to feel the magnitude of her mistakes!

"Leah, I ..."

"We have all lost people," Leah cut her off curtly. "Those are the fortunes of war." She turned and set her instruments back on the tray. "There is much to do," she said coldly, ignoring the tears that were running down Edith's cheeks, leaving red streaks on her pale skin. "See to it!"

Edith remained where she was for a few moments, trying to suppress her sobs, then all at once, she turned and fled.

"Return to your station!" Leah barked at her back, anger flaring anew. *I am working with a broken heart, so can you!* She wanted to scream at the retreating girl. *And unlike you, I did nothing to bring this about! And now in my deepest grief, when all the barony should be in mourning with me, I am suffering alone. The most painful tragedy of my life is pushed aside because of the attack. My betrothed is not here for me, and even Edith, who supposedly loved Eve too, can only think about the villain that she had treasured more than my sister.*

But as the hot flash cooled and the anger receded, Leah realized that her bitterness and anger had not entirely filled her soul; there was still room enough for guilt.

Nine

eil stared at Salena. Against all odds, they had made it out of Dawning Court without incident. They were never even challenged. That did not seem right, but Neil consoled himself that it was because of the attack on the castle that the enemy did not have men to spare; perhaps monitoring the gate for people *leaving* Dawning Court was the least of their worries. Now, with leagues between him and the castle, and the possibility of pursuit becoming ever more remote, Neil's thoughts were on the woman beside him driving the wagon in silence.

He had no idea what to make of it. Neil had always gotten on well enough with Salena even when they were younger, but now they did not speak. He would have assumed—had he given her any thought at all—that she had left the castle with the other nobles. But the fact that she was here now, filthy, stinking, and studiously ignoring him, suggested there was a lot more to this story than he knew.

"Did they capture you trying to flee the castle?" he finally ventured.

Salena did not move her eyes from the road.

"Hans ... captured me," she said slowly.

"And Rachel?"

Salena dropped her eyes at the mention of her daughter. "She was not with me; I pray for her safety."

Neil was surprised by that. Salena had always been an overprotective mother, and the idea that she would not have kept her young child close during the chaos of a mass exodus seemed strange.

"Do you believe that Aden can save the castle?" Salena asked to change the subject.

"If what Thomas said is true ..." he trailed off, realizing how ridiculous that sounded. "It seems unlikely."

"Then where are we going?"

"I do not know if Aden can save the castle. I do not know whether he is actually being pursued by Collin Braddock as Thomas indicated. I do not even know for certain that he has left Runnymede. But what I am certain of is that he is the last hope for Dawning Court.... Why are you stopping? Is there danger ahead?"

Without explanation Salena brought the wagon to a stop off the side of the road. Neil noted the firm set of her jaw and suddenly had the sense that he was in danger, but not from anyone who might be lurking in the trees. "Lady Abelin," he said slowly, working himself up from the half-reclined slump he had been in to reduce the pain in his torso, "are you unwell?"

She turned cold eyes on him. "I will not help you to save the Dawnings."

"You—you are helping the Braddocks?" He could not keep the incredulity from his voice, but he suddenly felt very vulnerable and wished for a weapon. "Salena, you are a Dawning."

"I am *no* Dawning!" she hissed. Before he could say more, she added, "and do not dare accuse me of complicity with that despicable bastard, Hans Braddock!"

Neil was confused, but recognizing that he was in uncharted waters, he spoke delicately. "Yet by not helping the Dawnings, you are helping the Braddocks."

"If our goals happen to coincide, then so be it. But do not ever accuse me of being party to that loathsome viper!"

Neil forced his voice to remain calm. "Lady, I do not understand. Is this because of David?"

She did not look at him when she spoke. "The Dawnings are the vilest, meanest sort of people. I will do nothing to protect their legacy that, were there any justice in the world, would have been stripped from them decades ago!"

"Salena," Neil said, choosing his words carefully. "This is bigger than the Dawnings. You must see that. There are innocent people who will suffer greatly if Thomas takes that castle."

"Listen to yourself!" she almost screamed at him. "You are trying to protect the Dawnings from the Dawnings!" Then in a low voice pregnant with rage she added, "I heard the guards talking; William lives!"

"You know about that?"

"I will not help that murderer."

"Salena ... I, too, miss David very much." Her head snapped around at the mention of her late husband's name. "I understand the injustice of it all. I understand your desire for revenge—truly I do—but you do not know what it is you do. It is not William that you are punishing; it is the *people* who will suffer."

Salena looked uncertain for a moment, but then her face hardened back into resolve. "I have sacrificed too much to see the Dawnings destroyed; I will not now be the instrument of their salvation."

Anger flared in Neil. He and everyone else he cared about had given their all to preserve Dawning Court, and now this silly woman was going to make it all for naught because she was throwing a tantrum! He suppressed the urge to snatch the reins from her and simply drive on; he was too weak for that. He had to accept that he was at Salena's mercy, and she was clearly in a dark place.

Neil took a deep breath to calm himself. Understanding and compassion were hardly his fortes, but this was a situation that would not yield to force. "Salena," he said softly, though he could not entirely keep the suspicion out of his voice, "how did you come to be in the company of Hans Braddock?"

Salena's jaw tightened with resolve, "'Twas I who authored the Dawnings' destruction!" she said with relish. "I told the Braddocks of the west wall. That is what gave Hans the confidence to march on the castle."

Neil was stunned. "You ... told Hans? But your friends, your family, David's legacy—"

"I care nothing for them!" she screamed at him. "Why should they live while my David is dead? He died at the whim of an evil man. And rather than stand up for David and decry William as the murderer he is, all those people celebrated him as some great hero. They did not have the courage to do what I did. And what I did, I did for David!"

Neil stared at her. The shock of the revelation was rapidly giving way to blinding rage. "Do you know what you have done?" his voice rose with each successive word. "Had you not done what you did, Hans would not have marched when he did, and Thomas' Saracen army would have been defeated. It is because of you that Richard is dead! It is because of you that we are all suffering this waking nightmare!" At that moment, if Neil had had a weapon, he would have struck her down without a moment's hesitation. "You are a ... traitor!"

"Traitor?" she shrieked. "I sacrificed everything to see *justice* done!"

"*You* sacrificed everything?" Neil shot back, ready to unleash his fury. But Salena suddenly wilted before him, dropping the reins and hugging herself.

Neil froze, confusion washing over him. When she had been matching his anger tit for tat, he knew how to respond, but seeing her suddenly wither before him left him once again uncertain.

"Hans," she whispered quietly, "would not let me go until he was certain that I was not part of some elaborate Dawning plot." She shuddered and looked away in shame as she said the next part. "He then forced himself upon me. Again and again. Day after day. Long after it was clear that I had been truthful with him, he continued to gratify his disgusting appetites at my expense. I did not bathe or change my clothes, or tend to my grooming in any way, with the hope that I would repulse him, but he only seemed more pleased at my debasement."

Neil was sickened by the image. His noble side felt to challenge Hans on her behalf, but then he remembered that she only came to be in his control by willingly betraying her own people—Neil's own people—and his anger at Salena blazed again. He wanted to revile her, to condemn her, to make her feel the weight of the thousands of lives that should be laid at her feet. But it was clear that she was already suffering, and what was more, he realized that she was his only hope for getting to Aden in time to warn him. He could not risk piling more on her just now; she was clearly on the verge of breaking as it was. "Salena," he forced himself to speak softly again, "if your aim was to punish William then you have failed."

"What?" She looked at him sharply. "You said yourself Dawning castle will fall to Thomas and Hans this very day."

"Salena, William is *with* Thomas! He, too, is a traitor!" It seemed there was a lot of that going around.

She stared at him. "I do not believe it!"

"It is true," he said. "William pretended to stand with Richard, but he was in league with Thomas all along. It may very well have been William himself who murdered Richard after the army had returned to Dawning Castle."

"No—that cannot be true."

"You *know* William. Do you really have any trouble imagining that of him?" Even as he asked the question, something about it nagged at him. William was many things: arrogant, selfish, brash, hot-tempered. But Neil had known William his whole life, and William was always fiercely loyal. *But*, he reminded himself, *William changed a lot in the years he was away. And I saw him there by the river with my own eyes.* But those doubts were not important at the moment; what mattered now was that he win Salena's support. "In point of fact, William is the reason that I am here now, in this state." He gestured to his bandaged stomach.

Salena's eyes narrowed. "You did not mention that back at the house."

"The wound was not delivered by William. But I was captured because he attacked us when we went out to break down the dam," his frown deepened, "the dam that was flooding the west wall!"

She did not lose her suspicious expression. "Then either you or William should be dead."

Neil stopped at that. He had not had much time to think back to it, but she was right. Why wasn't he dead? Why had William run off when he had both knights at his mercy? It could not have been fear. Perhaps he thought his identity was still unknown and was trying to keep it that way. *But if that were the case, would it not have made more sense to kill us?* Neil shook his head to clear it. "He left Timothy and me for dead. In my case, it almost worked. By the time he was done with me, I could not climb the rope back up to the battlements."

Salena's mouth had formed into a tight line. "Your story only strengthens my resolve."

"But do you not see?" Neil's voice rang with desperation. "You are not punishing William; you are helping him to get what he wants. You are punishing Leah and Eve—your friends!"

Salena's face fell at that, and Neil took heart that perhaps he might reach her after all. "If you truly want to punish William, you must see to it that his schemes are foiled. If the castle endures, then he is defeated. Even if he survives the battle, he will have no country that he may call home. He will be a pariah to all who know him, hated by his own people as much as he is hated by the Saracens. The 'white warrior' will become an epithet, and you will be a hero to those you care about." He could see that she was considering his words and leaned in for emphasis. "Salena, we must get to Aden before it is too late."

Salena thought for a long time until at last, she shook the reins and wordlessly directed the horses back onto the road.

Ten

Thomas watched with a growing sense of dread as the knights operating the battering ram fled from the barbican in flames, and then two of the three towers tipped over. And the third tower—Amir's tower—rolled to a halt scarcely outside of camp, still not even in the wall's catapult range. It had been spared only because Amir had been staging the fight with Thomas for Neil's benefit, causing him to be late; so he had not been alongside the other towers when they hit the trap.

The problem was that Hans was supposed to defeat the castle before the Saracen army turned on them. But as it was, victory over the castle was looking less and less likely.

Thomas looked around for someone with whom to consult, but he was alone behind the catapult line save for the soldiers scurrying to and fro to keep the weapons firing. He had remained back deliberately, biding his time until victory was assured, at which point Amir was supposed to give the order for the Saracens to turn on the Braddocks. The surprise attack from within their own ranks should make for a quick and decisive victory, leaving Thomas and his Moor army to take the castle. That was the moment Thomas planned to step in: when he could stroll through the open gate as conqueror.

But now, for the first time, he was forced to consider something that had never even crossed his mind since Richard's death—the possibility of defeat. He had never considered the possibility that they could lose to a peasant army, nor had they even discussed the idea. After all, one siege tower had very nearly overwhelmed the battlements; it was inconceivable that three should fail. But now two of the towers lay in ruins, never having reached the wall, and the barbican had again repelled the ram.

They were in serious trouble. The difficulty was not so much manpower, though that was dwindling rapidly, but time. They absolutely had to take the castle before Collin arrived with his army.

Thomas could only pray that his ploy to have Neil convince Aden to dig in against Collin would buy them the time they needed, which until this moment he had assumed would be no more than a day. But now he was not sure how long it would take because he was not even sure what to do.

Naturally Thomas always had the option to run, but beyond escaping with his person intact, running left him with nothing to show for all his sacrifice and very limited options for remounting an attack. It might take him years to raise an army to try again, and by then the defenses would be rebuilt, and he would have to start all over.

Hans came galloping back toward Thomas. Behind him soldiers were scattering in every direction. Some were running to join the ladder teams, some were running back toward the safety of the rear, and some did not seem to know where to go.

"This is a disgrace!" Thomas yelled at him before noting the wild look in his eyes. Hans looked at Thomas without seeming to see him. "Hans, what has happened?"

Hans glanced behind him as though he were afraid someone might be following him. "That fool, Ranalph ..."

"Yes?"

"He led the towers into a trap," Hans said almost as though he were talking to himself. He reached up and dragged his plumed helmet off his sweaty head. His hair was disheveled and only added to his wild appearance.

"Those towers cannot be easily replaced!" Thomas growled, dropping all pretense of deference to this man whose incompetence was putting Thomas' own goals at risk.

Hans looked at him, and his unfocused eyes suddenly focused. "There is still one more tower. We may still win the day!"

"The battle is lost, Hans," Thomas muttered reluctantly. "Our men are scattered. It is better to regroup and attack fresh. Sound the retreat!"

"*I* will decide when the battle is lost!" Hans bellowed at him.

"If we lose any more men, we will be sacrificing any hope of taking the castle at all! Stubbornness today will cost us the war tomorrow!"

"There is no tomorrow!" Hans shrieked in a shrill voice.

"If it is Collin you fear, Hans, what will enrage him more: To find that you have failed to take the castle and have killed off his entire army, or that you and the army live to fight another day?"

"How dare you?" Hans choked out. "I fear no man!"

"We still have time," Thomas reassured him. "I have received word that your brother is engaged in battle with Sir Aden a day's march from here.

Hans regarded Thomas, apparently trying to decide which of his statements to respond to, but he finally said, "I have heard no such thing."

"Of course not. You said yourself this morning that your scouts have not reported in...." That gave Thomas pause. He had not thought much about it at the time, being so keen to see William's attempt to undermine the Braddock-Saracen pact undermined, but surely that could not be a coincidence. "Your scouts still have not returned?"

"We have your brother to thank for that," Hans snarled, but Thomas frowned.

Suddenly that seemed strange. William had already been imbedded with the Braddock army. What reason would he have had to track down the scouts? What had seemed a simple enough explanation only a few hours before suddenly seemed a terrible omen. "We must send scouts out at once! We are in grave danger!"

"But you only just said that your—"

"Not to Collin," Thomas said urgently, "to check the surroundings for an army. *Another army!*"

Then, as if speaking it aloud had brought it to pass like some terrible incantation, they appeared, streaming in through the gates and the breaks in the outer wall of the Dawning lands like water through a crumbling dam. Hundreds of soldiers flying a red banner with a white cross sitting beside two yellow flowers became visible.

"Who is that?" Hans shrieked, but Thomas knew at once what he was seeing.

William's wild-sounding accusations were not simply a deception to undermine the trust of his enemies. They were real, and Thomas had not spared a moment's thought for what he would do if they proved to be true. And now it was too late. "Mayfield!"

At that same moment, Hans must have been coming to the same conclusion because he rounded on Thomas. "You mutinous dogs!" He went for his sword.

Without time to consider, Thomas acted. He reached up and yanked Hans from his saddle and slammed him to the ground. The weight of Hans' armor caused him to hit harder than Thomas had intended, and his bare head snapped back and collided with the earth, knocking him unconscious.

Thomas was not sure if Hans was dead or not, but he did not take the time to find out. Climbing into the now-empty saddle, he rode toward Leon's house. He had just been betrayed by Amir, and Hans believed that Thomas was part of it, which meant that Thomas was a man without an army in a three-way battle for the barony. Thankfully, he knew where he could get an army of his own only a day's march away.

When Hans came to, he was lying on the ground, and his head was pounding. A look at the encroaching Mayfield army told him that he could not have been unconscious for more than a minute or two. He climbed to his feet, a wave of giddiness causing him to stagger. He reached for his horse for support, but it was gone. *That scoundrel has absconded with it!* What was he to do now?

Think, you fool! He heard the voice in his head forcing him to focus, as it so often did. But it was not his own voice; it was the voice of his father correcting, denouncing, and spurring his bastard son on to greater heights than he would have otherwise attained.

"I—I do not know what is happening," Hans muttered, holding his pounding head between his hands.

Of course you do! Daniel Braddock's voice snapped back. *Concentrate!*

Hans realized that his father was correct, as he always was—usually was. When Hans forced down the feeling of panic long enough to consider, he *did* know what was happening, he had simply not wanted to face it. All at once three very important things occurred to him: He had been betrayed, his army was now outnumbered by a new enemy, and Collin might only be a day away.

What do you see? The voice, ever impatient in death as it had been in life, interjected itself into his thoughts.

"Thomas betrayed us," he breathed.

Of course he did. Now what is to be done about it?

Hans looked around. The attacking army had already overrun the mostly deserted camp, burning and looting everything they passed and killing any unfortunates who did not get clear in time. They were now pouring onto the battlefield, attacking any English soldiers they encountered.

Hans watched in horror as the Saracen army, instead of helping to fend off this new enemy, turned on his men who, having no inkling of what was happening, did not even offer up any resistance as their former allies cut them down in droves. It was very clear that if he did not do something quickly, he would have no force left to salvage.

"Regroup," he muttered uncertainly, "we must retreat and regroup."

As if it were some divine confirmation of his decision, a young page with a trumpet strapped about his chest came riding from the camp, fleeing the certain death of the attack on the camp for the relative safety the chaos of no man's land offered.

"You there!" Hans called, his voice sounding shriller than he would have liked. The young man, recognizing Hans, reigned in his horse with a nervous glance at the Mayfield soldiers in pursuit. "Rally the men," Hans growled.

"We must flee!" the boy cried, his horse prancing in a nervous circle.

Hans grabbed the boy and yanked him from the saddle, dropping him roughly to the ground, much as Thomas had done to him. "Do as I say! Call the men!"

The small group of Mayfield soldiers racing toward them were running wild after the page in no formation, just raiders out to pillage rather than trained foot soldiers. *Mercenaries!* Hans realized. He could deal with that; he just needed an appropriate weapon. He climbed onto the boy's horse. "Keep sounding the retreat until I return."

He spurred the animal into motion. Galloping over to a nearby weapons rack, he snatched up a lance that had been left behind because it was useless in a siege. It was, however, exactly what he needed at this moment.

Setting the weapon, he charged the closest Mayfield soldier, a swarthy-looking man with long, greasy hair. He took the man in the chest and was shocked by how easily the weapon tore through the man's chest beneath his leather armor. He did not even need to break stride to bring the lance back up for his next kill.

The next four men fell almost as easily as the first, and Hans cut a wide swath through the first ragged line of mercenaries before his lance broke. But it was enough to turn the soldiers away from his own disorganized soldiers and back to the camp in search of reinforcements.

For a moment Hans felt untouchable. *This is where I should have been all along!* he thought as he discarded the broken shaft and drew his sword. *I belong where the battle is fiercest. I am a Braddock!*

He wanted nothing more than to keep thrashing the line, answering the indignity of their treachery with Braddock steel, but now was not the time for that. There were too many for him to take on alone, no matter how angry he was. Instead, he turned and raced back to the page who was still dutifully trumpeting his rallying call.

Hans yanked back on the reins of his horse and drew up beside the boy, still panting from the exertion but elated at the triumph. He met the boy's eyes, expecting to see awe there, but the boy had not even seemed to notice. He still just looked terrified.

"Why do you stop?" Hans demanded when the boy left off the horn as if expecting Hans to take up the call.

"Nobody is responding," he cried frantically. "They either do not hear or cannot answer back!"

Hans twisted in his saddle and buried his blade in the chest of an approaching soldier. It angered him that this boy was attempting to instruct *him*. "Do as I say, or you are of no use to me!" The page pressed the horn to his lips and continued to sound the call, like a condemned man being forced to summon his own executioner.

Hildebrant was with the ladder teams crowding around the base of the Dawnings' inner wall. Hans had assigned him there as punishment for allowing William Dawning into their camp. More than just a simple demotion from the towers to the ladders, this was tantamount to a death sentence since the casualty rates were far higher trying to scale unprotected fifty-foot ladders compared to pushing a sixty-foot shield up to the wall.

Nevertheless, Hildebrant had not argued. He was ashamed that he had not detected William sooner. Yet even now, he could not shake the image of the broken boy he had found on that battlefield only a week before. *Could that have been a ruse?*

When Finn had led him into that ghastly graveyard with only one weeping survivor, Hildebrant had felt that he had been walking back in time to that fateful field where, in a moment of passion, he had allowed his own headstrong, belligerent son to perish.

Calvin had defied Hildebrant's orders and attacked too deep into the enemy line. Though he was only fifty yards away, he was surrounded, and it would have cost many lives to try to rescue him. So, in a moment of vengeful anger, Hildebrant had stayed his men from helping and instead stood and watched his son get overwhelmed by the enemy, even while screaming to his father for help.

Though Hildebrant had not wanted Calvin to die, in his anger he had wanted Calvin to suffer for his disobedience; he wanted the headstrong, disrespectful, arrogant boy to feel the repercussions of his own defiance.

Then, the moment before Calvin had died, when it was too late to do anything but mourn, Hildebrant's anger melted away, and he was left with an unobstructed view of what he had just done. Calvin was cut down before his eyes in an image that he could not but carry with him the rest of his life.

Was I not seeing Calvin in William in that graveyard? The version of Calvin that I wished a thousand times to find—

humbled, weighed down with regret, but alive? But as he considered, he realized that it was not a proxy for Calvin he had found weeping over his dead in helpless misery, but for himself. He was seeing himself all those years ago, shattered, staring over the remnants of what he had just sacrificed. In that moment, he had been William, and when he came across that broken boy, he decided to be for William what he himself had needed back then—the comforting angel that had never appeared to carry him from that nightmare.

Instead, he returned to Braddock Court a broken man. His wife died of grief not long after, and Hildebrant himself had very nearly drunk himself into the grave beside her. He had finally decided that since there may be no balm that could heal his soul, perhaps he could be that good angel to others with what time he had left.

No, he decided, William had not played him. What he had seen on that battlefield was genuine. That boy had lost everything, and Hildebrant had never stopped to consider that he might not be a Braddock. William had then taken advantage of the situation.

But now Hildebrant was here, in the middle of a frenzy at the base of the wall, with death raining down upon them from above, and his foremost concern had to be staying alive. Their ladder had already been pushed over once, but they had just gotten it resecured when the trumpet sounded retreat behind them.

The trumpeted call came again. Hildebrant's men paid it no heed amidst the clamor of the battle, but Hildebrant was attuned to it. He realized now that he had been half-expecting it. He looked around to get the lay of the land before ordering the retreat. That was the only warning he had of the Saracen attack.

The ladder team beside them was made up of Moors, and almost as though the call to retreat was a call to battle, they turned their focus from the wall and cut into Hildebrant's men.

His squad was so shocked at the unexpected blitz that half of them were cut down before they even reacted. "Fall back!" Hildebrant shouted as he cleaved through a Saracen shield.

In the excitement, his brain was slowly starting to put together what was happening. They had been betrayed; the Moors had probably sabotaged the siege towers and were now turning on his men! He needed a minute to think, to regroup, to see who else was still standing, but they were depriving him of that.

"We have been betrayed, men!" he shouted. "Retreat! We must get clear of the wall! Retreat! Retreat!"

The fierceness of his cry startled his men into action, and they pulled themselves from the immediate fight to follow Hildebrant out into no man's land amidst the falling stones and arrows from above.

Hildebrant led them from the most immediate danger, but where could he go? With attacks now coming from every direction, what ground did that leave them?

Then the trumpeting began again in earnest. Hildebrant set a course toward the sound, shouting warnings to as many Braddock men as his small crew could find along the way, and entreating them to fall in with him.

Hans' blade cut to both sides of his horse as the enemy soldiers began to swarm around him. Even the trumpeter snatched a mace from the hand of a dead soldier and began laying about him. His movements were not inept, but he was young and managed little more with the weapon than keeping a few soldiers at bay. Hans knew that the youth would soon be cut down, but while the boy still lived, he would serve as a distraction, which could only help Hans. So he called encouragement to the lad even while he searched for an escape for himself.

He would have to move quickly, or it would be too late. But where could he go? The entire field was mayhem. The Mayfields had taken the camp and the village, the Saracens were on the east, and the castle was shooting at anything that moved. There was no Braddock stronghold left, and there was no safe quarter in which to create one.

Suddenly Hans' knights were streaming around him, pushing back the Mayfields who were on the brink of hemming him in. Hans was so relieved that he was only marginally annoyed to see it was Hildebrant leading them. "Lord Hans, are you hurt?" the burly knight inquired perfunctorily.

"I am well enough, Hildebrant. Is this all the men you have gathered?" he demanded of Hildebrant, who had turned and laid an affectionate hand upon the trumpeter's shoulder.

"It was a well-planned attack," Hildebrant admitted, his smile fading as he turned back to Hans. "The enemy knew just when to hit us when we would be most vulnerable."

"So what is to be done? This is intolerable!"

"We must send to Lord Collin for help before they block the road if we are to have any hope of salvation."

Fear spiked Hans' heart at the mention of his brother finding him like this, and that fear turned to rage an instant later. His gauntleted hand flew of its own accord, striking the bearded knight across the face and drawing blood from his cheek. "How dare you attempt to undermine me? I should have you executed right here for this sedition!"

Hildebrant touched his fingers to his cheek and inspected the blood. "This is not a question of leadership," he said with carefully controlled fury, "it is a simple matter of arithmetic. Even if we had our entire force, we are outnumbered by at least three to one. As it stands now, it is closer to ten to one. Our escape is cut off, but a man or two could get a message through to Collin provided they go now! If you care for the lives of your men, you will appeal to your brother for reinforcements."

Hans reared back to again strike the insubordination from Hildebrant's cowardly maw, but Hildebrant was upon him in an instant. The large knight snatched Hans by the breast plate and yanked him from the saddle, dropping him to the ground and splattering mud in all directions. Hans found himself looking up at the sky for the second time in as many hours.

"How dare you?" he screamed when he had regained his wind. "Somebody help me up!"

Several of the men dutifully started forward but stopped at a word from Hildebrant. "Do not touch him!"

You are losing control of the situation! Daniel Braddock shouted in Hans' head. *Put that man in his place.*

"I will kill you for this!" Hans growled, but he was still on his back, his movement seriously restricted by his heavy armor. He rolled onto his stomach and climbed onto all fours to get to his feet.

Hildebrant, still towering over him, set a foot on his back and shoved him back down.

He is making you look like a fool in front of your men!

Hans roared an inarticulate sound of rage and started to push himself up again, but Hildebrant kept his foot on his back to hold him down in the mud.

He is humiliating you!

In his fury, Hans refused to acknowledge the futility of his effort and struggled frantically to get free. But between mud-laden armor and Hildebrant's foot on his back, it was hopeless. Nevertheless, he struggled desperately until he felt Hildebrant's fingers snatch his hair and yank his head back, causing tears to start in his eyes.

"Now listen to me, you little fool!" Hildebrant hissed, his mouth close to Hans' ear. "Look at those men!" Hildebrant indicated another group of enemy soldiers not two hundred yards away who were at that moment forming up to attack them. "Those men are coming to kill us!" Hildebrant yanked Hans' head harder still, pulling his chin up so far that it felt like his neck might snap until Hans found his gaze resting farther up the field by the battlements. "You see that?" Hildebrant growled into his ear. "Those are our brothers being slaughtered up there— betrayed by the heathen army with which *you* insisted on allying yourself. I care nothing for you or your feud with the Dawnings; I care about my brothers-in-arms, who are at this moment being slaughtered!" He lowered his voice low enough that only Hans could hear his treasonous words. "Now either you are going to help us save as many of them as we can, or you are on your own. As you are so quick to point out, I abandoned my own son to an enemy force; do you think I would have the least compunction about doing the same to you?"

Hildebrant released Hans' hair and stepped back. Hans knew the big knight was waiting for a response—they all were. Hildebrant had made him look like a fool. He had called him out for joining his army to Thomas and the Saracens, but Hans had done what was necessary to win. And he *would* have won if he had had men he could count on.

Hans staggered to his feet, sword in hand. "You will pay for this insult!" he screamed at Hildebrant. "Kill this traitor!" he roared at the men looking on. But nobody moved; they just watched.

They are waiting to see who is stronger.

"You must obey me!" Hans screamed at them. "This man has assaulted me—your lord!"

Still no one moved.

You are making a fool of yourself! Hans' father berated him. *They are not certain whom to follow. The only way for you to regain your power is to kill Hildebrant. Do it! Do it now!*

Hans locked eyes with the burly knight. This was the moment. If Hans backed down, his authority was gone. But if he attacked Hildebrant and could not best him, he would forever carry the shame of losing not only to a subordinate but to a branded coward.

Kill him! Daniel Braddock screamed in Hans' head, but the exultant feeling of power Hans had been feeling just minutes before, when he had ripped through the enemy soldiers from the safety of his saddle, was nowhere to be found in his leaden limbs. Had Hildebrant ridden out on the field to joust with Hans just an hour before, Hans would not have hesitated to engage him, but now he felt feeble and ineffectual before the seasoned knight. Hildebrant had humiliated him, and Hans had been powerless to stop it.

Your only response can be to gut him like a hog!

In a rare moment of clarity, Hans could see himself as his men must be seeing him, standing there with his newly burnished armor covered in mud, his blonde hair a filthy tangled mess, having just been unhorsed by an unarmed man. His shouted orders must have seemed less like the command of a mighty leader and more like the tantrum of a spoiled child who was not getting his way.

Hildebrant, who had not taken his eyes from Hans, recognized the defeat in Hans' eyes and turned from him for the first time.

"Finn," he ordered the young trumpeteer, "continue to sound the call. We need to draw every soldier we can to us."

"What is the plan?" one man asked, and every eye that had been watching Hans turned to Hildebrant. And just like that, the question of leadership was settled. Hans knew he had lost the battle without a single blow being exchanged.

Collin would not have hesitated, Daniel Braddock castigated Hans in disgust. The truth of the accusation only added to Hans' mortification because he knew it to be true. Had his brother been the one standing there, Hildebrant would now lie broken at his feet, and no one would even think to challenge Braddock authority. *That is the difference between you and the real Braddock men!*

"We have not the men to fight this army head-on," Hildebrant was saying to the soldiers, sliding very comfortably into the leadership role. "We must send word to Collin for help and regroup before they pick us off a few at a time."

"Even if we do manage to assemble," someone asked, "how are a few hundred to triumph against a few thousand?"

"Forget about victory! Our cause is to stay alive, and our chances of that increase with each new man that can get to us. We need to distract the Saracens and Mayfields long enough to allow our men to find us."

"How do you know they are Mayfields?" Hans demanded, absently trying to wipe the mud from his armor.

Hildebrant stared straight at him and said simply, "because this is exactly what William Dawning told you was going to happen."

Just then a shout went up from the group of Mayfield troops that were assembling nearby, and the band charged Hildebrant's group.

"You!" Hildebrant made a chopping motion as though he were cutting his small force down the middle. "Divide into two groups! I will engage the main force and then fall back, while you," he stabbed a finger at another man who was notably not Hans, "will lead the others around to flank them. Remember, the goal is to incite, not confront. If we can, we want every man on that field chasing us! Hurt them until they turn on you and then fall back. Listen for Finn's horn, that will lead you to us. Now go!"

Eleven

illiam lay in the dark, staring up at the ceiling. Suddenly, there was a pounding at the window. He started up and looked. "William, let me in!" a muffled female voice called urgently.

William slowly stood. He sensed that something was not right, but he could not pinpoint what it was that was making him uneasy. Warm light was filtering through the pane. It was a glorious spring day outside. Everywhere he looked, flowers were sprouting among the green grass. The river path he had walked so many times was in full bloom. The trees were a vibrant green, and the water from the river a crystal blue. Puffy white clouds drifted lazily across a piercing blue sky. It was a perfect day, the kind of day that he only wanted to spend with one person. And here she was.

"Hurry!" Leah's beaming smile was visible through the glass, chestnut hair pulled back on the sides and cascading down over her shoulders, except for the one rogue lock that hung in her face, exactly as he loved it. She wore a dress of light blue and pink that perfectly matched the spring blossoms blooming all around her. She was radiant, but William stopped a few feet from the window, afraid that if he moved, this perfect moment would somehow evaporate.

"William," she laughed, "you are missing the most glorious day."

William continued to stare. It was all over, the war, the fighting, all of it, and she was here for him. His heart swelled at the thought. It was all how it was supposed to be. It was as though he had never plunged his family into this nightmare. Leah was still his, and the promise of a blissful life together was not lost. Everything was going to be all right.

"Let me in, silly."

Finally, William moved. He rushed to the window to throw open the sash, desperate to be with her again, unfettered and unrestrained for the first time in his life. He would shower upon her all the love he had withheld, tell her all the things that he should have told her before. There was a lot of lost time to make up for. But the window would not budge.

"We are going to lose the day!" Leah laughed again, a light, carefree, wonderful laugh such as he had not heard since before fleeing Dawning Court all those years ago. How he used to love making her laugh!

He tried the window again, but still nothing. He could not see any obvious reason it should be stuck, but it would not budge. Everything William wanted in the world lay beyond that glass, but no matter what he did, he could not seem to reach her.

"William," she said, her smile fading, "we haven't much time."

A sudden desperation overcame him, and he reared back and struck the windowpane. It shivered but did not break. He hit it again and was able to wriggle the stubborn sash open an inch but no further. He hit it again and again, but he could not quite get his hand through to reach her.

He tried to call to her, but his lips too were sealed. "Leah!" He tried to form the name but could only seem to moan. He needed to tell her that he was trying and beg her not to give up on him. He needed to tell her what she meant to him, but he could not make the words come.

Terrible fury born of frustration welled in him. He drew back and struck the pane with every bit of strength he could muster. The window reverberated with a deep booming sound ... but the glass held.

He turned back into the room to find something with which to break the glass. He reached for a chair but stopped. Standing only a few feet away, watching him, was Jurou, William's old mentor. Jurou had been forced to leave Dawning Court in disgrace after William accidentally killed Vincent Braddock while cheating in a duel. Jurou had looked upon William's inability to control his anger, which led to Vincent's death, as a personal failure—a failure of the promise he had made to William's parents to harness the boy's spirit while stripping him of his demons.

A flood of emotions filled William at the sight of his old friend. He had never expected to see him again; it was almost like having his father returned to him.

"That life is gone to you, William," Jurou said sternly. "There is nothing you can do to get it back."

"Why would you say such a thing?" William demanded, forgetting the chair and stepping toward him. He could see the judgement behind Jurou's eyes, and the joy at seeing him again was soon replaced by anger. "Why would you return now when it is too late to help me? You wish to witness my final defeat? To see me at my lowest ebb?"

"I did not wish this for you, William. This is the very outcome I sought to prevent."

Another deep, booming sound reverberated through the room, but William did not notice. "You hoped to prevent this?" he almost shouted at Jurou. "You left me when I needed you the most! You taught me the tools of destruction and then abandoned me when I used them to destroy. You did not remain to teach me to temper their use. My life fell apart, and the only tools you endowed me with made everything worse each time I used them!" William was screaming now. "Now you come back to tell me that the life I have long dreamed of is forfeit?" William took another step forward. "I loved you like a father! But just like my real father, you were not there when I needed you. But he at least left me innocent. You made me a monster and then fled in embarrassment at your creation!"

"Did I also not try to teach you peace?" Jurou asked, still with no particular emotion in his voice. "The fist and the empty hand, war and peace, they are two sides of the same coin. Both must be present for the coin to be balanced."

William leapt at his former master, but as he did so, he tripped over some unseen object in the darkened room and crashed to the floor.

William's eyes snapped open when he hit the floor. He bounced instantly to his feet, scanning the room anxiously for Jurou, but it was empty. He spun toward the window, suddenly remembering Leah, but it was boarded up— nailed shut from the outside. It had only been a dream.

"Leah! No!" he cried in anguish. It had felt so real that even now his heart ached with yearning for her—yearning to return to the simple, idyllic life they had once known, whiling away the days in blissful wonder. "Why did I ever leave?" he moaned at the darkness. "Why did I ever give her up?"

But he knew the answer. He had run because he was afraid. Losing his first real battle to Amir had cut a deep gash of fear in him that had been torn wide open by Daniel Braddock howling for his blood. He was afraid and he ran.

Tears of frustrated anger started in his eyes. The feelings of sadness, remorse, anger, and confusion overflowed. He could not contain all the emotion and was desperate for an outlet, some way to vent the self-loathing and regret, some way to escape the heartache of the past. He needed to lash out at something, to destroy something, but what? He was locked in this room awaiting his execution.

Then, as if his wish were being granted, the bolt was drawn back, and the heavy door locking him in slammed open. He recognized the hulking silhouette that filled the doorway at once, though in truth it almost did not matter who it was; it was the outlet he sought. Like an animal, William vaulted over the small table between him and the door and leapt upon the form in the doorway.

Though Thomas had his mace in his hands, he was not prepared for the sudden, ferocious attack that came before his eyes had even adjusted to the darkness. He dropped his weapon in shock when the feral creature flew at him from the black, and he instinctively threw his hands up to protect his face.

William bowled into Thomas and sent him reeling back across the passage to crash into the wall. He leapt upon his brother and slammed his elbow into his surprised face again and again.

Thomas thrashed against him, but William was everywhere, savagely beating him, making it impossible for him to get his feet underneath him or mount any counterattack with any sort of force.

A soldier coming in the door that Thomas had left open cried something William did not understand and ran toward them, sword in hand.

When the soldier was still several yards away, William sprang from Thomas' flailing form, pouncing on the man while he was totally unprepared, just as he had done to Thomas. William grabbed the sides of the soldier's helmet and slammed his head back into the wall, cracking the plaster and leaving a helmet-sized impression in the wall. The soldier's body went limp in his hands.

William snatched the man's short sword, barely noting the unusual weapon and armor that marked him as a foreigner but not a Saracen.

Suddenly, the sounds from the courtyard began to penetrate the fog filling William's head. More men were approaching the house. William did not wait. He ran the last few feet of the passage and burst out of the manor house into the courtyard to find all of Dawning Court in commotion. The battlements were in upheaval as expected, but so was no man's land. And the camps. And the village.

He could see no order to any of it. Everywhere he looked, men of uncertain allegiance were fighting other men, some Saracens, some not. This, too, felt like some fever dream.

I am still not thinking clearly! Then he remembered that he had been running a severe fever when they had dragged him off the field that morning. He realized that he was still frail from the physical toll he had been subjected to over the past week and likely to be extremely vulnerable when the surge of adrenaline wore off. Now that he was free, he needed to get somewhere safe where he could recover properly, and he needed to do it quickly.

Thankfully he did not have to look far for his means of escape. Tied in the yard, grazing on the remnants of the yellowed lawn, stood a beautiful warhorse barded with Braddock insignias everywhere. William did not even pause to consider before taking up the reins, leaping into the saddle, and galloping toward the road.

Men armed like the man he had attacked in the hall came running from around the yard and outbuildings, but William did not even break stride, forcing them to leap aside with curses and exclamations of dismay. He reached the road and turned toward the castle.

A hundred separate skirmishes had broken out everywhere, as if the armies had fallen to infighting. It was total pandemonium. Even the smiths and pages left behind in the camps were now involved in the fight, using whatever weapons were at hand to defend themselves. But William really did not care. That could only be good for Dawning Court.

He rode toward the castle but stopped when he realized that the castle gates were still sealed. The enemy had not breached.

William's mount turned in a nervous circle as he considered what to do next. He could already feel his strength waning and needed to get to safety soon. But if these were the last hours of the resistance, could he just abandon his people?

Yet what good was he to them in his current condition? Even if he did manage to scale the battlements one last time, which was doubtful, what could he even do against a fresh army of ... who? Who were these newcomers?

And that's when he made the connection through the sludge in his brain. *The dark-complected men with the strange swords and armor are mercenaries. This must be the Mayfield army!* But how was he to fight an entire army?

Aden! The answer sprang unbidden into his mind. He could not save the castle by himself in any condition, but Aden had an army.

William turned the destrier back toward the main road and galloped back the way he had just come.

Twelve

Hildebrant brought his axe down upon the mercenary's shield, splintering the battered wood. The mercenary braced for death, but Hildebrant only dropped him with a kick to the stomach, as he was forced to turn and parry another blow from the opposite direction.

Hildebrant's tactic of using his small force to draw off the enemy was not going as smoothly as he had hoped. In his mind's eye, their small squad would continue to fall back while the pockets of Braddock knights united themselves to his group until they had a sizeable enough force to withstand the disorganized Saracen-Mayfield rabble.

But that was not what was happening. Instead, the enemy would start to engage, and Hildebrant would stand up to them just long enough that they would think it was a real fight, and then he would fall back. But not all his men could disengage, often being overwhelmed and left exposed by the retreat. So even though other soldiers were joining themselves to him with each passing minute, he was also losing men with each feint. He felt more like he was dragging the battle along with him like a fishing line behind a boat.

t was obvious that this was getting out of hand. He needed to retreat far enough that he could get a clear separation between friends and foes, but there was nowhere to run to. He was contained within the field of Dawning Court's outer wall, and although that was a large field, the scattered Saracen-Mayfield troops made it impossible to find a safe corner.

He had no choice but to make a stand and maybe, possibly, gather enough men to him to survive the coming storm.

Hildebrant stopped on the relatively smooth footing of the main road and turned on his enemies, while Finn continued to blare the trumpet call to whomever could hear it.

Hildebrant and his men fought ferociously. Though age had taken some of the speed from his sword-arm, it had done little to diminish his strength; nor did losing his taste for battle decrease his skill at it.

At last his small force managed to exploit the mercenaries' disorganized state and send them running for reinforcements.

Hildebrant, Finn, and a few others stood trying to catch their breath while the rest of his soldiers pursued the fleeing enemy, trying to capitalize on their vulnerability. Hildebrant knew that he needed to call his soldiers back before they were cut off and he found himself right back where he had started; but for the first time, his men were racking up an enemy body count, and that was a victory they sorely needed.

Though they had temporarily routed the Mayfield army, it was mainly due to the scattered mercenaries' fear rather than a result of the death toll. Despite their efforts, the Mayfield force was not significantly diminished.

"We had best rally the troops," he said to Finn. "Where is Hans?" While he was not particularly concerned for his lord's safety, he wanted to ensure that that moron was not drawing off the troops on some other short-sighted endeavor.

As if in answer to his question, Hans' regal warhorse, bedecked in Braddock crests, came galloping toward them from the castle, its rider tucked low behind the neck of the beast.

"He is fleeing!" Finn said, echoing Hildebrant's own thought.

Hildebrant was having none of it. "Block the road, men! Do not let him pass." This fool was the one who had gotten them all into this mess, and Hildebrant was not going to let him flee and leave them to deal with the disastrous consequences of his folly.

His men did as instructed, barring the road moments before Hans' horse reached them, forcing the rider to rein in hard. The animal protested loudly and reared up so dramatically that the rider was forced to slide off the saddle or be thrown. He landed on his feet but, unable to catch his balance, he fell to the ground in front of them.

"Hollis?" Hildebrant asked incredulously.

William bounced back to his feet, looking like a man possessed in his black armor, short sword held aloft, ready to take on Hildebrant's entire squad if need be.

Hildebrant was shocked. He had never known William the warrior; he had only known the diminutive squire. Even when Hildebrant had last seen him, William had been rolling around on the ground at the mercy of the Moor giant. He had seemed like a boy caught in a battle of men, someone who needed protecting. But that was not the person who stood before him now, evidently ready to take on a dozen men at the same time.

William spoke first. "I have no quarrel with you, Sir Hildebrant," he said with a force that Hildebrant did not recognize from the diffident boy he thought he knew. "Let me be on my way before it is too late."

"William Dawning." Hildebrant addressed him by name for the first time and felt the tension level rise in the men around him, who had not understood until that moment whom they were facing. "I understand why you did what you did, but you acted without honor. You pretended to be someone you were not and abused my trust to murder my men. You must pay for your crimes."

"I have no wish to harm you," William said flatly, "but if you do not stand aside, I will take that sword from you and kill you with it."

It was unsettling the way he said it so matter-of-factly. There was no blustering or posturing. This boy—man, Hildebrant corrected—really believed that he could do just that.

"I will give you one last chance," William said, his voice growing softer and more menacing. "Now stand aside ... please!"

"I cannot do that, William. Honor demands—"

William pounced, descending on Hildebrant with a flurry of strikes so fast that the older man barely even saw them.

Hildebrant threw his sword up to defend. His honed instincts managed to block the first half-dozen cuts, but William did not stop at half a dozen or even a dozen strikes. He drove relentlessly forward, forcing the older, slower man to stumble backward until his heel caught in a rut on the road, and before any of his men even had a chance to move, Hildebrant was on his back.

William kicked the sword from Hildebrant's stunned fingers, sending it bouncing away, and jammed the point of his own weapon into the older man's coif, twisting it through the links of the mail until it bit into the flesh of his neck.

The soldiers, recovering from their shock, started to close in on William, but he dug the point in far enough to draw blood. "Get back!" he roared.

The soldiers stopped and withdrew a pace.

"If you kill me," Hildebrant warned William quietly, "my men will overwhelm you."

"Are you so certain of that?" William growled ferociously and twisted the sword point even further.

Now Hildebrant could see it. For the first time he recognized the raw animal rage hidden behind the youthful countenance. William's face was the cast of a boy in his early twenties, but the bitter, violent rage behind his eyes bespoke devils many times that. In that moment, Hildebrant could believe all the heretofore unbelievable claims of the whirlwind of death that cut down scores of men for hours on end. *This* was the man who had humiliated Daniel Braddock before striking him down like a child.

Some detached part of Hildebrant's mind pointed out that he had just made the same mistake that Daniel Braddock had when the baron had naively challenged William. Daniel had thought he was challenging William the boy, only realizing too late that he had just unleashed William the demon, a fact that some part of Hans must have known when he chose to pit Hildebrant against William rather than avenge his father personally. But Hildebrant determined not to make the same mistake as the late baron. He was not going to pick a fight that he now understood he could not win. Not if there was any way to avoid it.

"'Tis alright, William," he said softly.

Hildebrant thought he saw William's eyes soften for just a moment, and took heart that perhaps he could reach the boy he had seen on that first day. "'Tis alright," he repeated gently. "Do what you must do. I do not hate you for it. We are victims of circumstance, you and I. I am attacking your home, and you killed my men. This is right."

Some of the rage in William's face turned to uncertainty. "You fool," his voice was quavering with unexpected emotion, "why could you not just leave me be? I never wanted to hurt you! We were friends."

Hildebrant smiled sadly. "Friends though we might have been, we are duty-bound to do as we have done. Kill me if you must. There is no shame in it. But William, the anger, it cankers the spirit. You can never kill enough to chase it from your soul."

William blinked at that, and Hildebrant could see that he had struck a nerve. "You can kill me, kill Hans, kill Amir, Kill Thomas; do you delude yourself that that will bring you peace?"

William's eyes looked distant as he stared at the prostrate man, who waited, barely daring to breathe, aware that his fate hung on a twitch of this unstable young man's hand.

"Finn!" William barked suddenly, "my horse. Bring it to me."

Finn looked nervously between William and his master, indecision showing plainly on his face.

"Do as he says, Finn," Hildebrant said, not taking his eyes from William's.

Finn nodded with relief and hurried off after Hans' horse, which was grazing just outside the area of commotion.

"William," Hildebrant said urgently as soon as Finn was out of earshot, "if you are leaving Dawning Court, take the lad with you. I would that he should live, and you well know there is naught but death awaiting those who remain."

William made no reply but stabbed his sword at a knight who had managed to find a horse on the field. "Surrender your mount!"

Finn led Hans' horse back to William and extended the reins toward him with a hesitant hand.

William reached for the proffered straps. "Finn, you will take that horse," he said, thrusting his head at the newly empty saddle, "and follow me out of Dawning Court."

At that moment, assuming that William was distracted, the knight who had surrendered his horse rushed William from behind.

"Stop, you fool!" Hildebrant barked, but it was too late; he was already in motion.

The knight's armor made him both loud and slow, and William hardly spared him a glance before pivoting and slamming the hilt of his sword across the bridge of the man's nose, dropping him instantly, and pressing the point of his weapon back into the mesh of Hildebrant's coif again as though nothing had happened.

"Perhaps I do not make myself clear," William said quietly at first before roaring, "YOU ARE THE ENEMY! YOU ARE THE REASON MY BROTHER IS DEAD AND MY HOME IS ABOUT TO BE OVERTHROWN! I WILL NOT HESITATE TO KILL EVERY LAST ONE OF YOU!"

The men closest to him took an unconscious step back, and William turned again to Finn. "Mount up. You will ride before me but will follow my cues. Try anything clever and you die, no discussion, no bargaining. Just dead. Do you understand?"

Finn cast a glance at Hildebrant, who nodded reassuringly. He then looked down at the bleeding man writhing on the ground with his hands over his face, blood pouring from between his fingers, gulped, and obediently climbed into the saddle.

William leapt onto Hans' horse, and the two rode away at a brisk trot.

Thirteen

Six Years Earlier

"Relax," Jurou told William, who stood stripped to the waist in the snow. "Embrace the cold," he said as he could see William tensing, on the verge of shivering.

"How is freezing to death supposed to help me overcome my demons?" William grumped, wrapping his arms around his bare torso and rubbing his hands over his skin to try to generate some warmth.

"Your body's reaction to the cold is exactly the way your mind reacts to your past traumas. At the first touch of the cold, you remember the coldest you have ever been and instantly react as if it were a life-or-death situation."

"I *am* going to die!" William blurted without thinking and earned himself a swat to the back of the head.

"Are you?"

William glared at Jurou. Who was he to drag William out into the cold without explanation, force him to strip down, and then abuse him for complaining about it?

"Well? Are you?"

"Am I what?" William muttered, not even bothering to try to understand the gist of the question.

"Are you going to die from exposure?"

William glared a moment more, but then, seeing that it was having no effect upon Jurou, looked around at his surroundings. They were in a stand of trees by the river, not more than a quarter hour's walk back to the warmth of Jurou's training house or the castle. William was cold, but he was dry and in no imminent danger, which he grudgingly admitted to his mentor.

A sly smile crossed Jurou's lips, and William found his annoyance rising again.

"In fact," Jurou rejoined, "you are not even really cold; you are so intent upon your anger with me, that you have forgotten all about the cold."

William realized with a start that Jurou was right. In that moment, he had been so focused upon the injustice of the situation that he had not even been thinking about his physical discomfort. But William was not about to acquiesce that easily. "I am still cold," he said, deliberately rubbing himself again to make his point, "it is only that I was thinking about something else."

"Precisely. And that is exactly how your mind works. It gets stuck upon whatever most attracts it. The cold was still present, but it receded into the background when you allowed your anger to consume your thoughts. Had you been in imminent danger of freezing to death, would you have been able to dwell upon something as trivial as your anger?"

William was embarrassed. As usual, he had acted impulsively, only to find that that was exactly what Jurou was expecting. Jurou had been playing him; and his predictably surly response, rather than derailing the lesson as he had hoped, had only furthered it.

William sighed in resignation. "What do I do?"

"Sit," Jurou said, lowering himself to the ground without bothering to clear the snow away first.

William did as he was told, but he did sweep the bulk of the snow aside before sitting gingerly on the frozen ground, which immediately penetrated his pants, causing him to feel even colder. "Now what?" he asked, afraid he already knew the answer.

"Breathe," Jurou said, taking a deep breath and slowly exhaling, "and just be aware."

"Aware of what?" William asked sarcastically but was not surprised when he got no answer. He had done these meditations in the training house a hundred times after a workout and had come to despise them. They were so mind-numbingly dull that whenever possible he would make up some excuse to cut them short and escape back to the castle. Nevertheless, he knew the routine and began to breathe deeply, filling his lungs and belly with air before slowly exhaling.

"Let yourself feel the wet ground," Jurou said softly through a jaw that had gone slack as he relaxed every muscle in his body. "Feel the breeze blowing over your skin, but do not judge it. Do not think of it as uncomfortable or something to dislike; simply observe it—like a cloud floating through the sky. What would be the point of deciding that you like one or hate another? The clouds are beyond your control and will change, regardless of what you think about them. When you feel your body tensing up to shiver, breathe relaxation through your limbs."

William did as he was told, and much to his surprise, he found that he could stop himself from shivering by simply calming himself. Shivering was such a natural reaction that he had never even considered that he might have control over it.

"Now, let yourself be aware of the sounds around you," Jurou mumbled softly as part of an exhalation of breath. "Tell me what you hear."

William started to respond that he could not hear anything. The snow not only muffled all sound but it had also sent the animals that were usually scurrying through the brush or chirping in the trees into hiding, leaving William and Jurou as the only two idiots not to get out of the cold. But before he could make his snarky reply,

William realized that he could pick out sounds all around them. "I can hear the sound of the snow dropping from the trees. I can hear a small creature rooting through the snow for food."

"Do you know it is in search of food?"

"I can hear a small animal rooting through the snow," William amended. He listened some more. "I can hear the echoes of the voices of the teamsters on the road beyond the trees."

"And are those sounds good or bad?"

William hesitated. "They are neither good nor bad. They just are."

"They just are," Jurou repeated between deep, slow breaths. "So are all things.... Imagine that you are walking along the road, enjoying the day, feeling very good, and a castle steward arrives to tell you that your family has been attacked, and some of them are dead."

William's stomach instantly knotted up at the thought.

"How do you feel?"

"I feel ... afraid," William admitted slowly, "and that makes me angry."

"What makes you angry?"

"That someone hurt those I care about."

"Incorrect," Jurou retorted, still in the same easy, slow voice. "You made yourself feel that fear and that anger."

"What do you mean?"

"In this example, your family was attacked, but you felt just fine until you learned of it. Did your knowing of it change the fact that it happened?"

"Well ... no."

"Then that means the attack cannot affect your state of mind."

"Should I not care that they were killed? Should I feel nothing?"

"You will feel what you will feel, William. Our aim is not to stifle your feelings but for you to understand that those feelings are not you. You do not have to be carried away with them. They are simply your mind's natural reaction to a stimulus, much like your body naturally wants to shiver in the cold. You are aware that it wants to shiver, but you do not *need* to shiver. You can simply be aware of the urge while maintaining your state of peace."

"I do not understand."

"Your consciousness is like this riverbed, and information is like the water. It never stops flowing through it. But these events, these moments, these feelings that you will not let go are like rocks in the stream. Instead of the stream flowing smoothly, the rocks create ripples, rapids, and waves. Until you can separate yourself from these things, you will continue to ride the waves of your consciousness like a twig on the rapids, without any control over whether you rise or fall, feel happy, sad, or angry. You are simply being carried along with the flow of incoming events."

"But *I* did not put the rocks in the river; I do not even want them there!" William protested.

"Yet it is you who keeps them there. If you will simply let them go, they will be washed away, and your consciousness will again flow smoothly. Your only aim is to let things go so they are not allowed to disturb your peace."

"But how do I do that?"

"By not resisting them! By not trying to shove them back down. When these painful experiences come up, let them come. That is your spirit trying to purge the rubbish from your soul. But you are using your mind to shove it back down and hold onto it. When they come up, let them come up; do not turn away; face the feelings that arise. Do not justify, argue, or shift beneath the indictment. If they make you feel shame, feel that shame; if they make you feel fear, feel that fear, and keep feeling it until the pain softens. And then do it again and again until these memories no longer come back with pain."

Jurou left off speaking. William knew he was supposed to be focusing on his breathing but found it hard to keep from thinking over what Jurou had just said. It was not that William did not want to find peace; he just had never noticed any difference in his peace of mind after these meditations.

"Now return to the river of your mind," Jurou said softly after an indeterminate amount of time. "Pick a stone and turn it over. What is there?"

William visualized a stream full of rocks running very roughly. He noted that not all the stones were of the same size. The closer he looked, the more he could see that there were hundreds, maybe thousands, of these stones everywhere, some small, some quite large.

In his mind's eye he stepped up to the first of the stones and turned it over, ignoring the voice in his head that complained that this whole thing was ridiculous. Without even thinking about it, a knot formed in his stomach.

"What do you see?" Jurou asked in the same barely audible voice.

"Callum," William said simply. The feeling of betrayal he felt at being ratted out by his former friend returned to him as though it had happened yesterday. William and his friends had all vandalized the tailor's shop in a fit of late-night, youthful indiscretion, but Callum had blamed William, and Martha had made William do the repairs by himself.

"Face your feelings; do not turn away. Tell me what you feel."

"Anger at being betrayed."

"And what is causing the anger?"

William wanted to snap back that that was a stupid question, but he stayed focused on the memory. "Fear," he finally admitted. "I thought I was safe; I did not expect that my friends would turn on me."

"Anger keeps you from needing to feel fear. But feel it now, William. Do not resist it. Do not judge it. These feelings are neither right nor wrong; they simply are. So let them be, let them flow through you, and simply observe them."

William felt an uncomfortable tightness in his chest. His first instinct was to push it away, but he forced himself to remain focused on it.

"Do not push those feelings down," Jurou said. "Sit with them and let them be. Let the energy pass through you; only then will you be able to release them and be free."

William did as he was told, and after a few minutes the tightness in his chest began to relax. He was still aware of the emotions, but there was a separation from them, as though they were happening to someone nearby.

As he sat with that, new thoughts occurred to him, things he had never considered before. With the emotions of the memory no longer clouding his judgement, he could see with a new perspective. He suddenly realized that Callum and Tyler had likely been punished as well. In fact, they had protected David and Neil by only informing on William who, as the leader of the group, would have been the prime suspect anyway.

"Is that it?" he asked Jurou, hardly daring to believe it. While the exercise had not been pleasant, it had not been particularly difficult. "Is that stone gone from my river?"

"Only you can answer that. The bigger stones may continue to create ripples from time to time, but as often as they do, you will repeat this process until one day, the memories they represent no longer hurt you. They are simply memories of something that happened, devoid of pain and guilt, fear and anger. But be warned that the bigger the stone, the more things around it get stirred up when you displace it, and that can sometimes overwhelm someone who is new to this. What else do you see?"

William relaxed into his breathing again and returned his mind to the river. Almost immediately another thought sprang up. His eyes watered suddenly as he remembered the pain and surprise of his hair being wrenched back as he pummeled Callum and Tyler in their own house. He could feel the coarse ruffles of Salena's dress beneath his knuckles as he spun and delivered a devastating blow to her abdomen. "Shame," he said without realizing he was saying it, "I feel shame."

"Sit with that shame," Jurou breathed. "Like the cold, it is unpleasant; but when you relax in the face of it, it is deprived of its power over you. Do not push it away; simply sit with it until the energy that ties you in knots dissipates."

After a few minutes, these feelings, too, had passed. The pain grew less acute until it was like he was seeing it from a distance. Like pressing on a bruise, initially it hurt, but then after a moment it became a tolerable, dull ache. What William did not know was whether the pain would be acute again the next time he pressed on these spots, but he was content to be free of them in the moment.

"Now ..." Jurou said slowly, "in the middle of the stream, there is a giant boulder."

Without the need to conjure it, William could see it, but he did not dare approach. He knew what it would uncover. "I am not ready," he breathed in a pathetic voice, "I cannot face that now."

"But you must."

Slowly William splashed through the current toward the boulder that stuck well up out of the water. He felt weaker with each step but knew that Jurou was not going to let him off the hook without an honest attempt. He set his hand on the top of the rock, thinking he was going to have to devise some means of levering this stone to turn it over, but touching it was all it took. Amir's scarred visage sprang up before him, leering down at him. This one did not simply tighten William's chest or twist his stomach. It hit William like a punch in the gut, his eyes snapped open reflexively, and he was halfway to his feet to defend himself before he realized what he was doing.

Jurou did not move. "Breathe, William."

William drew a long, shuddering breath, but a cold spasm shook him at the same time.

Jurou opened his eyes and looked at him. "You must deal with this, William."

"I cannot," William said, dropping his eyes to the ground as he began to shiver uncontrollably.

"It is not the giant that haunts you, William; it is the power you give to the memory that robs you of your peace. Until you deprive it of that power, it will continue to control you. It will force you to mask your fears beneath levity, bravado, and rage."

"I am not ready." William did not look up. "My first tournament is in a few weeks. I am competing in an exhibition match before the knights take the field. That will restore my confidence. Maybe after that."

Jurou sighed, stood up, and threw a heavy cloak around William's trembling shoulders.

"Why is that bad?" William grumped, standing and beginning to dance from foot to foot to try to warm up.

"The future never comes, William! The only time you have to make peace is now. This moment right here! Right now! Future William will not be magically imbued with some power to battle the demons you are not willing to face now. In fact, it may be harder for him because he will have lived under this burden longer than you."

"But I am just learning this. Will I not get better over time?"

"That is a true principle," Jurou admitted as they started to walk back toward the training house. "Ordinarily I would not advise a pupil to attack his deepest, most difficult memories immediately. But William, time is not on your side. Circumstances are changing, and the political landscape is shifting beneath your feet. Upheaval is coming, and you will need to be centered and whole if you wish to weather the coming storm."

Fourteen

England, near Dawning Court
Present Day

William shivered despite Hans' heavy cloak that he had found in the saddlebags. They were an hour outside of Dawning Court, and the anger and adrenaline that had fueled his escape had given way to a reflective melancholy that made everything seem bleak and hopeless. He desperately wanted to stop for a while—what he needed more than anything was sleep—but he trudged on. He had to get to Aden to warn him that Dawning Court only had hours left. So he trudged on.

"You—you do not look well," Finn commented hesitantly.

"Are you still here?"

"Well, I—that is, Sir Hildebrant said—"

"You are safe now, Finn. Go your way."

Finn continued to ride a pace behind him in silence, and William forgot about him. His mind was occupied with thoughts of his family, of Leah and Eve, of Amir and Thomas; and his aching and throbbing wounds were all vying for their share of attention as well.

But more than all that, William was troubled by Hildebrant. William had wanted to kill the big knight when Hildebrant had tried to stop him from escaping. But even faced with the prospect of his imminent death, Hildebrant had not returned William's anger with hatred. He had not breathed out vitriol against William; rather he had shown concern and sympathy for William even after William had abused his trust. Hildebrant had not been thinking of his own life but rather of William, Finn, and his men, just as Richard's final thoughts had been for William and the people of Dawning Court.

At the time, William had wanted to believe that it was some trick Richard employed to win others over, but he could not make himself believe that any longer. Richard had changed. He had become a selfless, good man. And Hildebrant was of the same cast.

And to make matters worse, as much as William wanted to hate him for revealing him to Hans, Hildebrant had been acting dutifully. It was Hildebrant who had the right to feel betrayed; but even then, when the old knight had every justification to want revenge, he had still stood up for William against Hans, Thomas, and Amir. Had the roles been reversed, William likely would have thought that the knight was getting what he deserved. But Hildebrant had not done that, and William had repaid him by almost killing him.

He remembered with shame how he had treated his friends whom he felt had betrayed him. He wanted to believe that his retribution against Callum was youthful rashness, but had he behaved any differently when he demoted and humiliated David, or with Neil, whom he had pummeled as an effigy for all his own pain? He had beaten Neil exactly as he had done to his friends all those years before.

I have not grown at all, William admitted to himself. *I am still haunted by the same demons and still reacting to them exactly as I have always done. I have not learned a thing!*

"Y—you look fevered," Finn pulled up beside him, startling William from his reverie. Before William could respond, the boy reached out and felt William's forehead with the back of his hand in a decidedly motherly fashion, reminding William that Finn had likely been living at home with his mother until very recently. "Your fever has returned."

William only grunted in response.

"I really think you should rest. You need a warm fire, food, and sleep."

"What is more important to you, Finn," William grumbled, "my health or Hildebrant's life?"

"What do you mean?"

William sighed; the effort of speaking was expending more energy than he had to give at present, but seeing no way around it, he explained, "The only hope Hildebrant and the others have is if I can recruit aid against the Mayfields."

That silenced the convivial young man, but William continued. "I meant what I said before, Finn. You are free to go. You need not remain with me, particularly as I am riding into a Dawning encampment where you may not feel especially welcome."

Finn stayed where he was, which only triggered William's irritation even more. "Go home!" he barked.

"No," Finn said quietly.

That surprised William enough that he turned his head to look at Finn despite the effort it took.

Finn kept his eyes studiously fixed on the road ahead of him.

"What?"

"I am not leaving."

William might have been amused had he not felt so terrible. As it was, he was more curious than anything else. "May I ask why?"

"You said it yourself: we are on the same quest to get reinforcements. And in your present condition, I am not certain that you will make it without help."

William snorted. "I assure you, Finn, though it be my last act, I will deliver this message."

Finn remained stubbornly at his side.

"Are you not afraid I will kill you?"

"No," Finn replied after a moment.

"Why not?"

"If you had wanted to kill me, you would have just left me behind in camp. Besides, I am not certain you could best me at the moment."

William laughed despite himself. He really did like this boy.

They rode in silence for a while before Finn's urge to talk overcame his reticence. "Thank you," he said, "for saving me."

William felt even more guilt at that. "Hildebrant saved you, Finn; I simply did not object."

"Well, you did not have to take me with you," he pointed out. "Can I ask you something?"

"Can I stop you?"

"Wh—why are you so angry?"

That question startled William. It was as though he had been wearing his thoughts on his sleeve. He was slow to answer, but when he did he answered frankly, too tired to play it off with humor. "Because I am scared, Finn."

"Scared?" Finn was incredulous. "But you are not scared of anything!"

"I am scared of *everything*. I am afraid of being afraid, and when anything touches that fear, I lash out. I do not even think about it. It has taken me this long to even realize that it is not merely anger I feel, but in that instant before the rage rises in me, it is fear that fills my heart. Or at least it has taken me this long to admit that to myself."

"But you are about the greatest fighter in the kingdom, maybe in all the world; what do you have to be scared of?"

"Most things in life are beyond our control, and that terrifies me. Even with all my skill, I could not keep my friend from dying by the Saracen giant's hand; I could not keep your people from pillaging my home; I could not keep Richard alive," he did not add, *nor keep Leah from marrying someone else.* "I took refuge in the Crusades because all I had to do was keep myself alive. I did not know the people we were fighting, and I never got too close to those with whom I fought; it mattered little to me whether we won or lost, lived or died. I convinced myself that indifference to life was the same as overcoming my fear; but since returning home, I have found all the old ghosts still waiting for me, bigger and stronger than ever. But I am still that same scared boy who fled Dawning Court all those years ago."

Finn looked confused and then finally shook his head. "If I could fight like you, I would not be afraid of anything."

"You only say that because you have not yet met your fears."

"I have things I fear," Finn protested.

"Such as?"

"Such as ... Cynthia," Finn said the name, deliberately not looking at William.

William cocked an eyebrow. "Cynthia?"

"The cobbler's daughter." Finn flushed crimson. "Whenever she is near, I cannot speak; I can hardly remember my own name."

I am not sure that counts as real fear, William wanted to point out, but instead said, "You see, then? Being a great warrior would not help you overcome Cynthia."

"But it would!" Finn insisted.

"Are you going to bludgeon her into liking you? Believe me when I tell you that does not work."

"No, but I would not need to be scared because I would know there is something that I was great at, so I would be respected.... And if that did not impress her, *then* I could bludgeon her into liking me."

"Women, you will find, Finn, are not so impressed with prowess on the battlefield as we men would like to believe."

"What do you mean? The queen of the lists always bestows a kiss on the winner, and fair maidens offer tokens to be worn for luck by their favored knights with the hope that they will win."

"Naturally a woman wishes for the object of her affection to be victorious, and many appreciate the trappings often bestowed upon successful warriors. But at the end of the day, that is not what captures most women's hearts."

"Then you are without a lady?"

"Recently, I may have been seen in the company of a young woman," William said slightly defensively, then added without thinking, "Lady Evelyn may be the most beautiful woman in all the realm.... except for Cynthia," he added wryly.

Finn flushed again.

"But she is a perfect example of that which I speak," William reluctantly continued. Since he had revealed something personal, he figured he might as well make his point. "She is smart and clever. She does not want a man that only seeks her as a trophy to be possessed and put on display."

"But why would she love you, if not for your fighting prowess?"

William glowered at Finn, who immediately grew befuddled and tried to backpedal. "What I mean is that, well, of course you are—er—clever and charming, but, well, you know, you are—disgr—that is to say, not in the good graces of ... some of the nobility...."

William waited for Finn's explanation to peter out and then sighed. "The truth is, Finn, I do not believe that Lady Evelyn does love me, nor I her. I think we have both felt on the outside of the nobility for much of our lives, having little taste for the empty formality and ceremonies of court. I think we recognized in each other kindred spirits and were drawn to that. Her because she was tired of being sought as a prize, and me because I could not be with the person I truly wanted to be with. I do love Evelyn, but not romantically. It is easy to get those feelings confused with such a bright, stunning creature. But alas, my heart has always belonged to another."

"Lady Leah," Finn nodded.

William looked at him in dismay. "Is there anything about my private life that is not a matter for gossip?"

"I cannot say," Finn said without sounding the least bit embarrassed, "because everything I know about you I learned through gossip. But you must know that many men in the kingdom sought Lady Leah's hand. Why, even Vincent Braddock himself was intent upon her."

"Is that so?" William replied ironically, "Vincent Braddock confided in you, did he?"

"Well, no. I was only nine when you kill—when he died. Why would he confide in a nine-year-old?"

"Why indeed?" William was awash in conflicting emotions. He had never meant to kill Vincent, of course. But he well remembered the fear he felt when Daniel Braddock was challenging him across the lists. He remembered the shock and guilt he felt when Jurou had told him that Vincent was dead. His entire life had changed that day. He remembered the devastation with which he learned that Jurou was refusing to teach him any longer, and the heart-wrenching farewell he had said to Leah that night when they had shared their first and only kiss, the memory of which was so sweet, he wondered how he ever could have left after that.

"Many say that the reason he challenged you at that tournament was because he sought Leah's hand and you were in the way," Finn said, mistaking William's silence as the need to argue his case further.

A memory returned then, something he had barely even registered until now. William was suddenly standing before Amir on the banks of the river, about to breathe his last breath. "If your brother John had not been such a coward," Amir had said, pontificating upon how they had arrived at that moment. "If Baron Braddock had not failed to rid us of you, or even if Vincent had succeeded...." The memory of those words echoed in William's head. Had

Vincent deliberately goaded William into that duel as a means to kill him? *If so, what does that mean?*

It meant that William may have unknowingly saved his own life that day. But it also meant that Vincent had known exactly how to set William off. He was an open book, and his enemies were using his inability to control himself against him.

"That day ruined my life," William muttered aloud.

"If you could go back and do that day over again, would you?" Finn asked.

Jurou's voice was suddenly in William's head as though he were standing beside him. *It does not matter now, William! It is done. It cannot be taken back, it cannot be undone, and it cannot be relived. Yet here you remain all these years later, reliving it over and over. Is it any wonder that you fail to progress?*

"I am not sure what I would do differently," William said finally, "but I can tell you this. I am tired of thinking about it. I am tired of flagellating myself for all the mistakes I have made and all the trouble it caused. I am done wishing it were otherwise. What happened, happened. I have accepted it and am ready to let it go."

"Let it go?"

"This may be difficult for you to understand, Finn, as you are of a temperament which does not cling to your mistakes and failures. For you, they are like a bad stint of weather. You may not like it; it may inconvenience you; but when it is past, so is all the thought you are going to put into it."

Finn shrugged uncertainly. "Why would I want to keep thinking about bad experiences?"

"That is exactly right, Finn. But what comes so easily to you takes some of us a lifetime to learn."

They rode on in silence for a while, which William welcomed, until Finn again spoke up. "William? What will you do after you deliver your message to Sir Aden?"

"Rest," William said, feeling his body slump at the very thought. How wonderful would it be to finally put this responsibility onto somebody else's shoulders and let someone older and wiser carry it for a while?

Fifteen

**The Kingdom of France, near Avignon
Eight days earlier**

Henry had not left his room since his carriage ride with Edward the previous day. After returning to the house, he had retired early on the pretext of not being fully recovered from his long journey. He had found sleep difficult, however, and wound up drinking in his room alone until he had passed out. He then proceeded to sleep through the next day, only to take up the bottle again upon waking.

Henry was not ordinarily one for drink, but he sought solace in it now, or at least amnesia. He wanted to forget that the world was again demanding things of him that he was ill-equipped to give. He did not want to think about the fact that his ideal society—the society of discourse and diplomacy to which he felt uniquely suited—was a lie, and he would have to function here, in the real world—a world for which he was malformed. And he did not want to see Edward and be reminded of that fact.

Edward, he acknowledged, was revolting, both physically and morally, but he had managed to strike at the heart of the fear that Henry had harbored since his first major defeat. Since that fateful day, Henry had begun to doubt all that he was and all that he believed about himself. But he continued to march the path of virtue because it was all he knew to do. It was the one thing that he felt separated him from his brothers. But Edward had made him question even that. What if the one thing he thought made him superior to his brothers was the very thing that was keeping him from success and happiness?

How oft had he resented the others for the accolades which were heaped upon them, which they neither earned nor deserved? But what if his brothers were simply lesser manifestations of what Edward had become? Edward had abandoned all pretext of social, cultural, or religious mores and had unabashedly sought for pleasure above all else. But not in the short-sighted way, as a brute attacking a woman on a darkened street, a method that would inevitably catch up to him. Instead, Edward had cleverly and single-mindedly created the means of supplying himself with all the pleasures of the world for as long as he lived. He did not even pretend to care for anything else. Family, religion, public perception and sentiment held no sway with him. He had succeeded in building a small empire where he was surrounded by beautiful women, delicious food and drink, and the most comfortable living conditions anyone could ever ask for.

Richard, too, had pursued his desires despite religion, his family's objections, or any other obstacles that might stand in his way. He wanted to be the greatest general in the world and would not be discouraged by anything. Even the Pope's edicts had not dissuaded him in his course. And despite his failure, Martha could not wait to thrust the barony upon him, once again unearned and undeserved.

William had plunged headlong into disaster after disaster, murdering the unfortunate victims of his displeasure, only to be immortalized as a legendary warrior and have the most beautiful woman in the kingdom throwing her life away pining for his notice.

Perhaps it was the wine or the late hour, but it seemed to him now that the only Dawnings who had amounted to nothing were those with some prick of conscience, those who felt that they should be doing more, that they should be better than they were, even though they failed at it: John, Thomas, and of course ... himself.

But what would I be, he asked himself frankly, *if I were completely unfettered by any compunction or inhibition of any kind whatsoever?* He didn't know. As much as he often dreamed of being a great general, he could see now that he was *not* a great general. As much as he loved the idea of having women fawn all over him, what he really wanted was a bosom companion, someone with whom he could share not just his bed but his heart. Would he really be content, as Edward had suggested, spending the rest of his life slaking his basest desires but never having the listening ear of someone who actually cared about him, someone he could confide in?

Is Mary that person? He didn't know and did not want to think about it.

Katriane could be that woman. The thought leapt into his mind unbidden but was rapidly followed by the sickly image of Edward laying his libidinous hands upon her, corrupting her simple, wholesome innocence.

What had she said? *Lord Ambroise provides for my family so long as I am in his house?* That innocent-sounding statement took on a completely repugnant meaning now that Henry understood what sort of house Edward kept. Everything about her manner and her reserve made sense now. She was trying to keep from drawing Henry's attention for fear that he would ...

Henry felt ill.

A soft knock came at the door. Henry could not face Edward now, with his mind so full of revulsion, so he did not respond.

The knock came again.

"Yes?" he called in a faltering voice, planning to plead ill health if challenged.

The door opened and Katriane stood there. "Lord Ambroise wishes to know if you will be joining him in the dining hall for dinner, or if you would prefer to take it here."

Henry stared at her. There was an understated, tantalizing beauty to this girl—woman. With her flaxen hair, naturally red lips, and demure, deferential manner, she really was irresistible. Henry suddenly had an overwhelming urge to rescue her. But how? He could not buy her freedom; he had nothing with which to barter. And it seemed apparent that Edward could not be reached through any appeal to conscience.

"Katriane," Henry said suddenly, removing his foot from where it was resting on the chair opposite him and wiping off the cushion, "join me for a moment?"

She looked back over her shoulder as though she might make a break for it but then ducked her head and walked over to sit across from him. As before, she sat rigidly on the very edge of the chair with her hands in her lap, eyes on the floor.

"I told you before, you have nothing to fear from me. You should know that I am a knight. A knight values a woman's virtue as a treasure to be protected at all costs."

She did not respond.

"You do not believe me."

"Forgive me, Lord Dawning, but I have known many knights."

Henry grimaced, preferring not to think too much about the implications of such a statement. "Katriane, you must believe that I did not know what my broth—what Lord Ambroise required of you. I truly believed you an ordinary house servant ... before today."

"And now that you know?"

Henry looked away in shame. What could he say? A real knight—as he had just proclaimed himself to be—would be obligated to rescue a woman who was enslaved to an evil lech. But this lech was not only his brother but someone whose help he desperately needed, even if he despaired of getting it at this point. So Henry did what he always did; he tried to learn more. "Did you come here willingly?"

She shrugged. "I was working as a scullery maid in a house in the north when Lord Ambroise came to visit. He took a fancy to me and said that if I were to come and work in his house, my family would be provided for so long as I remained. I did not understand what it entailed, but my family was starving. As the eldest daughter, what choice did I have?"

"You could have married," Henry suggested. "Surely a woman with your charms must have had suitors."

"I was dowerless, a poor match for any man of means. Had I married a man of equal station, I would have remained poor, and my family's position would have sunk lower still without me there to help provide for them.

"And does he provide for your family? Lord Ambroise, I mean."

She nodded.

"Yet you are free to leave if you so choose?"

She shrugged, but a deep blush came over her. "You must think very little of me now," she mumbled.

Henry sighed and refilled his cup from the mostly depleted wine bottle, which he had been working on all evening. He offered some to Katriane, but she declined. "As I said before, sacrificing for your family is something that I understand very well." He gulped down the wine.

Every fiber of his being screamed that this situation was wrong—that he needed to do something about it—but what could he do? Though the arrangement was abhorrent, she was not a prisoner. She could leave anytime she wanted. Edward was evidently doing all that he promised, and she was willingly selling her beauty and virtue in exchange for her family's well-being.

Henry felt terrible guilt. Even a few years ago, he could have taken her back to Dawning Court with him. He could have provided a decent life for her and her family. But now? Not only was he penniless but he did not even know if there was still a Dawning Court to return to. What could he promise her?

His long silence caused Katriane to look up. "Your family is in some distress?"

Henry's eyebrows shot up in surprise at the question, not only because it was somewhat forward but also because, up to this point, she had only responded to his queries. She had never freely engaged with him.

She blushed again. "Forgive my impudence, Lord Dawning."

"That was not impudent," he hastened to assure her. "I did say that...." he sighed. "It is complicated, but I suppose the simple explanation is that our army was defeated, and I came here seeking succor from Ambroise, while leaving my home and people exposed to the aggression of hostile forces." He looked down at the mostly empty cup of wine. "I am speaking very freely," he muttered in embarrassment.

"Is that why you arrived here in such a ... condition?"

"I can only imagine what you must have been thinking," he laughed. "I am amazed that you even conveyed my message to Lord Ambroise."

She put her hand to her mouth to stifle a giggle. "I must confess that I thought you a vagabond."

He grimaced. "Your assessment is not as far removed from the truth as it might have been a fortnight ago. Why did you not slam the gate on me?"

"Your accent," she said, "you were English. English guests are not uncommon, but poor Englishmen are not frequent visitors."

"Well, you have my sincerest thanks for being willing to grant me the benefit of many doubts."

She smiled again.

"Katriane," he said suddenly, "will you do something for me?"

Her expression instantly fell.

"Have I not told you that you are safe with me?" Henry asked, his exasperation at her incredulity plain in his voice, though he knew perfectly well that he could not blame her for that. She likely had very little opportunity to meet chivalrous men while working in this house.

"Forgive me," she apologized, though she did not completely relax. "How may I serve you?"

"Will you make my apologies to Lord Ambroise and tell him that I would prefer dinner in my room?"

She stood. "Of course. Will there be anything else?"

"Will you join me for dinner?"

Her mouth opened to respond, then it snapped shut. She clearly did not know what to make of this invitation.

"If it will make you uncomfortable, I understand," he said. "It has just been some weeks since I have had anyone to talk to, and Lord Ambroise turned out to ... not be the confidant that I had hoped for."

She considered for a long moment. Then with a slight duck of her head as her only answer, she withdrew.

You should not be doing this, a voice in his head told him, but he pushed it aside. Katriane was beautiful, and he would not pretend that the idea of spending the evening in her company did not fill him with excitement. However, it was not his lust but rather his loneliness which made him desire her company. She was simple, kind, and unassuming. He had not met a person like her in too long a time, and at this moment, when he was wrestling with profound doubts about his own character, he just wanted companionship that did not require putting on airs to impress. He wanted to be with someone with whom he could just be himself.

It was almost an hour later when Katriane reappeared, carrying a large tray of food.

Henry, who had all but given up on seeing her again that night, jumped up from his seat and moved across the room to meet her. "Let me help you with that."

"Please do not trouble yourself," she said quickly. "I can manage well enough." But he would not hear of it and took the food from her.

He grunted under the weight. "I can barely manage this. How ever did you carry it up all those stairs?"

She smiled her shy smile but said nothing.

He set down the food and was pleased to see that there were place settings for two. He spread the pewter plates out and dished a generous helping of meat, bread, and cheese onto each one. He then poured from a fresh bottle of wine. Katriane remained standing deferentially behind him.

"Please, sit," he said, moving out of the way and pulling the chair she had previously occupied out a bit further for her.

She did so but once again remained with her hands in her lap.

"You are having second thoughts about dining with me?"

She nodded. "But it is you for whom I fear," she said. "You are married, are you not? It does not look well, a married man in the lone company of a—of someone like me."

"Someone like you?" he repeated. "A lovely, sweet young woman?"

She colored again. "You are making fun of me."

"I most certainly am not," he insisted vehemently but then sat back with a sigh. "I suppose I simply do not care what others think."

"You do not understand," she said quietly, casting a glance over her shoulder at the door to ensure they were alone. "This is precisely the sort of situation that Lord Am—that can be used to gain leverage over you. I have seen it many times before."

"But we are not doing anything wrong!" Henry protested.

"That does not matter! All know the sort of house this is, and all know the sort of men who frequent this house. Few would believe the truth."

"Katriane, I thank you for your concern. And if you are not comfortable, again, I do understand. But let me explain to you where I sit. I hail from a failing barony in England that at this very moment I believe to be under attack. It very possibly has already fallen to our enemies. My wife—a noblewoman that I brought to Dawning Court only a year past—is quite possibly among the casualties. That burden has sustained me across an ocean and hundreds of leagues to your door. And in all that time, I have had no one to whom I might unburden myself.

"And now, through some accident of fate, I am here with you. I am drawn to you, not for your beauty but for your sincerity. You understand sacrifice and … mistakes. Mistakes which we may not take back, however much we might wish so to do."

Their eyes locked, and Henry held her gaze for a long time. He was not sure what calculations were going on behind her soft brown eyes, but she must have reached some decision because she finally reached up, took a scrap of bread from the plate, and began to nibble on it as if signaling her decision to remain.

He smiled in acknowledgement. "Thank you," he said, scooping up a chicken leg. "I am ravenous, and I was beginning to think that you were never going to eat." She returned his smile, and he asked about her home.

As the evening wore on, Katriane slowly opened up and relaxed. She even indulged in a little wine. The two swapped stories of carefree times until the food lay forgotten on the table and an evening chill entered the room.

Henry suggested they take the wine over to the sofa in front of the hearth. He stoked the fire and sat on one side, expecting that she would take the far side or even the chair opposite, but was thrilled when she sat in the space right beside him. He took it as a sign that she—who likely did not trust any man—was coming to trust *him*.

It grew late as the two talked in the warm glow of the hearth. Henry could not remember ever having such a natural, comfortable conversation with a beautiful woman in his life. With Mary, he had always been intent upon impressing her with every interaction. And even with Leah, while he had often forgotten himself and spoken too freely, her perfect properness and his extreme awkwardness every time they spoke made it impossible for him to just be himself with her. But with Katriane, he felt totally at ease.

He had to repeatedly force down a nearly overwhelming impulse to pull her close to him, not only because it was wrong but because he was afraid that she would take it as a sign that this whole night had been nothing more than an elaborate charade to hide his real motive.

But then, as if reading his thoughts, Katriane leaned against him and let her head rest on his chest. He slid his arm around her and squeezed her tight, reveling in her closeness, in her smell, and in the warmth of her body.

What made the moment even sweeter was that he knew that this woman had no ulterior motive; she was making no calculation; She was simply being swept up in the moment, just as he was, for no other reason than the fact that she liked him. Not for what he could do for her, for he had made it clear that he was not even able to help himself, but because she liked him as a person. He pressed his face into her perfumed hair while she stared into the fire.

"Tell me about your wife."

Whether or not she intended it, the mention of Mary snapped Henry back to reality. He raised his face from the bouquet of her scent and sipped his wine. Mary was the last thing he wanted to talk about, but if he were really intent on this being nothing more inappropriate than an evening of flirtation, he could not shy away from the topic. "What would you like to know?"

"What is her name?"

"Mary."

"Is she beautiful?"

"Mary is beautiful of face, but she is a hard woman."

"What do you mean by that?"

He considered how to explain and realized that he was not entirely sure that he knew what to make of Mary. At times she seemed his greatest, most loyal devotee, and at others she seemed to almost resent him. "She is very clever," he said at last. "She is always planning, always calculating; but when things do not work the way she would like them to, she does not bear it well."

"Things? Like you?"

He chortled involuntarily. Had he been so obvious? "I think that I do frustrate her."

"Why go against her wishes?"

That gave Henry pause. Why did he go against Mary when he knew it would cause him grief? Why not simply give her what she wanted? After all, she did seem to want what was best for him. She wanted him to rule the barony. Wasn't that what he wanted? He was not certain anymore. Edward was making him question everything he thought he believed. And he had always believed that if he were ruling, he could usher in a new, more refined society. That suddenly seemed impossibly naive. "I suppose that her plans and my conscience do not always coincide."

"Do you love her?"

Again, Henry was taken off guard. This was the first time he had ever been asked that question by someone who did not already have an opinion or an agenda of their own. With Katriane he did not have to defend his decision; he could be completely honest. But could he be that honest with himself? What if he looked inside and realized that he had only wed Mary to show Leah and his family that a beautiful, intelligent lady was interested in him; to show Leah that she had missed the boat? Could he accept that? He was not ready to find out, so he evaded the question. "I made a marriage vow to her."

It was impossible not to feel guilty talking of Mary while holding another woman, but he did not release Katriane. He had never felt this comfortable in the presence of a woman, and he was not yet ready to relinquish that feeling.

He set his wine goblet down, wrapped his now free other arm around her, and leaned back, pulling her into a reclining position with him.

She settled with her head on his chest, and idly traced patterns on his tunic with one finger. "Your heart is beating very fast," she said. Henry could almost hear the smirk on her face. "What are you thinking about?"

"In truth," he said, peering down into her brown eyes. "I am thinking that I would like to stay right here forever."

An irresistibly adorable smile played across her lips, and he surrendered to his next urge. He gently raised her chin to face him. He looked down into her eyes for a long time, wanting to draw the anticipation out as long as possible, and then leaned in and kissed her soft, red lips briefly, putting both of their willingness to the test.

She looked surprised but did not pull away. He thought he read a mixture of desire, fear, and uncertainty in her expression. She really was thinking about him and the consequences this might have for him!

He felt an overpowering rush of affection for this woman. He wanted to hold her, to protect her, to love her. He wanted to feel closer to her than words could express, and he only knew one way to do that; he pulled her in and kissed her a second time, longer and deeper than before. This time she did melt into him and returned it with a warm, wet kiss that flooded his entire body with excitement and thrilled him to his very toes.

After a long time, he pulled back and looked into her eyes. Her expression was a mixture of expectation and fear, but still she did not pull away. She knew that he wanted her, and her failure to move was her signal of surrender to him. He could have her. She was willing and ready, and there was nothing to prevent them. No one would ever even need to know.

Suddenly, as if hit by a bolt of lightning, Henry's burning desire turned to stomach-churning disgust. "What am I doing?" He pushed her from him and jumped to his feet, feeling utterly ashamed of himself. "What am I doing?" he repeated to the air. "I am married!" he said to her as if accusing her.

Katriane stared up at him from the couch in wide-eyed confusion, but Henry did not notice. He was pacing in agitation, speaking as rapidly as the thoughts flooded into his mind. "What will come of this? Will I defile my marriage vows only to prove Edward's assertion that every man is corruptible? Or will I return to Dawning Court with a lady of ill repute on my arm? That would be perfect. Prove that I am as base, weak, and disgusting as my brothers!"

Katriane's expression dropped when he said *lady of ill repute.* She looked as though he had struck her across the face. That same lovely face that had been inviting only a minute before was now so full of pain and betrayal that it stunned him into silence.

She looked like she would say something, but instead her eyes brimmed with tears, and she pushed past him.

"Katriane! Wait!" he called, chasing after her and snatching her arm. She stopped but did not look at him as she spoke.

"Many men come to this house and treat me like a trollop, but none of them was ever so cruel as to make me feel as though I were still pure and desirable, only to then reject me because I am soiled and therefore beneath them." She pulled her arm free and escaped through the door before he could even recover himself enough to respond to the brutal indictment.

He ran to the door after her, but she was already disappearing down the stairs. He briefly considered chasing after her, but the thought of the scene that would create for the other servants stopped him at the door.

Instead he went back into the room, slamming the door much harder than he intended as if to shut out the shame and self-loathing that he knew was waiting for him in the silence. His embarrassment at letting himself get this far was compounded by the pain he had thoughtlessly inflicted upon Katriane.

But wait! Maybe this is what Edward wanted all along. What if his plan was to plant this idea in my head and then use Katriane to work on me? "They must be conspiring to tear me down! To corrupt me and prove that I am no better than my brothers. But I *am* better." He ran to the door, flung it open, and shouted down the stairs after her, "I am not my brothers! I cannot be corrupted so easily!"

He then immediately felt ridiculous and slammed the door again. He hoped that she had not heard. *My thoughts, they are muddled.* His eyes fell on the empty wine bottles. *It is the wine! That too is a tool of Edward! This was all part of his plot!* But that explanation did not completely satisfy his conscience. A voice in his head whispered that it was he who had insisted Katriane remain with him. It was he who had moved them to the divan and he who had kissed her. Whether or not Edward had wanted that to happen, Henry had willingly escalated it.

"No!" He shook his head. "It was she who leaned against me! It was she who made herself irresistible. This is all part of their ploy. I would never willingly defy my vows had they not entrapped me! I must leave this house at once!"

He started to gather his few belongings, heaping them on the bed, but he soon ran out of steam and sat on the bed in defeat. He gazed out over the balcony. He could not leave now anyway as it was very late, and he had had far too much to drink. He turned onto his stomach. "Once again, you have made a mess of everything," he mumbled groggily. "You have not helped the family, and your only friend here now hates you. Well done, *Sir* Henry." He took a deep breath to control his emotions and realized that he was completely exhausted.

"I just need to rest for a few ..." and he was out.

Sixteen

enry slept late the following day and awoke feeling groggy and hungover. He wished that the previous night had been just a bad dream, but the sick feeling in the pit of his stomach could not be ascribed completely to the aftereffects of the wine.

He pressed his hands over his eyes. "What am I doing here?" he called out to the ceiling and immediately regretted it, as his head threatened to split in two at the sound of his own voice reverberating in his skull.

He rolled on his side and pulled the pillow over his head to try to shut out the world. It did not work; it only left him alone with his own thoughts, and one thought above all rang out: *I must flee this house before I am permanently corrupted!*

That resonated with him, and he climbed to his feet, waited for the room to stop swimming, and tried to collect his thoughts. Was it possible that not twelve hours before he had been thinking that he might like to stay here in Katriane's company? All he wanted now was to run and forget that any of this had ever happened.

He stumbled over to the wash basin and splashed water over his face. It had little effect, so he dunked his head as far as it would go, immersing most of his hair in the cool water.

When he could hold his breath no longer, he raised his head and let the cold streams of water running down his back shock his mind back to clarity. "You cannot leave," he mumbled aloud, as if someone else were speaking. "If you leave now, you are no better off than when you first arrived; you've now wasted all this time, and you are still unable to help the family!" Was it already too late for that?

"Okay, think!" he commanded his reflection in the mirror above the washbasin. "What must you do? You must force Edward to grant you temporary command of his army ... and you must apologize to Katriane." Where had that last part come from? Had he been thinking that? Hadn't she been helping Edward ensnare him?

An image of her hurt and betrayed expression from the previous night flashed into his mind. He knew at once that she had not been faking that. He had drawn her in and then blamed her for it. *But was it not her fault? I would not, in my right mind, have done something as low and crass as consort with a peasant of ill repute! But* she *does such acts as a matter of course.*

He passed his hand over his eyes. "I cannot be concerned with such things! I have a barony to save!" But still the thought nagged at him until he finally relented. *Very well! I will settle it with Katriane in order that I may focus on the more important issue.* Before he could think better of it, he walked over to the bell rope and gave it a tug.

He, of course, heard nothing, but he was certain that somewhere in the bowels of the house, Katriane was being summoned. While he waited for the knock on the door, he endeavored to make himself presentable. He put on fresh clothes and smoothed his hair into a manageable shape.

He was still fighting with a particularly stubborn cowlick at the back of his head when there came a soft tapping on the door. He straightened, took one last look at himself in the mirror, decided it would have to do, and walked over to let her in, deliberately not thinking about what he was going to say when he saw her. *Perhaps she will apologize? That would make it simpler.*

He took hold of the latch, took a deep breath, and opened the door. Words started to tumble from his mouth before he was even aware of it. "Katriane, I beg..."

Outside the door stood a tall, red-headed woman with a small stack of folded clothes in her hands and a confused expression on her face. "Oui?"

"Er ... where is Katriane?"

"She was not feeling well this morning," the redhead explained. "I am Miriam. How may I serve you?"

Henry had not even considered that it would not be Katriane who answered his summons, as she had been the only servant to attend him in his room since his arrival.

Was he disappointed or relieved? *Relieved,* he decided. After all, he had tried to do the proper thing and make amends. He could not help it if she refused to face him. Now he had more important things to worry about. "I need to see Lord Ambroise at once," Henry said instead.

"Lord Ambroise is preparing for the ball this evening and is not to be disturbed."

Henry vaguely recalled Edward mentioning some sort of social function the last time they were together, but Henry had been far too distracted at the time to give it any thought.

"Lord Ambroise has asked that you attend if you have recovered sufficiently."

The last thing in the world Henry wanted to do at that moment was attend a party, but if that was the only way he could see Edward, what choice did he have? "Very well. When does he expect me?"

"The evening will begin with supper."

Henry looked out the balcony at the sun. It was well past its zenith and already descending toward the horizon. He had been toying with an idea to make gaining Edward's consent as easy as possible, but it would take some time to prepare. It was later than he would have liked, but it would have to be time enough. He could not afford to wait any longer, or rather, his family could not afford for him to wait any longer. "Bring me ink and paper at once."

"Of course, monsieur," Miriam nodded and held up the clothes in her hands. "Garments for the ball," she said by way of explanation before placing them in Henry's hands and retreating to find writing implements.

Three hours later, Henry sat alone at a banquet table in the corner of the dining hall watching guests arrive in the ordinary fashion—the same as at a hundred other balls Henry had attended. Each of the noble attendees was announced upon entering the banquet hall in their lavish regalia. Henry thought it was mildly interesting that it was a female courtier that announced them; he had never seen that before. But given that females were all Edward kept in the house, he supposed that was not too strange. It occurred to him, in fact, that the first time he had seen any male servants near the house was just this evening on his way to the hall, when he noticed soldiers stationed in the courtyard. Perhaps to keep the peace, or maybe as a show of force to remind his guests that there was a hard backbone to the soft, decadent lifestyle? Whatever the case, those soldiers were apparently only stationed outside, as he had seen none within the walls of the house.

Henry watched with little interest as the guests arrived, some in pairs, others alone, but all looking the part, dressed in the latest fashions. Henry remembered a time not so long ago when this would have fascinated him, but now it all seemed so superfluous that it bored him out of his mind. He just wanted an opportunity to talk to Edward, but at the moment his brother was busy greeting the guests.

Edward did not introduce Henry, and few paid him much attention, likely due to his dour countenance and relatively bland clothing. Though Edward had provided him with an elegant long-tailed, cream-colored waistcoat with golden stitching, Henry felt invisible standing beside the guests in their ornate gowns, wigs, and makeup. He thought that he might have been mistaken for a servant had he not been a man.

The ball progressed as expected. A small string ensemble began to play as the guests took their seats at the table piled so high with food and drink it was difficult to see the people sitting on the other side.

Great quantities were consumed, continually replenished by serving girls dressed in extremely revealing tunics that hung down to mid-thigh over bare legs and were stitched of a gauzy material that hid just enough to make the shapes beneath even more enticing.

The partygoers, however, paid the help little attention. Though pretty or exotic looking, each of the serving girls, with their plain garb and hair that flowed over their shoulders without embellishment, were—no doubt by design—plain by comparison to Edward's guests. Every woman attending the ball wore bright, elaborate gowns that flared out wide or dragged in long trains behind them. Their hair was done up in elaborate braids and knots, and most of them wore thick layers of makeup that made them appear like flawless figures from a work of art rather than human women.

Henry, though, had no interest in this ball and even less interest in socializing or feasting. Rather, his attention was fixed upon Edward. All he needed were a few moments without interruption to press him into helping, and Henry did not want to become distracted and miss his opportunity.

So focused on his brother was he that he hardly even noticed as the music became livelier and the guests became noticeably excited, leaving the table to partner up on the dance floor.

As he paused to watch what was happening, it seemed to Henry that there was an air of eager anticipation in the room that was much more electric than an ordinary dance warranted. Dancing was often relished by young ladies, but it was generally a chore that gentlemen accepted as the price of being able to interact with the object of their affection. It was not usually known to arouse excitement. But here, the men seemed every bit as eager as the women, if not more so.

The nervous laughter, the knowing glances exchanged, even the calculated positions that each person seemed to take in line all bespoke a subtext that Henry was not privy to. *Perhaps they have all done this so often that it is a familiar ritual to them,* he thought dismissively.

As the music started up, even those vying for Edward's attention began to peel off in search of a place on the dance floor, leaving his brother mostly alone at the head of the table when the dance started. But there was a petite blonde woman sitting at Edward's right hand to whom he was paying more than passing attention. In fact, now that it was just the two of them, Edward was positively doting on her. And she was equally effusive in lavishing attention upon him.

Henry sat by himself halfway down the table, debating about what to do. If only the blonde girl would join the dance! He considered recruiting someone to invite her to dance, but aside from the three of them, he could not see anyone who was not holding the hand of some other guest or participating already.

But it probably would not have mattered, Henry admitted to himself, as Edward had made it clear that he was determined to woo this particular woman. "See that exquisite creature there?" Edward had said to Henry when the guests were first arriving, indicating the girl with whom he now sat. "She is the niece of the Earl of Montague. I have had my eye on her since she first began to blossom, but the scurvy earl has deliberately kept her out of my reach. He only brought her into his house to entice me and then refused to let me near her. He has been pressing the ministry of affairs for a shipping charter to the spice coasts. When he was denied repeatedly, he sought out my assistance. But he had nothing with which to barter until now." Edward's eyes had burned with lust as he looked upon the girl. "She will finally be mine." He licked his lips in excited anticipation.

"I do not understand," Henry said, trying not to see the obvious but revolting implications. "Are you going to wed her?"

Edward had laughed and slapped a meaty hand across Henry's shoulder. "If I were going to wed her, I would not have had to arrange the trade agreement," he said, waving a folded sheet of paper in the air, affixed with the seal Henry had seen him using upon his arrival. "But I will give the earl what he wants in order to get what I want. Feel free to enjoy, Henry. You will find most everyone more than willing. But do not spend your strength on the servants," he added, looking meaningfully at Henry, who was not able to hide his blush. "The servants are day-to-day fodder to slake one's appetite, but tonight we sample the prized cuisine of the nobility."

Now, hours later, Henry felt his impatience growing until it bordered on anger. He was agitated enough that he was about to march over to Edward and demand that he help the family, but he knew that interrupting his brother was guaranteed to put him in a sour mood. So Henry sighed and sat back. He was just going to have to wait.

Behind him, the music changed. What had been a light air for dancing had been joined by a steady drumbeat. It had started low at first, but it gradually grew louder and more intrusive until it was driving the rest of the music to keep up with it.

Henry looked back at the musicians and was surprised to see that the alcove in which they played had had the curtain drawn over it. He could see now that some of those curtains whose purpose he had wondered at the first time he was in this room were being used to shield the party guests from the prying eyes of the uninitiated. As the visitors continued to eat, drink, and dance, they became rowdier and more raucous until all semblance of decorum had utterly fled. The men were openly accosting the women, and the woman either reciprocated—or in some cases initiated—or laughed and made the men chase them through the hall, dodging in and out of the columns and tables until they were caught and drawn into the draperies that were hung throughout the hall, which would then be pulled closed to create a makeshift private chamber. Here, those who were concerned about being viewed by others could indulge their debauchery in relative privacy, though it seemed that most of the guests did not care at all about being seen engaging in such acts, at least not in this setting. The partygoers seemed determined to perform every libidinous indecency at once, and while Henry had already learned from Edward's own lips that he was such a man, what Henry found so disturbing was the open way in which the members of the nobility participated, with no hint of shame or self-consciousness over their sybaritic surrender to their depravity. They seemed to abandon all vestiges of their better selves in pursuit of their lusts.

Though every person wrestles to control some passion— some weakness, Henry thought, *the surrender to such has always been done in secret, shrouded in darkness to hide his shame from the world.* This function, however, seemed to operate on the idea that if everyone were degenerate, then all vices could be embraced openly. That notion disturbed Henry to the very core. He knew he had weaknesses, but he had always feared letting his weaknesses rule him. These people were reveling in theirs! Instead of struggling to control their passions, they simply found a place where they were free to be as depraved as they liked.

Henry had always believed that nobility was a divinely bestowed right, the bestowal of which endowed the recipient with certain gifts of status and wealth in life, but in exchange required that they use their life of privilege in the pursuit of excellence, trying to be better than other men, to live up to their God-given privilege. What did it matter if a serf wiled his life away in a tavern with ladies of ill repute? The serf's life accounted for but little. But the people in this room were important dignitaries, lords, and knights. They had an inherent responsibility to be better— to make a contribution—because their lives, their examples, mattered. *These nobles are no better than the most wretched peasant!*

Henry remembered this feeling well from when he had found Thomas and John drunk in that seedy tavern in the company of trollops. The idea that his brothers, who were supposed to be better than others, who should be setting an example for the commoners who depended upon the Dawnings, would willingly debase themselves for all to see, had struck at Henry's deepest fears at the time. His brothers' behavior was embarrassing and disgusting, but it was more than that. Did his brothers' low actions mean that they were mean men, no better than anyone else? And if it did, what did that say about Henry, who already felt inferior to his station? If all the advantages consequent to his noble upbringing were still not enough to make him superior to even the most debased men, what did that mean? Was he even less than they?

Maybe Edward is correct after all. Maybe nobility is nothing more than a facade concocted by the wealthy to allow them to indulge while insisting that the lower classes live morally upright, hardworking lives so they would continue to produce. Am I the only fool who pretends otherwise? Is that why I am so miserable?

Do I feel so terrible because I hurt Katriane, or because I refused her rather than surrendering to my desires? After all, were not the hours sitting with her last evening as close to bliss as I have ever felt? Am I only wretched now because I failed to see it through, humiliating her and leaving me the worse for my discipline?

Henry looked at the wine on the table before him. He had seen many men throw their lives away in pursuit of the mindless stupor that spirits produced. Wasn't lust just another vice, the pursuit of which would steal a man's life away just as surely as drink?

Yet, as he looked around the room, he was the only one who seemed to be unhappy. Granted, he was very nearly the only one still in his right mind, but maybe he *was* too extreme in his ideals. Perhaps it would not hurt to indulge just a little. *Who would know?* The thought came as Edward's voice whispering in his ear. *What if I did just indulge this one time? Whom would it hurt?*

Henry again scanned the room, but with different eyes, eyes that were not judging the participants this time but were instead seeing the opportunities available to him if he were to cast aside everything he had always professed to believe. What a relief it would be to no longer need to wear the badge of responsibility, to no longer need to try to be something he felt completely ill-suited to be. And many of these women were very beautiful....

Henry was just reaching for the heretofore untouched goblet of wine in front of him when a beautiful brunette dropped suddenly into his lap, draped her arms over his shoulders, and planted a wet kiss on his lips. Henry lowered his eyes in embarrassment only to find that he was staring down her décolletage at her ample bosom. For a moment, he wanted her desperately. She was beautiful, raven-haired and curvaceous, though she reeked of wine and too much perfume. But she was right here, ready and willing for whatever Henry might wish. He did not even need to go looking for it.

His mind was clouded with conflicting thoughts and emotions such that he did not fight her when she again kissed him. It was warm, wet, and exciting, but the smell of wine on her breath was so overpowering that he was forced to turn his head aside to catch his breath. When he did, he found himself staring into the face of Katriane. She had been refilling the dishes beside him but was openly staring now that she recognized the man beneath the noblewoman. She looked sick.

"Katriane," he said, quickly trying to disentangle himself from the strange woman's arms.

Katriane turned and rushed for the door.

"Katriane, please. This is not what it looks like! Let me explain!"

The woman grinned and wrestled back against Henry as he tried to free himself, as though it were part of a game. She leaned in to kiss him again, and on impulse, Henry bounced her off his lap.

She landed on the floor on her rear and blinked in surprise as though she did not know what was happening. Nearby, another couple that was on the table necking and groping each other, stopped their wrestling session long enough to laugh uproariously. The jilted woman on the floor started to laugh as well, as though this were all some wonderful jest.

Henry, though, was not watching them; he was chasing after Katriane. "Katriane, one moment!" he said, catching up to her just before she reached the door and spinning her around to face him. "This is not ..." he started but trailed off. How could he explain? "I know this must appear the height of hypocrisy, but you must believe me when I tell you that I am not like these people."

Her eyes blazed until it looked as though she might lose control entirely. "You rejected me because I was a common trollop; your tastes clearly run to those of your own class."

"What? No!" He was trying to figure out how to explain any of this when she started to turn away again. But he still had a hold of her arm and spun her back again to face him, more forcefully than he had intended. "I did not reject you because you were a ... because of your class. I stopped myself because I am married."

"It only violates your vows if it is a woman beneath your station?"

"No! I do not break my vows with anyone. I honor them," he said, realizing how ludicrous that declaration sounded at this moment. His shame was acute under her scarcely concealed sneer, and he released her arm. "I did not mean to hurt you," he said in a softer voice. "I ... just need to get out of this house before I lose myself entirely." He looked over his shoulder at the partygoers, and his eyes fell upon his brother seated at the head of the central table. Edward's physique prevented him from taking part in the more active games that occupied many of the others, so the young woman accommodated him by sitting in his lap, feeding him grapes while he groped her lasciviously. Henry's desire turned to revulsion. There was no freedom in feeding vice; it only enslaved these people, forcing them to sell themselves to people like Edward.

"I believed myself a good man when I arrived here," he said, shaking his head as though he were shaking off the remnants of a dream. "Does this make any sense to you?" He turned back to Katriane, but she had used his moment of inattention to slip away.

Henry was hurt. She clearly did not believe he was anything more than the rest of these debauched degenerates. And given the thoughts he had been having only minutes before, perhaps there was not as much difference between him and them as he would like to believe.

The nearly irresistible temptation that had almost claimed him only minutes before turned to disgust. The sights, sounds, and smells emanating from every alcove of this room suddenly turned his stomach. Human debauchery in its lowest form assaulted his senses like physical blows. "I cannot stay in this house another instant!"

He turned to go. He was done with Charles Ambroise and done with France. In the space of only a few days, he was on the verge of sacrificing every ideal he had ever fought for in order to participate in this grotesque parody of happiness.

Henry knew that he would always look back with shame on this visit. This had been a test of temptation that challenged him to his core. And within the space of a few days, he had very nearly thrown everything away to plunge headlong into its embrace.

It stung him to know that Katriane had seen his failure firsthand. Instead of remembering Henry Dawning as the model of manhood, a good man who honored his vows in a sea of weak-willed frauds, she would know him as one more hypocrite, who in the end was just like all the other debased men in her life.

He exited the dining hall without looking back and began to mount the stairs to his room, where he had already packed the few belongings he would take with him: the clothes that Edward had provided and a basic travel kit he had assembled, including a bed roll and some dried meat and beans he had set aside in anticipation of his return journey.

He reached his room, fully determined to depart at once when he felt, tucked neatly under his tunic, the orders he had written to Edward's men on Edward's behalf, instructing them to follow Henry to England.

He slumped. He had again completely forgotten his purpose. His friends' and family's lives hung in the balance while he debated over whether to abandon them for the fleshpots Edward offered. "I am a despicable man," he muttered aloud.

But it was not too late! He could still win the day, even if he had lost the battle up to this point. Orders in hand, he turned and hurried back down to the dining hall, opened the door, and marched across the floor, dodging around two women who were wrestling in petticoats to the delight of a group of cheering men, and made his way to where Edward sat at the head of the table with the girl still on his lap.

As Henry looked upon his brother's scabrous, bloated form, he knew once and for all that he would never be like this. The remainder of Edward's life would be devoted to the pursuit of his next pleasure. Like an insect bite that itches unbearably and always returns no matter how much you scratch it, Edward would never be free from his lusts. This was not the life of freedom he espoused; it was a life of chains and bondage to a master that could never be satisfied. Henry would not submit to that life, no matter how tempting it looked in the moment.

He took a deep breath and steeled himself. "Pardon me, Lord Ambroise," he said loudly enough to be heard over the noise of the room.

Edward stopped fawning over the girl long enough to look at him. "Henry, have you not found yourself a companion yet?"

Henry unfolded the document he had written earlier that day and plunged in. "Lord Ambroise, I can delay no longer; I must return to England at once. This document is an order to secure command of your garrison. I would naturally leave enough of a force to ensure your security here until your men return. Three months. That is all that is required."

"What is this?" Edward demanded, his face falling abruptly.

"Edward," Henry reverted to his brother's real name, hoping that it might spark some old sympathy in him for the life he left behind. "I beg of you, I must rescue my wife and mother. If there is any hope left for them, I must go at once. The walls of Dawning Court are strong, but Richard will not be able to hold a siege party off forever with a depleted force. I have no one else to whom I may turn for help. You are my last ally." He could see that Edward was not moved, so he added, "I will recompense you threefold any losses you incur as a result of this endeavor."

"Threefold?" Edward scoffed. "And how will you pay?"

"Well, I mean once Dawning Court is liberated, of course."

"And if you fail, then I am out an army and any prospect of remuneration."

"Edward—"

"Ambroise!" Edward corrected him peevishly.

"Forgive me, Lord Ambroise. But you must understand that now is the moment when we cannot fail to act. Your generosity in this matter will win you the forgiveness of the family and maybe even the Church. We have a rare opportunity to make amends for all our past wrongs and put everything right. All your shame will be washed away in this one glorious deed."

"Shame?" Edward almost choked. "*I* am not ashamed! My choices have brought me everything life has to offer. Why would I risk all that I have to save a people that would have denied me all of this if they had had their way? Why, even now I might be with them, dying at the hands of enemies with whom I never had a quarrel until I created one by doing my *'duty.'"*

"Surely, you must take some thought for your origins. You may resent them, but had it not been for the family, you would have none of this."

"How dare you?" Edward's flaccid face began to quiver in rage. He used the arms of the chair to push his great bulk up onto his feet. The earl's niece was pushed to one side as he did so, and she flashed Henry a dark look at the interruption.

"Everything I have," Edward began in fury, "I have earned. I only took from the family what they would have squandered on a fool's errand for a church that holds them enslaved to its own dogma. I took the silver that our mother threw away in a show of pretended piety, and I used it to build a church of my own, a church where any man or woman is free to come and indulge any passion which God has given them without fear of judgment or reprisal. This is religion the way God intended it!"

Henry shook his head in despair. Edward was so far removed from his own ideals that he could think of nothing to say that might reach him.

Edward continued, "You still do not understand. That society of peace we spoke of is not some distant dream; I have achieved it. Look around you, Henry. These men are not at war with each other because they have found another form of trade that is more amenable to all of them—a world in which we all win. No man here would ever dream of lifting a finger against me."

"Then why keep an army?"

He looked piteously at Henry. "I see now that you are not worthy to live in this paradise. Everything you ever wanted is right before you, but you are still a slave to the traditions of our fathers and will ever be. You do not belong here. You will remove yourself from my presence and the presence of this enlightened company this instant."

Henry could see he was wasting his time. He took the orders off the table and folded them again. "I am sorry to have offended you, brother. I will leave your house this very night."

"No, you will not."

Henry blinked. "Pardon?"

"Henry, it was you who tracked *me* down and called on *me* unannounced. Need I remind you of that fact?"

"I do not understand."

"You pierced the veil that I placed between myself and the family." He motioned to someone over Henry's shoulder. "I cannot very well have you return with that knowledge and jeopardize my little empire, now, can I?"

A moment later Katriane and Miriam appeared on either side of him, each woman hugging one of his arms as though he were escorting them—the dashing noble with a beautiful lady on each arm. Henry still did not comprehend what was happening and started to shake them off when he felt the tip of a blade pressed into his side, hidden beneath the casual way Miriam was hugging his arm.

Edward waited until he saw comprehension dawn in Henry's eyes before saying more. "I had so hoped that you would join us, Henry, and remain here of your own accord; but as you have chosen to spurn our enlightened society, you will remain here as my prisoner."

"Your prisoner?" Henry still could not believe what was happening.

"When you succumbed to Katriane's charms last night, I thought that perhaps you were starting to see the light. She is fetching, is she not?" Henry looked at Katriane, but she would not meet his eyes. "Better men than you have fallen for that innocent air. It makes her positively irresistible, would you not agree?" Edward smiled fondly at Katriane. "But what am I saying?" he laughed. "You agreed last night in your chambers." Henry started to protest that no such thing had happened, but Edward cut him off. "Now, these two lovely ladies will show you back to your room, where you will remain until I decide what is to be done with you."

Henry looked at the relatively small female figures. Each was lithe and lean, and assuming he could evade the first dagger strikes, he expected that he could overpower them without too much difficulty.

"I see what you are thinking, Sir Knight," Edward said in a dangerous tone, "but if you resist my cordiality now, you will find yourself fertilizing my vineyard before sunup. You noted the soldiers in the courtyard, I trust. They can be here in an instant, and it will not go well for you if you force me to embarrass my guests by bringing soldiers into my house. Now be a good lad and go with the ladies."

At a nod from Edward, Katriane and Miriam led Henry back toward the door. Henry was too stunned to resist. "Edward," he cried over his shoulder, "this is a mistake!"

"Relax, my friend," Edward said, taking his seat again and patting his lap for the blonde girl to return to it. "If the Dawnings' plight is as dire as you say, you will be free to go your way very soon, once the Moors have eliminated the threat for me."

In his state of heightened anxiety, Henry's mind refused to accept what was happening. Nevertheless, he tried one last time to reach Edward. "You must release me! With each day I delay, our family's chance of survival diminishes! The deaths of all our people will be squarely on your shoulders!" But Edward was not listening. The last thing Henry saw before being pushed from the room was Edward locked in a savage kiss with this night's prize.

Seventeen

L adies, this is a mistake!" Henry turned his protests to the women once they were out of the room. "I am only here to acquire help for my family back home!" Neither woman looked at him as they led him up the stairs, still clutching his arms. "Katriane," Henry pleaded, "you know this to be true." She flicked a glance at his face but otherwise gave no indication that she heard him.

"You must believe me," he said as they ushered him back into his room and closed the heavy oak door on him. "My family is in grave danger!" he called through the door as the lock clicked at the sound of the key being turned from the outside. "Every hour I delay may cost them their lives!"

Henry slammed his hand against the door before slumping helplessly with his back against it. His disbelief was beginning to give way to alternating fits of rage and despondency. He remained where he was for a while, staring across the room and out over the balcony.

Henry felt the fool for not having seen from the first that Edward would help no one but himself. After all, hadn't that been his character from the beginning? As much as Henry had tried to justify and excuse it, Edward had always been deeply and truly selfish. Henry was just a naive fool to believe that his brother's estrangement was all part of some colossal misunderstanding. William and Thomas had both seen it in him, but Henry had never wanted to see Edward for what he truly was.

Perhaps if I had not refused to see, he thought, *I would have known that he would never be willing to help the family.* On the contrary, Edward had been overjoyed by the news of their impending demise because it meant the end of the fear that had likely weighed upon him since fleeing Dawning Court.

Could it be, Henry wondered, *that Edward's real reason for keeping the garrison is to guard against the family's retribution?* Henry snorted. "I should tell him that while he lives his life in fear of them, they have all but forgotten he even exists."

Henry could still hear the music playing and the raucous voices from the ballroom. He cursed himself for going back that last time. *I would be free now if I had just not gone back!*

"Stop pouting, you fool! Now is the time for action. You must strike now while Edward is deep in his debauchery. Now think, what do you do from here?" He had to get to the stable, get a horse, and get it out the main gate without the alarm being raised, but how to do that?

Henry expected that he could overpower the girls of the house that apparently served double duty as guards, but he doubted that he could do it before they raised a general alarm. "Where is William when I need him?" *What would my insane brother do in a situation like this?*

That gave Henry an idea. He moved to the balcony to look for some means of escape. He was about twenty feet above the east end of the vineyards. The rows of grape vines below him were cast in darkness, but the courtyard to his right—which he would have to pass through to reach the stable—was aglow with light and abuzz with the coachmen and footmen of the nobles attending the ball, as well as a score of Edward's soldiers standing guard.

Henry scanned the dark rows of the vineyard to his left. There was a high wall surrounding it on the two sides, with a natural wall created on the backside by the house and the steep hill that the house was built into.

Up and to his left was the balcony of the room where Henry had first met Lord Ambroise sitting in his chair, putting the seal on some document, maybe the very document he had shown Henry tonight, which had secured the company of the blonde woman on his lap at the ball.

Henry looked down at the orders still clutched in his hand, then looked back to the darkened balcony, and a wild idea suddenly seized him. He ran back into the room, picked up a chair, and stole over to the main entrance, where he braced the chair against the door, hoping to impede any unexpected visitors while he worked.

He then pulled the bedclothes from the mattress and began knotting the ends together as fast as he could manage. When he was satisfied that the knots would not give way the moment his weight was applied to them, he extinguished the lights in the room to hide his movements from anyone on the outside and hopefully made it appear he had retired for the evening.

With only the moonlight to work by, he placed the orders in the pack he had prepared for his trip and slung it on his back. He then moved onto the balcony and tied a heavy knot on the end of the makeshift rope to give it some weight.

It took him only a few tries to successfully throw the end around the railing of the balcony of Edward's study. Then he let out enough of the makeshift rope for the knotted end to swing back within his grasp.

Taking a deep breath to steel himself, he put his weight on the rope and let himself swing out into the open air. The knots tightened, the blankets stretched, and he heard a tearing sound as the threads threatened to give way under the strain they were never intended to withstand; but it held, and he found himself swinging in the air ten feet beneath Edward's balcony.

He grabbed the other end of the rope, clutching both sides together, and then awkwardly kicked himself around in circles a few times so the blankets would twist into a single strand. He hoped it would be stronger that way, but at the very least it would be easier to climb.

Henry began to pull himself up the blanket rope. He felt ridiculous and wondered if William ever felt the same in those moments when he was carrying out one of his wild, overly elaborate schemes that should never work but somehow always did. But maybe that was why William's schemes so often succeeded—they were so far outside any expected norm that no one could even conceive of someone trying them. Hopefully that same incredulity would allow Henry to pull off his plan as well.

He pulled himself over the edge of the balcony and immediately ducked for cover in the shadows. He waited to see if anyone in the courtyard had noticed him but did not see anything to indicate that he had been seen.

Henry breathed a sigh of relief before removing the pack and retrieving the orders. He stepped carefully into the dark room and stopped to listen. If someone were to enter at that moment, he could still hide on the balcony, but a few steps more and he was committed. He stood motionless for a full minute before he dared move any farther.

Finally, Henry walked into the room. The only illumination came from the moonlight streaming in from the balcony and bathing everything in a pale glow that silhouetted the furniture but hid smaller items in shadow.

He felt his way over to the plush chair where Edward had been sitting that first day. He tried to ignore the residual odor of his brother's musk, which clung to the seat as he squatted beside it.

Henry said a silent prayer that Edward's official seal was still there, took a deep breath, and pulled open the drawer.

The drawer was empty. The wooden stamp carved with the seal of Charles Ambroise was not there.

"No, No," he whispered frantically. Without that seal, his forged orders would never be taken seriously. Without it, he had no army and no salvation for Dawning Court or himself. He shoved the chair aside, dropped to his knees, and felt around on the floor in desperation. And then his hand fell on something hard and smooth. With an audible cry of relief, he picked up the stamp and laid it on the table.

Henry jumped to his feet and drew the curtains before lighting a candle he took from a wall sconce. He unfolded the orders, laid the page across the end table, and forged Lord Ambroise's signature. He was sure that it did not look particularly authentic, but he gambled on the fact that no order with Ambroise's seal affixed would have the signature overly scrutinized. *On the other hand,* he thought, *of all the orders they were likely to look closely at, this was the one.*

Henry pushed the doubts from his mind. None of that mattered. He was not going to get another chance like this, and he had to take it. He refolded the document, dripped wax onto the folded edge, and waited just a moment for it to begin to harden before pressing the seal firmly into it. When he was satisfied, he blew out the candle and replaced it in the wall sconce. He then stooped down and set the seal beneath the end table exactly as he had found it.

Henry inspected the room for any remaining trace of his presence. *With any luck,* he thought, *I will be out of the country before Edward has any idea that his army is missing.* He threw back the curtain to the balcony to make his escape. That's when the door behind him opened.

Henry froze, one hand still on the drapery. He realized a moment too late that he was undoubtedly outlined against the moonlight.

There, limned in the light from the hall, stood Katriane, staring at him in shock.

"Katriane," he said softly, taking a slow step back into the room. "This is not what it seems." His mind was racing furiously. Was this girl the mercenary seductress that Edward had made her out to be, or was she simply an innocent victim of circumstances as Henry had believed? He needed her to be the latter if he had any hope of escape without her raising an alarm. "My family really is in trouble! I came all the way from England to enlist help, and now I must return. I know you understand that—acting for the good of one's family?" Still she did not respond, and an idea struck him. "You could come with me," he said suddenly, surprised that he was excited by the idea. He took a step forward. She stirred on the verge of bolting. "You would not have to live here like this any longer. You would be free."

He took another tentative step, and for just a moment, he thought that he might be getting through to her. "Katriane." He took another step and she bolted.

Henry started after her. He made it into the hallway just in time to see her disappear down the first staircase, which led to his room and eventually the main hall. He could not possibly stop her before they were seen or heard.

He cursed, bolted the door, and sprinted to the balcony. He dropped the orders into his pack and tossed the whole thing over the edge, hoping it would not burst apart on impact.

He then grabbed his makeshift rope and almost leapt off the balcony. The bedclothes were not up to the extra strain and made an audible tearing sound under his weight. This time, however, the tearing did not stop, and he could feel it giving way.

He dropped hand over hand as rapidly as he could, but with a final tear, the rope gave out. An involuntary cry escaped his lips as he plummeted the last ten feet and landed hard in the dirt between two rows of grape vines.

Whether roused by his cry or because Katriane had raised an alarm, he did not know, but there was no mistaking the sudden excited shouts from the courtyard.

Henry performed a brief check to ensure nothing was broken before rolling to his feet and snatching up his pack. He ran deeper into the acres of grapevines, finding his legs only slightly rubbery after his fall. He knew this was a dead end, but he could already hear men scattering into the rows of grapes behind him, and he needed time to devise a plan.

He pressed deeper into the vineyard, dodging in and out of rows until he found a spot deep in the shadows, where he crouched to consider his options. The stone walls were too high to scale without aid, and the hillside behind him had been cut away to make room for the vineyard, leaving only a sheer wall that was at least forty feet high, quashing that as an option as well.

But even if it were possible to climb the wall, he could not escape on foot. If he had any hope of the garrison finding the unusual order to follow him to England credible, it would not do to approach them on foot, sweaty, filthy, and panting from his narrow escape. Henry had to be on horseback and appear as though he was prepared for the journey, which meant he would have to get across the courtyard to the stable and then out the main gate without anyone noticing. But how was he to do that?

Time was also becoming a factor, he realized, not only because he needed to make his escape before the search intensified but because embarking on such a journey as this in the evening was already strange. If he were to approach the garrison in the middle of the night, it would be sure to arouse even more suspicion.

The lights carried by the search parties were moving down the rows toward him. The shadow he rested in would not hide him from direct lantern light. He had to move again.

Henry stood upright. Taller than most men, he could just see over the top of the trellises that supported the grapevines if he stood on his toes. He was dismayed to see that there were already men on both sides of him. They were spreading out through the vineyard, searching in a haphazard fashion, which made it impossible for him to anticipate where they were going to appear at any given moment.

He dropped back down to keep out of sight as a light on the next row bounced by. It was unlikely that they would press through the tangled grape vines and find him here, but it was very possible that they would see him through them if they were looking hard enough.

As soon as the lantern on the next row passed, Henry bolted from his hiding place, trying to suppress a panicked feeling that he was trapped.

He cut across the rows in the opposite direction the light had gone and was rushing so fast that he did not see the soldier until he was almost upon him. The soldier was running along the ends of the rows, shining a light down each one in search of the intruder.

Henry was running out the end of one row of grapes at the same time that the soldier was coming upon it. They both skidded to a halt only a few feet from each other.

The soldier turned his head back toward the house to cry out, but Henry was upon him. He struck the man hard with his fist. The soldier's cries were choked off as his jaw snapped sharply sideways, followed abruptly by his head. Henry stepped past him and slid his arm around the man's neck to choke him into unconsciousness.

The lantern slid from his fingers, and the light was extinguished when it hit the ground. Henry let the body slide gently down before bolting back into the vines. Though the soldier's cry had been cut short, it was still enough to draw attention, and he could hear others approaching in response.

Henry ran along the last row with the cliff wall of the chateau on his right, working his way toward the courtyard, but he stumbled to a stop as light appeared from the row in front of him. He turned to go back the way he had come, but here too men were appearing, drawn by the cry. Henry was trapped! He threw himself into a shallow depression in the cliff wall and held his breath as the two groups converged upon him from both sides.

"Oi," the three men emerging from the row in front of Henry shouted to the two who appeared from the other direction.

"Eh?"

Henry pressed his body back into the shadow as the two lanterns drew closer together, chasing away the shadows that were his sole concealment. He willed himself to become part of the wall behind him.

"You find anything?" one of the men said in French.

"Of course I did not find anything," the man in the row ahead snapped, and he stopped where Henry's outline was just faintly visible against the black wall. "You hear me call out that I found someone?"

Henry tensed in preparation to spring from his hiding place. Only half-concealed in shadow now, if even one of the men glanced in his direction, he was going to be seen. He needed to act now, as that split second of surprise might be the difference between life and death. He held his breath and prepared to shove past the two arguing men before they could stop him. He started to push away from the wall.

"Ahhh!" The man closest to him cried suddenly in dismay, pointing back over the heads of the two who stood on Henry's left. Every eye turned to look in the direction he was pointing just in time to see flames erupt over the rows of grapes in the deepest part of the vineyard.

A fire in a vineyard, if not squelched immediately, could not only destroy a fortune in unrealized product but could easily consume everything in its path, including the house and stable. All at once Henry was forgotten as the five men raced toward the blaze, shouting at the top of their lungs.

Henry waited until they were well out of sight before he dared to breathe again. He slid down the wall in relief and remained there while he recovered himself. That had been entirely too close. What were the odds that a fire would break out at the precise time he needed a diversion to make his escape? That did cause him to wonder, but he could not worry about it now.

He ran toward the courtyard along the back wall while every available soldier raced toward the blaze along the main row.

With all efforts focused on suppressing the blaze, Henry could move more quickly now; but he still had the problem of crossing the courtyard without being noticed. He paused to inspect the furor.

A bell had begun to toll from the guard tower near the gate. Henry hoped and prayed that this was a different alarm than the one that would bring the garrison up. The bell did, however, cause all the nobles at the party to start pouring from the house.

Edward was already outside hollering orders by the time the other nobles from the party began to emerge in various stages of undress and dishevelment. Edward rode in a small, two-wheeled buggy pulled by a single horse. The compact size allowed him to maneuver up and down the rows of the vineyard and coordinate the fire suppression efforts. As Henry watched, Edward's buggy bolted into the vineyard on the opposite side from where Henry was concealed.

As soon as he disappeared, Henry slipped from the shadows into the group of nobles collecting near the house, who were staring bemusedly at the commotion. Some were attempting to call for their carriages, only to learn that every servant—theirs included—was engaged in fighting the fire, leaving the nobles with little to do beyond staring and gossiping about what they were seeing.

Henry kept his head down and made his way slowly but steadily across the courtyard to the stable. The alarm bell had called all the stable hands as well, so Henry entered the stalls unobserved, chose a strong-looking mare, and saddled it as quickly as he could manage in the dark.

When he emerged a quarter of an hour later, a fire line had formed to pass buckets of water from the well in the courtyard out to the blaze in a long human chain. Despite these efforts the flames had risen even higher, curling twenty feet into the air in some places.

Henry quietly led the horse by the bridle to the deserted main gate and opened it just far enough that he and his mount could fit through. He took one last look at the house. Every eye that was not engaged in the fire suppression effort was fixed on the blaze. Every set of eyes save one.

With a jolt, Henry found himself once again staring into the eyes of Katriane. She stood across the courtyard with some of the other servants, but while they were all looking toward the rising flames, she was turned toward him. He froze, but this time it was different. She was not nervous or fidgeting. She was deliberately staring at him, and he suddenly knew, without knowing how he knew, that the flames were her doing. She had created the diversion that allowed him to escape. Perhaps she was the person he believed her to be after all. And, maybe, that meant she understood that he too was the man she thought he was.

Their eyes locked for a long moment. Henry raised his hand in a simple, sad farewell salute. After a pause, she returned the gesture.

Henry led his horse through the opening and closed the gate softly behind him. He found himself smiling as he galloped down the road toward the guard houses.

Eighteen

England, near Dawning Court
Present Day

alt!" the guards ordered, weapons coming up instantly at the sight of the Braddock crests covering William's horse. A warning horn was already on its way to one of the guards' lips.

"Take your ease, brothers," William said to head them off. Though sounding the alarm might be the fastest way to get Aden's attention, it would do William little good if someone ran him through before he could say his piece. "It is I, William Dawning!" he added when they did not appear to be dissuaded.

All four men looked hard at William in the fading light.

"I must see Sir Aden at once," William insisted, though he could not seem to muster the emotion that should accompany such a statement. He was utterly spent. His wounds throbbed, his entire body felt like it was one massive bruise, and he was fairly certain that Finn was correct, and his fever had returned. In short, he did not want to be doing this anymore. But if he could just deliver his message, in an hour he could turn the responsibility for it over to Aden. Then, maybe, he could rest.

"Can you prove you are really who you claim to be?" one of the guards asked.

William could not even muster the strength to roll his eyes. Instead he turned back to Finn, who had stopped a pace behind, not at all certain, as a Braddock, about the wisdom of riding into a Dawning encampment. "Finn, tell the men who I am."

Finn stared at him in confusion until William jerked his head toward the guards as if to say, "Well, come on."

"You did not tell me what to sa—" he started to whisper to William but stopped when he realized everyone could hear him.

"My thanks, Finn. Now please answer the question."

"He is William Dawning," Finn said lamely.

"There. You see?" William turned back to the guards, whose weapons had not lowered an inch. "Incontrovertible proof that I am he whom I profess to be."

"Why you ridin' a Braddock horse then, eh?"

William heaved a great sigh and called to Finn again without turning around. "Finn, tell the men whose horse this is."

Finn stared at William's back, unsure of what William wanted him to say, but finally muttered, "Er—the Braddocks'."

"And how did I get it?"

Finn hesitated only a moment this time, "You stole it."

"There you have it. Now if you would be so kind as to direct me to Sir Aden's tent; time is short."

The guards took a step away and began to confer in hurried whispers. Finally convinced that the Braddocks would not send just one man and a boy into the camp with the intent to stir up trouble, they agreed. "Dismount and surrender your weapons."

William dismounted, but instead of handing his sword to the guards, he turned and gave it to Finn along with his horse's reins. "You wait there," he said, nodding toward a rise in the road back the way they came.

The guards looked unsure if they should protest but apparently deemed the young man of little consequence and let him ride away unmolested.

William walked between the soldiers as they led him through the camp. It was odd to now feel like a stranger in the Dawning camp when for days he had moved freely among the Braddocks'. But in truth, he was so displaced—the world he had known so shattered—that he barely noticed the faces of the men who looked on curiously. He absently noted as he trudged through the dank camp that Aden had been digging in. Tall mounds of earth were thrown up around the perimeter, with sharpened wooden balustrades sunk into the tops of them.

William's escort stopped suddenly, causing William to bump into the man in front of him and blink in surprise. Only then did he register the aging canvas tent and hear one of the guards part the tent flap and say, "Sir Aden, this man wishes to see you." The guard hesitated a moment before adding, "It is—er, that is, he claims to be William Dawning."

A moment later the flap was thrown wide and into the firelight stepped the tall, spare form of Leah's father. He regarded William with a deep frown.

It was at this moment that William was reminded that Leah's father had never particularly liked William and had taken no pains to hide that fact. William had never really understood where Aden's dislike came from but had always assumed it was a result of the budding relationship between Leah and himself.

Aden had been a peasant soldier who had served with distinction under William's father and had been landed and knighted as a result. As the son of Aden's greatest benefactor, one might have expected that Aden would welcome a marriage between the two, even push for it, but that had never been the case. William had always felt that it was somehow personal with him and had not understood it at the time. Sure, when he considered the mess he had made of things recently, he had no trouble understanding it; but Aden couldn't have known that it would all lead to this.... Or could he?

It had never occurred to William until this moment that Aden's personal dislike of William might affect his decision in the current matter. *But surely he would not let such a thing cloud his judgement, would he?*

"Our report said you were dead," Aden said without preamble, as though it were an accusation.

"I am only partly dead."

"You think this amusing?" Aden demanded. He looked to be on the verge of striking William.

"I watched Richard cut down by a horde of Saracens and Braddocks. I have spent every moment of this past week trying to prevent Dawning Castle from being overthrown by that same horde. Now they are within hours of accomplishing their designs. So no. I do not find this especially amusing. But I have done all I can do for them. You must march to her defense at once—this very night!"

"I know all about the castle," Aden said shortly. "But Collin Braddock is camped only a thousand yards to the north, and I will not expose my men by ordering them from our defenses. We cannot withstand Collin in open combat."

"I understand the danger. But if we do not march now, there will be nothing to march home to, and victory here will mean nothing."

"The lives of my men may be of no value to you," Aden snapped, "but they very much matter to me!"

William ignored the slight. "What is it that you fail to grasp? Is it me? Am I failing to convey the urgency of the matter? Then I will speak plainly. The castle and all the people of Dawning Court who have sought shelter within her walls are hours away from being slaughtered! I know it is dangerous. I understand that Collin is waiting to pounce, but we must risk it. We can leave enough men behind to deceive Collin into believing that the army is still camped here. If we hurry, then we can save Dawning Castle and be inside her defenses before Collin can catch us up. But I swear to you, Sir Aden, if we do not march now, all will be lost. My mother, Leah, Evelyn, they will all be at the mercy of our enemies...."

William trailed off as the blood drained from Aden's face. William sensed he had just made a major misstep but was not clear what it might have been until Aden spoke again.

"My daughters," his voice quavered with scarcely suppressed fury, "are in the castle?"

William felt that Aden was directing this accusation at him personally and was unsure how to respond.

"The messenger at Runnymede said the castle was warned of the siege. He told me that you were given several *days* in which to prepare!" Aden's voice was rising now, and he stepped close to William until he was towering over him. "What fool would have allowed young noblewomen to remain in a besieged castle?"

William felt his own anger begin to rise in response. How dare this man—his subordinate—suggest that William should have done something to prevent that? After everything William had been through! But William forced himself to remain calm. He had to stay focused on the goal at hand, and letting his anger take control would not accomplish that.

"There is enough blame to go around, Sir Aden," William said softly.

"You have much to answer for!" Aden shouted back.

"That is also the truth, but I think you will agree that what matters now is saving those who can be saved— rescuing Leah and Evelyn." Aden continued to glare his naked hatred down at William, so William pressed on. "Dawning Castle is about to fall, but in rushing to take the castle, our enemy has over-extended itself. If we strike before they take control of the battlements, they will be vulnerable. We can overwhelm them, and they will never expect it."

Aden continued to glare down at William.

"Perhaps, Sir Aden, we should hear the lad out."

Behind Aden stood Martin, the aging but still powerful man-at-arms who was serving as Aden's second-in-command.

Aden glowered down at William one last time before stepping back.

"Tell us what is happening, lad," Martin suggested.

"We have been betrayed!" William said to Martin emphatically, grateful to have a listening ear.

"We are well aware of that. Thomas has allied with the Saracens."

"No, not that. There is a new army, the Mayfields. They have allied with the Saracens and double-crossed the Braddocks."

"The Mayfields?" Martin blinked in confusion. "Henry's wife? Should they not be fighting *for* us?"

"Yes, Henry's wife!" William snapped impatiently. He could feel his tolerance waning along with the last of his energy. But he took a deep breath to get control of himself. "Listen to me. It is complicated, but time is very short. The Moors have made a deal with the Mayfields. They have mobilized an army that is even now attacking Dawning Court."

"Then they are fighting for us?"

"No! Their intention is to overthrow the remnants of Hans' weakened army after he has defeated the castle. They will then take the battlements and install their own baron." William deliberately omitted the name of who that was going to be, as he realized that—for whatever reason—his credibility was already weak enough with this group. "Lord Aden, if we do not stop them before they take control of the battlements, we will find them quite unstoppable—a professional army of fresh troops protected by the defenses of Dawning Court!"

Aden looked at Martin, and something unspoken seemed to be passing between them. William could feel a tension in the crowd of men who had gathered around, attracted by the exchange, but it was not the expected tension that came from hearing that they were about to lose their home. There was something going on here that William was not privy to, but he did not have to wait long to get the answer.

"Lies!" Every eye turned to see Neil hobbling through the assembly. William could not hide his shock at seeing his childhood friend here. But if seeing Neil was surprising, seeing Salena Abelin following behind him was positively astonishing.

"Neil?" It was half a question and half an exclamation of surprise. "How ... the last time I saw you, you were riding away from a pack of Braddock knights, bareback on a plow horse."

"And how, pray tell, would you know that?" Neil demanded.

Everyone looked at William as though he had just fallen into a trap. William blinked. It took him a moment to realize what he had just said. Without context, there was no way they could understand. "Neil," William hesitated, casting a confused glance at Salena, who was striding toward him, "I am not your enem—"

Salena slapped him across the face. "This man is a murdering liar!" she screamed. "He is a traitor! He and Thomas betrayed us all!"

She turned to hit William again, but at a motion from Aden the guards grabbed her and pulled her back.

"Sir Neil, explain this!" Aden commanded.

"This man was not in Dawning Castle, as he would have you believe!" Neil lurched up to William with the help of a walking stick and looked him in the eye. "The only reason he stands before you now is because he has betrayed us. It was likely William himself who killed Lord Richard. You can be certain that if he wants you to march, then the best thing you can do for Dawning Castle is to remain where you are!"

William's brow furrowed. He was not surprised that Neil thought him a traitor, but he had not really expected to face those accusations here, in front of Aden. He opened his mouth to proclaim his innocence, but as he turned back to Aden, he was struck again across the face. Not a slap this time, but a vicious blow that knocked him to the ground.

He looked up to see Aden standing over him. "I might have known," Aden growled through clenched teeth. "It is because of you that Hans Braddock attacked *my* home. It is because of you that I cannot employ my army in defending my own people because the enemy you made of Collin Braddock hounds our steps. And I swear to you, if my daughters are harmed, you will wish that you had died on the battlefield with Richard."

William could feel what little energy he had left draining away along with the last vestiges of his hope for Dawning Court. "You do not know what you do!" he protested. "Much has happened of which you are not aware! The Mayfields are counting on you delaying Collin in a futile stand that will lead to your demise, weaken his force, and allow them time to secure the battlements before he arrives; and you are playing directly into their hands!"

"Why would either party consent to such an alliance?" Martin asked. He seemed to be the last one who was still listening to William, everyone else having dismissed him as a lying traitor.

William sighed, sitting up and touching his lip to see if it was bleeding. He knew that he had lost this battle and telling them the truth was only going to make him sound more unbelievable; but he told them anyway. "Because they each get a barony out of it. With Collin's army defeated, there is no one left to defend Braddock Court. Hans left Braddock castle with so little defense that a small band of highwaymen could overthrow it."

Martin, seeing that Aden was still in his passion, glanced at Neil for confirmation.

"William well knows that we cannot verify his story without risking our entire remaining army. He has devised his tale in such a way that time does not permit us to even send scouts to substantiate his words but insists that we act now, trusting solely to the strength of his word."

"And we might have done, had you not been here, Sir Neil," Aden said, tearing his smoldering gaze from William for the first time. "He could not have known that there would be anyone among our camp who would know of his duplicity. He believed that we would welcome him as a hero."

"This is about the type of hero's welcome I have come to expect," William muttered, spitting blood in the dirt.

"Guards!" Aden roared. "Remove this swine from my sight before I gut him here and now!"

The guards, who had withdrawn a pace during the confrontation, moved up and surrounded William again.

"Do what you will with me, but heed my words!" William called as they dragged him to his feet. "It is our last chance!"

"Keep him on minimal food and water," Aden ordered, "and bind him fast, with a dozen guards watching him at all times! If the Lord should spare us, then William will face the justice of the people of Dawning Court—the people he has betrayed! And if we are destroyed at the hands of the Braddocks, then we will see to it that the author of all our misfortunes suffers the same fate."

The soldiers began dragging William away. "Aden," he shouted over their shoulders, though he knew it would do no good, "kill me if you must, but you are Dawning Court's last hope! This is your last chance to save Leah!"

"Hold!" Aden commanded, loathing plain on his face.

The guards stopped in place, still holding William by the arms. Aden crossed the distance to William and struck him a brutal blow to the stomach, doubling him over painfully. But Aden did not give him time to catch his breath before wrenching William's head up by the hair, forcing him to meet his eye.

"You dare to use my love for my family to manipulate me?" he growled. "Know this. I am holding you personally responsible for anything that happens to them. If even a hair of their head is harmed, I will exact payment upon you an hundredfold."

William felt the resolve in Aden's words, and he felt the fear of having such a powerful man intent upon his personal harm. And as it so often did, the fear flashed into rage in an instant. He knew he needed Aden's help as the only man who could save Dawning Castle, but in that instant, he did not care. "Why not release me here, if you think you are man enough to stand up to me, and I will gladly plant the body of the man who is letting our home be destroyed beside a thousand other fools who thought they were strong enough to face me!"

A twisted smile crossed Aden's face, and just for a moment William thought he was going to be beaten again; but Aden only shoved his head back down. "Remove this rubbish from my sight."

The four guards who had escorted William into the camp dragged him away. William did not resist, the frustration of defeat draining what little energy the exchange with Aden had generated in him.

In the past, the attacks and sieges that William had helped organize, when he had neither cared about success nor worried over survival, had always just seemed to fall into place for him with very little effort. But now that he was trying to do something good—trying to make amends for his mistakes—nothing was going his way. Why was God, who had protected him through everything up to this point, not helping him now that he was trying to save so many innocent people? Why, now that he was working to put things right, was he failing at every turn? If God had preserved him for this, where was God's hand now?

The guards put William's back against a tree and lashed his arms around the trunk behind him. He was finished. He had done everything that could reasonably be expected of him to help Dawning Castle, but it was out of his hands now. Sure, they were doomed, but that was not his fault. What was there left to do other than watch it happen?

And when it had all collapsed, William fantasized about standing in front of Aden to gloat before William struck him down for his defiance. "Damn fool!" But that fantasy did little to lessen the sick feeling in the pit of his stomach.

William slid down to a sitting position at the base of the tree. He was torn between his crippling exhaustion, his rage at Aden, and the fact that every square inch of his body hurt. His injuries on his hip, arm, and ribs where Amir and Najid had cut him felt like they were torn open; his head throbbed from where he had been hit with the rock at the dam; and his mouth hurt from where Aden had struck him, to say nothing of the fever that still raged. But all of that was not enough to keep oblivion at bay. William leaned his head back against the tree, and within a minute he was out.

Nineteen

"Lord Braddock," Bertram, Collin's second in command stirred him from sleep late that night.

"What is it?" Collin asked at once, not even a hint that he had actually been asleep in his voice.

"A messenger from Braddock Court, he—well, I think you had better hear this."

Collin rose and stepped out of his tent. There before him stood a young blonde boy who looked to be about fifteen years old.

"What is all this?" Collin demanded, not bothering to hide his irritation. "Who are you?"

The boy's eyes were wide as he looked up at Collin and swallowed hard. "F—Finn, Lord," he squeaked.

"I did not ask for your name! Who are you? What is your business here?"

"Yes, Lord. Sorry, Lord. Er, the Dawnings are attacking Braddock Court."

It took Collin a moment to register what he had said. "That is impossible. Their only remaining force is bivouacked not a thousand yards from where we are standing, and the rest of their army is defending against Thomas and his heathen mercenaries. They do not have men enough to besiege Braddock Castle."

Finn looked uncertainly at Bertram, obviously afraid to contradict Collin.

"Just tell him what you told us, lad," Bertram instructed him.

"Well," Finn spoke hesitantly, looking up at the two seasoned knights as though they were giants, "perhaps you are not aware that Lord Hans took the defensive force left at Braddock Court and is besieging the Dawnings."

"So it is true." Collin was seething with fury, but much to Finn's relief, he was addressing Bertram. "It seems that Saracen merchant was telling the truth."

Bertram spoke then, giving Finn a much-needed reprieve. "The Dawnings are likely exploiting Braddock Court's weakness in order to use it as leverage should they be overthrown by Hans."

"They will have no such leverage over me!" Collin growled. "Awaken the men! We break camp at once!"

"Your orders, Lord?"

"We will secure our home and then ride to Dawning Court and tear it down stone by stone."

"And Hans?"

Collin got a cold look in his eye. "Hans had better pray that the Dawnings get to him before I do."

"Should we not leave part of our force here?"

"That is exactly what the Dawnings are hoping we will do. With only half our force, we will be outnumbered by Aden, and it will be even harder to take back my castle from them. Instead, we will do that which they do not expect; we will take the entire force, rip down the gates of Braddock Court, and then march upon Dawning Court with the entire might of the Braddocks before they even expect it!"

Twenty

"Lord Aden!" Martin burst into Aden's tent, startling him from sleep.

Aden was instantly up. "What is it? Attack?"

"Collin is leaving," Martin said. He had been personally overseeing the night watch, given the precariousness of having the Braddocks camped so close. They could not afford any mistakes from their peasant army. Though they had proven themselves at Runnymede, that did not replace years of training.

Aden was already reaching for his armor but stopped at that. "What do you mean, leaving?"

"I mean leaving. His camp has pulled up stakes and ridden out."

Aden resumed strapping on his armor. "They mean to bypass us entirely and reach Dawning castle ahead of us."

"No, Milord," Martin shook his head. "I thought of that as well, so I had our scouts follow them. They are on the road to Braddock Court." When Aden did not respond, Martin fidgeted uncomfortably. "There is something else, Milord. William Dawning has escaped."

Aden's face went from thoughtful to dark in an instant. "A ruse, then? William has defected to the Braddocks and warned them that we were not to be moved from our stronghold so long as their army was nearby? They mean to lure us out and attack us in the open."

Martin shrugged uncertainly. "Perhaps, but the scouts confirmed that the entire army is more than a league away and still on the march."

A tense silence hung in the air. Both men recognized this as the crucial moment that it was. If Collin had really pulled out, they had just been given an opening to save the castle. But if it was a ploy, and they fell for it, they were sacrificing Dawning Court's last fighting force.

"Your orders, Milord?"

"Send more scouts. I want continuous updates on Collin's movements."

"Done. And our army?"

Several thoughts were vying for Aden's attention. He was thinking that he wished he had put William down while he had him. He was thinking about the danger to his men; but he was also thinking of his daughters trapped inside Dawning Castle, where every moment might mean the difference between life and death for them. He was so tied up in knots that he could not see clearly. He looked seriously at his second-in-command. "What would you do, were you in my place?"

"The safe thing would be to wait it out," Martin replied carefully.

"You did not answer my question."

Martin frowned and then said, "I would break camp and march for Dawning Court."

"And if it is a trap? If Collin doubles back upon us immediately?"

"It will take us an hour to break camp. Our scouts will warn us if they turn back or stop before that. If not, then we will march hard through the night; they will not catch us before we reach Dawning castle."

"I need not point out the exposed position this puts us in," Aden said seriously. "We may find ourselves trapped with Hans and the Saracens before us and Collin at our rear, and nowhere to turn for cover. This might be the very outcome Collin—or William—desires. We might be doing exactly what William expected all along."

"If William is behind this, then you are likely correct," Martin agreed, "but Collin is not so devious. And consider that we only dug in here out of necessity. If the danger has passed, then Dawning Court needs us now. Tomorrow may be too late."

"And if Collin does turn back on us?"

"Then we better be inside the walls before he arrives."

"Rouse yourself!" a gruff voice called, startling Neil from a fitful sleep. His stomach wound did not allow him to rest well for very long.

Neil blinked. It was still dark out. He had an instant sense of foreboding. "What is happening?" He was in a cot inside a small tent shared by several other recovering soldiers who had been wounded at Runnymede but were well enough to travel with the larger company. It was not comfortable, but he was at least being attended by someone with actual medical training.

"We are breaking camp." The sergeant was already turning to go.

"Pardon?" Neil sat up, heedless of the pain that lanced through his stomach.

"We are breaking camp. We ride for home within the hour."

"No!" Neil exclaimed, climbing painfully to his feet. "I warned them. This is exactly what William wanted."

"William Dawning?" the sergeant groused impatiently. "He has gone. Fled."

"And what of the Braddocks?"

"The Braddocks have marched for Braddock Court."

"William has escaped and now this? How can you fail to see this as the trap it almost certainly is? William is the author of this confusion."

"Well," the sergeant said, losing interest and turning again to leave, "you may wait here to see if they return. But if you intend to ride with the army, we are leaving within the hour."

"This is all wrong," Neil said to his retreating back, but the sergeant ignored him. Neil turned, pulled on his cloak, and hurried out into the night.

Everywhere he looked, camp was being actively struck. Tents had been dropped, bedrolls were being bound up, and wagons were loaded with gear.

He looked around desperately for someone who would listen to him, but no one who could do anything about this disastrous mistake was around.

The carriage that he and Salena had used to escape Dawning Castle was parked nearby. It stood out distinctly among the utilitarian equipment of the military camp, parked beside a horse paddock where the horses had been unhitched and corralled for the night.

He moved reluctantly over to it, thinking that he had better hitch up the horses before they were commandeered by the soldiers.

He had just reached it when a head poked up out of the back, startling him. "Salena?"

"What is happening?" she asked in a groggy voice.

Neil looked down at the blankets she had gotten from somewhere to fashion a bed. "Did you sleep here? It is freezing!"

"There are not many accommodations for a single lady in a military encampment. I thought it better to remain out of sight rather than draw the attention of a thousand lonely men. Now tell me what is happening. Are we under attack?"

Neil did not understand. As a noble of Dawning Court, Salena could have simply demanded accommodations be made for her, and Aden surely would have seen to it; but it only now struck him that given what she had been through with Hans, this camp must be a terrible place for her. She must have felt safer simply hiding rather than announcing her presence to everyone in the camp. It was a horrifying thought, and he felt a deep sense of pity for her in that moment but forced himself to shake it off.

"William!" he exclaimed. "He has escaped. And I do not know how, but he must have convinced Collin to pull back far enough that Aden feels secure to leave the safety of the fortifications."

"We must stop him!"

"I agree, but thus far no one is listening to me." He shook his head in disgust.

"I will hitch up the horses," she volunteered, "while you seek out Sir Aden and attempt to talk some sense into him."

Neil nodded, impressed by Salena's assertiveness. He made his way through the camp as fast as his injuries would allow. By the time he reached it, Aden's command tent had already been collapsed and packed up. Aden was talking to a group of soldiers, apparently giving them marching orders.

"Sir Aden!" he called, but it was Martin who answered, stepping between Neil and Aden.

"What is it, lad? As you can see, we are very busy."

"Martin, I must speak to Sir Aden. This is a mistake!"

"Why? What do you know?"

"I know William!" Neil exclaimed. "Think about it. He tried to convince us to march immediately, but we refused. So he escapes, the Braddocks then mysteriously pull out, and now we are doing exactly what he wanted. Surely you must see that this is a trap!"

"Do you *know* that it is a trap?"

"Well, I—" Neil started, but Martin cut him off.

"Do you KNOW that it is a trap?" Neil fell silent. "Because this much I do know. Our families and everyone we care about are packed into a castle with insufficient food, supplies, and soldiers—you told us that yourself. And every hour we delay here could be the difference between life and death for them. So, unless you *know* that we are making a mistake, we are going to take this chance."

"But William," Neil protested weakly.

"Is a wild card. You forget, lad, that I know William too. Though he trained with Jurou instead of with me, I watched him grow. I was marshal of the tournament where Vincent Braddock was killed. I know something of his character, and I have been thinking much on that since you arrived in camp."

"Then you know as well as anyone how dangerous he is."

Martin shrugged. "I am not certain what I know, and neither are you. But I do know that had he wanted power for himself, he had ample opportunity to see to it that Richard did not make it back from Persia alive. 'Twould have been a small thing for him to sell out the lot of you to the Nizari. There were only fifty of you, after all. That would have removed Henry and Richard, and no one would have asked too many questions since the quest was believed doomed from the start. So why wait until now to betray his people?"

Neil hadn't had much time to think on these matters since fighting with William at the dam, but he still felt certain of his conviction. "It would have raised too much suspicion if he was the only one to return."

"Suspicion would have been irrelevant because only Thomas would have been left for succession. If that is what they had planned all along, they would have had it. And if William were looking to take the barony himself, he could have simply challenged Thomas, and the barony would be his. All the suspicion, machinations, and rumors in the world would not have changed that because there was no one else in line."

"John was still alive," Neil offered weakly.

Martin grimaced to show what he thought of that. "John was disavowed. He was no longer in contention for the barony."

"He could have led a revolt if he believed that William had murdered his brothers—what is your point?" Neil demanded suddenly. "You believe William innocent?"

"My point is this: There is bad blood between you and William, is there not? Because of David's death?"

Neil reluctantly nodded.

"I wonder, then, if you are determined to see the villain in the man because you *wish* it to be so." He held up a hand to forestall Neil's protests. "I do not know for whom William fights, but I will wager you have not asked yourself this question since William's arrival: What if he speaks the truth?"

Neil opened his mouth to argue, but a hundred thoughts collided in his mind at once. He remembered his surprise at seeing William alive; he remembered coming to blows with him; he also remembered William as a youth who had no apparent interest in ruling. None of it made any sense. How was he to reconcile that?

Seeing the conflict in his eyes, Martin patted Neil on the shoulder. "There is much to do now. You should be making preparations as well. See that you are ready to travel, and do not burden Sir Aden with these things unless you have some solid proof."

Neil was too immersed in his thoughts to even notice Martin leave. This had to be a trick! There was no other explanation. But how could he prove it? He hurried back to Salena, determined to find proof before it was too late.

"This is not the way to Dawning Court," Salena protested a quarter of an hour later as Neil drove the wagon out onto the highway. He held the reins in his free hand while his other hand protected his wound, but it was still hurting him. "Where are we going?"

"To prove William Dawning's guilt once and for all."

It took Salena a moment to realize what he meant, but then it clicked, and she reached over and snatched the leather straps from him. "Why did you not say so before?

Sit back, this is going to be a hard ride!" She snapped the reins on the horses' backs to start them into a gallop.

Twenty-one

You told us that Aden and Collin were neutralized!" Mary shrieked at Amir. It was very late, and the Mayfields and Amir were in the sitting room of the manor house, where an out-of-breath scout had just reported that Aden and Collin were on the move and could be there within a few hours.

"So they were," Amir frowned. "The threat of the other was keeping both armies at a standstill."

"Hmmm," Mary said acidly, "and yet they approach."

"It is well," Amir replied calmly. "This is all part of the plan."

"It was part of the plan when we were *in* the castle, you heathen dullard! We are not ready!"

Amir's face tightened at the insult, but he did not respond to it.

"You were supposed to already have taken the battlements when we arrived!"

"What was supposed to happen," Amir corrected her, "is that we were to raise the Mayfield flag over Dawning Castle. But William's interference forced us to adjust that plan. Your army arrived too early."

"You assured us that you would have taken the battlements by late morning. We attacked when you told us to!"

"We did not anticipate that a Dawning trap would cripple two of the towers," Amir admitted.

Mary shook her head in disgust. "I am tired of hearing about your incompetence. What do we do now? Are we to be caught between two armies?"

"There is no need to fret, my love," George assured her.

"No need to fret?" she screamed at him. "In a matter of hours, Aden's army will be upon us!"

"Mary, my dear, you worry over nothing! You are the wife of the rightful heir and the people's salvation. You vanquished the Braddocks! On the morrow, we will simply present you at the gates, and they will welcome you with open arms."

"And if they do not?"

"It will not come to that," George assured her.

"You are a fool!" Mary spat and turned to Amir. "What of you? What is your plan if the castle does not surrender itself to me?"

"If they do not open the gates to us," Amir said, thoughtfully stroking his beard, "we will have no choice but to attack!"

"Attack?" Mary's eyes bulged. "Are we to do in several hours what an army twice our size failed to do in two weeks?"

"All will be well," he assured her. "We still have one siege tower. We will overthrow the castle with one bold, all-out assault should it come to that. Their diminished, ragtag army of peasants will not be able to withstand us. But as I say, it will not come to that."

George smiled at her smugly and took a self-satisfied swig of the wine.

"But will we have the time to use the tower?" Mary demanded in exasperation, as these two morons were failing to grasp the real problem.

Amir shook his head, a faint smile on his lips. "The value of the siege tower is not as a weapon but as a symbol! When we demand entrance to the castle with the tower at our backs, they will know that we are going to take the castle one way or the other, and they will have no choice but to acquiesce."

Twenty-two

ear down that gate!" Collin urged on his men as they crowded around the closed drawbridge, hacking at it with axes and maces, desperate to get through the thick wooden barrier before the next round of death was poured upon them. They had not had time to prepare properly for a siege. In fact, they had no siege equipment at all beyond some hastily constructed siege ladders that they had built in the woods around Braddock castle just before the attack, and a makeshift bridge to allow them to cross the mote.

And though the castle had repelled Collin's first and second waves, as Collin had known it would, the manner of defense employed had told him all he needed to know about their defenses. The Dawnings had not brought enough men to defend the castle properly. But then they likely had no other option, given that the bulk of their army was with Aden on the road from Runnymede. As a result, the sparse arrow, catapult, and ballistae fire were erratic and unevenly paced. The pitch attacks, while destructive, were only coming intermittently. The sporadic attacks obviously meant that they did not have enough men to keep the stations manned and supplied properly. Collin judged that he had a quarter of an hour before the next round of boiling pitch was poured down upon them. They might be able to get through the drawbridge in that time, but even if they could not, it did not matter. They would simply keep at it. Though the losses were devastating, they were relatively meaningless when weighed against the combined might of his army.

"Fools!" he muttered aloud. "Do the Dawnings not realize that this insult is only ensuring their eradication?"

"A ploy for time," Sir Bertram, Collin's second, said from his side as they watched the proceedings.

"A last desperate grasp for survival that has only ensured their speedy destruction," Collin growled.

"A ruse, perhaps," Bertram suggested, "to allow Aden to surprise us and trap us here?"

Collin snorted his derision. "So much the better. Without protective fortifications, we will wipe Aden's peasant army from the earth in an hour."

Collin was mounted behind the foot soldiers. He was in full armor and had his Golden Sword arrayed around him, ready to pounce the moment a hole was opened in the defenses. It was a dangerous place to be. Though the arrows from the wall had little effect upon them, the ballistae could punch right through armor and shields. But Collin was confident that the disorganized defense of the walls would offer little threat to him. The Dawnings had even failed to destroy the bridge. Where Dawning Castle had a barbican to restrict and trap attackers around the gate, Braddock Castle had a mote for that same purpose. But the two had to be defended differently. So long as the castle kept the attackers from getting any sure footing over the mote, the drawbridge was almost unassailable by foot soldiers. But the Dawnings had botched even that.

Collin cast his eyes upward. The eastern horizon was already beginning to brighten. It could not be long before the next round of liquid death was poured from the wall, but they were so close. If they could just break through in time, they might be spared that horrible fate. "I want the Dawnings' heads on a pike before daylight!" he shouted over the tumult.

Under their renewed efforts, great chunks of the drawbridge began to splinter and fall away. "The ram! Now!" Collin ordered as a matter of course. He had been in too many of these attacks to get excited at this early stage. There was still much to be done, and there was no telling what other traps the defenders might have prepared for them.

The crowd around the gate stepped aside as the trunk of a hastily cut tree was carried forward, and twenty men holding rope handles that had been nailed into the side began ramming it into the weakened drawbridge.

The wooden fragments did not withstand the pounding for long, crumbling and falling free from the iron banding. Minutes later, the drawbridge was decimated, exposing the portcullis that lay behind it.

The battlements had yet to answer back with the next round of pitch, so the ram crew kept on slamming the massive log into the iron grating until it began to bend and flex beneath the strain.

Collin knew the pitch pots must be near boiling, but they were so close! "Harder! More!" he roared. "Break it down!"

The ram crew backed up onto the makeshift bridge. More soldiers crowded in around them, and some took up position in the rear to add their strength to the assault. As one they charged forward, slamming the tree trunk into the portcullis with the combined force of thirty men.

The strain was too much. Iron rivets popped, and the portcullis was ripped from the stone wall and hurled ten feet into the courtyard, where it clattered down onto the cobbles.

The force of the charge propelled the ram crew into the courtyard, where they immediately cleared the area to make room for Collin and the Golden Sword who charged in right behind them, the golden knights fanning out in a semi-circle to hold the gate from the defenders' inevitable attempts to reseal it.

Only the expected retaliation did not come. The courtyard remained eerily deserted with only a few torches burning around the perimeter. It felt almost as though there was no one in the castle at all.

The men looked around in confusion. "A ploy!" Bertram, ever present at Collin's side, suggested. "They intend us to break our line by forcing us to ferret them out of their burrows."

"That is a trap that I do not fear. If they are too weak to hold us here at the gate, then we will easily drag them from hiding."

Then they heard it. The footfalls of the mailed boots clinking on the stone as armored men began to pour into the courtyard to defend the castle.

Collin's horse reared, sensing its rider's anticipation. "Yes!" Collin shouted encouragement at the squad of soldiers streaming into the courtyard. "Fight to the death! That is a good death!" There was no mockery in what he said, for he sincerely meant it. He would kill them all for the insult they had inflicted upon his noble house and by extension him personally, but it was right that a warrior should die in battle. It is how warriors were meant to die. He trained his lance at the foremost of the Dawning foot soldiers and spurred it into a charge.

The foot soldiers drew up short at the sight of Collin charging ahead of his magnificent band of knights, burnished armor glowing in the torchlight of the courtyard. They were overwhelmed at the sight and stunned into immobility. Collin exulted and charged even harder. But while the men looked scared, they were not behaving as they should. They had stopped their charge, but they were not taking defensive positions or brandishing their weapons. Many of them even raised their visors. Something was wrong.

At the last moment Collin realized what it was. They were wearing Braddock tabards! By itself, he would have just assumed this another level of subterfuge; but that, coupled with the strange refusal to fight, was too much. He pulled up his lance just in time to keep from impaling the foremost guard, but that did not prevent his warhorse, which could not come to a stop so quickly, from trodding down the man he had intended to skewer.

Collin's horse skidded sharply to a halt. He ignored the crushed man behind him and raised his visor to get a better look around. The remnants of the castle guard stood in stunned silence, staring up at him and the rest of the Golden Sword, who had also realized their mistake and pulled up short around the group of foot soldiers.

Collin leapt from his saddle, snatched the closest soldier by his mail shirt and heaved him off his feet until he was eye level. "What is the meaning of this?"

The guard looked utterly petrified. "I swear, Lord, we did not know it was you. We had no word that you were returning, and in the darkness, we could not tell."

What he said was true enough. Collin, too, had been so certain that he was fighting an occupying army, he had not bothered to verify the fact; but his fury was not so easily quelled. "I identified myself and you fired upon me!" he growled through a jaw clenched in rage.

A strange expression crossed the soldier's face, but Collin hurled him aside. "How many men did we lose fighting ourselves?" he shouted to those around him, but it was a rhetorical question as no one could have possibly tallied the death toll yet.

He turned back to his horse, grabbed the saddle as though he would remount, but only dropped his forehead onto the worn leather in distracted thought. *How could this possibly have happened?*

"Tend to that man!" he shouted in response to the agonized moans of the man whom he had ridden down moments before. Every wail of pain was a reminder that he had just wasted an entire night and hundreds of lives fighting his own forces.

The guards who had stood frozen in shock and fear sprang into action around the half-crushed man, checking the extent of his wounds and eventually moving him out of the courtyard and away from Collin.

Collin did not look up when Bertram stepped up beside him. "You have put it together, I trust," Bertram said softly. "It *was* the Dawnings." He paused for a moment to let that sink in. "They deliberately led us here and made us believe they had seized the castle. They played us for fools, and we acted our part flawlessly." There almost seemed to be a trace of admiration in his voice, which only added to the fury that was growing in Collin's mind.

Collin spun on him, needing to lash out, to break something, to kill, but he stopped. The guards that had not yet had the sense to clear the courtyard saw the warning signs and finally fled. Even Bertram took a step back. "We ride tonight! Now! I will dismantle Dawning Castle stone by stone, and I will slaughter every last Dawning!"

Just then, Finn, who was now acting as a runner for the army, raced up to Collin and Bertram. "Your Lordship," he said, pausing to catch his breath.

"You!" Collin suddenly fixated on him. "Who did this? Who perpetrated this evil upon my people?"

Finn looked around, not yet comprehending what had happened, and Collin snatched him up by the tunic and shook him. "Who made me look like a fool?"

Finn's eyes bulged with fear. "I—it was William Dawning who led the attack," he squeaked, not sure what else to say.

"William Dawning is dead!" Bertram interjected.

"He is not," Finn said, struggling to keep Collin's fists from pressing into his throat as the material from his tunic stretched beneath his weight. "He infiltrated the Braddock camp at Dawning Court and sabotaged it. He then led the attack here."

"William Dawning?" Collin repeated the name as though it was unfamiliar to him. He then dropped Finn and turned back to Bertram. "Is there no end to the slights my family suffers at his hand? I swear that I will drink the blood of William Dawning or relinquish the barony!"

Bertram nodded and looked past him to Finn, who was just getting back to his feet! "What did you wish to tell us, boy?"

Finn flashed a nervous glance at Collin, afraid he might explode on him again, but then answered Bertram, "Escapees were spotted, a dozen of them riding through the trees."

Bertram looked at Collin. "Deserters?" he asked.

"No," Collin said quietly, "not deserters. Instigators. Golden Sword!" he roared. "Mount up at once!" He climbed into his own saddle and turned to Bertram, who was rushing to follow suit. "They can only be circling around to the highway. We will cut them off, and we will make them suffer!"

Twenty-three

Dawning Encampment
Earlier that night

"I call it peculiar."

The sound of voices nearby brought William back to consciousness sometime later. It was dark now, his shoulders were screaming at him for being propped behind him for so long, and it was cold. A group of soldiers—presumably his guards—had made a fire about ten feet from where he sat and were gathered around it on three sides, with William being on the fourth so the soldiers would not have their backs to him. "How can soldiers take their noble captive?" a sandy-haired man said to the others.

"You call it peculiar," a stalky, dark-complected man who was chewing on a stalk of grass said into the firelight. "The nobility would call it mutiny."

Silence fell over the group at the mention of the word. "Mu—mutiny?" a younger man squeaked in fear. "We could be hung?"

The dark man shrugged. "Looks as though death is inevitable either way. If we remain here, Collin's Golden Sword is going to ride over our defenses at dawn. But if we flee to Dawning Castle, we will be trapped between Collin and Hans Braddock."

"I do not want to die," the young man said after a moment, echoing what they were all no doubt thinking. "Not like this. Not for nothing."

"'Tis a pointless death," the grass-chewer muttered into the fire. An air of depression seemed to settle over the group like a pall, and they all went quiet.

It was late enough that the rest of the camp was asleep, or at least settled down for the night; so when this group stopped talking, all was still.

William was not certain how long he had been asleep, but it had been long enough to take the edge off of his exhaustion. As much as he had all but decided to ride out the rest of this conflict as an observer, it was very clear to him, sitting here now, that it was not enough to simply sit by and wash his hands of this. The only chance he had to be right before God, or Leah, or his mother, was to keep fighting right up until the final bell tolled.

"You are not cowards," he said into the silence. He did not look at the men but kept his head back against the tree, eyes half-closed, as though he were talking to himself. "That is what weighs on your minds, is it not? Does the fear of death make me a coward? It does not. It is only if you let that fear keep you from your duty that it becomes cowardice."

"You are suggesting," the sandy-haired man said, "that we should be proud to die in a ditch, the victims of noble duty. Is that it?" The unspoken implication came through loud and clear: *What else would a noble say?*

"I am suggesting," William said, opening his eyes to peer at them, "that your death need not be a pointless, unsung death in a mass grave! That notion causes your hearts to shrink in your breasts, but I say to you that it need not be so. We may all be dead by the next sunset, but why not depart this mortal sphere in a way that minstrels will sing about, that generations will celebrate, that will cause your kin to utter your name with reverence? Is that not a better death? A warrior's death?"

It occurred to William that he was manipulating these men with ideas of honor and glory that he well knew, at the moment of death, were a cold comfort at best, as he had witnessed with David. But the truth was the idea of glory and honor did motivate people, as long as those people had not seen the things that he had seen.

The dark man, who looked to be in his forties, peered at William closely in the same way one would look at a snake that might be venomous. "What are you proposing?"

"Instead of standing to face Collin's Golden Sword in a contest of might, which we cannot hope to win, let us use cunning."

"What does that mean?" the sandy-haired man demanded irritably.

"We need not defeat Collin. All we need do is distract him, divert him with something he cares more about than settling an old grudge." The soldiers waited expectantly. "Braddock Castle is only a few hours' ride from here. It is virtually undefended. I promise you that if Braddock Castle were under attack, Collin would lose all interest in us."

Many glances were exchanged around the fire, but it was the sandy-haired man who finally spoke. "Preposterous."

"No," William shook his head, "a small force using subterfuge is all it would take. What have you to lose in the attempt?"

"Our lives!"

"By your own word, your lives are forfeit at sunup. Remain, and you may only hope for a senseless, unsung death; follow me, and if all goes well you will rescue your friends, help your families, and maybe—just maybe—live to fight another day."

"We will all die just as surely as if we were to remain here," the man groused.

William shrugged. "Perhaps. But with my plan, at least there is a chance. And what if we were to succeed? Think on that! That is a glorious hope not available to you here."

"Then we are heroes," the young soldier said with a dreamy air in his voice. "We alone will have saved the army and maybe the barony."

"Wait a moment," the sandy-haired man said, shaking his head. "Consider what we are discussing here. Not only are we trusting in the word of this suspected traitor, but if we free him, we will also be branded traitors. And worse, we may be helping him to overthrow our own people."

"Fair point," William agreed easily, "so it is time to ask yourself what you believe. Did I betray my people, my own mother, and the woman I love all to help my brother take the barony with no apparent benefit to myself? Or am I the man you believed me to be before today? The White Warrior, the Moor Scourge, the master strategist offering you your last opportunity to save your own people from destruction."

No one spoke as they again passed uncomfortable looks around. Finally the dark man tossed the stock of grass into the fire. "Silas is the name," he introduced himself, standing up. "As far as I am concerned, this is your army, Lord William." He executed a bow from the waist, and the other men awkwardly followed suit, though with some obvious hesitation.

"What are your orders, Lord?"

"Why don't we start by cutting me loose. I will explain the rest while we ride. We have very little time."

"Oh, there is one more thing," William said, massaging his newly freed wrists where the ropes had rubbed them raw, "my squire is waiting for me outside of camp."

"So?"

"So, he is a Braddock."

Twenty-four

hy will you not tell me what we are about?" Finn whispered across to William when they slowed from a gallop to allow the horses to walk before pushing them again. William had not said much since returning from Aden's camp two hours earlier. All Finn had been able to get out of him was that he had managed to recruit some men that were sympathetic to their cause. William had only grunted at Finn's protestations that this small band was not enough to make any difference against the Mayfields. "We are only getting farther from Dawning Court with each passing league!"

William slowly exhaled. "I have a plan, Finn. But you will not like it."

"So, what else is new?" Finn quipped, though he was in no way prepared for what William said next.

"We ride to conquer your undefended home."

Finn blinked, but then snorted. "You mean to take the castle with..." he looked back to count the men riding with them, "...with fewer than a score of men?"

William said nothing, and Finn's smile faded.

"You are in earnest! You actually mean to do it! That is madness!" he added when William still did not respond. "We will all be killed!"

"Quite possibly," William agreed.

"William," Finn said after a long silence, "I know Sir Hildebrant said that I was to remain with you, but I cannot be party to an attack on my own home."

"I know," William said.

The group rode for another minute with no indication of stopping. "Er ... please desist," Finn said, not quite able to manage the command he had intended.

"Finn, I do not wish to split your loyalty. Answer me this, if you were under no obligation to me, what would you do?"

"Do?" Finn asked lamely.

"Do," William repeated. "What would you do at this very moment?"

"About your plan?" Finn clarified, trying to determine if William was baiting him. "Well, I could not really best you in combat, so it would do me no good to challenge you," he began to talk through his options. "I could ride with you and attempt to foil your attack as you did to us at Dawning Castle," he suggested. "But that was only effective because we thought you one of us, so that would not work."

"Then where does that leave you?"

"I suppose my only remaining option would be ..." Finn clamped his mouth shut, but William finished the thought for him.

"To warn Collin."

Finn grew pale.

"Finn," William said seriously, "that is what you must do."

"What must I do?"

"Ride back and warn Collin."

"I never said ... er ... is this a ruse? Are you having me on?"

"No," William said simply.

"Then you mean to stop me. You will not let me go?"

"No ruse, Finn. You are my friend, and I would not have your conscience twisting you into knots forever more."

"But—but if I warn Lord Collin—" Finn began, but William cut him off.

"It will not matter. We have enough of a lead that he cannot stop us now."

Finn looked around at the others as though they were all in on some jest that they were not sharing with him. "You are in earnest? You mean for me to ride back and warn Collin that you are besieging his home?"

"I do. Though I would not mention this conversation or the size of our force to him if you wish him to take you seriously."

"William," Finn said earnestly, "he will descend upon you with all the might of the Braddock army. Even if you somehow did take the battlements, you would never be able to hold them with so few men." His voice dropped to a whisper. "You are a great warrior, William, but Sir Collin's rage is truly terrible to behold. He will not simply slay you for this insult; he will make you suffer horribly."

William smiled a strange smile that Finn did not understand. "Finn, are you content to remain with us while we besiege your home?"

"I—I suppose not."

"Then do what you must, my friend, just as Sir Hildebrant did when he discovered my true identity. I release you from your obligation to me."

Finn slowed his horse and began to drop to the back of the pack, fully expecting someone to intervene or to order him to keep riding. But when the two columns of soldiers parted around him like a stone in a stream, he stopped, completely dumbfounded.

William turned back and gave a final farewell salute before kicking his horse into a gallop. His men did likewise, and Finn watched the small band disappear down the highway, leaving him sitting alone in stunned disbelief. He still did not understand what was happening, but as their hoofbeats receded into the distance, he began to accept that it was neither a trap nor a prank. They were not going to stop him, nor were they going to come riding back, laughing and slapping him on the back.

He remained where he was until his incredulity was replaced by loneliness, which shortly turned to fear. Alone on the King's Highway at night was no place for anyone, particularly a young squire who still felt much more a page than a warrior-in-training. Finn turned and galloped back the way he had come. Though he did not understand what was happening, his duty was clear. He had to warn Collin that Braddock Castle was under attack.

William scurried over the log they had laid across the mote to Braddock Castle, followed closely by Silas.

Silas pulled it across after them and laid it aside by the base of the wall for later use while William unspooled the rope around his shoulders and hurled the grappling hook toward the parapet high overhead.

The metal claw thudded back to earth beside him. He had wrapped the metal tines with strips of cloth to muffle any noise, but the heavy thunk still made him cringe.

"You missed," Silas, the swarthy soldier, observed helpfully.

"My thanks, oh wise one," William snapped as he reeled the hook back in. "What count?"

"35, 36, 37," Silas counted aloud. "You should hurry."

"Again, you have my thanks. The additional pressure does wonders to clear my head!" William began to spin the grappling hook in a vertical circle. He released it as the hook neared its zenith, and the momentum whipped it up into the darkness before again falling back to earth.

Silas stared at it for a moment. "I thought you said you had done this before!"

"You are aware, I presume, that under normal conditions besiegers have catapults or bows with which to throw these things up to the ramparts?"

"Normal attackers usually have more than a dozen men, too," Silas added dryly. "You can use my bow if you like," he offered.

"That's loads of help," William grimaced, looking at the grapple in his hand, which, unlike the ones he had used to gain access to Dawning Castle, was devoid of any means of fitting it to a bow string.

"Wasn't much call for grappling arrows in Runnymede," Silas shrugged. "I considered it fortunate to even find that one."

William glowered at him. "Don't you have something better to do?"

"The others can handle it; I'm here to look after you."

"That is loads of comfort," William groused. "What count?"

"221. And not to pile on, but if Collin rode ahead of the army with his Golden Sword, they could be here within the hour."

William started to snap at him, but Silas pressed his back into the shadows of the base of the wall, pulling William after him, while they waited for the guard patrol to pass above.

"Remind me to insult you later," William whispered when the guards had presumably passed. He then stepped away from the battlements as far as he dared and hurled the hook up a third time.

To his relief, it did not come back down. He tugged on it a few times, then looked pointedly back at Silas, as if to say, "I told you so."

"I never doubted you for a moment, Lord," Silas said with no hint of irony.

William scowled at him again but then turned back to the task at hand. "I will distract the guards, you do whatever it is you do," he said dismissively and began to climb the rope.

William could not ignore how heavy his limbs felt compared to when he had climbed the Dawning walls only two days before. Or was it three? He could not seem to remember, but it really did not matter. Though his nap back in Aden's camp had taken the edge off of his fatigue, he was realizing that it had done little to address the bone-weary exhaustion that had built up over the course of the previous week.

But he pushed those thoughts from his mind with the reassurance that the walls of Braddock Castle were only half as high as Dawning Court's. *So why do I feel like I am scaling the Tower of Babel, with walls so high they were intended to reach Heaven itself?*

By the time he pulled himself over the edge of the battlements, he was dizzy from the exertion. *What count?* He wondered. *234.... I think.*

He dropped onto all fours, focused on his breath, and silently willed the giddiness to pass.

"You there! What are you doing?" A gruff voice demanded. William heard the rapid footsteps, but before he could react, he felt himself being jabbed in the back with the tip of a spear. "Who are you?"

"You are early," William muttered.

A boot to the side told him that the guards were not in a playful mood. "Get to your feet! Slowly!"

William did as he was instructed, forcing himself to suppress a groan as he pulled his aching, exhausted body up before the two mailed guards. "I am one of you," he said, glancing down at the Braddock crest on his tabard, which he had taken from Finn before telling him what he was planning.

"Who are you?"

He smiled at the two gruff-looking, thirty-something soldiers wearing white Braddock tabards that matched his own. Each of them was armed with a spear and a sword. He could see the confusion on their faces. William just needed to think of a reason for his presence on the wall that would sound the least bit plausible. Maybe it was the fatigue, or maybe it was because he just didn't care anymore, but at that moment a heady recklessness at the impossible task he had set for himself seized him. This plan was so far-fetched that it would take a miracle to pull it off. And in that instant, rather than overwhelming him, the idea that he could not possibly succeed without a hundred different things working in his favor was somehow liberating. This was out of his hands, and he had no choice but to accept that.

"I am William Dawning," he said simply. "I have a dozen men with me, and we are here to take Braddock Castle."

The two guards stared for a moment before bursting into laughter.

William also started laughing, which seemed to take some of the fun out of it for the guards as one of them abruptly slammed the butt of his spear into William's stomach, sending him stumbling backward, gasping for breath. "I thought we were becoming friends," William wheezed.

"How did you get up here?"

William took a moment to recover himself. His armor had absorbed the brunt of the blow, but it had still knocked the wind from him.

The guard took a menacing step forward. "Do not make me ask twice."

"I climbed," William said, forcing himself to stand erect again.

"He is obviously mad," said the first guard. "What should we do with him, Travis? Do we take him down to the stocks?"

"Forget it!" Travis snapped. "That will take half the night. He is obviously an intruder. Let's throw him off the wall."

"May I ask a question?" William interrupted.

The guards paused, which he took as close to assent as he was likely to get, and proceeded, "If I am mad, does that mean that you do not see that man behind you?"

The guards spun around automatically, but it was too late. Silas fired his bow at close range. The arrow embedded itself in Travis' chest, and William stabbed his knife into the other guard's kidney while covering the man's mouth with his other hand.

William shoved the limp form toward Silas, who was just dragging Travis' body up onto the crenel for disposal over the side of the wall. "Quickly now. Strip his tabard before it is covered in blood, dispose of the body, and get out of sight."

"The guards work in pairs," Silas pointed out as he knelt to strip the tabard, helmet, and sword from the body. "Should I not be here to back you up?"

"If they are suspicious of me, I do not want them to see two unfamiliar faces." William pulled a nearby cart over to hide the grappling hook. "You will be employed to greater effect when you respond to my distress call with the others and confirm my fears."

The two tossed the defrocked guard from the battlements, and William took a deep breath to prepare himself while Silas hurried away.

William gave Silas a minute to get clear before turning and running for the closest guard tower, shouting, "We are under attack!"

There was a tower at each corner of the square wall that surrounded Braddock Castle's square keep. The turrets jutted up ten or fifteen feet above the main battlements, with watch platforms at the top of each, though they were not always manned, as was the case this night.

William ascended the tower with other guards already hurrying toward him. Once he had topped the tower, he pointed into the darkness and shouted, "Close the gates! We are under attack! We are under attack!"

A big, burly guard with a wiry, black beard panted up the stairs shortly after William, a handful of other guards in tow. "What attack?" he demanded.

"There!" William pointed at the silhouettes of his men moving out in the darkness. Knowing what he was looking for, he could see them easily, but it was not as apparent to the others, who were squinting into the night.

"So?" the big guard asked, his tone thick with irritation. "Why do you assume that is an attack? And why are you alone? Where is your partner?"

William made a show of forcing himself to calm down enough to speak coherently. "That is just it! Travis has disappeared! I think he might be dead." He let his voice crack a bit to sound like he was on the verge of panic.

"Dead? Why would you say that?"

"We saw some movement around the base of the wall. It looked like men skulking around—scouts, perhaps, or saboteurs. I said we should sound the alarm, but Travis was afraid of looking foolish for panicking over nothing, so he went down to see for himself and said that I was to raise an alarm if he was not back in a quarter of an hour. He went down to check, and ..." He trailed off as though he were afraid to utter the obvious conclusion.

"And what?" someone asked.

"He did not return," the bearded guard supplied for him. "We will send someone out to investigate."

He started to look among the faces for good candidates, and William started to genuinely panic. He had not considered what he would do if they simply called his bluff and sent someone out to check. They would find Travis dead as expected, but beside him would be his defrocked companion. How would William explain that? The entire ruse might unravel.

Thankfully, Silas showed up at that moment. "Is that not exactly what they are hoping for?" he said, stepping from the stairs onto the increasingly crowded platform. "Gives them a chance to pick off our small force a few at a time."

"Why not seal the gate first," William nodded, "as a precaution."

The bearded guard looked between Silas and William and then narrowed his gaze on William. "Who are you?"

"Me?" William asked incredulously, casting nervous glances at the horizon, hoping to remind the soldier that he should be more concerned with the invading army than with William's identity. "Hollis, squire to Lord Hildebrant!"

"I have stood guard with Sir Hildebrant's squire. He is a young boy."

William nodded quickly. "Finn, yes. He was Sir Hildebrant's page until recently. Obviously I know Finn. But Sir Hildebrant took me on as well. Now, are we going to discuss mutual acquaintances," William threw his arm out dramatically toward the darkened horizon, "or are we going to prepare the castle to defend against the attacking army?"

The big guard kept his narrowed gaze on William. "Sir Hildebrant is with Lord Hans at Dawning Court."

"That is true," William nodded impatiently.

"Why would he not have his squire with him when going into battle?"

"Because," William said in a flabbergasted tone meant to convey how obvious the answer should be, "he is traveling with Sir Ranalph, and I ... got crossways with the surly knight. Sir Hildebrant thought it better to relegate me to guard duty here rather than incur Ranalph's wrath in the field—as though anything might prevent that," he added wryly.

The big guard's pursed lips spread into a grin. "He is ornery, is he not? Sir Ranalph?"

"Well, we must not be too critical," William grinned back. "Were I as ugly as he, I suspect that I would be equally as unpleasant."

The big man barked a laugh as other guards from farther up the wall began to arrive on the tower. "What is all this?" one of them snapped.

"Young Hollis here believes we are under attack," the guard announced. All of them began to scan the darkness in earnest.

"There!" one of them exclaimed, pointing a gloved hand at a spot about three hundred yards away.

The bearded man squinted after him. "There are definitely people out there, but who are they and what are they about?"

"A returning army?" someone suggested dubiously.

William had to bite back hard on his response. *We could not make it any more obvious!* Thankfully, Silas came to the rescue again. "I suppose Collin's army returning from Runnymede made it this far and decided to make camp until morning."

"Should we not at least seal the drawbridge?" William suggested. "If we are wrong, we can open it again, but if not...." He left the implications of that hanging in the air.

Finally, the bearded guard nodded. "Lower the portcullis," he said, and two men descended from the tower to relay the order.

"Look there!" someone said, pointing to a small group of men on horseback riding toward them, illuminated only by the light of a single torch.

"They fly no pennant," the bearded man observed.

The group reigned in in front of the mote on the smooth patch of earth where the drawbridge—which had been raised for the evening but was not yet sealed—would land. The lead member of the party shouted up to them. "Braddock Castle! I am an emissary from Lord Hans. We bring news. Open the drawbridge and allow us entry!"

The guards breathed a collective sigh of relief. "It is only Lord Hans," someone almost laughed.

"They are probably just here to resupply," another man said.

"Tell the gate guard to let them in."

William could not believe what he was hearing. So shocked was he by the credulity of the guards that he spoke without thinking, "Are you mad?" he demanded.

The others turned on him with obvious irritation, not wanting to accept that they might actually be in danger.

William wanted to point out all the signs that this *was* an obvious ruse—the signs that he himself had designed on the assumption that they would see right through it—but he stopped short, afraid that he might seem a little too perceptive. Thankfully, Silas again spoke up to say what William could not.

"How do we know that they are from Lord Hans? Where is their banner?"

"That's right," someone agreed, "and why are they here in the dark, when they know we cannot identify them?"

"I am certain that there are more men farther out," someone else added.

The bearded guard nodded. "Identify yourself!" he called down.

The men on horseback conferred for a moment before shouting back up, "I am Sir Olaf of Braddock Court!"

"That is not Sir Olaf," William said quietly. "I would know Sir Olaf's bulk from a league away."

The bearded man grunted agreement. "This is a ruse to get us to let down our defenses."

"But," William swallowed hard, once more reverting to the frightened young guard role, "if we tell them we know what they are about, will they not simply attack?"

"Do not challenge them," another man added quickly. "We have not the men to hold off an army."

"A ruse of our own, then?" Silas suggested. William thought that he blended with the men completely naturally. He looked, sounded, and acted like them, and no one even seemed to look twice at his unfamiliar face. "Tell them the drawbridge has jammed, and we are working to repair it, but it might take some time."

"Will they not eventually get tired of waiting and attack anyway?" the same panicky guard asked.

"Perhaps, but we only need time to see what size army we are dealing with. Once we know that, we can decide how to proceed."

The big guard considered for a moment and then turned. "Welcome home, Sir Olaf," he called down. "The mechanism on the drawbridge has stuck. You know what a problem it is in the cold. Go into town, refresh yourselves, and rest for the night. We will get it fixed in the morning."

More conferring, and the men on the ground called back, "We will do as you suggest and refresh ourselves. We will return on the third watch, by which time we expect entrance to the castle."

"What hurry? Rest yourselves for the night. You have had a long journey, and the repair will be easier by the light of day."

"We have urgent information that cannot wait. We will return soon."

"They do not believe us," the bearded guard said. "We must prepare for an attack. Quietly man the defenses but sound no alarm."

Soon word was passed down the wall, and a great commotion arose as the full complement of soldiers left to defend the castle was awakened and quickly sent to man their stations. They collected arrows, filled pitch pots, and quietly wheeled carts full of stones out onto the battlements.

William and Silas helped with the preparations right alongside the other men. But they assisted further by adding to the frenzy that was already beginning to take hold by speculating wildly about what army or armies might be at their gates and about all the abhorrent things that might happen to them if they failed to repel the attackers.

"They are surely going to try something more. Something we do not expect," William commented to the different groups of men around him as he and Silas unloaded sheafs of arrows from a cart at different stations along the battlements.

"I bet this is a mercenary army from King John come to exact revenge for Runnymede," Silas added. "I heard that they are attacking weak baronies and gutting every man inside as vengeance for the nobility's betrayal of the Crown."

"I bet this is the Dawnings come to repay Hans' attack on Dawning Castle."

The two men continued to spread rumors of the terrible things the enemy army was likely to do to them if they gained access, until they had the other guards near panic.

"Men approaching!" someone called. William ran back up the wall to the top of the drawbridge near the bearded guard, whose name he had learned was Bennett. It was clear that Bennett would be making the decisions, so he needed to be near him at this crucial juncture.

Both men looked over the wall, and William's heart skipped a beat. There were indeed men advancing on the castle, but far more men than he had left on the ground. In the inky blackness, it was impossible to count, but it seemed obvious that there were hundreds of men moving into position around the front wall of the castle. They were making no effort to hide their numbers or conceal their movements. On the contrary, they seemed to be intent on making it clear that not only were they there but also that they were not the least bit concerned.

William took a deep breath. This was it. The Braddocks were here. This was the critical moment when he needed things to go badly. If calm, collected heads prevailed, this could be over before it began. He needed everyone to panic and act as rashly as possible. "The enemy is upon us!" he hissed to Bennett but made sure it was loud enough for the men on either side of him to hear it. "We must attack!"

"Patience," Bennett said without looking at William. His eyes were fixed upon a small party that rode into the clearing before the drawbridge and stopped at almost the exact spot William's men had an hour before. To William, who understood what was happening, the central figure limned in the light of a torch could only be Collin Braddock;

but he prayed it would not be as obvious to the confused, panicky soldiers.

The vanguard trumpeted an elaborate fanfare.

The activity on the wall stilled in nervous anticipation as every ear strained for what was to come next. Tension mounted as the silence lengthened.

"What are they playing at?" the man beside William whispered. William was too nervous to reply. His very life depended on what happened in the next few minutes.

Suddenly, a great booming voice rang out in the silence, decidedly more powerful than the one from before. "You in the castle! This is Baron Braddock!"

Shocked silence prevailed as Collin gave that statement time to sink in.

"That's not Collin Braddock," William whispered hoarsely. "We would recognize his voice! Another trick!" He could hear urgent muttered snippets running down the battlements, but he had no idea what the men were really thinking. William edged his way toward Silas, who had taken up position on a nearby ballista.

"You will throw open the gates to me at once, or I will tear them down and cleanse my castle by slaughtering every living person inside. You know that you have not the force to hold against my army, so do not sacrifice yourself to a fight that you cannot hope to win!"

"I think that *is* Collin," someone ventured. "Can you see the banner they carry?" They squinted into the darkness at the pennant flapping above the group, but making out any detail was impossible.

"You fools!" Silas whispered harshly. "This is obviously a ploy. Why would Collin threaten to attack his own castle? That army is desperate to get us to open the gates before the sun rises and we can identify them. Why else would they attack at night?"

"Collin is at Runnymede settling matters with King John!" William added. "Everyone knows that."

"I, for one," Silas added, "will not be party to handing Braddock Castle over to our enemies while Collin is fighting in the Barons' war."

Arguments broke out among the men until Collin spoke again. "You have until this torch burns down to decide what your lives are worth to you!" He threw it down on the hardpacked earth.

It was William's turn to panic. Given time to calm down and think rationally, it was almost certain that the guards would figure out that that was actually Collin; and if he could not buy Aden more time than that, that was the end for Dawning Court.

William did not think about his next move, he just acted. "We will never surrender to the son of a liar!" he shouted over the wall, and Silas, taking his cue, let fly with the ballista. William had no idea what "son of a liar" meant exactly, but it was generic enough that he hoped it would be interpreted appropriately by all who heard it.

"What did you do?" Bennett grabbed William roughly by the shoulder but fell into stunned silence with the rest of the wall when Collin moved back into the circle of torchlight.

No one could tell if the ballista bolt had hit anything, but it had had the intended effect. Collin tore his sword from its sheath and pointed it toward the castle. "Attack!" he roared.

From the darkness, men poured in like the tide rushing the beach. They swarmed the base of the walls, throwing down bridges and planks to cross the mote and putting up hastily constructed siege ladders. Dozens of grappling arrows began to land all over the battlements.

Seeing very clearly that the time for deliberation was past, the men upon the wall sprang into action and began raining death down upon the attackers.

An hour later, the attack was well underway. The defenders had no choice but to fight or die, which gave the conflict a momentum of its own. As they were no longer needed to stoke the fires of the battle to keep it going, William and Silas quietly let themselves down by the same rope they had used to climb the wall. They dropped from ten feet up, pretending they were Braddock men who had been knocked off the rope, and retreated from the wall amidst the fray as though they had been injured. Their Braddock tabards made them blend in perfectly with the group swarming the wall below. Silas clutched at his left arm, and William dragged one leg behind him and leaned on Silas to help him from the battlefield.

They joined up with the rest of their group half a mile away and remounted for the hard ride to Dawning Castle.

"That was a stroke of brilliance!" Nolan, the sandy-haired soldier, laughed as the men congratulated each other.

"You realize," Silas said to William with a more serious air, "that when Collin realizes the deception you have just perpetrated upon him, he will stop at nothing to exact revenge?"

William recognized that as the formidable threat that it was, and in truth it made him uncomfortable. But he had done what was necessary, and now he had other concerns to focus on. "It would seem," he sighed, "that I am destined to be at odds with every member of that family."

"At this rate, there will not be any members of that family left to be at odds with," Nolan snorted.

Twenty-five

The sun had not yet risen when Thomas pulled his horse off the road just in time to watch the young riders gallop by. He was not even a mile outside of Dawning Court when he heard them coming and pulled off the road to hide. The riders went by without so much as a glance in his direction.

Thomas had reluctantly given up and fled Dawning Court when it was clear that the Mayfields would take the castle unopposed. But now, seeing what looked to be advanced scouts gave him the first indication he had had since the Mayfields' arrival that things might again turn his way. This might be a sign that William had inadvertently done exactly what Thomas had wanted, despite Thomas never getting the chance to manipulate him into it.

When he had decided to release William to warn Aden of the betrayal, he had expected to find his brother in a similar state to when he had seen him a few hours earlier as he was carried away by the guards, beaten, bloody, and so woozy he could barely stand. He had not even imagined the explosive attack that William launched against him the moment he opened the door.

It angered Thomas that William had gotten the jump on him and beaten him without Thomas answering back with even a single blow. But he consoled himself that it was only because William had surprised him and because he, Thomas, had not really been interested in hurting his brother since he needed him to deliver a message. That was why Thomas had made such a poor showing. *Had I been there to fight,* he told himself, *William would be a dead man.*

Be that as it may, however, the real problem he was facing due to William's mode of departure was that he had no idea where William had gone. And with no expectation of reinforcements, Thomas was escaping. But if those were scouts, then they almost had to be Aden's or Collin's, and that could change everything.

If he was right, then that meant that somewhere not far down the road was a large army that would not welcome Thomas. But it also meant that the balance of power was on the brink of a rapid shift, and Thomas had better be nearby if he wanted any hope of affecting that shift.

He hesitated only a moment more before galloping back down the road after the scouts. The fleet-footed Arabian steed he had commandeered to make his escape should be able to catch the scouts on their tired, less powerful animals with relative ease.

None of this had gone the way Thomas had hoped, but maybe there was still a chance to salvage something.

He caught up to the scouts just as they left the road in opposite directions from each other before reaching Dawning Court's outer wall. One went left and the other right, no doubt intent on sneaking into Dawning Court to get the lay of the situation.

Thomas followed the smaller man to the right. When the scout dismounted to move on foot, Thomas did the same, keeping him just in view as the man felt his way along the wall until he found a rough portion of the outer wall and began to climb.

Thomas decided that this was his chance. Drawing his dagger, he hurried from the trees, intent on seizing the scout; but to his surprise, the lithe young man was already clearing the top of the wall before Thomas had reached him.

Thomas cursed, resheathed his weapon, and began to climb up after the scout. It was easy at first, as the wall was wider at the base than at the top. But shortly Thomas found it necessary to pull himself up using cracks that were barely big enough to fit his fingertips. He almost fell several times but finally managed to make it to the other side, dropping the last ten feet with an audible grunt rather than continuing to stress his overtaxed fingers and arms.

He was on the east side of the castle, away from the encampment where the Mayfield army was now stationed. It was definitely the safer of the two directions the scouts could have taken, but it would also be harder to collect accurate information given the distance from the enemy camp. But that was neither here nor there, as this scout would never make it back to report.

Thomas found the young man working his way through a stand of trees toward no man's land. He was so intent upon the field in front of him, he did not even notice Thomas coming up from behind until it was too late.

Thomas wrapped a hand over his mouth and pulled the scout against him with a knife to his throat. "Quiet now!" he hissed to the boy, who looked to be about seventeen. "Answer my questions, and you might live. Do you understand?"

The boy nodded, eyes wide and shining in the darkness.

"To whom do you report?"

The boy did not immediately respond, so Thomas made it easier for him. "Are you with Aden or Collin?" he growled.

"Aden!" the boy said when Thomas uncovered his mouth.

"How far is he behind you?"

"F—Four leagues ... perhaps three by now."

"And Collin? Where is he?"

"I—I do not—he returned to Braddock Court."

"What?!" Thomas demanded. "Why? How?"

"I do not know."

"You are lying!" Thomas twisted the knife in the flesh of his neck.

"I am not!" the boy squeaked in alarm.

"Why would he do that?"

"I do not know. We were dug in ready to defend, and he pulled up stakes and took the road to Braddock Court, leaving no one behind."

"A ploy then?"

"I cannot say."

Thomas considered this new information as he slit the boy's throat and let his body drop silently to the ground. Collin's withdrawal had to be a ruse, but to what end? He could not guess with so little information, but it seemed obvious that Aden was intent on overthrowing the Mayfields before Collin could arrive. However, if Collin's departure was a trick, it was possible that he might only be a few hours behind Aden. Surely Aden would not be so foolish as to assume he could defeat an enemy of equal size within a few hours? Or was he just that desperate?

What is my play here? If the Mayfields took the castle before Aden's arrival, then Aden would be too late. But if he were to arrive in time to press the Mayfields against the battlements, he might be able to break their line and join his forces to the beleaguered defenders before Collin arrived. But if—

Thomas froze when he felt something sharp in his back.

"Drop the dagger!" an English voice ordered.

Thomas did as he was commanded and raised his hands slightly to show that he was no threat. He silently cursed his stupidity for allowing himself to be distracted. "I am not your enemy, brother," he said, trying to crane his neck to see who was behind him.

"Turn around."

Thomas slowly turned to face what turned out to be a Braddock patrol. *Of course, the remnants of the Braddock army have taken shelter in the eastern trees.* He cursed himself again. *Where else could they have gone?* He looked at the four Braddock soldiers that had moved in around him, weapons out, dirty, exhausted, bloody from battle, and not in a patient mood.

"Well met, brothers!" Thomas said in a hearty voice. "I am not your enemy," he repeated when he was greeted with only tense silence. "You know me! I am Thomas ..." he hesitated only a moment before adding "Dawning. We fight on the same side." Still there was no reaction. "I too have been betrayed by the heathens!" he said, stabbing his arm at the castle. "We are allied in our cause to drive these brutes from our land!" Still he got no visible reaction. The men did not lower their weapons. "This," he said, pointing at the body that was now behind him, "is a Dawning scout. Their army is preparing to attack at this very moment." Still no response. "I beg leave to speak with Lord Braddock and apprise him of this development."

"Surrender your weapon!" the man with the sword still held only inches from his chest demanded.

"My weapon?" Thomas asked as though he were genuinely befuddled by the request. "Surely you do not think me so foolish as to attack an entire patrol by myself." When the guard did not budge, Thomas sighed and turned over his mace.

Minutes later Thomas was being led into a clearing where the Braddock survivors had congregated. He eyed the guard with his weapon to see what it would take to overpower him should things go badly. Despite not having done anything directly to betray the Braddocks, he was not at all certain what reception he might receive from the mercurial leader, and he wanted some means of defending himself in case Hans flew into a rage as he had done after his first defeat in the siege, when he thought Thomas had sabotaged him.

Thomas smiled wryly at the memory. *Who knew but that it was a Dawning to blame after all? Hans just had the wrong Dawning.* Part of him wished that he *had* been responsible for bringing William into the camp right under their noses.

That would have been intrigue too delicious for words— the Dawning men working together against their enemies three levels deep. But alas, none of that mattered now. As usual, fate had dealt him a terrible hand, and, also as usual, it was up to him to salvage anything from it.

He looked around at the ragtag group of survivors. He estimated there to be 200-300 present, many of whom were wounded, all of whom looked the worse for wear. The Braddocks had been decimated. Instead of the orderly force of professional soldiers who had set up camp, prepared weapons and armor, and built siege engines only a week before, this was a group of refugees with no military order at all.

Realizing that he stood out in his relatively clean armor, Thomas made a show of tightening the grieve over one shin and used the opportunity to rub his hands in the dirt and spread it over his armor. William had graciously provided him with wounds on his face, but he had to appear as though he, too, had only just survived the day. He needed to look like one of them, a victim of the Moors' treachery which, ironically enough, he was.

They entered the center of the clearing where Hans was conferring with a small group of battle-weary knights. The blonde man's eyes widened in disbelief when he recognized Thomas. "You?"

Thomas held up his hands. "I come in peace. We fight the same enemy."

Hans' shock passed a moment later, and he reached for his sword. "I will kill you, you traitorous dog!"

Thomas fell back a pace, looking for the guard who held his weapon; but before he could make a grab for it, the bearded knight who Thomas recognized as the man who had stepped in to save William from Amir grabbed Hans when he was still several paces away.

"Release me!" Hans cried. "That coward struck me from behind the moment the Mayfields attacked to prevent me from organizing a resistance. He is the reason we were caught off guard. Stand aside, Hildebrant, that I may dispatch him!"

"You mistake me," Thomas said, relaxing from his defensive posture. "As I recall, it was you who attacked me. But I understand," he added quickly. "You had every reason to believe I was privy to the attack. But as you can see," he said, gesturing around as though he were part of the unfortunate survivors, "I, too, was betrayed."

"You struck me!" Hans roared, twisting in Hildebrant's grasp.

"Only to protect myself. If I may say so, you were quite beyond reason. Now consider, had I been part of this conspiracy, would I not have slit your throat while you lay at my feet?" He said it as though he were speaking to Hans, but he was appealing to Hildebrant as the obvious level head of the two.

After a moment Hans' rage seemed to subside, and he began to calm down.

"Why have you come?" Hildebrant asked.

Apparently Hildebrant had not picked up on the fact that Thomas was not there willingly, so he chose not to call attention to it. "Where else would I be? Hildebrant, is it? Well, Sir Hildebrant, much like Lord Hans, I too sacrificed everything for this chance at the barony. All of my remaining hope to claim what is mine lies in this clearing." Thomas had meant that last statement to sound inspiring, but as he gestured around at the dismal scene, the reality of the situation stole the enthusiasm from his voice, and he ended up sounding more hopeless than encouraging.

"Hope?" Hildebrant asked incredulously. "Look around you. Our only goal is survival."

"Why not flee then?" Thomas asked. Though he well knew the answer, he needed to buy time because he had no idea what to do next. *Think, you fool. Where is the advantage?*

"We are hemmed in," Hildebrant murmured. "The wall to our east is still intact, and the main gates to the highway are guarded by the Mayfields."

"That wall is only twenty-five feet high," Thomas pointed out. "You could scale that under the cover of darkness."

Hildebrant shook his head. "Too many wounded. They cannot climb, and they are too numerous for us to pull over."

"Leave them," Thomas said without thinking. "The Mayfields will likely take pity on them."

Hildebrant's jaw tightened at that. "We do not leave our comrades behind!"

Thomas looked at Hans, who was no longer looking at him but glowering at Hildebrant. There was obvious resentment there. Thomas knew how much Hans hated being upstaged. *He resents the fact that Hildebrant is not deferring to him.* That gave Thomas an idea. "You need to know that our situation is about to change drastically."

"Change? How?"

"I have only just intercepted a scout. He reported that his army was fewer than three leagues from us. That's less than three hours' march." Thomas could see the anxiety on their faces and let them stew in it for a moment.

"What army?" Hans demanded.

"It must be Sir Aden's peasant army," Hildebrant answered for him. "This is exactly the distraction we need to get our wounded men to safety."

Hans had gone white as a sheet. "How—I mean—Collin ..."

"I believe what Lord Hans is trying to express," Thomas said helpfully, "is that Lord Collin is likely following behind Sir Aden's army and will most assuredly look upon our failure here with displeasure." *And he is likely to be in a murderous temper,* Thomas did not add, but he well knew that Hans was thinking it.

"Our men are the priority," Hildebrant insisted. "We must get them to safety. Some of them may not survive another night out here."

"Sir Hildebrant," Thomas objected, "let us not be hasty. May I suggest that the arrival of Aden's army presents us with a unique opportunity."

"Opportunity?"

"To salvage something from this disaster. To demonstrate to Lord Collin that we are men instead of worthless dogs."

Hildebrant frowned. "We have our own lives to think of. We are in no condition to go to battle."

"I am not suggesting that we march out to meet either force head on." *This force could not conquer a nunnery, to say nothing of three different armies,* he did not add. "But think now; the castle is ready to fall. By my estimation, the ladies from a brothel could overwhelm the defenders. But what happens if a well-trained force takes control of those battlements?"

"It will cost Collin many lives to take them back," Hildebrant muttered.

"Surely you are not suggesting that we attack the castle!" Hans' voice was bordering on panic.

"I am not," Thomas assured him. "And until an hour ago, I would have agreed with you that there was little that we could do to prevent the Mayfields from taking it. But now we have an opportunity. We need not defeat the Mayfields, we need only prevent them from taking the battlements long enough for Aden to arrive."

Hildebrant considered that. "That would force the armies to face each other in the open field. Casualties on both sides will be much higher."

"And," Thomas added with satisfaction, "it will leave an easy victory for Collin when he arrives. All we need to do is nudge the battle in either direction to keep either side from prevailing long enough for Collin to arrive."

"Thomas is correct," Hans said, his tone starting to change from panic to excitement. "And I know how we will do it!"

"Has my dear brother not already shown us the way?" Thomas smiled, but Hans' excitement was making him nervous. "Through sabotage and strategic raids, we can cripple whichever side—"

"We will do better than that!" Hans was staring toward the castle that was visible above the tree canopy. "We will present the castle on a platter for Collin when he arrives. There will be nothing left for him to do but simply take it...." He was almost whispering now. "We will bring down the west wall. With the wall destroyed, we give our query nowhere to hide from Collin's Golden Sword."

Hildebrant's jaw tightened and released as he considered it. "And assuage Collin's anger somewhat, I should think," he muttered.

"What matters the motive if we are saving thousands of our own people?" Hans demanded with uncharacteristic persuasiveness. "The reasons we came to these circumstances are of no consequence; all that we should focus on is preventing any more of our people from dying needlessly."

"All the equipment we would need should still be in place from our prior attempts," Hildebrant suggested thoughtfully. "And I'll wager that the foundation is thoroughly compromised by now."

Thomas did not like what they were planning, as it would make the plan that he was beginning to form in his head more difficult. What he wanted was for the Mayfields' and Aden's armies to mostly destroy each other. The victor of the two would then take control of Dawning Castle's fortifications and decimate Collin's army before they were inevitably overthrown. Thomas could then return later with whatever army he might muster up and overthrow the feeble remnants of Collin's once great force. But with the battlements compromised, they would be handing the barony to Collin, even while making Thomas' future claim that much harder. But he could not exactly tell Hans and Hildebrant that. So instead, he said, "I was given to understand that my brother had interfered with your attempt to dam the river?"

"He did, indeed, ruin the dam," Hildebrant nodded, "but not before we had saturated the base of the wall. All that water has had time to seep into the soil now. The wall may not topple in a single piece, as we had hoped, but I'll wager that we can bring it down."

"Precisely!" Hans snapped. "And I will wager that no one on the battlements is worried about the west wall with the arrival of the new army. The guard detail will almost certainly be light."

"Very well," Hildebrant agreed. "Leave a small force to watch over our wounded, and the rest of us will see to it at once. We have not much time."

Thomas sighed as they began to give orders with a renewed sense of purpose. He had managed to save his own skin once more but may have done so at the cost of his future claim on the barony. But all was not lost yet. If he stayed close, he might be able to swing things his way, given the right opportunity.

Twenty-six

It was just after dawn. Tendrils of smoke still rose from the town and camp. The battle between the new army and the Braddocks had raged until night had made it impossible to tell friend from foe. Only then had the newcomers reluctantly withdrawn, leaving the beaten and broken remnants of the Braddock army alive, but only just.

Anthony watched with disbelief as the new arrivals—perhaps unknowingly—lined up on the same spot the Braddock-Saracen army stood before every attack. Whatever hope Anthony had held onto that this new army might be a liberating force rather than an occupying one had just vanished. Now, instead of facing the waning strength of the Braddock-Saracen army, he had to contend with fresh soldiers.

He had welcomed the respite when the new army attacked just as the battlements were on the verge of being overthrown. But not being certain whether they were friendly or not, Anthony had not been able to take advantage of the conflict to diminish their ranks. He had done what he could to attack the Saracens and Braddocks, but mostly he had used the time to regroup with his own demoralized troops.

The situation with the defenses had not improved since yesterday. They were even more ragged, the soldiers even more beaten down and exhausted; but now barely half of the war machines mounted on the walls were still functional. They had either been smashed by the enemy onagri, burned by the enemy's flaming arrows, or had their torsion chords broken; and they had no replacements since their stores had been sabotaged by the assassins in the castle.... by William.

William! The name twisted in his gut like a knife. The pain and impotent rage at the betrayal caused Anthony's jaw to clench in anger. To think that William had been planning this all along and that he could be so cold as to murder the woman who loved him was more than Anthony could contemplate. It was not only a personal afront to Anthony, Leah, and his sister—Richard's wife—but it also violated everything Anthony stood for as a knight. It was selfish, despicable creatures like William that caused the peasantry to fear and hate the nobility rather than respect and honor them for their selfless sacrifice.

For the hundredth time since learning of William's treachery, Anthony had to force these thoughts from his mind. He needed to focus now more than ever, but the pain and anger of the betrayal kept intruding regardless of the situation, souring his mood and fogging his attention.

Now, though, he had a fresh army arrayed in attack formation just outside of catapult range. It was depressingly clear that the force that had seemed their salvation the day before was just another opportunistic baron hoping to take Dawning Court while it was weak.

Anthony shook his head. How could it be that they had somehow, against all odds, survived this long only to face a third enemy in as many weeks?

But what unsettled Anthony even more than the prospect of facing fresh troops was the siege tower that had not attacked on the previous day with the others and had subsequently not been destroyed with the others.

Movement from the line caught his eye—not the all-out attack he was expecting but a group of about a hundred mounted riders who broke from the rest and approached, a parley flag flying overhead. *Could this mean salvation after all?* Nervous anticipation welled up in him. But he quickly quashed those feelings. It was more likely that they simply recognized their advantage and wanted to achieve their aim without sacrificing more men by demanding the castle surrender.

The advanced group stopped outside the barbican, and Anthony ran to get a closer look. The lead rider called up to the men on the wall, and Anthony did a double take. It was not so much what she said, which Anthony had not yet registered, but the fact that it was a woman's voice that shocked him. She was outfitted in armor with a sword at her side, as were the others, but there was no mistaking the alto voice for that of a man.

"Dawning Castle," she repeated, "I am not your oppressor but your liberator! Open your gates to me!"

From this close, Anthony could see clearly the white cross on the field of red that flew on their banner, and though he was not English, he placed the crest even as the woman identified herself. "It is I, Mary Dawning, here to bring salvation to my people!"

Anthony could not believe what he was hearing. *Could it be that we have just been delivered from destruction?*

Spencer came running toward him, flushed with the same excitement that Anthony himself was struggling to control. "Shall I give the order?" he asked.

"Steady now!" Anthony cautioned. "Only the lord of the castle may order the gates to be opened during a siege." While that was true, the primary reason for mentioning it was to give himself time to think. "Not everything here may be as it seems."

Spencer squinted down at the envoy. "That really is Mary Dawning," he confirmed. The jubilation was evident in his voice. "We are saved!"

"If that is Mary Dawning, why does she not fly the Dawning Crest?"

"I believe that is her father beside her. That is the Mayfield crest. Surely this is his army."

"If she had intended this from the beginning, why did she not say so to Martha before fleeing the castle?"

"Perhaps she did not dare commit her father's armies without speaking to him first."

Spencer's excitement was undiminished, which only made Anthony more reticent. "How did they get here so fast?"

"Dawning Castle!" Mary called from the ground. "We await your response!"

Anthony looked to a nearby runner who was gawking over the edge of the wall along with everyone else. "Fetch Martha Dawning at once," he ordered the runner before turning back and shouting down to Mary. "I must plead for patience, Lady, while we apprise Lady Dawning of your arrival!"

Noting Anthony's reluctance, Spencer said, "we cannot withstand her army. If she is an enemy, she is going to get the castle one way or another."

"That is not our decision to make. Find Timothy and meet me in the courtyard."

A quarter of an hour later, after a quick conference with Anthony, Spencer, and Timothy, Martha arrived at the same conclusion as Spencer. "We will open the gates."

"I do not trust her," Anthony murmured.

"Nor should you. Make no mistake about this, Sir Knights, we are trading one devil for another. And just to hedge our bets ..." she trailed off thoughtfully.

"Lady?"

"Sir Timothy, prepare the gate, but do not open it until I give the word."

"Should we not be here by your side?"

"No. I want you on the walls, out of immediate harm's way. Quietly prepare the men for battle. If this proves to be something other than what it seems, I expect we will soon know. If that is the case, upon my signal you are to close the gates, trapping the envoy in our courtyard, and prepare to repel borders."

Timothy looked uncertain. "That violates the rules of parley. The code says that we may not attack or imprison an envoy if we have opened negotiations with them beneath the flag of parley."

Martha looked at him levelly. "Did I say anything about imprisoning the Mayfields? If we happen to close our gates because we are under siege, that has no bearing on them. And if they choose to violate the pact by attacking us, well then, we will have no choice but to defend ourselves."

"Such a course will put you in tremendous danger, Lady," Timothy rejoined. "*I* will greet the Mayfields."

"Your concern for me is appreciated. But I have not the constitution to lead the men on the battlements. You must do that. Moreover, the Mayfields will be immediately suspicious if I am not present."

Timothy looked to Anthony for guidance, but Anthony was watching Martha closely.

"Er—if that is the case, Lady," Timothy argued, "should not Sir Anthony be on the battlements?"

Martha shook her head. "Sir Anthony will prepare the castle to be the last line of defense."

"But if I seal the castle, will you not be left exposed in the courtyard?"

"If circumstances permit, allow me in," she said simply.

Martha's gray eyes met Anthony's. He could read in them the very sentiment that he had not been able to shake. This *was* the end. They both knew it. What did it matter if she died in the courtyard now or hiding in the castle in two hours? If Mary was anything other than what she claimed, there was only one way this could end for Martha.

"Do as Lady Dawning instructs," Anthony said without taking his eyes from her.

"Sir Spencer," Martha turned to the youngest of her remaining knights. "Collect an honor guard of some of our less harried-looking soldiers and return here to greet our *liberators.*"

Spencer turned to obey only to be stopped by Timothy.

"Lady," Timothy said earnestly, "I pray thee, grant that I may lead thy honor guard."

"Why does it matter?" Spencer asked, mildly irritated by the delay.

But Timothy did not take his earnest eyes from Martha's. "I have failed to prove my valor before," he admitted frankly. "Grant me now the chance to make amends for that."

Martha considered him for a long moment before assenting. "Very well. Sir Spencer, man the battlements. Sir Timothy, collect the guards."

Both men saluted and hurried off to obey. Martha watched them until they were out of earshot and then turned back to Anthony, who was waiting expectantly.

"Sir Anthony, there is one last thing."

"I suspected there might be."

"At the very moment that I give the order to seal the gate, I give you one last charge. The enemy—whoever they prove to be—will not be watching for escapees at that moment." She paused, expecting him to protest at the very insinuation; but when he made no reaction, she continued. "At that moment, this final charge I place upon you. You are to find Grace with the unborn heir of Dawning Court. I deliberately did not learn where she was intended so I could not be made to reveal it should the worst come to pass. Inform her of all that has befallen us and get her to safety in your homeland in the Kingdom of Sicily."

Anthony let that wash over him. She was asking him to do precisely the same thing Richard had asked him to do in his final moments, the very deed that had haunted him since that day—abandon the fight and leave people he was sworn to protect to die. "I will do no such thing," he protested, though it came out less emphatically than he had expected. "I will not abandon this people—my people—in our final hour."

Martha's face softened at that. "Anthony," she said, dispensing with his formal title, which gave her a motherly air. "You have done well. You have fought the good fight. I could not be prouder of you were you my own flesh and blood. So I will say to you what I would say to you if you were Will—my son. There is no more fight to be had here. You will do more to ensure the Dawnings have a future by doing as I ask than by staying here and perishing with the rest of us. You will see to it that the Dawning line lives on through your sister, perhaps one day to rise again. Go now!" she ordered in a more commanding tone before he could argue further.

Anthony vacillated. Every bone in his body protested that this was violating his oath to protect these people. He felt that he should resist, that he should protect Martha despite her protests as he had failed to do with Richard. *But what does it matter?* The voice of defeat popped into his head, as it had done with increasing frequency over the past week. But now he found it impossible not to give place to it. He was emotionally, physically, and mentally spent and could not summon the energy to fight it. *We are all doomed. What does it matter if my body molders beside the rest of these people or not?*

"One more thing," Martha said as he turned to go. "Take Leah with you."

He barely managed a nod before shuffling away. All he had done, all he had fought for, had only succeeded in preserving the people long enough to be taken over by a different despot. All his efforts were for nothing. Even the men whose legacy he thought he was honoring—the men in whose name he took charge of Dawning Court and whose ideals he strove to live up to, were nothing but duplicitous traitors. Well one of them was, anyway. Maybe it was fitting, then, that Anthony should fail. After all, why preserve the legacy of one such as William, who willingly turned on his own family? Why not let it die or even burn it to the ground with the rest of Dawning Court?

Maybe that was the reason Anthony had failed despite his best efforts. Maybe God had ordained that the wickedness of the Dawnings should be exposed and destroyed, and Anthony—albeit unknowingly—had been fighting against that very thing.

Anthony's head hung low as he walked dejectedly toward the Great Room.

Twenty-seven

They are in formation, ready to attack," Martin announced. It had only taken him a moment to assess the situation. It was already well after dawn when he and Aden stopped off the side of the highway where it descended into the town before climbing back up to the castle.

Martin turned to order the army forward, but Aden grabbed his arm.

Martin looked down in surprise. "They will attack at any moment! We have no time to lose!"

"The battlements are weak," Aden agreed. The highest parts of the wall were illuminated by the rising sun, bringing the damage to the crenelations into sharp relief. "But they will stand for half an hour. If we attack now, we are two armies of roughly equal size meeting in an open field. We have no advantage. But if we wait until the enemy is engaged at the battlements, then they will never see us coming."

"Hold it!" Martin said, looking past Aden toward the castle. "What is happening now?" Aden spun and squinted toward the castle gates where a small envoy had approached and appeared to be speaking with the soldiers on the wall. "Are they negotiating?"

"Demanding the castle's surrender, I should say," Aden muttered darkly. "Why else line up in attack formation with their siege tower except as a show of force?"

"Surely the castle will not give in."

Aden watched anxiously. "They are obviously near defeat. They have no indication that we are here, or even that we received their original message. It may be that they feel they have no other choice."

"But if they surrender now, then ..."

"Dawning Court is lost," Aden completed the thought. "Bring the army up at once." A dark fear was spreading through him.

Martin rode back to obey while Aden remained where he was, transfixed by the events at the castle gate, silently willing it to remain closed. A quarter of an hour later, he watched in horror as the portcullis blocking entry to and from the barbican began to rise. "No, you fools! No!" he cried. "Force them to attack!" But the iron grating, heedless of his commands, continued to rise. "We must go now!" Aden said and wheeled his horse to ride back to coax the army on faster, thinking that it may already be too late.

Martha stood with Timothy at her side, facing the gate. A semi-circle of soldiers spanned the space around her from wall to wall, effectively sectioning off the gate from the rest of the courtyard. Behind the soldiers hundreds of peasants filled the lower ward, pressing in upon them, anxious to catch a glimpse of their salvation, anxious to see for themselves if the rumors were true.

Mary and George rode through the gates side by side, helmets off, at least three-score soldiers flanking them. The soldiers overflowed the limited space Martha had left for them in the courtyard, spreading through the barbican and spilling out in front of the wall, as though waiting in a giant queue to enter the castle.

"Lady Dawning!" Mary said with overblown affection. She did not dismount, however, but instead stayed in the saddle and the position of power it afforded her. "I cannot tell you how pleased I am to find you well. We did so fear for your safety."

"Mary. George," Martha nodded to the couple. "We are very pleased at your timely arrival," she said evenly.

"We are only too glad to be of service," George said with as deep a bow from the saddle as his paunch would allow. "I have been looking for some means of repaying Braden since the day I left his service." He sat up and looked around at the frazzled group of peasant-soldiers that surrounded them. "My dear Martha," his voice quavered with scarcely suppressed laughter, "is this all that remains to you? I commend you for holding the Braddocks off for even an hour with a force such as this."

"The hearts of my people are as valiant as any," Martha retorted. "There are no more spirited people in all the realm than the Dawning people!"

Mary looked at the hundreds of dirty faces staring at her with a mixture of curiosity and wariness. She noted the stinking trench running the length of the yard and wrinkled her nose in disgust. "No noble should have to live in such conditions."

"We did what was necessary, Lady Mayfield," Martha said flatly.

Mary grimaced at the sight before raising her voice to all those looking on. "The danger is past!" she told them. "I, Mary Dawning, and my father, George Mayfield, have delivered you from harm. You may return to your homes. Go now in peace."

"Is that not a bit premature?" Martha asked, though whether she was referring to Mary's taking command or to her promise that all was safe was unclear.

"Not at all. We are here to guarantee their safety."

"With a garrison?"

"Let us call it a protective force," George interjected.

Martha leveled a serious gaze at the pair. "Mayfield is a very long way away. It is fortuitous that you could assemble an army and make the trip so quickly."

"Astute as ever, Lady," George smiled, though there was decided malice in the expression now. "Except, perhaps, where your husband's indiscretions were concerned, but that is neither here nor there now."

Martha's expressionless façade darkened ever so slightly. "Come to the point, George," Martha snapped. "I have no stomach for games."

George clucked his tongue at her. "That always was your biggest fault, Lady, if I may presume to call it so. You have no appreciation for the game itself. Because Dawning Court was strong, you disdained such things; but now that she is weak, you know not how to navigate the politics of the realm, nor do you now have the power to participate as a formidable opponent."

"Power, George?" Martha asked quizzically. "I may have little taste for politics, but I do make it my business to stay abreast of the affairs of the realm, and I know very well that Mayfield does not have sufficient strength to garrison two baronies so far distant from one another."

George seemed to deflate a bit, but his smile flickered for only a moment before returning even brighter than before. "Lady Dawning, you do have a way of cutting right to the heart of a matter. And while I thank you for your concern, you may rest assured that we have made arrangements for that. We thought perhaps we would relocate back to this vicinity."

"You mean to take control of Dawning Court," Martha said without a trace of surprise.

"Take control of Dawning Court?" George looked appalled at the very notion. "Why, Milady, I have no right to Dawning Court. It is Braden Dawning's legacy. I served under Braden, and I intend to see his legacy honored!"

Martha stared at him expectantly. He was obviously baiting her, but she was unwilling to give him the satisfaction of taking the bait.

Unfortunately, Timothy, who was less seasoned, spoke up. "Lady Dawning is Braden's legacy, and she has preserved the barony in the absence of a worthy male heir!"

George turned his gaze from Martha to Timothy. "Who are you?" he asked and then shook his head, "Oh, it really does not matter." He looked back at Martha. "This young man has asked the right question. With Braden gone, and his sons all such bitter disappointments, who is there to carry on the legacy?"

He grinned from ear to ear as he extended his arm back toward the gate, and his troops parted to allow a towering figure on horseback to ride through.

Martha's eyes widened in shock. "How dare you?" she hissed at the Mayfields. "Was this your plan all along? Were you in league with this fiend from the beginning?"

Mary met her eyes coolly but said nothing.

"Lady Dawning," George grinned, "allow me to introduce you to Dawning Court's *rightful* heir and new baron, Amir Dawning!"

Amir half bowed from his saddle, unable to conceal his triumphant grin.

Martha looked between the three of them as if trying to determine whether this was some terrible joke. "This is madness!"

"Madness?" George repeated. "Martha, Amir is Braden's eldest son. Braden fathered him in the Holy Land before your John was born. I can attest to it, as can Sir Aden. Surely, you were aware of it?"

Martha's brow darkened, and Amir's grin only deepened. "He did not tell you," his raspy voice almost purred.

"Braden was a man of great passion, Lady," George said, as if he were excusing Braden's actions rather than twisting the knife in her. "He spent years campaigning. It should not surprise you that he had ... dalliances."

"This is an outrage!" Timothy stepped forward, quivering with indignation. "We will not surrender the castle to the likes of you or this heathen scum!"

"And how do you mean to stop us?" Mary spoke up, sounding amused.

"You are here under the flag of parley," he spat. "Lady Dawning granted you access while still in parley. Any aggression committed toward her people would be violating the terms of such and is therefore forbidden by any code of honor you might still claim!"

"Your parley," Amir rumbled, "is with the Mayfields, not with me."

A discontented murmur rippled through the courtyard.

Perhaps fearing a bloody revolt while they were so outnumbered, even if it was only by peasants, Amir stood in his stirrups and addressed the crowd. "Good people of Dawning Court, I am your new leader, and I bring with me peace."

"You are not our leader!" someone called, "Richard Dawning is our leader!" A general murmur of assent passed through the crowd.

"Richard Dawning is dead!" Amir called over the group and waited for that to settle them down. "Yet even were he alive, as a man of honor, Richard would be the first to acknowledge that, as I am the eldest Dawning male, my claim to the barony supersedes even John Dawning's, which proof I will offer before the week is out. Yet I do not wish to rule as a tyrant. I will not force you to accept me as your new baron. You may choose for yourselves. Only hear my terms: You may accept me as your leader and return to your homes this very day, or you may deny my claim and continue to languish here behind these dilapidated walls, living in your own filth, praying that death from cold, privation, or trebuchet does not find you while your weak, aging leader hides away in the castle, hoping that your blood will not be spent before you deliver her."

An uncomfortable silence spread through the yard, as Amir had obviously hit upon a nerve. "Decide now your future!" he yelled and stabbed his arm toward the gate where the soldiers cleared a path. "All those who are prepared to accept me as their rightful ruler are free to return to their homes unmolested and unharmed. Any who wish to remain will be sealed once again into this castle, and the siege will resume."

For a moment Martha worried that Amir might be about to incite a revolt against her. Many exchanged uncomfortable looks or fixed their eyes on the ground. Was it possible that anti-Dawning sentiment had grown so much that it would overwhelm even Richard's legacy?

She was relieved when no one moved. For the moment, at least, they were not ready to throw her overboard in favor of this evil foreigner. For all the discontent there had been under her reign, facing down a common enemy together was galvanizing.

"Decide!" Amir barked sharply.

No one moved. Martha looked at the exhausted, hungry, and scared faces of the people and felt an overwhelming sense of love for them. Despite whatever misgivings they may have about her, they had done everything she had asked of them. They had put up a good fight, but they were beaten. She did not have the heart to subject them to any more suffering when it would be meaningless. This fight was over.

"My people," she raised her voice over the crowd, "you have served faithfully. We have vanquished the Braddocks—*you* have vanquished the Braddocks! They pitted their chivalry against our peasantry, and you sent them running for the hills. You are to be commended for your bravery. But there is no more fight to be had this day. You may return to your homes in good conscience, knowing that you have served well!"

Still the people did not move; nobody wanted to be seen as the first to desert the cause.

"You are Dawnings! You have proved that beyond question. Return to your homes, return to your lives, be fruitful; worry not over what happens here."

Some of the people exchanged dark looks, and for a moment Martha wondered if they would revolt against this command. It occurred to her that they might be feeling betrayed by this order. After sacrificing so much, perhaps they viewed this as a sign that she valued their offering cheaply and was simply giving up. Nevertheless, the crowd did slowly start to disperse, as they began to file away to collect their families and belongings. But there was no celebratory air or even any detectible feeling of relief. To all present, this felt like defeat.

Twenty-eight

Inside the castle, Anthony was going through the motions of preparing to defend. It was not that he did not feel a sense of urgency, for he knew that time was short. If things went badly at the gates, the Mayfields could be breaking down the door to the Great Hall very soon, but that only added to the overwhelming feeling of hopelessness.

He had divided the castle watchmen into two groups and instructed them to man the main entrance in the Great Hall and the postern entrance. But he did not really know what he might do beyond that. There was no time to gather supplies or weapons into the castle, so he issued orders about trying to escort Martha to safety, when and if the attack came, before barring the doors, and then left the watch to it.

It was insufficient instruction for an insufficient force, and Anthony knew that, but he consoled himself with the thought that none of it mattered. This show of making a last stand in the castle was little more than theatrics, whether Martha saw it that way or not. The best this ragtag group of old and injured men could do was delay the inevitable for a few hours, but they could not possibly affect the ultimate outcome. And what were they even protecting? If Martha was killed and Grace gone, there was nothing to protect save the castle itself.

Anthony ducked into the castle and found his way to Leah's room. He knocked and was surprised that she opened the door a moment later, surprised not because she was awake—all the castle was awake—but because she did not even bother to verify his identity. It seemed that the last forty-eight hours had chased any fear of assassins or death from her. Though he understood it—he was surprised how much that numbness of spirit resonated with him at the moment—that sentiment might make his charge trickier.

As he looked into her hard eyes, it struck him that the thrill upon seeing her that he had always felt was nowhere to be found. She was objectively still exquisitely beautiful, with large eyes and natural rosiness to her cheeks that made her appear made-up even after the worst week of her life; but it just did not trigger that same excitement in him.

"Yes?" Her tone was not rude but there was no warmth in it as there had been in the past.

"Lady," Anthony said, then paused. In that moment, he knew that she would never agree to this plan, so he decided not to explain. "Please come with me." He took her arm and escorted her down the passage.

"What is it?" she asked with a note of concern.

"The enemy is in the gates," he said into her ear. "They may be in the castle within the hour."

"What?" she demanded, pulling her arm from his grasp and turning to look him in the face. "So where are you taking me?"

"The Mayfields," he said, glancing behind them impatiently, "they are in the gates. They have a fresh army and a siege tower."

Leah frowned. "The Mayfields? I do not understand."

She has been in her room, he realized. *She does not know all that has happened.* "The Mayfields are the new army that arrived on the field. Mary has demanded access to Dawning Castle as her liberator. She will claim Dawning Court as her right."

"But it is not her right," Leah objected. "Martha Dawning is still alive, as is Grace."

"Are the Mayfields likely to be open to reason with an army at their back?" he snapped impatiently. "Do you not see what is happening here? We have lost! All our efforts at holding off Thomas and the Saracens were for naught. All we did was weaken them enough that another unscrupulous profiteer could sweep in and take over."

"What of my father?" she asked in a distracted tone, seeming to take no notice of his anger. "His army is sizeable, is it not?"

"Yes, yes," Anthony said, taking her arm again and trying to pull her toward the kitchens and the postern that led out to the upper bailey. From there they could mount the northern wall out of sight from any commotion that might be occurring around the front gate. "It is too late now. Even his force will be no match for a trained army in a well-fortified castle."

She wrenched her arm free again and stopped. "Then where are you leading me?"

"Lady Dawning issued strict instructions that I was to remove you from the castle while there is still time."

Leah stared at him. "Do you truly believe that I would leave now? There is nothing left to me but this." She stabbed a finger at the floor. "I have given everything in my life to this people and this cause. Nothing remains to me but what happens here in these walls."

"I know you believe that, Leah, but that is only because you are wounded to your very core and cannot now see clearly."

"I will not leave!" She turned toward the Great Hall.

Anger surged in Anthony, and he grabbed her and spun her to face him. "You listen to me, you naive fool!" he said, putting his face very close to hers. "I too have given myself wholly to this endeavor, and I too will live with the pain of having lived while others died. I will carry with me the shame and self-loathing forevermore for fleeing the castle at the very moment the people I failed to protect are to be conquered. I only obey Lady Dawning's order because there is yet one thing that I may salvage from this catastrophe; I can keep it from claiming you!"

He held Leah with such ferocity that she squirmed painfully in his grasp. "Sir Knight," she said, "you do greatly err if you believe that forcing me to abandon these people will salve your conscience. You may flee if you choose, but you will do so without me."

The pang of guilt that stabbed Anthony's heart almost staggered him, but he did not release her. It only made him more determined than ever to see to it that she made it to safety. He began to drag her toward the kitchens over her protests.

"What is all this?" an aging watchman, drawn by the sound of Leah's objections, appeared in the hallway before them, club in hand.

Anthony stopped and drew himself up to his full height to make it clear that he was no assassin. "I am merely escorting the lady to the courtyard," he said, feeling ashamed at what he knew must look like a knight forcing himself on a beautiful lady, which only made him angrier. "Why did you not turn out with the other watchmen?" Anthony demanded. "Report to the Great Hall to guard the entrance. All hands are needed there!"

The old man gulped but did not move. "Beggin' your Lordship's pardon, but it does not appear that the lady wants to go to the courtyard with you." He looked at Leah, but Leah glanced up nervously at Anthony, unsure of what she should say. She had never seen him in this state, and it scared her.

The guard took her silence as fear, and his grip on his club tightened. Anthony released Leah's arm and took a half-step away from her. "Very well," he said, raising his hands in surrender, "you escort her."

The watchman took a tentative step forward, and when Anthony did not move to impede him, he took another and reached out a hand to Leah. She looked sidelong at Anthony and stepped hesitantly toward the watchman.

Her suspicious glance triggered something in Anthony. Leah was going to leave with this man and thus perpetuate the idea that Anthony was nothing more than some brigand hiding in knight's armor—the very sort of man that Anthony despised. After sacrificing everything for this people, Anthony was trying—even against his own conscience—to do one last noble thing and save Leah from herself; but instead of complying and allowing him to snatch some measure of victory from this disaster, she was willing to paint him as a villain in order to get what she wanted!

In a moment of pure impulse, Anthony snatched the watchman's club from his hand with his left hand, while smashing his gauntleted right fist against the side of the old man's head. The frail old body hit the wall, and the man collapsed.

Leah gasped in horror. "What have you done?" She stooped to check on him.

"I am not the villain here!" Anthony's voice came out much louder than he had expected. This was all going wrong! But how was he to fix it? If he stopped now and let Leah go, then he would have failed even at that. There was no way forward but through. "I warned you that I was not to be deterred! I will see you to safety at all costs."

Leah ensured that the old man was still breathing and stood slowly before Anthony, locking eyes with him, like she might with a wild animal about to pounce.

The visible fear in her twisted in Anthony like a knife, but what else was he to do? "Is he alright?" he grumbled.

"He is alive," she said, not taking her eyes from Anthony's face.

"Then please come with me and make no more trouble."

Leah nodded, and Anthony stepped aside to let her lead the way, knowing that she would shy away from his touch and not wanting to see that his betrothed was actually afraid of him. "This is for your own good," he insisted as she hurried past him. "Can you not see that?"

Leah walked on in silence.

Twenty-nine

Rylan was young. At fifteen, he had been passed over the first and second time the Dawning knights came looking for fighting men. But as the older men continued to fall, they had had no choice but to recruit him. And now he was nowhere near the youngest boy on the walls. Boys and girls as young as ten were being used as runners and helpers. And though Rylan had been made an actual soldier, he was still relegated to the northwest corner—the furthest corner from the battle. Only the north wall had seen less action than this quiet corner.

In truth, however, it did not especially chafe Rylan that he was not called upon to fight. While he liked the romantic idea of being a soldier—defeating his enemy despite overwhelming odds and returning home in glory to the accolades of all the lords and ladies—the prospect of battle frightened him. And he thought the better he stood his post here in this dismal spot that nobody else wanted, the less likely he was to get reassigned to a more dangerous post. So even now, as his fellow guards along the western wall began to drift southward to get a better look at what was happening with the new arrivals in the courtyard, Rylan remained where he was.

The sun was not yet high enough to push back the deep shadows thrown by the castle and wall to the west. In the resulting mirk he could see little, and it was hard to stay focused looking for something where he never expected to see anything, particularly when all the other guards were clustering to the south.

Finally, pulled by his curiosity as though by a rope, Rylan turned and looked over the inside of the wall, but his view was blocked by the castle. He took a few tentative steps south and then a few more before standing on his tiptoes and craning his neck; but it was no use. The lower ward sat beneath the upper bailey, largely obscured by the upper court. And even if he had been able to see it from here, it would have been blocked by the crowds that had gathered to watch whatever was happening at the gate.

Glancing around to verify that there was no one nearby to tell him otherwise, Rylan climbed up on the inside of the wall; but even that was not enough. If he wanted to watch the events unfolding by the gate, he would have to abandon his post as the others had done.

He climbed down in frustration. Maybe if he just ran down with the others for just a minute or two, that would be okay? No attacks had come on the western wall in days. Surely in the few minutes he was gone, nothing would happen. Besides, it sounded like the enemy was in the courtyard negotiating with Martha, so why would they attack now?

Finally he could stand it no longer. He started to walk toward the others. But just as he did, as if in condemnation of his decision, the sharp clang of metal striking stone brought him up short. It was not the sound of an arrowhead, a coin, or even a sword but rather of something much heavier.

He turned back to look but could not immediately see anything. He clutched the horn around his neck for reassurance. "If there is trouble," the grizzled old sergeant had told him, "you blow this horn before anything else. If you even think there might be trouble, you blow this horn. If the wall is breached and you are about to be run through, before you draw your sword, you blow this horn!" Rylan had gotten the point. He should blow the horn. But he did not want to look like a coward by sounding the alarm over nothing when the castle may be moments away from peace. For all he knew, sounding a false alarm now might actually put the negotiations in jeopardy if one side or the other believed they were being betrayed.

Rylan glanced down the wall with the hope that he would see other guards coming his way, but as the only guard who had not left his post, he was the only one close enough to have heard the noise.

He peered over the edge of the wall. The long shadow of the wall still extended well past the river, but was that ... something? He squinted into the black, trying to discern—

He staggered back and fell against the inside edge of the battlement as a huge metal grappling hook flew up and over the parapet, missing his head by inches. It was large, too large to have been thrown by any man. It must have been machine-launched and probably would have taken his head off had it hit him.

The heavy metal hook slid back toward the edge of the wall with a grating sound and clanged into place as two of the claws grabbed onto the edge of a merlon. Now that Rylan knew what he was looking at, he recognized the black, spidery silhouette of another hook twenty feet down the wall from where he had first heard the sound. More hooks began to land on the wall farther down.

Rylan scrambled forward to dislodge the closest hook but remembered the sergeant's stern warning and instead brought the horn to his lips. He started to blow a warning note but found that his mouth was too dry to make the unfamiliar horn work, and he managed only a few weak squeaks.

Though the sound did not ring out over the battlements as designed, the sharp squeal had been enough to get the attention of his fellow guards down the wall, who descended upon Rylan in a fever, acutely aware that they had not been manning their posts as they ought. The first guard reached Rylan, who by this time was trying to dislodge the huge hook from the wall; but it did not budge. Something was wrong. Though it was undoubtedly heavy, he should have been able to at least set it to wobbling; but it did not even wiggle under his efforts.

The guard watched Rylan for a moment. "There is already pressure on it," he called in a voice that was louder than strictly necessary, a sign that the panic Rylan was feeling was not far from this guard's mind. "We must cut the ropes!"

The guard drew his sword and leapt to the crenel beside the grappling hook but stopped. Instead of the braided climbing ropes usually used by the men in escalade, which were about an inch and a half thick, these ropes were closer to six inches in diameter, and they had a unique metal sheathing over the first eight feet of them that prevented them from being cut. The sheathing was then attached to the grappling hook by means of two perpendicular fat, metal rings that allowed the sheathing to move independently from the hook at nearly any angle.

The guard glanced askance at Rylan, who had instinctively ducked behind the merlon for safety but caught the look with all the uncertainty and fear it conveyed. Though this soldier had served on the battlements since the first day, it was clear that he had no idea what to do.

He raised his sword and brought it down on the steel sheathing with no noticeable effect. He grunted and hit it again. Still nothing. He took his sword in both hands and reared up to strike at the rope with all the strength he could muster when an enemy arrow fired from the darkness below found its way into his neck, dropping him in place and sending Rylan crab-walking back from him as fast he could manage. They were in big trouble, and he had no idea what to do.

Rylan again put the horn to his lips, but this time it worked. A loud, long moan emanated from the horn, reverberating down the wall and over the courtyard.

Thirty

"That was a wise decision," Amir said to Martha as the crowd began to disperse.

Timothy watched the people start to shuffle off, burning with indignation. He had been feeling horribly guilty since Neil sacrificed himself to save Timothy in the very hour that Timothy had been trying to convince Neil to abandon Dawning Court to her fate.

Now that spark of guilt had ignited a conflagration in his brain. He felt the scar of disloyalty acutely as though he wore it on his tabard. But if he could just see Martha Dawning through this, then perhaps that would make amends for his weakness and prove that his character was noble, even if his birthright was not. He *needed* to prove that he was worthy, that his oath meant something, that his character was not of the mean stuff that his birth suggested but was as noble and self-sacrificing as that of Neil. Nothing else mattered now that he was certain he was in the last hours of his life. Like Sir Neil, he would go to his grave proving that he was, above all, valorous.

"I do not know what unholy alliance has brought you three together," Martha said to the trio, "but you have made it clear who our true enemies are."

"Baron," George said pointedly to Amir, "what shall we do with this usurper? She seems intent upon undermining your reign and fomenting rebellion."

"Fomenting rebellion?" Timothy could no longer restrain himself. "Lady Dawning just prevented this people from tearing you apart!"

"And she has surrounded herself with dissidents!" George added.

"How dare you! I will not endure this farce one moment more!" He ripped his sword from its sheath and started forward, determined to rid the barony of this threat once and for all, here and now.

"Timothy, no!" Martha shouted, but it was too late.

As though he had been expecting it, Amir reacted instantly. He rose in his stirrups and brought the curved blade of his sword down upon Timothy's unprotected head, cleaving his unprotected skull almost in two and dropping the young knight at Martha's feet. Martha reached out to him as he collapsed, but it was clear at once that there was no point. He was dead before he hit the ground.

The crowd that had been dissipating stopped and turned back. Seeing the faithful young knight who had fought so valiantly for them cut down right before their eyes turned the pall of discouragement dark in an instant. The feeling was palpable, like a storm cloud blocking out the sun.

Martha knelt over Timothy's body as blood spilt from his head. She glared up at the trio. "You murdered this man!" she spat. "A loyal, faithful knight, and you murdered him in cold blood!"

"We did nothing of the kind!" George replied indignantly. "*Baron Dawning* simply defended himself from the unprovoked attack of a mutinous soldier."

Amir's horse danced nervously, though whether it was from the smell of blood or the shift in the energy in the courtyard was unclear.

Martha glared up at them. "May God grant that I may see you repaid for this. Though it be with my dying breath, it will be worth it!"

Amir snorted and snapped his fingers. Four soldiers hurried forward. "Escort Martha to her new quarters in the dungeon and see that the castle is cleared by tonight. I wish to spend my first night as baron in peace."

"Amir," George said quietly, "is it wise to leave her alive?" He flicked a glance toward Martha. "She is the only remaining Dawning. Opposition may be raised so long as she lives."

"We dare not kill her with so many of the peasantry about," Amir replied. Then, realizing that Martha was listening, he looked directly at her. "We will dispose of her quietly, and no one will even notice she is gone, so relieved will they be to be free from her captivity. She will be lucky if they even spare her a passing thought at some point in the future." He leaned forward in his saddle. "That will be your legacy, Lady Dawning. Though you devoted your life to these people, they could not care less about you."

Martha did not reply, and Amir, pleased that he had found a chink in her carefully controlled façade, taunted her further. "Have you nothing to say to that?"

Their eyes were still locked upon each other while Martha struggled for the next move. What should she say, what should she do? At this moment she had options, but those were quickly disappearing, like the last rays of sunset.

As if in answer to her silent question, somewhere behind them—from the other side of the castle—a warning horn sounded.

"I do have one thing to say," Martha replied. "Close the gates!"

Thirty-one

Near Braddock Castle, earlier that night

e are almost to Braddock Castle!" Salena said, forcing down a shiver at the memory of the last time she was here. "What is your plan?"

Neil wasn't entirely sure. He had expected that within a league of leaving the Dawning encampment, they would find Collin's army waiting to pounce upon Aden the moment he left his stronghold, proving that this was all a ruse. But one league had turned into many, and there was still no sign of them. "Could they have left the road without us seeing them?" he demanded in exasperation without bothering to explain his thoughts; but Salena understood.

"There is no way an army that size could be hiding in the trees without us noticing. We would have seen or heard ... What is it?"

Neil motioned for quiet. It irritated her, but before she could argue she heard sounds coming from the trees. "Is that ... voices?" It sounded like excited chatter.

"They are close!" he hissed. "Quickly, pull off here!" Neil pointed to a small clearing just off the road that was behind a small stand of shrubs, and Salena obeyed. It would not have hidden them in the daylight, but maybe, with an army that was not looking for or expecting anyone to be there, it would be enough.

There was no mistaking it now. Men's voices were talking excitedly and approaching the road from the opposite side from where Neil and Salena were hiding. While they were not yelling exactly, they were definitely talking too loudly for the middle of the night in this sleepy hamlet of Braddock Court.

Salena suddenly felt very exposed with the wagon and the horses. She looked around for somewhere to hide, but the wagon was too big and slow to move without drawing more attention to them.

"Hide," Neil whispered to her, nodding toward a field farther off the road.

"What of you?"

"I am too slow, but I am in less danger at the hands of a lonely army than are you."

That thought turned Salena's stomach, but she was more irritated than afraid. "I will not be told to run and hide by a man who can barely stand! If there is trouble, I am the only hope you have."

Neil opened his mouth to retort, but it was too late. A group of men on horseback broke from the forest across the way and stopped on the road. Their leader turned toward his men, leaving his back exposed to the hidden pair.

"Men, you are to be congratulated. I do not know of another time in history when a dozen men deceived an entire army into laying siege to its own fortifications." A ripple of laughter went through the group.

Neil, though, had stopped watching the soldiers and was watching Salena for a reaction. The fact that she looked unmoved told him that Salena did not hear what he heard.

"That is William!" he whispered into her ear.

Salena stiffened in shock. That *was* William! He was here now, right in front of her. She had given everything to see him destroyed—her home, family, friends, even her honor—and yet, even as the world came down around her, William still lived!

She was not even conscious of drawing her dagger and only vaguely aware of what she was doing as she slipped from the seat. Neil whispered something to her, but she did not even pay attention; like the call of a distant bird, his words had no effect upon her. All that mattered was William!

And there he was, laughing and jesting with his cohorts despite the misery he had inflicted upon all those around him, not even sparing a thought for the lives he had shattered and the families he had destroyed. This was all his fault! If he had not sacrificed her David to save his own useless life, she would have never been forced to go to Hans, Hans never would have attacked, and she would be sitting at home by the fire with her family, blissfully happy. It was all his fault, and William did not care a bit! He was actually laughing!

Salena could not stand it one moment more. She bolted onto the road with her dagger poised.

She made it halfway to him before anyone even noticed or was able to cry out. But for William, whose back was to her, it was too late. She closed the distance to him, leapt up, and plunged the knife into the center of his back. There was a satisfying solidity as the blade connected.

Her triumphal moment was over in an instant, however, when the knife rebounded off the armor beneath his cloak, slipped from her hand, and spun into the dirt.

The dark man beside William who had been sitting perpendicular to him was the first to react; he wrenched his sword from its sheath and swung at Salena.

She lurched backward, just avoiding his sword, but the soldier immediately reversed his swing and hit her across the face with the flat of the blade. Her cheek exploded in pain, and Salena fell back with a cry.

She curled up on the ground with her hands pressed to her face. It was agonizing enough that she could not tell if she had been seriously injured or not.

Before she could recover herself, several soldiers dismounted and were bearing down upon her, weapons in hand. In that moment of pain and fear, she could see with clarity how disastrous her impulsive action had been. She had been so fixated on killing William that she had not even considered what might happen if she failed, the same mistake she had made when she convinced Hans to attack Dawning Court. And once again, she had not only failed to achieve her aim but had also managed to put herself in serious peril.

Tears of pain and defeat squeezed their way out. She would have given anything at that moment to be at home with Rachael, but she had been so focused on the empty hole in her heart that she had not recognized that she was sacrificing all she had left in an attempt to salve it. And now it was too late.

"William, stop!" Neil staggered onto the road, waving his one free arm in the air to get their attention. "It is Salena! She is a Dawning!" he added to the others, who would not know her name. "She is overwrought from exhaustion and grief."

"Neil?" William's voice was incredulous. "I know this man," he said to the questioning looks from the soldiers. But nothing in his tone suggested they should stand down, so they remained where they were. "What is all this about?"

Neil wiped his hand across his face. "I do not even know where to begin."

"I suggest that you decide quickly," the dark man who had struck Salena groused, "considering that she just tried to assassinate the heir of Dawning Court!"

"It was not enough to metaphorically drive a dagger into me back at camp, labeling me a traitor and robbing me of any credibility." William was scathing. "You also found it necessary to pursue me and see to it that my evisceration was complete?"

"They are obviously conspirators," the dark man said, "and we've no time to lose. Let us dispatch them and move on!"

"After our encounter at the dam," Neil said in a loud voice meant to call the men's attention back to him, "what was I to think but that you were working with Thomas?"

"Had I been working with Thomas," William said without sympathy, "I would not have left you alive, and I certainly would not have protected your escape."

That stopped Neil. "Wait ... what do you mean?"

"Who do you think it was pestering the enemy with arrows while you and Timothy rode for the castle?"

"That was you?"

"But the next time I see you, you are denouncing me to Aden and convincing him that I am a liar who is not to be trusted!"

Neil could not get his mind around the events as William was laying them out. There were just too many questions, so he pushed them aside to focus on more immediate concerns. "We did not understand. Even now, I must confess that I do not really understand what is happening."

William leaned forward in his saddle. Neil could not tell if it was just a trick of the moonlight, but his face looked drawn and pale. "What is happening is that I am attempting to save Dawning Court, and my two old friends, who should have been the first to assist me, have shown that they are not only working against me but are determined to murder me as well."

"William, please," Neil said, raising both hands to stall the men who were stepping toward him. "I swear to you that until this moment, we did not know that you were working *for* Dawning Court!"

"You doubted my loyalty?" William demanded. "You? Of all people?"

Neil dropped his hands in a show of surrender. "In earnest, William, I do not know what to believe," he said plaintively. "When we were locked in the castle, desperately manning the battlements with women and children, when we could have used you the most, you were not with us. We thought you dead, only to discover that you were yet alive when you attacked us at the dam. You say that you are trying to save Dawning Court, but in her final hours you are here, closer to the Braddock army than to Aden's." Neil spread his hands before him in a show of helplessness. "So tell me, William, what are we to believe?" His voice was not a challenge but a plea for some explanation that would make it all make sense.

William dismounted and approached Neil, the scowl on his face unchanged. "Get her to her feet," he ordered as he passed by Salena and stopped in front of Neil.

Salena was dragged up by the men around her and held fast. William looked angry, and Neil was in no position to defend himself.

"No, William, please!" Salena, recognizing that Neil was the closest thing to a friend she had left in the world and that William was about to take him from her too, began to beg. "Attacking you was my idea! I swear to you that Neil knew nothing of it. It was me, William! It was all me!"

William watched Salena without comment until her protests petered out. He then turned back to Neil, who was standing barely a foot in front of him, and their eyes locked. Neil was taller than William, but he was hunched enough that they were almost eye to eye. It was obvious to all that there was nothing Neil would be able to do to protect himself.

"Is this true?"

Neil flicked a nervous glance toward Salena, obviously torn between admitting the truth and letting Salena take the blame, which was almost certainly tantamount to a death sentence, or choosing to take some of the blame upon himself.

"I—I was not aware that she meant to attack you," Neil admitted. "We—I—only intended to detect whether you were in league with Collin." In the dark he could scarcely see William's face and began to fidget under his stare. "I had no notion of Salena's intention. Come to that," he added softly so she would not overhear, "I am not certain that even she knew she would do that before she acted. She ... has not had an easy time of it since David's death."

William's frown suddenly deepened.

"For David's sake, please—" Neil cut off at a curt motion from William.

"We must go!" William snapped suddenly and turned back to his men. "Mount up at once!" he said urgently.

Neil felt it then, the dull rumbling underfoot. The men surrounding Salena ran toward their saddles, leaving her standing in the road in confusion.

"Salena, come quickly," Neil motioned to her, but they had not made it two steps back toward their carriage before a group of galloping knights came charging around the bend so fast that they almost collided with them.

The lead rider drew up sharply, his horse rearing back angrily to avoid trampling them. He was a huge man on an oversized warhorse. His golden armor glinted in the moonlight which, Neil thought, made him look like a demigod from Greek mythology.

The forty similarly clad knights reined in behind their leader and, despite the surprise stop, instantly moved into a perfect "V" formation.

William cursed himself while he and his group stood motionless in the middle of the highway as Collin surveyed them under his raised visor. All he would have had to do was move twenty paces into the trees, and Collin would have flown right by them, never the wiser. But he had not done that, and now they were all going to die.

His men would not have been any match for Collin's meticulously trained knights, even had the numbers been equal; but at four to one, they had no chance.

Collin's gaze fixed upon William, and his eyes hardened. "Kill them!" he snapped.

William looked around desperately as swords were drawn on every side. This was going to be a disaster, but what could he do? Even in peak fighting form, he could not possibly make up for the difference in numbers and training. If only Collin had challenged him personally... And that's when it hit him. "Stop!" he called suddenly, throwing both hands in the air.

Much to his surprise, that worked. Collin stopped with his hand on his visor, and his men froze too, watching their leader for their cue.

"Collin Braddock!" William said dramatically, "I challenge you ... to a contest of honor."

There was a collective gasp from his own people, which was not reassuring. Collin guffawed and his men laughed.

"William," Neil whispered urgently, "what you are you doing?"

"Saving your life," William answered out of the side of his mouth, then raised his voice to Collin again. "Do you accept my challenge?"

"William, no! He is going to kill you!"

"Do you think I do not recognize this for the ruse that it is—a desperate ploy to preserve your worthless lives a moment longer? No, I do not accept your challenge; You are an honorless coward and therefore cannot make a challenge of honor."

Then Neil understood. If Collin accepted William's challenge, that gave William leverage to barter for the rest of their lives. "Honorless?" He shouted, hobbling up beside William. "Collin Braddock, you claim to be a man of honor; so *you* must answer for the dishonorable conduct of your family toward the Dawnings."

"What are you doing?" William whispered.

"Helping Collin take you seriously!" Neil retorted.

"What dishonorable conduct?" Collin sneered. "This man has murdered my father and brother!"

"You claim moral superiority over the Dawnings, but was it not Vincent's improper challenge to William that began this travesty?"

Collin glared at him. "I might strike you down for speaking ill of my brother, but it appears that time will silence you soon enough." His men chuckled.

Neil ignored the jab and continued, "What do you imagine Vincent intended, jousting with someone who had never ridden on the lists? Do you suppose his intentions were noble? And what of your father?" Neil pressed on before Collin could respond. "He challenged William to a duel only minutes after the Dawnings' wedding party was attacked. Rather than offer succor to his brethren as gallantry demanded, he took advantage of the moment to settle an old grudge. He demanded that William face him then and there, upon threat of war, despite the fact that William was freshly wounded! Defend his actions as noble, if you can!"

"My father had no choice but to seize the rogue before he fled again," Collin shot back, the litany of charges against his family obviously beginning to agitate him.

"And now," Neil continued, undeterred, "your brother Hans aligns himself with a traitor and an army of heathens in order to overthrow the family that you had heretofore been unable to conquer. Is such opportunistic behavior a reflection of the Braddocks' fine, noble tradition?"

Collin drove his heels into his horse, causing it to leap forward, very nearly landing on top of Neil.

William pushed Neil aside, as his friend's compromised reflexes could not react in time. Neil crashed down on his rear, pain exploding through his entire torso.

"Hans is no brother of mine!" Collin roared. "Another word from you," he said, jabbing his sword at Neil's writhing body, "and I will finish boring that hole through you!" He then turned his rage on William, swinging his weapon back to point at him. "You have murdered my kin, killed my subjects, and humiliated me in front of my own people. No amount of rhetoric will spare you from meeting your well-deserved fate this very night. If you are so simple as to believe that your chances of survival are improved by facing me one on one, then I welcome it!"

"One condition!" William interjected. "Regardless of the outcome, my friends are left to return to Dawning Court unmolested."

Collin snorted. "Your *friends* are guilty of the same offense as you, but perhaps if their lives are at stake, you will have some incentive to see the challenge through instead of fleeing like the coward you are. So, I will let your friends live provided you best me." Collin paused for a breath just long enough for hope to begin to settle upon them before adding, "As the challenged, I select the method of combat, and I choose the joust!"

Whatever vague hope William might have retained that he may somehow manage to come off victorious drained from him.

"How much sweeter the victory to cut you to pieces one pass at a time! Choose your second from this rabble. We joust now! Bertram," he called over his shoulder, "bring him a lance!"

Thirty-two

Collin turned and rode back down the road fifty yards while William helped Neil struggle to his feet. "So, what about it?" William asked with a levity that he did not feel. "Be my second?"

"William," Neil said seriously, "what are you doing?"

"You cannot do this!" Silas said as he, Nolan, and the others hurried up to William. "Lord Richard is the only one to ever best Collin in the joust!"

William was suddenly transported back to the lists years before, where it all began, when Leah had made a similar plea after William's mouth and pride had landed him in a similar contest with Vincent Braddock. He could not help smiling wryly at the situation.

"Why the smile?" Neil demanded. "You know nothing of such things. And even if you did, one look at you tells me you are not fit to stand up to him. Collin is going to kill you."

William dropped all pretense of flippancy. "I know," he sighed, "but if I refuse Collin's challenge, everyone dies."

"You heard him; we will die regardless," Silas pointed out. "At least together we can make a stand."

"Yes, 'tis very romantic," Neil snapped sarcastically. "The bards will surely sing of it. But we are trying to save your life! Perhaps you would like to assist us!"

William smiled at his friend sadly. "You were always a good friend to me, you grumpy old dog. A better friend than I deserved. I am grateful that I had a chance to tell you that."

Neil's sour countenance did not change at all. "And you are a selfish, ungrateful lout! But you deserve better than this!" he flicked his head toward Collin. "This is not right what he is doing."

"Too often," William said, "as you have pointed out, I have put my own interests before that of my people; I will not do so now, when one life might save many. It is okay, Neil. I think some part of me has always known that I would have to face this. It is only right that it should end this way."

William mounted his horse and looked down at Neil. "Now, my old friend, will you act as my second?" he asked seriously this time.

Neil looked down at his wound dubiously. "William, I am not fit for this."

"Neither am I," William grinned. But when Neil did not return it, he said, "These are good men, but they are not trained in the etiquette of the lists. We must not risk Collin declaring victory based upon some innocent mistake. I fear it will have to be you, if you are able?"

Neil glowered at him, but William recognized the gesture for what it was, disgust with the situation rather than with William personally. "Since you have left me no choice," he growled, "I would be honored."

William nodded his thanks, then looked around at the nervous faces of his men and saluted them. "Thank you, men. You have served honorably. Your hearts are as noble and brave as any I have ever known."

"May God be with you, William," Silas said gravely. The others wished him well or saluted and then withdrew a few paces to await the outcome of the duel and their own fates.

He turned back to Collin, who was watching impatiently. William recognized the inevitability of what was about to happen. Maybe if he were fresh and uninjured, he could devise something; but as it was, he had nothing left.

He chuckled softly to himself. How many times had he stood on the precipice of battle, wondering if the Angel of Death was there for him, only to be denied the escape he so desperately sought from the life he had created for himself? He had always assumed it was because he was rejected of Heaven; Richard had said it was because God was not done with him. But either way, he had always survived, even when he should not have. And he had always resented it.

But now that he was staring certain death in the face, William was shocked to realize that he wanted to live! He wanted more time to make amends with Leah, to assure his mother that he had remained faithful; but that was not to be, and he had to accept that.

He had given almost everything to try to save his family, home, and people, so it was only fitting that he should be required at last to give the only thing left to him. He did not want this, but he was ready for it.

"It is time," Neil said without enthusiasm.

William settled himself in the saddle while Bertram, acting as Collin's second, stuck a lance in Neil's hand. Neil looked it over to ensure it was sound.

Silas took his shield and helmet off and offered them to William.

William strapped the shield to his left arm but refused the helmet.

"What are you doing, you bloody great fool?" Neil growled at him. "Collin is an expert! One strike to the head without a helmet ends you!"

"The odds are stacked against me regardless," William said. "I would rather meet him in a way that I am comfortable."

"We will see how comfortable you are without a head." Neil reluctantly handed the lance up to William, leaving Silas with his helmet in his hands.

William accepted it and tested its heft. While it vaguely resembled his beloved spear in appearance, it may as well have been a log for how familiar it felt to him. It was too thick, too long, and too heavy.

Down the road, Collin lowered his visor in preparation to charge. William knew his time was down to seconds. He was feeling something bordering on panic. One of the things he had always hated most about the joust is the basic premise that it was simply a contest of who could withstand more abuse. Though there was skill involved, in the end one of them would have a tree trunk rammed through his body by the other. And since Collin was both stronger and more skilled than William, William knew he did not have a prayer.

"Any advice that will help me keep my head?"

"Other than a helmet?"

"Right. Other than that."

"Alright, listen," Neil said seriously, "if you are planning any trickery like you did with Vincent, I urge you to rethink it."

"I doubt I even have the strength for something like that," William told him honestly, remembering the roll he had done off his galloping horse to surprise Vincent. "But why, exactly?"

"Because it will not work with Collin. Had Vincent been more experienced, his lance would not have been trapped on the wrong side of his horse's neck, and he would have impaled you clean through before you ever got a chance to swing your spear."

"Oh," William said lamely. He had never really thought about it before, always considering his move to be a supremely clever act that had exploited the obvious stupidity of the joust as a form of combat. But now that it was pointed out to him, he could see that perhaps he had been far more vulnerable than he had ever realized. "Um, what do you recommend instead?"

Neil looked at him pitifully. "Try to hit him before he hits you."

"Am I wrong, or is that not a tremendous amount of help?"

Neil gave him a slight smirk. "You are not a tremendously good student."

"Fair," William admitted with a sigh. He took a deep breath to calm himself. He had to accept that there was really nothing that Neil could tell him that would make any meaningful difference at this point. Whatever was going to happen was going to happen.

Then Collin charged. His huge horse's hooves churned up the soft earth as the massive knight bore down on William.

William reluctantly followed suit, spurring his mount into motion a moment after his rival. The two men rushed toward each other in the moonlight.

William struggled to get the lance fixed under his arm as the two flew toward each other. It was not just that it was awkward, but in his present condition, with his strength depleted, he worried that he might not even be able to hold onto it through a collision.

Every possible advantage went to Collin in this contest, but William realized moments before they collided that by removing his helmet, he may have inadvertently given himself one small benefit. He had all but guaranteed that Collin would try for a head strike, which meant that William just needed to ensure his head was not where Collin expected it to be.

Of course, if he was wrong, and Collin did aim for his chest, William might find that he was ducking directly into the tip of an unblunted lance; but that would be a mistake he would only have to live with for a few seconds. A very unpleasant few seconds, to be sure, but few nonetheless.

William braced behind his borrowed shield, training his own weapon on Collin's chest. At the last second, as expected, Collin's lance rose up, aiming for his head. William folded over the handle of his lance, once again moving in a way that was inconceivable in the stiff plates of Collin's armor, and he was gratified to feel Collin's lance slide over the top of his shoulder, even as his own weapon crashed into Collin's shield.

Unfortunately, Collin was ready for the impact and turned his shield to deflect the strike outward, causing the tip of William's lance to slide off with no visible effect.

The horses raced past each other, and William drew up at the opposite end of the circle of knights, where Collin had started. He turned to line up for another pass, recognizing as he did that he could not repeat the same ploy twice. It had worked once, but now Collin would be expecting it, which meant that a second attempt would likely end in disaster. He had to think of something else. Maybe he could force Collin to the ground? The problem with that was that given his current condition, William could not be certain that being on the ground was an advantage.

He ground his teeth in frustration. In a way, this death by joust was worse than an execution because instead of being able to simply surrender to the inevitable, like a prisoner might surrender to a headsman, this contest gave him the illusion that if he were just clever enough or strong enough, he might somehow survive. It forced him to marinate in his inadequacy through every second of the contest, and at the last moment, just before he died, he would inevitably be thinking of what he might have done differently to have avoided this outcome.

William considered several unconventional options, such as striking Collin's horse or even leaping from his saddle to tackle Collin; but he dismissed them. Meeting Collin's challenge was not just about fighting him; it was about meeting him honorably, playing by the very rules he had failed to follow with Vincent. Had he done that all those years ago, then even if Vincent had died, there would have been little ground for the Braddocks to quibble. But because William had violated the rules, it had set this chain of events in motion that was now culminating with his death, but maybe not with the defeat of Dawning Court.

Then they were charging again. This time William employed no trickery, trusting that Collin would aim for his shield, hoping to catch his head. They collided, and again

Collin shrugged off William's strike, while directing the point of his lance directly into the center of William's shield. The inferior metal of the borrowed shield buckled noticeably, and the impact reverberated through his body as he was flung backward in the saddle, falling back over the rear of his horse and barely keeping hold of the reins.

He was just righting himself when he made it back to Neil. "It is going very well, don't you think?" he asked with feigned cheeriness as he watched Collin turn to face him again, looking none the worse for wear.

"Er—yes," Neil muttered, "I think you have him nearly beat."

The two warriors flew at each other again. This time William did manage a satisfying impact on Collin's shield, but Collin directed the tip of his weapon with expert precision into the precise spot on William's shield he had hit before, where it tore through the weakened metal, ripping a gash down the center and out the bottom, missing William's body by an inch.

The two men again circled and stopped to stare at each other. Collin's burnished armor still shone bright and untarnished in the moonlight.

William, on the other hand, felt less like a knight and more like a practice dummy in the training yard. His shield was shredded, his horse was lathered, and he was visibly panting and having a hard time even holding himself erect in the saddle.

He knew he was outmatched, but there was nothing to be done about that now. In a tournament, he could acknowledge his opponent's superiority and submit, but that was not an option in a real joust. His only chance was to try to score a headshot. It was a ridiculous gambit for a novice like himself, especially against an opponent as experienced as Collin. Headshots were hard enough to land on an immobile practice dummy, let alone on a live opponent. But if he did manage a sound hit, he might be able to take Collin out with his last pass. And it was even possible that Collin would not expect it because it was such a foolhardy move. And that's just what William needed right now, some good, old-fashioned beginner's luck!

Then Collin was moving again. The two men closed in on each other. Collin stiffened behind his shield, preparing to absorb the impact while he lined up his strike perfectly.

William kept adjusting the position of his battered shield, hoping that it could protect him from one more blow. But at the last moment, he forgot about that and raised his lance up to point at Collin's visor.

Collin did not expect the sudden movement and failed to defend against it, but William's lance did not land cleanly, glancing instead off the side of Collin's helmet.

Though it failed to inflict any serious damage, it did surprise him enough that his own aim was thrown off, and rather than driving his weapon through the battered remnants of William's shield, he hit the outside of it, again piercing the weakened metal. This time, however, Collin's lance did not pull free. Instead, the force of the pass violently tore the shield from William's arm, and the two men were again past each other. William's tattered shield hung from the end of Collin's lance until he shook it loose and it was kicked aside by his horse's hooves.

William's left arm was numb and hung limply at his side. It did not respond to his commands to move, as though it were not there at all. He did not know if it was broken, if the muscles were torn, or if the nerves had just been so violently shocked that they were temporarily numbed. What he did know was that he was totally vulnerable now as he turned to face Collin for what could only be the final pass.

"This is it, Dawning!" Collin gloated. "This is what happens when a Dawning meets a Braddock in a fair fight."

William did not respond to Collin's jab. What could he say? He was no match for Collin in a joust, and explaining that Collin was exploiting him while he was at his weakest would only sound petty.

Instead, William led out the charge, determined to put an end to this farce once and for all. His horse sprang forward, leaving the gloating Collin to belatedly start after him in surprise. William leaned over his horse's neck. Collin drew a bead on him with no less earnestness than his previous attacks.

William made no attempt to evade or deflect Collin's lance, instead using every bit of focus to aim his own weapon. As such, he made an easy target, and he took the full force of Collin's lance to his chest. He was hurled from his saddle back onto the turf, but not before his own lance hit home, directly in the center of Collin's facemask.

The visor crumpled, and Collin's head snapped sharply back, followed by his body. He toppled off his horse and crashed down on the muddy road, where both men lay motionless.

Thirty-three

Neil raced over to check on William, and Bertram did the same for Collin.

The duel was not over until at least one man was dead. It may be that both men had been killed, but it was far more likely that at least one of them had survived. If that were the case, all the survivor would need to do was recover himself enough to declare victory or finish off his helpless competitor.

Collin's strike had completely dashed to pieces the protective plates from the already weakened chest of William's armor, leaving an oblong, eight-inch circle of exposed, bloody flesh beneath. William was not moving.

Neil examined the wound. It was not terribly deep, but William's face was deathly pale, and his lips were blue.

Neil was suddenly transported back to their childhood, when William had fallen from the rope swing and they had feared him dead. He felt every bit as helpless now as he had then. But unlike then, when he had been able to run for help, there was no one to whom he could turn now.

A sudden feeling of despondency passed over Neil as he realized that, for all their differences, William too was his oldest friend. But his death here meant so much more than that; it was the end of Neil and the others, and possibly the end of Dawning Court.

Neil looked helplessly back at Silas and the others, who were watching anxiously but did not dare interfere for fear that the other side would claim William had violated the terms of the duel by receiving help. Even Salena's face showed open concern, though she might have been thinking more about her own well-being. But she too now had a vested interest in the outcome of this duel.

Neil looked down helplessly and finally did the only thing he could think to do, the same thing he had done as a child when he had felt so scared and helpless; he prayed.

Nothing happened. Neil looked over at Collin, whom Bertram was attempting to revive. Apparently, Collin was not dead. Neil glanced heavenward as if to say, *I suppose I cannot ask for another's death while asking for salvation for myself, but it would sure make things a lot simpler.*

"William!" Neil finally snapped in exasperation. He glanced over and saw that Collin was stirring under Bertram's ministrations, and a jolt of panic went through him. "William!" he said with more force and reached over and slapped William's cheek.

William's eyes fluttered open. "Did I win?" he croaked.

"Not yet," Neil smiled with relief. "Can you stand?" He took William by the arm and started to force him up.

William winced at the pain. "Give me a moment! My ribs might be broken."

"That is not surprising. But you must get to your feet, or Collin may declare you unable to continue and claim victory by default." Neil had William halfway up before his friend turned and wretched on the ground.

Neil let him fall back on all fours. "Er ... take a moment," he said lamely. He looked over at Collin, whom Bertram was half-helping, half-dragging to his feet. Collin, too, had his helmet removed, and Neil could see that his face around his right eye was shredded, almost certainly leaving him blind in that eye. Blood was running down his neck and coating his gold breastplate.

Neil motioned to Silas, and Silas took the cheap guardsman spear they had taken from Aden's camp and threw it to Neil.

"William, listen to me," Neil said, bending down close to his ear. "It is down to the blades."

"I—I am too weak," William breathed into the ground, still trying to catch his breath.

Neil could not tell if the quaver in his voice was from pain or if he was ... emotional. "You do not need to best him if you get to your feet now!"

William made no move to comply.

"Collin is in bad shape. He only stands with the help of his second. If you engage him now, he is all but defenseless."

"Neil ..." William pleaded weakly, "I cannot."

Neil wanted to scream at him that he had been given this one tiny chance at success, at redemption, if he would just act now! But Neil did not say that. He found that he actually understood. He knew firsthand that pain, fear, and exhaustion could make one feel helpless and as vulnerable as a little child.

Neil crouched down beside William, put his hand on his shoulder, and spoke softly to him. "It is not right that it should come down to this, that all this responsibility should be heaped upon your shoulders in this moment, when you are least able to bear it. But here we are.... I am starting to think that life is just a series of trials designed to strip us down to our basest elements to see if we will continue when we have neither the desire nor the fortitude to continue...." He trailed off, unsure why he should have gotten philosophical in this critical moment. Such thoughts seemed inadequate to the moment, like offering a man whose boat was sinking a ladle with which to bail himself out.

He cast another glance at Collin, who was now standing under his own power, resting only a hand on Bertram's shoulder to steady him, and sighed in defeat. He dropped into a sitting position in the dirt beside William and set the spear down. If this was the end, he might as well be comfortable.

"May I tell you, William, what I have learned about you?" Neil dusted off his hands as he spoke. "Well, I suppose you are not in any position to stop me, so I will tell you. You may not want to hear it, but I have come to know the truth of it for myself. You, William ... are a good and honorable man. Stupid? Yes," Neil could not resist adding, "but good. You just put your life on the line to save mine and a handful of other meaningless souls—albeit in the worst gamble that anyone could make—but when the moment of truth came, you were not thinking of yourself but of others!"

"I am sorry, Neil." William spoke into the dirt. "I am sorry about David. I am sorry about us. I am sorry that I let everyone down."

"We all could have done better," Neil mused, "yet however much we might wish it otherwise, the past is past. We can do nothing to change it; the one and only thing in the cosmos that we have power over is this moment right before us. The moment that all of time and space has conspired to create for you is this moment here."

Collin was walking toward them now, dragging the tip of his huge sword in the dirt behind, the weight seeming too much for him. But he was moving under his own power.

Neil was so distracted by the sight that he almost did not notice William struggling to his feet. Neil followed suit, chortling as they both grunted and groaned like old men from the effort of standing up.

Neil pressed the spear into his friend's shaking right hand.

"The world is spinning," William whispered, putting a hand on Neil's shoulder for support, "and every breath feels like a knife in my lung."

"Just take it slow."

Collin continued toward them. His steps were slow, as though he were ensuring each foot was firmly planted before lifting the next one; but he looked stronger than he had only a minute before."

"Neil, I can barely lift this thing," William whispered, referring to his spear. "How do I fight him?"

"Listen to me now, you must end this quickly. He is blind on his right side, which means he will be expecting you to attack him there."

"So attack his left?"

"No. Give him what he expects. Feint to his right, and then swing for his unprotected neck."

William nodded and took a deep breath to get control of his nerves.

Neil met his eye. "You can do this!"

A dubious smirk flashed across William's face, and he took his first tentative steps without assistance to meet Collin, who was only twenty paces away.

Neil watched both men drag their injured and disoriented bodies once more into the fight. William's balance was affected, which meant that his only advantage over Collin, his ability to move like a cat, was compromised. Collin, meanwhile, though he appeared to be more severely injured, was also much stronger, and his armor was in better shape than William's and would offer him more protection. Neil felt ill at the thought that this might be the end for all of them.

William carefully placed one foot in front of the other to keep from falling. The world was swimming before him, and if he moved his head too quickly, it started pounding and his vision narrowed as though he were on the verge of passing out. Neil's tactic was sound given Collin's injuries, but it did not take into account William's own limitations. He was seriously doubting he would be able to execute on the plan, but neither could he meet Collin toe to toe. Collin was similar in size and ferocity to Richard, and William well remembered Richard's last moments, fighting with a dozen wounds, any one of which would have dropped an average man.

I might be in trouble, he had to acknowledge. William felt small and weak and alone at that moment. He wished that one of his big brothers would burst from the trees to save him as they had done in his fight with Amir. But he knew they would not. He had to do this himself. But how? Collin was in a bad state, to be sure, but he was still massively strong.

Jurou's voice was in his head then, chastising him for giving up. *Everyone has weaknesses that can be exploited. What are Collin's?*

I can see a dozen weaknesses! fifteen-year-old William's petulant voice snapped back in his mind. *But I am barely on my feet, and Collin is so much stronger than I am!*

Then you have surrendered before you have even begun. Your fear is handing him the fight.

He is too big! William cried.

And you are too weak! Too tired! Too injured! Lay down your weapon and give up! Let him have your home, your people. Let him have Leah!

As it so often had when they were together, instead of arguing with William's self-defeating mentality, urging it to its extreme forced William out of his pouting, victim mindset and caused him to reframe his position. Neither man had a shield any longer, and Collin would certainly be looking to end the fight quickly. He would undoubtedly rely upon his superior strength, so maybe—

"Help me remove my armor," William said over his shoulder as he tried to lift the heavy shirt. But his left arm was still not cooperating.

"Are you insane?" Neil hissed from his elbow.

"I cannot breathe!"

Neil glanced toward Collin, who was only ten paces away, and reluctantly did as William asked, leaning William's spear in the crook of his arm while helping him to raise his left arm, which William did only with obvious pain. Neil then slid the heavy mail shirt over his head.

"Put it in my hand," William said, flexing the fingers of his left hand.

Neil looked dubious but did as he was asked. He held the heavy shirt up so William could close his fingers around it, but as soon as he released it, the weight of it pulled William's arm down with a painful intake of breath. He did manage to hold onto it, but it was dragging in the dirt.

Neil placed the spear in William's right hand and looked like he would ask more, but Collin was only five paces away. So with one last, nervous glance at William, he withdrew, leaving William to face the much bigger and positively gruesome-looking challenger alone.

"Collin," William said to the bigger man, "'tis not too late. Let us call this a draw and return to our homes, if not as friends, at least as peaceful neighbors."

"Coward!" Collin rasped. "You insult my honor by the very suggestion that I will not see this through to its end! The cowardice in the Dawning blood will always tell."

William shook his head and immediately wished he had not as needles of pain lanced through his temples. "Are you a fool?" he demanded, his angry voice more a consequence of his pain than any surprise at Collin's stubbornness. "You see what this has cost us. I am offering you a chance to preserve your family's legacy and perhaps to save your own life!"

"Dawning dog!" Collin's voice rose an octave. "Do not mask your cravenness as a boon for my benefit!" Collin lumbered forward, raising his one-and-a-half-handed sword in both hands and swinging a downward stroke toward William's neck.

Gritting his teeth against the pain of the still-shocked nerves in his arm, which screamed in protest, William brought his mail shirt up in his left hand like a shield.

Collin's blade crashed against the makeshift shield. The pliable metal plates folded around the blade and blunted the blow so much that it bounced harmlessly off William's torso, causing Collin to be thrown off balance and stumble forward.

William stabbed his spear forward as Collin fell forward, letting Collin's own momentum run the spear through his exposed neck.

In that instant before Collin struck the spearhead, William could see with perfect clarity that though Collin's actions may have led to this outcome, it was William himself who had set all these events in motion. And now, seeing the once-mighty warrior so pathetic and weak that he could not even arrest his own fall in time to save his life was something to be mourned, not celebrated. For the first time William could remember, he did not feel anger or hatred for his enemy but rather pity for a fellow sufferer in misery.

In that last instant, William turned the killing thrust aside, slicing Collin's neck but not piercing an artery.

Collin fell forward on his face with a grunt of pain, and everyone froze.

William's head was swimming from the sudden exertion. He knew he was in serious danger of passing out, and if he did, all was lost. He was endangering everyone by letting Collin live, but he had to try one last time.

"I say again, Collin," William said as he drove the spear into the ground beside Collin to make it clear that the knight only lived because of his lenience. "We are cousins, you and I. I take no pleasure in your death. Withdraw your men from Dawning Court, ride against us no more, and I will grant you your life.

Collin pushed himself up onto all fours, his head hanging down and his labored breathing audible. "You," he growled slowly, "are a coward! If you do not finish this duel, then I will claim victory!"

"Are you mad?" Neil cried from fifteen feet away. "He is offering you your life!"

Collin struck out with his left forearm, snapping the shaft of the spear a foot above the head that was buried in the ground. He then came up on his knees, swinging the sword still clutched in his right hand toward William.

William reacted on instinct. In one motion he spun behind Collin and out of the path of the weapon, his dagger coming into his hand. Ignoring the whirling world, he drove the blade through the back of Collin's exposed neck with such force that the tip of the blade tore out the front of his throat.

Collin remained motionless for so long that William began to wonder if he would somehow continue to fight through this wound that should have been instantly fatal. Visions of Richard's seeming indifference to his own critical injuries filled his mind. But then, all at once, Collin's limbs went slack, and he pitched forward onto the road.

The onlookers fell silent as the shock of this momentous, unfathomable outcome settled over them. Collin's men's stunned expressions shortly turned to fury. Bertram's blade flew from its sheath, and he ran forward, with the other members of the Golden Sword right behind.

In response, William's men reached for their own weapons.

Seconds before it all devolved into a bloodbath, Neil raised his arms and roared, "Stop! You would dishonor Lord Collin while his blood is yet warm?" he demanded of Bertram and the knights.

Bertram skidded to a halt only a few paces from William, naked rage plain on his face. It was clearly taking every ounce of restraint he could muster not to cut them down where they stood.

"Lord Braddock's challenge was met honorably. More than honorably, as my man gave him every opportunity to save himself. Per the terms of the agreement, you and your men are to withdraw."

Slowly Bertram sheathed his sword. "Out of respect for Collin, I will leave the field; I will not butcher your worthless hides here and now as you deserve."

Neil was just starting to relax when Bertram made his next pronouncement. "I will instead return with my army and burn Dawning Castle to the ground!"

Bertram gave orders for Collin's body to be wrapped and tied over his saddle for transport back to Braddock castle. He then remounted and directed one last glare at William and the others before turning and galloping back toward Braddock Court.

Whatever joy the small band may have felt at having their lives spared was restrained. Silas hurried up to William and Neil. "Lords, did we just make the situation even worse?"

"We bought Aden time," William said. "Not as much as we had hoped, perhaps, but it will have to be enough."

"Perhaps we had better be on our way," Neil suggested.

"I—I am not certain I can ride," William admitted.

"You will ride in the carriage with me so you may rest." *Your fight may not be over,* he did not add.

"Lord William, what shall we do with the traitor?" Silas nodded toward Salena.

William had forgotten all about her. It was the last thing he wanted to deal with now, but given the severity of her charge, he could hardly leave it for later. The appropriate and necessary punishment for her sedition was death.

Salena, too, had momentarily forgotten what awaited her in the drama with Collin. She had even had a stirring of feeling that she had not expected as she watched Neil defend William, not only because of what Neil had said about the injustices the Braddocks had perpetrated on the Dawnings, which William had simply been reacting to, but because of the act of defending him.

She knew that, like her, Neil did not like William; he was injured and could and probably should have declined to participate in the duel. But when he was called upon, he put all that aside and did his best to serve William because that was how he could best serve his people.

Salena could make no such claim for herself. Even if she did believe that the people would have been better off without William around, she could not honestly say that anything but her own wounded feelings were dictating her actions. She had not been thinking of others; she had not even considered Rachael's fate; she had only thought of revenge.

She dropped her eyes under the judgmental scrutiny of the soldiers. She wanted to plead her case, to ask for mercy, but how could she? She deserved her fate. Hopefully they would make it quick.

"Leave her to me," William finally said. "The rest of you ride on ahead. The carriage will not be able to keep up with you, and the castle may need you."

"But Lord William, the way may be dangerous," Silas protested, nodding in the direction the Braddocks had ridden.

"Perhaps," William acknowledged, "but in my current condition, my loss would not be much of a hindrance to Dawning Court. But you and your men can still do some good. Make haste."

Silas looked like he wanted to argue but did as William instructed.

When the men disappeared down the road, William turned toward her.

Salena braced herself for what was to come. *Will he execute me himself? Or will he order Neil to do it?* she wondered. *Will Neil comply?* For while she and Neil were friends after a fashion, so were Neil and William, or at least they had been once; and it was Neil's duty to obey his lord. Salena held her breath but could not bring herself to look him in the eye.

"You are free to go, Salena," William said in a voice heavy with exhaustion. He then turned toward the carriage, as though the matter were settled.

Salena looked up sharply. "Wh—" she could not quite form the question.

"There has been enough blood spilt for one night."

Salena could not have said why she did what she did next, but in this moment, after watching Neil selflessly serve a man he hated, a man who had wronged him and taken his best friend from him; and then watching William, the lowest of the low, repeatedly try to make peace with the family's oldest enemy rather than fight him, it just did not seem right that she should be pardoned under false pretenses.

"I am the reason the Braddocks attacked Dawning Court when they did!" she blurted, then stopped as though she would take it back; but it was too late. The confession hung there in the night. She glanced at Neil, who was watching her in astonishment. "I—" she explained in a much quieter voice, "I told the Braddocks of the weakness of the west wall. That is what convinced them to attack when they did."

William, who had been about to mount the carriage, stopped with his hand on the side. Salena thought she saw his already wavering form slump even lower, if that were possible. He looked at the ground as though praying. Silence hung in the air for a long time.

"Forget it," he muttered abruptly.

"What was that?" Salena and Neil asked in chorus.

"But I deserve death for what I have done." Salena knew it was insanity to speak this way, but at that moment she found it impossible to hold her tongue. "Why?"

"I could not give David his life back," William said, the fatigue draining all emotion from his voice. "But I can give him something that he prized even more highly than that; I can give him your life back."

Without another word, he boarded the carriage, signaling the matter was closed, and was instantly asleep.

Salena did not move.

"I do not understand."

"You have been pardoned," Neil said flatly.

"But after what I did ... I should be dead!"

"Yes, you should be. But you have been given a second chance. I hope you will not throw it away."

Neil turned and climbed up in the carriage beside William, leaving Salena to awkwardly mount William's horse and trail after, trying to sort out a sea of conflicting thoughts and feelings.

Thirty-four

Dawning Court
The next morning

I do have one thing to say," Martha replied. "Close the gates!"

It took Amir a moment to register what was happening. He heard the heavy chain begin to unspool, and the portcullis, now bent and damaged from the many previous attacks, begin to grind down its stone tracks into place. The Dawnings were trapping him in the courtyard!

There was no time to think. Yanking his horse's neck around, Amir drove his spikes violently into the animal's flanks, forcing the men in his way to dive aside or be ridden down.

The spiked end of the portcullis was already halfway down when he entered the barbican. He was not going to make it. In desperation, he drove his horse harder until a collision with the steel grating was inevitable. He then dove off the side of his mount only a yard from the descending spikes. He hit the ground hard and rolled, even while the gate crashed into his mount's back, breaking its spine and driving the animal to the ground under its weight. Amir used the gap his horse's body created to roll beneath the grating, ignoring the piercing cries from the dying beast.

Once clear, he leapt to his feet and ran to the nearest mounted soldier, hurling him from the saddle. "Attack!

Attack!" he screamed as he jumped onto the horse and galloped back toward the Mayfield-Saracen line.

Word spread, a horn blew, and the army charged, pushing the last siege tower out in front of them. It was there that Amir directed his horse. If the Dawnings were not going to surrender peaceably, he would cut the remnants of their pathetic army to pieces, and he would do so with great relish!

Even as he rode, the battlements began to resume operation. Slowly at first, but with increasing frequency, arrows began to fall from the sky, followed by stones hurled from the wall-mounted artillery.

Of course, Amir knew that the odds of victory were in his favor, but it was going to cost men—which were running low—and more importantly, time. And that he was certain he could not spare. At any moment, one or both of Colin's and Aden's armies might come storming through the outer gates.

An arrow shot from the wall struck Amir's pauldron with a sharp thud. The wooden shaft of the arrow snapped harmlessly against his armor, but it refocused him. The tower was already trundling forward in front of the army, and Amir circled around behind it.

As soon as they had successfully crossed the bridges laid down over the trench that had foiled Hans the previous day, Amir dismounted and pushed his way into the tower and up the stairs toward the egress. He felt the massive structure rumbling beneath his feet and reveled in its power and in the confidence the tower gave him that he would win the day.

He forced his way onto the top platform until he stood just behind the heavy plank that would act as the bridge over to the wall, then waited. He blocked out all the voices of the men pressing in around him, the sound of the battle outside, all the doubts, frustrations, and misgivings. This was his moment, and he was ready.

He grinned with satisfaction at the memory of Martha's face when the Mayfields had introduced him as the rightful heir of Dawning Court. He had waited his entire life to see this cursed family and all that they owned fall to him. He exulted that Martha had lived to see that he, the bastard abomination of the great warrior baron, had beaten them all, and he was going to take everything.

It had been so sweet, but of course Martha had attempted to ruin it before he even got a chance to savor it. Amir was determined to answer back immediately and show her that she had done nothing beyond sacrificing more lives to briefly delay the inevitable, for he was inevitable. And he would see to it that Martha would suffer tenfold for every hour she kept him from his rightful place.

Amir could feel they were getting close and took the time to deliver instructions to the men around him regarding tactics for taking possession of the wall. It was not necessary, of course, as these were experienced soldiers who well knew how to comport themselves, but it was less about instructing them and more about establishing dominance over them. He wanted it clear that he was in charge, and that this was his victory—his and his alone!

He waited impatiently for the tower to be pushed into place. He could hear the stones and arrows from the wall bouncing off the armored plating only inches from where he stood. He had seen firsthand how well these towers withstood attacks, so the sound did not bother him; rather, he was encouraged by how infrequently the strikes came. That suggested that the defensive forces were even more depleted than he realized. Taking them might be even easier than he had expected.

When he felt the tower slow, he knew they were getting close. He drew William's sword from his hip and again smiled with satisfaction at the memory of playing William. Watching that arrogant, smug little brat's shock when the Mayfield flag had not been found among Amir's belongings was one of the most satisfying moments of Amir's life; it almost made up for the fact that William somehow still lived. The boy had been so certain that he had outsmarted all of them. He had been so sure that the other Englishmen would automatically believe him over the Saracens, but Amir had outsmarted him.

"Ten yards!" someone shouted from the rear of the tower, and word was passed up the stairs. They were moments away from their final breach, and Amir found himself wondering what had become of Anisa. She had remained on the inside of the castle like the dutiful soldier she was. There was much mischief that could be perpetrated from inside, but Amir also knew that it was very dangerous for her. His sister was tall, dark, and beautiful, not the sort of person to walk through a crowd of pale English peasants unnoticed, particularly when an army of her countrymen was tearing down the gates.

Though she had obviously failed in her primary objective to execute Martha and incite a revolt, Amir had no doubt that she had used this time well...though it may have cost her her life. But if anyone was cunning enough to survive in such a precarious situation, it was Anisa. And that was good because there were very few people left that Amir could trust to support him when he installed himself as baron.

"Five yards!" came the strained call from below. The barrage against the tower was incessant now, but Amir forced himself to remain calm. He closed his eyes and took a deep breath—and then sniffed the air. He wanted to remember every single thing about this moment—the moment just before he stepped into his birthright.

A vague scent caught his attention. There was a tang of something above the odor of bodies, armor, and fresh-cut timber. *Is that ... oil?* He could not be sure. Perhaps he was only smelling the pitch that was doubtlessly coating the iron-clad face of the tower from the defenders' catapults.

But at last, the tower finally lurched to a halt, and everything else was forgotten. In his excitement, Amir himself began to remove the thick boards securing the bridge over the tower exit. He smelled the smoke only moments before he saw it begin to seep through the cracks in the wood. *Is the tower actually on fire?* It seemed impossible given how the other tower had withstood all efforts to ignite it during the previous attacks. But it really did not matter now. They had made it. The tower could not possibly burn fast enough to stop them.

The men around him pushed the heavy plank blocking the exit forward until it toppled over and crashed into place between the merlons, forming a bridge to the wall.

The smell of smoke filled Amir's nostrils, and a memory stirred. *Wasn't William in one of the towers when Hans captured him?* But all that was pushed from his mind when he saw the small party of petrified peasant-soldiers congregating on the wall just ten feet away from where he now stood. Unlike the last attack, where men had filled every inch of the wall, the battlements now looked almost deserted. This victory was going to be quick! The castle was all but his.

Amir paid no attention to the flaming pitch that had splattered across the armor plating of the tower and was running down its side. He did not even care that a rivulet of the stuff was streaming onto the newly exposed woodwork of the exit where he now stood. He gripped his blade tighter and bent his knees to charge.

The tower egress burst into flames.

Amir threw his arms in front of his face as the heat washed over him. He felt the hair on his face singe as the wood around him was engulfed as though it had been doused in oil. He tried to jump back but came up against the wall of soldiers behind him who could not make way for him because of the men pressing up from below.

His cloak was on fire now. Amir could feel it searing the skin on his legs and back. He was reaching for the clasps to release it when the first arrow lanced through the flame and pierced the leather jerkin of the man standing at his shoulder, missing Amir by inches.

The next arrow snapped against Amir's breastplate, but he hardly noticed, just as he was only dimly aware that the men behind him were starting to panic at the sight of the fire. Amir's conscious mind was completely consumed with the alarms being raised as pain seared through his body from each new nerve center affected by the heat; it was some deeper instinct of self-preservation that impelled his legs into motion, forcing him through the wreath of flames, heedless of the small band of peasant-soldiers who were waiting to greet him. His blind charge would have left him open had the undertrained soldiers not been so shocked by the sudden appearance of a giant figure with flames shooting over his head. Instead of rushing in to capitalize on his vulnerability, they froze in terror.

Amir plowed into them, smashing one aside with his shoulder while swinging his sword wildly at anyone who stood in his way. Deprived of his ability to think clearly, he was stuck in a paroxysm of desperation and did not think to drop to the causeway to try to extinguish the fire, even after breaking through the small cluster of peasant-soldiers. Instead, he cut his cloak loose and continued to run down the battlements, only dimly aware that the horrible shrieking he heard was coming from him.

He had never known pain like this. Surely death could not be worse than this! He just wanted it to stop at any cost.

Finally, he could stand it no longer; he must make the pain stop, it did not matter how. It was not a conscious decision; he did not even stop to consider before throwing himself over the edge of the parapet and out into the air above the courtyard fifty feet below.

Thirty-five

By the time Aden led his army through the outer gates of Dawning Court, the Mayfield-Saracen forces were already battering the walls, and the last siege tower was already in place.

"It would appear the negotiations with the Mayfields went poorly," Martin called wryly from where he galloped alongside Aden. "Where do we begin?"

Aden pointed toward the siege tower that was beginning to billow smoke. "There."

With that, Aden spurred his cavalry forward, charging ahead of his infantry. They drove toward the line of soldiers scrambling to escape the burning tower. At the last moment, Aden's men veered off, cutting off the retreating soldiers from behind instead of pushing them toward the castle walls and losing their momentum.

Aden's vanguard crashed through the rear of the mercenary line, cutting down fifty men before circling around for another charge. But this time the enemy had turned to meet them, and the cavalry ground to a halt as they became embroiled in the press of soldiers.

But then Aden's foot soldiers arrived, colliding with the Mayfield-Saracen army, trapping Aden and his cavalry between them. Chaos erupted as the two armies clashed in a whirlwind of violence. With their formations broken in the rush, Aden's soldiers lost all semblance of order, the battlefield devolving into a wild, tangled brawl.

Meanwhile, the battlements continued to rain arrows and stones down upon the fray, only adding to the pandemonium.

"Fall back to the castle!" Sebastian shouted, rallying his watchmen as they formed a protective circle around Martha.

She was equal parts shocked and relieved by the appearance of the ancient steward, who had raced down from the Great Hall with a group of watchmen as soon as the gates had closed.

"Lord Anthony sent us," he said, answering Martha's unspoken question.

Meanwhile, the Mayfield soldiers had formed a tight semi-circle around George and Mary, trapping them against the gate. Amir, ever the survivor, had managed to slip away.

Martha pushed her frustration about the Saracen aside. As long as Amir lived, he would continue to wreak havoc; but that was a concern for later. Right now, her focus had to be on getting to safety. Neither Sebastian nor the watchmen were seasoned fighters, and the sooner she was out of danger, the sooner they would be.

The group began to move through the crowd as best they could, watching outward for threats while they tried to hold a firm line against the panicking peasants, who repeatedly crashed into them in their frantic rush to escape the chaos at the gate.

Thirty-six

nthony followed close behind Leah as they pushed through the sea of people toward the stairs to the battlements, keeping near to the castle's wall to try to avoid the worst of the thronging crowds. She could feel him pressing in on her, but rather than comforting her as it would have only a day ago, his closeness brought only anger and frustration. Leah knew that his proximity was less about protecting her and more about ensuring that she did not bolt into the crowd. It felt like some strange dream in which she was a prisoner, but rather than her captor being an enemy, he was her betrothed. And instead of leading her to her doom, he was forcing her bodily to flee the castle while abandoning everyone else to their fate.

What do I do? she thought desperately. She wished Eve was there with her. Eve was not afraid of anything, which may have been why she was always getting into trouble. But she had to admit to herself that it wouldn't have mattered, even if Eve were here. There was nothing either of them could do to Anthony. He was bigger, stronger, armed, and armored.

Leah hopelessly scanned the crowd for some means of escape. The press of people would only work against her if she ran. Not only would they impede her flight, but they would also undoubtedly recognize Anthony; and none of the peasants were likely to challenge him.

She hated how helpless she felt against the very strength she had reveled in when it was vanquishing the assassins in the castle. That same strength that was of such comfort when employed to protect her was a fearful weapon when directed against her.

At that moment, Leah hated the chivalry and all their hollow, empty promises of valor. She chose to ignore the voice that whispered that protecting her is what Anthony thought he was doing.

Wait! That's it! Anthony is not some stranger; you know him! He is trying to do what he thinks is right. He is trying to protect you because he cares for you.

If she was correct about what he was feeling, then the way to reach him was not force but compassion, and that was the one thing she just could not seem to muster. Her natural empathy had been murdered with Eve, alongside her hope and faith.

As they neared the rear of the castle, they were impeded by a slow-moving cart going in the same direction. But there was a veritable river of people moving the opposite way, anxious to see for themselves what was transpiring in the courtyard.

They trudged along behind the cart until they passed a small alcove where the bell tower jutted out from the castle's main wall. There were no people in it because it had become a repository for unused wagons and equipment. Anthony steered Leah into it to try to get around the cart, only to find that the space between the slow cart and the equipment store was not wide enough to get by. Anthony cursed as they were again forced to stop and wait.

While they stood there, Leah scanned the alcove for something she might use as a weapon. She looked over the assorted tools and broken carts until her attention was drawn to a lump strewn over the sides of two adjacent wagons that had been backed into the alcove. Something about it caught her eye. *What was—*

Leah suddenly gave a startled cry and shrank back, bumping up against Anthony. Lying in a mangled heap across the pile of equipment, her robe making her blend in with the tarp covering the equipment, was Lindsay Dawning. She appeared to have fallen—or been pushed—from the bell tower. Her hood partially covered her head, leaving only part of her face and one wide, staring eye peering out from beneath the cowl. Her visible cheek had swollen and turned purple where the blood had pooled, but she looked as though she were watching Leah.

Anthony spun at her cry, his hand going to his sword hilt while his other arm wrapped protectively around her.

She covered her mouth and instinctively turned into Anthony's chest to block out the vision of that horribly mangled body.

"William must have pushed her off the tower," he muttered sullenly. "A punishment for failure, perhaps."

Leah felt sick. Lindsay was in death as she had been in life, lonely, abandoned, and forgotten. *No!* She chided herself. *You will not feel sorrow for her! Lindsay was a villain who was in league with William.* "I should rejoice at this," she muttered, but Anthony overheard it.

"Seeing that pathetic creature lying in a heap, without a friend in the world to mourn her or even to note her absence, is not a cause for joy."

A pebble of guilt rippled the surface of the deep pool of sadness that had filled her broken heart. The feeling unsettled her until she suddenly realized that Anthony still had his arm wrapped around her, and she shook it off with renewed anger.

"Eve showed nothing but friendship toward Lindsay," Leah spat, "and it was Lindsay fighting with her that left her vulnerable to William bringing the platform down beneath her. Had Lindsay not done what she did, Eve might still be here."

"Do Lindsay's poor choices cheapen the friendship that Eve offered?" Anthony asked flatly.

Surprised by his lifeless tone, Leah looked into his face, wondering if he was trying to instruct her or if he was genuinely asking, desperate for answers to whatever soul searching was going on inside him. But at that moment, there was a break in the line of people, and Anthony propelled her gently but firmly back into the flow.

Leah let herself be pushed along, her thoughts filled with the image of the pale face and dark, staring eye. She was forced to acknowledge that she did feel sad for Lindsay but was instantly angry with herself for it.

Why do you feel pity for that creature when all you can feel for everyone else is anger and hatred? Was it perhaps because of the sad, miserable life Lindsay had led, or was it due to the horrible, lonely, meaningless way it had ended? Lindsay was a simple girl from humble circumstances who could have married an ordinary man, raised a family, and been perfectly content with her simple life had she not had the misfortune to catch the eye of John Dawning.

The handsome, young noble had swept her off her feet, but instead of a life of comfort and luxury that such a husband promised, she had been disowned by her own family and never accepted by the Dawnings, ending up a penniless widow at John's death. She had been made miserable in life because of the Dawnings and then died a pawn to some evil Dawning cartel, and for what?

How many more poor innocents will die needlessly to this Dawning feud with none to note their passing or care that they are gone? She found tears welling in her eyes as Anthony steered her onto the stairs mounting the battlements.

"Please," she said, unable to hide her emotion, "please, I just need a moment."

Anthony stopped to let her rest near the top of the stairs that let out onto the northeast corner of the wall. He looked concerned but did not ask the reason why she was crying. After all, there were a dozen reasons that might have triggered it, and many of those were related to him personally or to what he was doing at this moment.

"You cannot believe this is right," Leah sniffed, wiping her cheeks, "to abandon this people at this critical hour when they need us the most."

"None of this is right," he croaked in a voice hoarse with emotion. "Our cause is just! We should have been victorious."

"Where is God?" she muttered, voicing a thought that she had been harboring and that she was sure must be echoing in Anthony's own head. "Why is he not punishing our tormentors and protecting our loved ones?" She found fresh tears on her face as she spoke.

"This," Anthony said with a gesture that encompassed all of Dawning Court, "has cost me everything: my belief in the chivalry, my heroes, and now ..." he trailed off, so Leah finished the thought for him. "And now your faith."

"I do not understand." His voice was anguished. "I know that God does not prevent the wicked from doing as they will, but I took it for granted that I would have divine help in championing the weak and fighting for right. When I accepted Lord Richard's charge to protect this people, I believed that I was doing Heaven's will. I was agreeing to protect a people in the direst of circumstances who no longer had a defender. Yet at every turn, we have only been beaten down further. The sabotage, the compromised stores of pitch, the rat-infested larders, the assassins in the castle, and then William kill—" He broke off and sank to a squat with his back against the wall, as though each thing he listed was adding a physical weight to his shoulders.

"William killing Eve." Leah took a seat on the step above him.

"I just ... cannot—will not accept it. Is nobody in this world truly good?"

"Eve was good," Leah said softly, "and you," she added, though she said it to the ground. "Anthony--" she sighed, trying to find the emotional energy to say what she knew needed to be said to him but finding that it was like prying the words from lips that were rusted shut. "You ... are the best man I have ever met. You are what I always wanted to believe of people. You did right for right's sake, not because it profited you or bolstered your reputation but simply because it was the proper thing to do. It was your example that justified my naive belief in the essential goodness of people long after the evidence suggested otherwise."

They both just sat and stared, each thinking thoughts that were not so far apart as they might have assumed. "And you," he finally said in a voice so soft that it was almost a whisper, "are good. That is why I was determined to save you from … this." He gave a half-hearted wave at the courtyard. "Even if my salvation has been lost with my faith, I thought if I could just rescue you from perishing along with these people, then I would have done something worthwhile—something that mattered. That is why I forced you." He dropped his eyes again in shame. "Forgive me."

Leah understood his plight better than she ever could have even a week ago. But what was there to say? She could not tell him that Heaven had not forsaken them, nor that the wicked would be punished and that good would ultimately triumph, because she too was bereft of the faith she had long enjoyed, the faith she now realized had been born of her once safe and easy life.

Instead, she sat with him in dejected silence. She leaned her head to the side, resting it against the cold stone, and let her gaze wander. *We are all only shadows of the people we once were,* she found herself thinking.

She was so awash in her own thoughts that she did not even register the distress call that sounded from the west wall until Anthony started to get slowly to his feet. His eyes were on the wall, and he climbed the last few steps past her to try to get a better view.

"What is it?" It took only a moment for her to sort out the frantic motion of the guards and the distress calls that she could now pick out over the cacophony of noise coming from every direction. The west wall was under attack.

"There is no one leading the west wall," he said but did not move. "They are undermanned and totally unprepared."

Leah stood, looking between him and the wall. "Should you not help?" she said, realizing that if she could persuade him to do so, it would mean the end of her captivity.

"Martha ordered me to see to your safety." He set his jaw firmly. "Besides, these people are done for. Helping them to resist for another hour will make no difference."

"Perhaps not, but will it help you lay your head down at night?"

"The battle is already lost," he cried, dropping his eyes in anguish.

"But there are still lives to be saved!" She was surprised to realize that she actually believed what she was saying. "Maybe we need to save them in order to save ourselves."

Anthony remained where he was, looking conflicted. She realized that he needed her to direct him—to be his moral compass when he was too shattered to trust himself. "Go," she said, "defend the wall."

He looked into her eyes, and a whole range of emotions passed there. She could see all the sadness, the regret, the doubt, the fear, and the uncertainty. "This is the right thing," she assured him. "I will be fine. Grace will be fine. See to your duty, Sir Knight."

He closed his eyes and exhaled a long breath, as though it were releasing all the doubt and fear into the air, and then he ran toward the west wall with renewed vigor.

Leah watched him go. She had been lying about herself and Grace, of course. She had no idea what she was going to do and knew nothing of Grace's fate, but she was not disturbed by the lie. It was what Anthony needed to hear. She knew that he may be running to his demise, but she also knew that even knowing that fact, he would not shy away from his duty. Perhaps that was the price of internal peace.

Thirty-seven

*A*nthony rushed down the wall toward the sound of the warning horn, grateful for action to distract him. The wall was woefully undermanned, and he knew part of that was his own fault, as he had pulled all but a minimal complement of guards to defend the southern wall.

As he neared the area where the call had come from, he watched a soldier crab-walk backward away from a dead comrade until he bumped up against Anthony's legs.

Anthony reached down, put his hands under the guard's arms, and threw him to his feet with so much force that the guard stumbled forward into the merlons before spinning to face Anthony. But the tongue-lashing Anthony had been about to deliver to the cowering soldier died on his lips when he saw how young the boy was.

"You sounded the alarm," Anthony said instead, nodding to the horn on the ground beside him.

The boy stared in stunned silence.

"What is your name?"

"R—Rylan, your Lordship," he managed to stammer.

"You did well, lad. Now stand strong. Remember that you are a Dawning," he added automatically, swatting the boy on the shoulder with a joviality that surprised even himself. There was something liberating, he decided, about staring death in the face and knowing that you were helpless to prevent his pouncing. Anthony wondered if that was not an insight into William's own flippant personality. Regardless, it gave him a heady sense of recklessness that was quite apart from his normal character and miles apart from how he had felt with Leah only minutes before.

"Y—yes, Lord."

"Why, William Dawning was only about your age when he became a hero in the Crusades. If we are to meet our end on this wall tonight, Rylan, we will do so as Dawning men. Like Richard, we will take as many of these bastards with us as possible!"

The previous days had been so wild that thoughts of the west wall and its fatal flaw had been pushed completely from his mind, which, he now realized, may have been exactly what William—or was it Thomas—was hoping for. And now the Mayfields, who had apparently double-crossed the traitors, were taking the castle. Or was this part of Thomas and William's plan all along? Use the Braddock army to smash the castle's defenses and then ally with the Mayfields to destroy the Braddocks? Trying to keep all the possible machinations straight made his head ache. How much simpler it was to live an honest, open life.... Or so he had always believed ... until now.

Anthony looked down the line of frantic guards scrambling and shouting to each other while vainly attempting to break the hooks loose from the wall. But the enormous iron claws, Anthony knew, were attached to horse or oxen teams straining against them, trying to pull the wall down. The combined force of the animals effectively sealed the hooks to the wall. No man or group of men would be able to pry them loose so long as the animals were pulling on them.

"We must attack the ropes," he shouted, starting toward the nearest group of guards. "Sever them!" But when he got closer, he saw the long metal sleeves that had been fitted over the ends of the ropes and understood the problem. It was impossible to cut through any portion of the rope that was within reach of the men on the wall. They would have to extend at least ten feet out from the wall, and even if they could manage that, they could not exert any leverage on the cut itself, as the men were aptly demonstrating by the clumsy attempts to hack at the ropes with blades tied to poles.

"We need to try something else!" Anthony pointed out needlessly. Rylan's face lit up, and he suddenly ran toward the south wall. Anthony wanted to call after him, but what was the point? Until they had some method of defending against this attack, one more soldier would make no difference.

Just then, the rising sun shrank the shadow cast by the west wall enough that the horse teams pulling on the ropes were no longer obscured in darkness. Due to the height of Dawning Court's wall, the ropes had to be made very long to avoid toppling the wall onto those pulling on it. As a result, the horse teams had to leave the cover of the trees by the river and were now exposed. "Artillery," he shouted at the catapult and ballistae crews, "aim for the animals!"

Anthony was asking a lot of the novice crews. Catapult aim was difficult enough for experienced soldiers to calibrate under the best of circumstances. Nevertheless, the crews did what they could, clumsily loading, aiming, and firing the weapons.

To Anthony, though, it seemed like they were working in slow-motion. He had to restrain himself from shouting at them in frustration, knowing that his anger would only fluster and slow them even more.

A few minutes later, Rylan returned, carrying a long, makeshift ladder consisting of two long planks lashed together with several ill-fitting cross-members. "Try this!" he panted. Without waiting for a response, he laid it over the edge of the wall beside the closest grappling hook. "Help me support it!" he shouted to no one in particular.

Anthony suspected that the boy had taken the ladder from some damaged part of the southern wall where it had been serving as an improvised bridge, but now was not the time to quibble over such things. He and several others rushed over to support the end while one of the smaller soldiers, knife clamped in his teeth, climbed out unsteadily toward the other end, hanging in space fifty feet above the ground.

"Lower him down!" Anthony directed, and the four holding the ladder let it slowly rise on their end so that the soldier on the other was lowered toward the rope.

But as the soldier felt the platform begin to dip, he dropped onto his stomach and clung desperately to the ladder, suddenly afraid that he was about to plunge to his death.

"Cut the rope!" Anthony shouted at him, but the young man was too afraid to relinquish his grip enough to even attempt it.

Then arrows started to slice through the air around them as the enemy on the ground realized what they were up to.

"Quickly!" Anthony yelled at him. "Every moment you remain, you—" he never finished, as the soldier suddenly stiffened and rolled off the plank with an arrow in his neck.

As if in retaliation for the arrowshot, a well-placed boulder from a wall-mounted catapult crashed down on top of the animal team that was harnessed to a grappling hook farther down the wall. The boulder smashed the yoke and scattered the animals that were not killed or injured by the skittering stone. The rope went limp, and the grappling hook drooped suddenly.

The soldiers did not lose a moment pulling it loose to drop it from the wall, but Anthony stopped them. "Hold!" he roared, running toward them in a slight crouch to avoid the arrows still coming over the wall. They were infrequent, nothing like the incessant volleys that protected the attacks on the south wall—this felt like it might be just a couple dozen archers—nevertheless, he did not fancy an arrow through the eye if he could avoid it. "Do not return that to them!"

The guards nodded their understanding and pulled the hook up enough to reach the unprotected part of the rope and begin cutting through it.

Anthony was just about to return to help Rylan when the grappling hook between him and the first crew tore loose from the wall, taking a six-foot-wide section of the battlements and one unfortunate soldier with it.

Anthony froze as the stone tore free and plummeted toward the earth. He gripped the merlon beside him while he waited to see if the damage would result in catastrophic failure of the architecture, taking more—if not all—of the wall down. But the structure held for the moment, though he wondered if even then there were cracks spreading out from the damaged section that would compromise its integrity.

But once again, he forced from his mind thoughts of things he could not control and instead concentrated on what he could. There were still four hooks firmly in place with the animal teams still straining against them. He could feel shudders running through the wall with each successive pull. Cracks were appearing in the mortar, and now that part of the wall had failed, the vibrations underfoot seemed especially ominous.

"We need those ropes cut now!" he shouted as he raced back toward Rylan, who was looking around for the plank's next volunteer. Not surprisingly, no one was anxious to oblige. All the nearby soldiers busied themselves with other tasks and avoided meeting his eye. No one wanted to take that risk.

Anthony resigned himself to what must be done. He checked that his dagger was secure in its sheath and was just stepping toward the ladder when Rylan placed a hand on his arm. "No," he said, "I will go."

"Nonsense," Anthony dismissed him, stopping short of adding, "you are only a child."

"I will be easier to support," he persisted, though his voice cracked with fear as he said it.

Anthony was about to argue further when a swarthy soldier, hatchet held between his teeth, ran by them and jumped off the wall.

The soldiers stared as he hung in space for a moment and then grabbed hold of the rope attached to the grappling hook. He wrapped his legs around it and with his one free hand took the hatchet from his mouth and began to attack the fibers of the thick rope just beneath the iron sheathing.

"Cover him!" Anthony ordered the soldiers, who all wore the same shocked expression that he likely wore. The men snapped from their surprise and began to shoot into the darkness below at anything that moved.

The fibers of the taut rope gave easily beneath the soldier's hatchet, and in less than a minute, he was two-thirds of the way through it. The teams on the ground, unaware that the rope was compromised, renewed their exertions, whipping the animal teams to drive them harder. The rope stretched one last time, and the remaining fibers failed, breaking between the soldier's arms and legs.

The soldier was just drawing back for another blow when it happened, and though he had one hand grasping firmly above the cut in the rope, he was not prepared for it to give way so suddenly. In a panic, he dropped the hatchet, flailing to get a hold of the metal sheathing which was now swinging back toward the wall. He managed to get some cursory grip with his second hand just before colliding with the wall.

"Pull him up!" Anthony shouted. Though he no doubt sounded desperate, he was encouraged. For the first time, he was starting to feel like they might survive this latest attack. That was when he glanced down the wall to see how the others were fairing, and his heart stopped.

There was daylight showing between the south and west walls. He did a double and triple take to ensure he was seeing clearly, but that's when the causeway lurched beneath his feet.

"No!" he cried. "This cannot be!" Though he was seeing it with his own eyes, he could not accept it. *Perhaps an errant catapult throw has simply broken that section away?* he thought desperately. Snatching up an arrow, he broke the fletching and head off and dropped it at his feet. It rolled unerringly toward the outside of the wall.

Almost as though the arrow had been the final weight to tip the scales, the wall lurched again, and this time there was no doubt that it had moved. Where there had been only a sliver of daylight a moment before, there was now at least a foot of space between the south and west walls.

Anthony spun back toward the north. There was an obvious crack there, too, where the causeway was no longer straight. Though the daylight was not yet showing through, the wall was flexing and bending in the middle as the animal teams continued to pull on the three remaining lines.

"Get those hooks loose!" he screamed, racing toward the next group of soldiers, who needed no urging. Every man on the wall had felt the movement beneath his feet and was scrambling in a panicked frenzy to pry, cut, or shoot the ropes loose before it was too late.

The wall gave another lurch and moved another foot outward.

"We have to give up the wall." The swarthy man who had cut the rope appeared at Anthony's elbow.

"We are not lost yet." Anthony continued to shout instructions at the soldiers.

"She will go at any moment!" The man's voice was urgent but did not carry the note of panic that marked all the shouted conversations across the rampart.

That got Anthony's attention, and he looked closer at the man. Stocky, swarthy, and middle-aged, there was little to distinguish him from any other soldier except that there was a seasoned look of competence about him. Anthony found himself wondering how he had not noticed this man before now.

"We need to evacuate the wall," the man said as the causeway lurched again.

But Anthony was not yet ready to surrender. He had spent weeks struggling desperately to keep these defenses intact, and if it fell now, it was all for naught. The battle for Dawning Court would no longer be a battle for possession of the castle but a wild, brutal, free-for-all battle of attrition, where everyone was a participant, and the outcome would only be determined by the last man standing. And in such a battle, Dawning Court would lose far more than anyone else because only Dawning Court had women and children on the field.

It was a wild, desperate impulse that gripped him, but he had nothing left to lose. Without another word, Anthony pushed past the soldiers, raced toward the nearest hook, and leapt off a crenel out into the air before grabbing onto the massive rope holding the hook in place, exactly as he had seen the swarthy soldier do.

"Are you mad?" someone cried, but he ignored it. He pushed aside the terror of hanging on a rope that might come loose at any moment and did exactly as the soldier had. He wrapped his legs around the rope, held onto the armored sheathing with one hand, and used his dagger to hack at the fibers.

The wall lurched again, and panic threatened to overcome him as the line swayed. The wall was now at least a yard away from the adjacent southern wall and offering less and less resistance to each pull on the ropes. The soldiers started to flee like rats abandoning a sinking ship.

Anthony cursed in frustration but focused on the task at hand. He cut all but the last of the fibers, sheathed his dagger, and started to climb the ten feet back up the wall.

The horse teams gave another pull, and the rope he was on snapped. Anthony clung to the metal sheathing as it swung back toward the wall. His back slammed into the stone harder than he had expected, and unable to keep his grip on the smooth, metal sheathing, he slipped.

Unlike the soldier whose leather armor offered some grip when he hugged the rope, Anthony's metal cuirass not only offered no resistance to sliding, but the extra weight made it even harder to hang on.

Anthony reached the end of the metal sheathing and was just able to snag the dangling end of bare rope to keep from plummeting to his death far below.

He had arrested his fall, but there was no way he was going to be able to climb back up. He glanced furiously around for another option, maybe some way he could climb the stones themselves. But even as he did so, the entire wall heaved forward even farther.

Anthony was now hanging at an angle from the battlements so that, instead of resting against the wall, he was dangling at least five feet from it, which gave him a good indication of exactly how far out of plumb the wall now was. At any moment, the fortification would no longer be able to hold its own weight, and the entire section would collapse, taking him and anyone else foolish enough to have remained with it.

From this unique vantage point, however, Anthony could clearly see the jagged crack that ran from the causeway near the center of the wall, where the first hook had torn loose, toward the ground where it tapered to a point near the southwest corner. The wall was lost. He could see that clearly now.

Why did I jump out here? he wondered, particularly when he knew better than anyone that the castle was lost and saving the wall was ultimately a meaningless gesture? *Was I trying to prove that it had all meant something? Or have I just come to value my life so little that I simply did not care?*

Another jolt through the rope almost tore the fibers from his fatigued and cramping fingers. He turned to look at the south wall as a reference, expecting to see that he was toppling inexorably outward. It took him a moment to realize that he was not falling but rising. Even as the wall lurched and shuddered toward its demise, Anthony was being lifted toward the causeway.

When he was close enough, he reached up and took hold of a merlon. The wall bucked again, causing him to struggle, but he was shortly hauled up onto the inside of the merlon, which was now tilted enough to form a V-shape with the causeway. The wall was deserted save for Rylan and the swarthy soldier who had appeared out of nowhere like a rescuing angel.

"We must go now!" he barked, shoving Anthony toward the north. "Run!"

Anthony did not argue. The three ran as fast as the tilting and bucking walkway would allow, struggling to find firm footing in the trough created by the tilting stoneworks.

They were forty yards shy of the northwest tower when the southern half of the west wall finally gave way. The three men did not see it peel away from the rest of the fortifications, but they knew from the weightless sensation they suddenly felt in the ground beneath their feet that it was coming down.

Anthony sprinted with renewed energy to get clear of it before it was too late, diving headlong to clear the last ten feet and reach the north side.

He landed hard but turned back just in time to see the final collapse. Everything moved in slow motion as the wall split in half. The northern-most side sagged outward and remained standing eight feet out of plumb, but the southern half of the wall toppled completely. Many tons of stone crashed to the earth, plowing up the saturated soil around the base as the thirty-foot-deep foundation tore from beneath the cobbles and lawn of the courtyard, displacing mountains of soil, smashing equipment, and hurling aside any who had been unable to get clear in time.

Anthony and his two rescuers stared in disbelief at the mayhem that ensued.

Thomas watched the west wall break in half and collapse with a mixture of foreboding and disbelief. Part of him could not accept that the impregnable Dawning fortress had at last been completely compromised. He had, of course, known that this was the plan, but for his entire life Dawning Castle's defenses had been a fixture, a permanent security blanket against the outside world. And he had always imagined that they would continue to serve the same purpose for him when he was baron. Now that the wall had fallen, he was not sure what to do next.

He was very clever, of course, able to think on the fly and snatch victory—or at least survival—from the jaws of defeat over and over, but he really did not have a plan now. He stood strangely mute while the dust settled, waiting to see what would happen, trusting that his instinct for survival would see him through if an army of peasant-soldiers came pouring through the breach, or the Mayfield-Saracen army raced around from the south to capitalize on the new vulnerability.

He was torn from his reverie when one of the guards who had been posted to warn them if the army to the south got wind of their movements came bursting out of the trees. Thomas was certain he knew what to expect. The guard was going to announce that everyone had seen or heard the wall collapse, and they were all charging this way; but what the guard actually said took him completely by surprise.

"Aden is here! He has attacked the Mayfields and Saracens!"

"That must be why no one answered the breach," Hildebrant said.

Hans and Hildebrant began to argue over their next move, but Thomas' thoughts were elsewhere. If Aden had arrived, then Thomas really was out of time. Just like the collapse of the wall, though he had known it was coming, he had not wanted to accept that it was really here, as it brought with it the end of all his plans.

Thomas stole up to the breach to peer into the courtyard. The wall had broken in a lopsided V-shape from the top center toward the bottom right, leaving a rough break about thirty feet wide where anyone could pass through, though parts of it would require leaping or climbing foundation stones that were still intact.

Thomas was surprised to see that not only were the people in the courtyard not preparing a defense, but they were actively fleeing from the wall, evidently expecting enemy soldiers to rush in upon them.

He hesitated. If Aden had arrived, then that meant that Collin would not be far behind. The prudent thing for him personally would be to run while he still could and begin recruiting a new army while the Mayfields, Dawnings, and Braddocks all tore each other apart. With any luck, he could return and fall upon the weakened victor before they had a chance to rebuild.

But Thomas was reluctant to leave. Being this close to the overthrow of Dawning Castle and knowing that it was not he who would sit on the baron's seat left him with a profound sadness. He had destroyed the world as he had known it, ruined it beyond repair, with the promise that a better one would emerge. But now that dream had been dashed, at least for the time being, and it was going to take tremendous effort to remount another attack. He was no longer just one battle away from having Dawning Court within his grasp, and he was tired.

Thomas still held the dream of being Dawning Court's next great warrior baron, with Leah on one arm and Anisa on the other, each woman representing the subjugation of their respective people: Leah, the delicate beauty of the Norman aristocracy; and Anisa, the exotic, savage beauty of the heathens. Those women not only represented his superiority over both—a feat that not even his father had achieved—but each represented a deep longing for what he had been denied by never being taken seriously as Braden Dawning's son. He wanted to possess what all other men longed for; what they lusted after!

He was not sure what had become of Leah, but he knew that Anisa and Martha were at that very moment inside the castle, where panic was certainly causing the same mayhem as was ensuing here in the courtyard. Thomas smiled grimly. If he were in the castle now, he could have his way with anyone—do anything—and there would be no one to deny him.

That's when an idea seized him. Why couldn't he do exactly that? It would take hours or even days for the armies to destroy each other. Why couldn't he salvage something for himself from this disaster?

Almost before he knew he had decided, he jumped through the break in the wall and pushed his way into the retreating peasants. Much to his surprise, he was not challenged on any hand. Whether it was fear of his menacing countenance or the Dawning crests on his armor that afforded him smooth passage he did not know, but not a single person even bothered to ask who he was or what he was about.

Upon consideration, though, this was not entirely surprising given that most of them were not even armed. He could have laid waste to dozens of these sheep before they even realized there was a wolf among them. But Thomas was not interested in fighting serfs. He was intent on getting into the castle before he was locked out.

He eschewed the main entrance into the Great Hall, as the odds of his being recognized there were too high. Instead, he turned for the postern near the kitchens.

"William, we are here!"

William slowly stirred in the seat of the carriage, where he had been dead to the world for the past several hours. He kept his eyes closed as sensations flooded him: the pain in his chest where Collin's lance had hit him, his ribs where he had crashed down, and his left arm that had been holding the shield that Collin's lance had torn from him. He realized as he reluctantly scanned his body that the many cuts and bruises barely even registered now due to the far more severe wounds that demanded his attention.

Other senses began to provide input then. He could feel the coarse fabric from a blanket that he could not recall having been draped over him; he could feel the chill air on his face. He could hear Neil in the seat beside him, the creak of the leather, and the snort of the horses. Birds sang nearby, and there was light behind his closed lids.

"Are you dead?" Neil asked, only half-joking, as he gave William a small shove to shake him awake.

"If I were dead, I would not hurt this much," William mumbled.

He pried his eyes open and sat up. It was indeed daylight, and he was relieved to see the Dawning flag still flying above the castle and a furious battle along the southern wall.

Salena rode beside them, but his soldiers were nowhere to be seen. "Silas?"

"You sent him and the others on ahead," Neil reminded him.

"Oh ... probably wise."

William threw off the blanket and gingerly climbed down from the carriage and carefully began to probe his many wounds and sore spots.

"You do not know that to be true, you know?" Neil said suddenly.

William looked at him, perplexed.

"Before. You suggested that in death, your pain will end. You do not know that death will relieve you of your pains."

"What?" William shook his head.

Neil shrugged, slightly embarrassed. "All I am saying is that everyone believes that death will relieve them of their troubles when it might do the very opposite; it could be that death curses you to live with all your pain and regrets while removing your ability to do anything about them."

William started to snap a flippant retort when it occurred to him that Neil was revealing something about himself. Though William could not guess what it might be, it was clear that this was something very close to Neil, the depths of which William did not have the time or energy to plumb just now.

"Er ... yes, well," he said awkwardly, making a show of checking his daggers, the only weapons he still carried. "I need to find a way into the castle; I do not think I could make the ascent in my current condition."

"Well, it appears that the Mayfields are taking care of that for you," Neil said, nodding toward the west wall that was even then beginning to separate from the battlements.

"We are out of time!" William murmured ominously before disappearing into the trees.

"Salena, I need your horse," Neil said, climbing down from the carriage and digging into a sack that had been at his feet.

"Can you ride?" Salena asked, speaking for the first time as she tore her gaze from William's retreating back and looked dubiously at Neil.

"If you will help me, I believe I can manage it." He set a sword aside and pulled out a cuirass and a gambeson he had gotten from Aden's camp.

Salena dismounted and helped Neil pull on the shirt of gambeson.

"It is too tight," she said, forcing it down over his stomach, trying to be mindful of his wound.

"That is rather the point," he said, picking up the cuirass and handing it to her. "The gambeson will keep pressure on my wound, and the cuirass will support that and hopefully serve as a replacement for my own stomach muscles, at least until this is all over.

"Are you certain about this?" she asked as she pulled the straps on the sides tight, an act she had done a hundred times for David.

"If we fail here, nothing else matters. All will be lost."

There was silence for several moments as Salena continued to adjust the cuirass; then she asked hesitantly, "Why did you say that? About death?"

Neil shrugged. "It is something I have come to believe." He hesitated and then continued, "After Ellen left me and took our infant daughter with her, I knew she was never coming back—knew that I probably deserved it—but I could not face a life of miserable solitude..."

"What did you do?" Salena asked, still focused on the straps of his armor, but Neil noted the intensity in her question. He did not like talking about this but thought that for her, particularly, this might be relevant.

"I had a rope around my neck, preparing to end it all, thinking that would free me from the calamity I had created of my life, when in that moment I had a vision. I thought I saw myself waking after the deed was done, free from my body, but every bit as haunted by the pain and misery I had created. Only now no one could see me, no one could hear me. I could travel the earth, still see those I cared about, watch them struggle. But now I had sacrificed any ability to right my wrongs, to repair any damage I had done. I was deprived of the means of finding peace, and that *truly* was hell."

"Do you believe that is what would happen?"

"I do not know, but I was not willing to take that chance. Though it is frightening and difficult, and I am terrible at it, I have decided that I would rather be here, trying to work out my salvation, than risk that eternal nightmare.... And say what you will about William, but he too is here, trying to put things right, when the easy choice would have been to run away."

Neil scooped up the reins of the horse. "Take the carriage, Salena, and get away from here. Go be with your daughter." With that, he gingerly mounted the horse and rode toward the castle.

Thirty-eight

Leah walked down the east wall, which was incongruously calm—still water in the maelstrom. She knew she should hurry back to the Great Hall as quickly as possible, as she would be sorely needed, which was why she had chosen to make her way back along this nearly deserted section of wall rather than fight her way through the packed courtyard. But now that she had a moment of peace, she could not bring herself to jump right back into the cacophony of horror, death, and grief just yet. She was unexpectedly isolated from it, even if only for an instant, and though it made it impossible to ignore how soul-sick she was, it felt wonderful not to have constant demands being made of her for a few moments.

A bracing wind blew over the wall, but rather than sheltering from it as she typically would, she inhaled deeply, breathed in the chill, and let it wash over her. All her senses tingled, and she realized that this was the first encounter she had had with the world beyond the castle since they had sealed themselves up against the siege.

It was strange to think that the world went on. People rose in the morning, worked, laughed, and ate, all without the slightest inkling that Eve was dead, William still lived, and Leah was in her own personal hell. How could the sun continue to rise and set, heedless of her suffering? How could she be expected to keep moving when all she wanted was for the whole world to stop and mourn with her? It did not seem right! It was all just another reminder that God was a presence in her life that she had always imagined but that appeared to her now to be just a fantasy. His divine hand may have set the machinery of the world in motion, but that machinery cared nothing for the people that were chewed up in its works.

Leah found herself ambling rather than running along the battlements, struck by the incongruity of the scene. If she looked to her right, all was chaos, death, and fear—a perfect metaphor for her inner state. But to her left, all seemed peaceful, almost idyllic, with very little sign that anything had changed, a representation of the pacific bliss of her life before it had all been torn apart forever.

She could almost see Eve laughing and running along the trails as a child, playing with the blissful naiveté of innocence. But Leah knew then that, even if she could somehow step back into that world, she no longer had a place there. Like trying to put on a dress from when she was a child, it no longer fit her. She had seen too much, done too much, changed too much to ever fit into that world again. *Will I ever feel joy again?* she wondered idly as she neared the south wall.

She stopped as the southern ramparts came into view. She had not been up here since the siege began and was shocked to see them so battered and pitted. She thought that the tattered remnants of the once proud stonework were a fitting metaphor for the people the walls protected. Only a few weeks prior, the Dawnings had stood proud, even in their declining power. The Dawning subjects had basked in the perceived invulnerability of the family, just as they had sheltered behind these walls for the same reason.

Are we all now doomed? Was trusting these ancient ramparts to protect them as disastrous a blunder as trusting the Dawnings had been?

She turned toward the stairs to descend to the courtyard as her sense of duty drew her back to the moment and dispersed the clouds of nostalgia that had provided a few precious minutes of respite from reality. She had known it could not last but wished that it would linger a bit longer. It had been the closest she had felt to peace since this nightmare had started.

Leah paused at the southeast tower. From here she could see the battles raging on both sides of the gate. Outside the wall especially, all was chaos, but there were Dawning soldiers contending with the enemy. *My father has arrived!* she realized with a flash of excitement. She started down toward the courtyard with a renewed sense of purpose that lasted for about sixty seconds.

She had descended halfway and was just stepping onto the landing that separated the two flights of stairs when she froze. She was looking straight across the courtyard at the west wall. Something about it did not look right. *Is it ... tilted?*

Before she could identify exactly what it was, the great wall shivered and bent and then broke apart like a stack of a child's building blocks. Half of the wall tore away from the rest, and in one ponderous motion, hundreds of tons of stone and mortar went tumbling to the ground with a rumbling, cracking sound like a great thunderclap that shook the causeway beneath her feet.

A great dust cloud rose up from the collapse, temporarily obscuring her view, but Leah did not move as she waited for the air to clear enough to get a second look. Though she had just seen the catastrophe with her own eyes, her brain would not accept it; it just could not be real.

She watched as the tide of peasants in the courtyard, who had been fleeing the battle in all directions, abruptly changed course and began to run from the collapse.

It was then that she remembered that Anthony had been intent on defending that wall. *Did he get clear in time?*

As the dust settled, a new horror appeared. There, standing in the breach looking into the courtyard, was Thomas. From this distance it was only his distinct shape that identified him, but she knew, without knowing how she knew, that it was him.

She stared in disbelief as Thomas surveyed the courtyard and then jumped down and disappeared into the frantic crowd. She looked to see what it was that had drawn his attention and spotted Martha, encircled by a group of watchmen, making a controlled withdrawal toward the castle. *Thomas could only be intended for her!*

Hiking up her skirt, Leah moved to intercept, descending as quickly as she dared and plunging into the chaos.

"Move aside!" she cried as she attempted to push and weave her way through the peasants. But there was no rhyme or reason to their patterns of movement, and since she could not anticipate them, she was constantly being impeded or forced to stop short to avoid colliding with people who stepped in front of her without warning.

I will never catch him in this muddle! She considered calling out that Thomas Dawning was in their midst, but even if she did manage to make them realize what danger they were in, all it would likely do is cause further panic, which would work against her.

So she reluctantly continued to push her way across the courtyard until she reached the upper bailey, where she was able to spot Martha's entourage nearing the main door to the Great Hall; but they were momentarily stopped by the press of people attempting to get into the castle. *They are going to seal it up!* Leah realized with sickening certainty. That was the only logical move with the walls compromised. For just a moment, she exulted that if the castle were sealed, then Martha would be safe; but just as quickly, her excitement waned. If Thomas got into the castle, she would be trapped inside with nowhere to run.

Leah continued to push through the crowd, but Martha's entourage was still twenty yards ahead and nearing the doors. She elbowed and clawed her way forward, but the press was too tight. For every two steps forward she managed, she was shoved back one.

I am not going to reach her in time! Leah panicked. "Lady Dawning! Lady Dawning!" she cried, but there was so much noise, so many voices begging and pleading for entrance, that Martha was never going to pick Leah's out of the cacophony.

Then Leah recognized one member of Martha's entourage. "Sebastian!" she cried. "Sebastian, wait!"

Sebastian was between Martha and Leah, pushing people back, trying to keep the area immediately around Martha clear. His eyes began to swivel across the crowd.

Was that because he heard me? She didn't know, but she redoubled her effort. "Sebastian! It is me, Leah! Please wait for me!"

Martha's group was entering the castle now. Only Sebastian and the two men beside him had yet to cross the threshold as they continued to shove the desperate mob away from the doors.

Leah dropped her head and made one last frantic push forward. "Sebastian! Wait for me! It is Leah!" She hated feeling helpless, hated begging for help, but that did not keep her from doing what was necessary.

She was nearing the front of the crowd when she was struck between the shoulder blades. She stumbled forward and fell, landing on all fours on the cobbled landing before the doors, the breath knocked from her. "Sebastian," she gasped at the ground beneath her face. "Please ... help ..."

She heard the doors scrape on the floor as they were being pushed closed, but she was being tromped on now; her entire attention was devoted to pulling herself up before she was trampled to death.

She clung to a large, sweaty man's vest and tried to regain her feet, but was again slammed to the ground amidst the crowd's last fraught surge.

It is too late!

Then she felt the area around her clear, and strong hands seized her by the arms and dragged her across the threshold, where she was unceremoniously dumped on the floor of the Great Hall, even while the watchmen forced closed the heavy doors and barred it with a giant oak crossmember.

"Lady, are you hurt?" Sebastian asked, helping Leah to her feet. She smiled fondly at the elderly man, who had been letting her into the castle since she was tiny. He looked sweaty and disheveled but unharmed.

"I—I am uninjured," she said after a moment. "I trust I have you to thank for my rescue from that mob?"

Sebastian looked embarrassed. "When I went to close the doors, I saw you lying on the ground. That's probably what saved you. Had you still been on your feet, I doubt I would have recognized you among the other faces."

"Leah?" Martha asked in surprise. "What has happened? Why were you in the courtyard?"

Leah was not sure how to respond. Was Martha referring to the fact that Leah should have already been in the completely packed Great Hall helping the wounded, or was she asking why Anthony had not removed her? Leah did not know how to explain, so she did not try.

"Lady Dawning, I was attempting to warn you."

"And what is it that I must know now, at this moment, Leah?" Martha demanded angrily. "That an enemy army is in our gates? That our defenses have collapsed? What is it that cannot wait?"

Just then something heavy hit the doors of the Great Hall, and a great commotion rose among those sheltering inside. Sebastian turned to take control of the situation, but Leah snatched his arm and held him fast while she spoke to the matriarch. "Lady Dawning, Thomas is near!"

Sebastian held up a hand to stop her. "Not here," he said, nodding at the press of people who could not help overhearing what Leah was about to say. "Follow me."

He pushed his way to the door leading to the interior of the castle, but the passage was not much clearer than the Great Hall, so he continued down the hallway until he came to the empty platform above the postern door.

"Speak quickly!" Sebastian said as he positioned himself between the women and the passage like a guard.

"Now," Martha started in, all business as usual, "what do you mean when you say that Thomas is near?"

"I mean," Leah said urgently, "that he is here! He was right behind you in the courtyard. If he is not in the castle now, he soon will be."

Martha took a deep breath and let it out slowly. "Very well, where can we go?" She looked at the passage full of anxious people. "No one would even notice Thomas in this fracas. He could move undetected."

Just then, the postern door in the alcove below them made a loud crashing sound. They looked over the rail to see that someone was trying to force open the door while those inside were struggling to close it enough to put the bar in place.

"Bar that door!" Leah ordered, a sudden sense of foreboding seizing her.

The watchmen were just raising the heavy wooden crossbeam to drop into place when it was violently shoved inward. The door bounced off the men holding the timber and slammed shut again. Unfortunately, it sent them staggering back, so there was no one holding the door closed.

Leah's knuckles turned white on the rail as she stared at the unguarded door.

"Block that entrance!" Sebastian cried. The two closest watchmen threw themselves against the portal, but they were too late. Another blow sent both guards sprawling as a hulking figure forced his way into the alcove.

Now it was Martha who did not move. It took her several moments to reconcile the form that was thrashing the aging watchmen like ragdolls with the image of her son.

It was only when he dropped the last man who did not have sense enough to flee and turned his face toward her that it sank in. Thomas' eyes shone in the low light, and there was a crazed look on his face that struck fear into her heart. Though she had been told Thomas was a traitor, seeing that her own son was here to kill her severely shocked her.

"We must go now," Leah said, pulling Martha's still stunned form back from the railing.

Thirty-nine

George Mayfield's men were vastly outnumbered and trapped against the closed gate where he and Mary were sheltering in the archway. They were trapped, but in truth, it was the safest place to be at that moment. In that one spot, he was neither exposed to attacks from above nor to attacks from the courtyard. And the cries of the Dawning soldiers on the battlements shortly after negotiations with Martha fell apart informed him of the arrival of Aden's army outside the gates.

Had the peasantry within the gates been organized or even armed, they would have easily overwhelmed the Mayfields. But the panic-stricken, disorganized rabble were more interested in fleeing than in fighting. Nevertheless, there were enough of them throwing stones or whatever was at hand that George did not dare break the shield circle around him and Mary.

"What is happening?" Mary cried.

"We are trapped!" George almost screamed at her. "And Aden's army has arrived!"

George continued to shout orders at his men regarding weak points in their line or warning them of impending attacks in an attempt to maintain the illusion that he was in control; but he knew that this defensive action would only last until someone did organize a coordinated attack.

"We cannot open it from here!" one of the men yelled back from where they had been trying to use the space between the cobbles and the portcullis created by Amir's crushed animal to lever it up enough to escape; but the metal grating would not budge.

George looked down the length of the courtyard. They probably could move as a protective unit to the stairs that mounted the battlements, probably fight their way to the top, and maybe even take the barbican and open the portcullis. The problem was that in allowing access to his army, he would also be opening the defenses to Aden's men. Was he better off here inside the wall with a large but disorganized peasant-army to contend with or opening the gate and possibly having enemy soldiers rush in upon him?

"What are we to do?" a panic-stricken Mary demanded as her horse wheeled in nervous circles beside him.

"Be still and let me think!" George snapped. He silently cursed Aden. Why did that man have to show up now, at this precise moment? Another half-hour and they would have taken possession of the castle! Then they could have easily repelled him.

George was not entirely sure what drew his attention to the west wall. Maybe it was the huge mass of stone slowly shifting, or maybe it was the cries of the peasants who had been sheltering at its base; but whatever it was, George's jaw dropped as he watched it slowly topple outward.

He was dimly aware that all fighting in the courtyard had ceased while the combatants stared in awe as the larger-than-life structure slowly tipped over. It was like watching a mountain get swallowed by the sea. One moment the mountain seemed so big and permanent that it could never be displaced, and the next it was gone.

But it was not the spectacle that made George temporarily forget everything else; it was the question of who would come through the breach. Neither his army nor Amir's had done this thing, as they well understood that Dawning Court's defenses were an essential element of their plan. They were counting on these very walls to break the backbone of Collin's army.

"What is happening?" Mary demanded in a shrill voice.

"Quiet, woman!" George barked at her without taking his eyes off the breach. Whoever emerged would turn the tide of the battle one way or the other.

Every eye in the courtyard waited for the dust to settle. But as the rumblings of the collapsing wall settled into silence, no one appeared. No army came pouring in upon them. It was almost as though the wall had collapsed from natural causes, and no one, either inside the wall or out, was poised to take advantage of it.

As such, when the shock of the moment wore off, the battle for the castle resumed as before, except that now even more peasants were attempting to flee the courtyard, retreating toward the northeast side of the castle as fast as they could manage.

"They are fleeing!" Mary's relief was evident. "Drive for the breach!" she ordered their personal guard, but George overruled her.

"No!" he shouted. "Out there only death awaits us at the hands of Aden and Collin. Our only chance is to take the castle while it is undefended. Drive for it! Now, men! Go!"

The castle was the last defensible position, and in this moment of blind panic, they did not have any real opposition. This was their best chance.

George leapt out into the open in his excitement, kicking one peasant aside and skewering another without so much as a single parry to slow him down. *Yes, this is going to be easy!* he thought with mounting excitement. Only a moment before, they had been trapped on the verge of destruction, but now they were going to change the tide of the battle.

He and his men cut their way almost entirely across the courtyard, slowed more by the mass of people than by any real resistance being offered by the panicking, screaming rabble.

George felt like he was in his prime again. In his mind he was back riding with Braden in the Crusades as they decimated city after city. He was invigorated by the certainty of victory. Nothing would stand in his way now!

Forty

The dust from the wall had not yet settled when Hans' moment of victory was shattered by the report that Aden's army had arrived on the field. Hans' heart sank. He had finally broken down the castle's impregnable defenses, only to hand the victory over to another. The best he could hope for now was that his efforts were enough to preserve him from Collin's wrath; but he could not be certain of that. Collin might simply count it a meaningless gesture, believing that he could have easily taken the castle himself, whether or not the wall stood. His brother would never know nor care what Hans had endured to grind the defenders down to this. All he would see is that Hans had been unable to prevail against a simple peasant army.

Hans was surprised that no one had yet come through it. Even after Thomas had disappeared through the opening, no peasant-soldiers had answered back.

He cautiously moved up to the break and peered into the courtyard, half-expecting to see Thomas being torn limb from limb; but there was no sign of him. The peasants inside were still giving the area a wide berth but otherwise seemed to be swarming in frantic but aimless waves away from the nearest threat.

Hans spotted the Mayfields with a small force trying to cut their way across the courtyard. They were making progress with shocking ease given the number of people they had to ride over to do it. Nobody was even trying to resist them. It looked as though their small force of soldiers would shortly force their way to the castle, and maybe, if the castle had not been sealed up properly, take control of it.

If the Mayfields get control of the castle before Collin arrives ... The thought turned to ice in Collin's stomach.

"Sir Hildebrant," Hans turned back suddenly, "prepare the men to attack!"

"Attack?!" Hildebrant was incredulous. "This was never about mounting an attack; this was about preventing our enemies from sheltering behind the walls. We have done that. We need only wait upon Lord Collin."

"I have no doubt but that Collin will arrive at any moment to reinforce us," Hans agreed. "But if those mercenaries take the castle before then, our triumph here will account for little in Collin's eyes. We must stall them."

"We have not the men to mount an attack!"

"We are nearly ten score! That is double the number that guard the treacherous Mayfields in the courtyard. We can stop them, and who is to say but that in this pandemonium we might even take the castle!"

Hildebrant glanced back at the exhausted men behind him and then at the Mayfields, who had already mounted the upper ward and were moving swiftly toward the castle. "Very well," he reluctantly agreed, "we will attack."

Forty-one

He is burned badly." A woman's voice broke through the black.

Amir felt himself swaying gently as if on a boat.

"He fell from the wall," the same woman explained, though who she might be talking about, he could not imagine. "He must have lost his senses when he caught fire."

"Fell from the wall?" a second woman asked incredulously. "And he is still alive?"

Something was beginning to encroach on the peaceful darkness that swathed Amir. He tried to nestle back into the safety of the black, but the voices continued to impose themselves on his consciousness.

"He became entangled in the protective canopy erected in the courtyard. It must have slowed his fall."

"Set him here."

Amir felt himself rise as if on a swell of water and then drop back down onto something hard. There was a loud clunk of something metal hitting the wood of the table. "Sword?" the first woman asked curtly. "Get rid of it!"

The protective veil of darkness began to lighten. He heard metal clatter against the stone floor. He knew there was something about that sound which should concern him, but all he was aware of was a dim sense of dread. He could not lose that blanket of oblivion.

He felt hands moving around his clothing and struggled not to let himself be drawn out of the dark. Someone started to remove his tunic, and it felt as though his flesh were being peeled from his body. The dam of oblivion burst, and in an instant, Amir was awash in agony, a terrible, unquenchable searing of his flesh. He heard someone screaming and lurched to his feet before realizing that the scream was his.

He clutched the table he had been lying on and looked around wildly, like a cornered animal desperate to escape a pack of hunters. He was in a large, vaulted hall that was packed with peasants. Several drawn, haggard women in blood-covered aprons stared at him in astonishment. Around the perimeter of the room were makeshift cots stacked with wounded and dying. Beside two great double doors lay a pile of bodies awaiting removal.

He finally realized that he was inside Dawning Castle. Someone had brought him here, presumably thinking him a wounded defender.

Then the next wave of pain hit. There was no way to describe the feeling of every nerve ending over half of his body shrieking at once. It doubled him over, overwhelming his senses and pushing him close to madness as the fever in his brain screamed that he must do something—anything—to quench the fire.

He collapsed onto the table again, remembering that he had hurled himself from the battlements in a desperate attempt to free himself from this, but clearly that had not worked; and here he was against all odds, alive and feeling every iota of the burn.

Allah is punishing me for my failures! That was the only explanation.

"Remain still," a rather plain blonde woman said with an authority that was not reinforced by her overwrought, drawn countenance. "We must salve your burns if we are to stop the pain." Then speaking to someone nearby she said, "We will need more of this. It is at least half of his body."

She then began to spread a cream onto his skin, and Amir did not resist. In that instant, he did not care if she were ministering to him or poisoning him. The result of either had to be better than this.

The salve had a cooling effect. Though it did not remove the pain, it felt like being dipped into a frigid river. Amir's wave of agony momentarily diminished, allowing him to think about something beyond his immediate misery.

He remembered his herbal mixture then. He had carried it with him into battle, knowing that the camp would be overrun by the Mayfields; it was too valuable to risk losing. He reached his unburned right hand down to feel for the pouch at his belt. It was still there and intact! *Perhaps Allah is yet watching over me.*

There was another commotion nearby, but given the chaos in the room already, it was not enough to distract Amir from his own plight. He did not even bother looking up until someone exclaimed, "Lady Dawning!"

He froze. Was she here for him? He was unarmed and extremely vulnerable and had just revealed to her that he planned to murder her at the first opportunity. Amir raised his head ever so slowly so as not to draw attention to himself, but she was not even looking around. Instead, she was being led from the room by a lady and a frail steward.

A steward! Allah *had* delivered her to him! She was only thirty feet away and completely unprotected. He had to act now!

Amir pushed himself off the table once again, but before he had made it three steps, he was hit with the next wave of pain. He gasped and fell back against a support column to wait for the burning to subside.

"You must let me treat those burns," the blonde woman scolded him.

"Water," he gasped through teeth grinding in pain, but the woman only stared blankly at him.

"Water!" he roared. He pushed himself away from the wall in defiance of the agony and shoved the blonde woman aside to reach the basin behind her.

He fell against the pedestal that held the large bowl and found himself looking down into the water where the surgeons had been washing the blood from their hands between patients. It was a thick red color with things floating in it, but Amir did not care; he could not stand this anguish one moment longer.

He worked open the pouch with trembling fingers and upended it into the bloody water. There was enough of the mixture for a dozen men. It was dangerous to take that much, but nothing beyond controlling the pain enough to chase after Martha mattered in that moment.

He took the basin in his arms and gulped down the red sludge. He was not sure how much of the gelatinous mass was his herbals and how much was other organic matter, but he swallowed as much as his stomach would hold before it threatened to come back up.

Ignoring the shocked and revolted faces of the onlookers, he dropped the basin and stooped to retrieve William's sword from where it had been dropped beneath the table and then staggered into the passage after Martha.

Anisa watched in astonishment the discarded washbowl crash to the floor and Amir lumber across the room and into the castle. Alone in a fortress full of enemies after Najid and Lindsay had died, she had been using the commotion as a chance to escape undetected. She had made her way to the Great Hall and was slowly working her way through the room toward the double doors, pretending to be part of the medical staff so as to go unnoticed, when she saw them carry in her brother.

Between his light skin and extensive burns, the others had not realized that Amir was a Saracen, but to anyone who knew him, there was no mistaking his giant frame.

Instead of fleeing as planned, Anisa busied herself around the perimeter of the room while watching for a chance to get close to him.

Before she had been able to do that, though, Martha Dawning had come in with Leah, either of whom she feared might recognize her; so she had retreated into the corner by the pile of corpses, one of the few places that was not filled with peasants.

She watched in dismay as Amir drank down that vile slurry and then rushed after Martha. Anisa hated to go back into the castle when she was almost free of it, but if Amir was intent on finishing the matron that Anisa had failed to eliminate, she was not going to miss that.

Forty-two

"Lady Dawning, you must hurry!" Leah urged the matriarch down the passage, but she still seemed stunned, moving mechanically as though she were not even aware of the urgency.

"Thomas will be upon us at any moment," Sebastian added, looking nervously back over his shoulder.

Leah found herself doing the same; she could not help it. They were both acutely aware that Thomas would soon appear, and when he did, he would spot them at once. Even with all the people milling around, Sebastian, standing a head taller than most everyone else, was immediately recognizable in his steward's garb. "We will never lose him at this rate."

"In here!" Sebastian pulled open the door to the chapel and hustled the two women through it.

"Sebastian, please," Leah pleaded as he gently but quickly pushed her in after Martha, "not here."

The chapel, too, was relatively full, though not so much as the other rooms. Shafts of light from the arrow slits high overhead dimly illuminated the room. The pews were still in disarray from where she and Eve had fought with William, though they had all been put upright again. The by-altar had been picked up and the candles swept into a pile in the same alcove where people, facing the imminent possibility of death, had begun to replace them one by one as they lit them in prayer.

Leah would not let herself look at the corner where the curtain divided the knave from the alcove with the stairs leading up to the bell tower. She tried not to think about the bloodstain that would certainly still be there, sticky and dark with that distinct metallic odor permeating the air.

She suddenly felt weak in the knees and found a lump in her throat that made it hard to swallow. "I cannot breathe," she gasped.

"Milady, I understand, but we have no time. I will lead Thomas away, and then you and Lady Dawning will climb to the upper floors. They are still empty, and you will be able to secrete yourselves there."

Leah desperately wanted to argue, wanted to yank back on the door that Sebastian was pulling shut, but she knew that to do so was to jeopardize all of their lives.

The door closed with an audible thud, and Leah leaned her head against it. She felt like a prisoner being locked in a dungeon. All the pain and devastation of her last visit here was rushing back in, depriving her of her anger and leaving in its place an overwhelming grief. She could not have that! She needed to be angry, needed the strength it gave her, needed it when she met William again. If she could not hold onto it, then she and Eve would fade into oblivion with the rest of the Dawning legacy, and William would never be made to pay for what he had done!

Leah could not tell if she was nearer to screaming and breaking something or bursting into tears, but one thing was certain: the last thing in the world she wanted to do was sit here, helpless and alone with her thoughts.

She reluctantly turned back to Martha. The matron looked less shocked than she had a few minutes before; her glassy-eyed expression had been replaced by one of deep sadness. Leah thought that was progress, but she still looked more tired and frail than ever before; she would not be much help if Thomas did find them.

Leah looked at the other occupants of the chapel. There were only about a dozen, mostly women, all elderly. Some were in the pews, a couple more were at the by-altar. A few had looked up when Leah and Martha had entered, but seeing nothing of interest, the worshipers had returned to their prayers.

Leah felt very unsafe. There were not enough people to hide them, and none of them would pose any obstacle for Thomas.

Then her eyes settled on the curtain, and all at once she knew what they needed to do. She recoiled at the thought; she could not even contemplate returning to the scene of Eve's murder, but she also knew that she had no choice. As it was, if Thomas even glanced in this room, he could not miss them.

Before she could think too much about it, Leah took Martha by the arm and pulled her toward the front of the chapel via the far side of the knave, opposite the by-altar, hoping to attract as little notice as possible.

"Leah," Martha protested, "you must not go back there. It is too soon."

"It is the only place to hide in here," Leah whispered back.

She approached the black curtain with a growing sense of dread, finally stopping involuntarily in front of it. Beyond that thin shroud lay death and despair. It was like facing the veil of death, unsure of exactly what she might find or how she might react to it. But she knew that every second of delay endangered their lives, so she took a deep breath and pushed through into the dark antechamber beyond.

It was mercifully dark. She could see the silhouette of the rotting staircase where the fight with Lindsay and William that had led to Eve's death had taken place, but she could not see the pool of Eve's blood left on the floor after she fell, as the entire floor was just a black mass of shadow.

"The staircase is dangerous," Leah said, trying to focus on the problem at hand, "but if we should be discovered, we may have to flee the way William did."

Martha stopped her inspection of the alcove and looked at Leah. "What do you mean, the way William did?"

Leah silently cursed herself for her slip. She did not want to deal with this now, but maybe it was just as well that Martha heard it from her. There was no telling when they would see him again or what Thomas might say to her if he found them.

"Forgive me for being the one to tell you this, now of all times, but it is probably better that you know now." Leah took a deep breath. "I recognized the assassin who was lying in wait for you in the chapel."

"Oh?" Martha seemed to brace herself for what was to come.

"It was William!" Leah cried as if the force of will it took to say it aloud was like a dam bursting. "It was William who was waiting for you. It was he who killed Eve!"

Martha's face did not change, but she froze in place, giving no indication that she had heard Leah at all except that she seemed to shrink with age right before Leah's eyes.

"Lady?" Leah said tentatively after a moment.

"If that is true," Martha muttered quietly, "then all my sons are dead to me."

Leah was still trying to think what to say when she heard the chapel door across the room bang open. She carefully peeked through the curtain, and there he was, looking just as dangerous as before, only now Thomas wore an angry scowl on his face.

Did he know about this alcove?

Thomas scanned the room, his eyes passing over the faces in the knave. He then turned and moved on, evidently intent upon not losing sight of Sebastian.

Leah gave a shudder. Had they delayed even a few seconds longer, Thomas would have found them.

"What is it?" Martha asked, looking over her shoulder just as another figure passed by the door that Thomas had left open. This figure was huge, at least a head and shoulders taller than other men, and Martha gasped at the sight. "He is here!"

"Who?" Leah turned to her as Martha stepped back as though reeling. "Who is here?"

"Amir," Martha said in disbelief.

It took Leah a moment to make the connection. "The Moor giant?" She automatically turned for a second look, though she knew that he had already moved on. Leah felt her jaw tightening in anger. "Of course all the rats would converge to feast on the dying carcass of the falling barony," she muttered to herself. "Now we just need William, and we will have a quorum."

"What was that?" Martha asked absently.

"Never mind," Leah dismissed it. "We cannot stay here. We must move before it is too late."

Then, as if to confirm her fears, the door was pushed wide, and a hooded figure stepped into the chapel and scanned the faces just as Thomas had done. Leah's heart stopped. It was William! And unlike Thomas, there was no question that he knew about this alcove.

His gaze moved over the faces of the people and then fixed upon the drapery from which Leah was peeking.

Reflexively she jumped back, only realizing her mistake a moment too late as she watched the curtain flutter back into place. The sick feeling in her stomach told her that she had just confirmed to William that there was indeed someone back here.

"What is it?" Martha asked, starting for the curtain to see for herself until Leah grabbed her arm.

"He is here!" Leah hissed.

"Thomas?"

"William!" She had not seen his face, but Leah would never forget what he looked like coming down those stairs to murder Eve. And there was no doubt in her mind that the figure moving up the aisle toward them now was the same person with the same murderous intent!

Leah looked to the stairs for a possible means of escape but changed her mind. Besides being extraordinarily dangerous for an elderly woman, there was no way Martha could climb it fast enough to stay ahead of William.

Instead, Leah frantically searched for something with which to defend herself. She snatched up a chunk of wood about the length of her arm that had fallen from the staircase and swung it experimentally. It felt solid and reassuring in her hand.

"Lady Dawning," Leah whispered, "climb the stairs to the landing. I will wait for him here." Leah put her back against the wall beside the curtain, while Martha, without seeming to comprehend exactly what was happening, climbed up the first creaky steps of the staircase.

She looked back to inquire if it was wise to trust the structure when William came through the curtain.

The ruse worked. William's eyes were immediately drawn to Martha on the stairs and did not even see Leah until the board in her hand was connecting with his head.

He crumpled to the floor, his arms going to his head, while the knife he was carrying clattered on the ground.

Leah did not wait. She had gotten the jump on this dangerous man, and she needed to capitalize on it. She conjured all the anger, fear, and betrayal and raised the board overhead to deliver a blow intended to dash out his brains onto the very floor where Eve had bled out her life. *How fitting!*

But just then, William turned his face up to her; it was not William at all but a woman.

Leah was so stunned, her killing stroke never fell. She had been so sure that it was William, so sure that she was doing the right thing; but now she did not know what to make of it. Was there some mistake?

Martha's voice brought her back to herself. "So, we meet at last," Martha said, having regained some of her customary composure. She stooped to pick up the knife. "Have you a name?"

Leah kept the cudgel cocked in both hands as the woman got slowly to her feet. Leah could see that she was unusually tall for a woman but still wondered that she could have failed to recognize the slender physique or the narrow shoulders that marked her as female.

The woman reached up and pulled back her hood to reveal the angular features and dark skin of a Moor woman.

"You may call me Anisa." She wore a triumphant expression as she performed a slight bow, but her face fell when it was clear that neither woman recognized her. "You do not know my face, perhaps," she said, recovering quickly, "but you are very familiar with my work." She purred the last out in a voice that dripped with self-satisfaction. "It was I who gave John the courage to claim the birthright that was rightfully his. And when the Dawning blood curdled in his veins, I watched with pleasure as Amir ran him through with the blade of one of your own knights."

Leah looked at Martha to see if the matron shared her shock, but Martha's face had returned to her customary unflappable mask.

"It was I who then persuaded Lindsay to avenge his death," Anisa continued, apparently determined to get a reaction. "It was her hand that threw the knife that almost ended your life."

"Where is Lindsay now?" Martha asked.

"Hiding in the shadows, plotting your destruction," Anisa smirked.

"She is dead!" Leah interjected. "Anthony and I ... found her body in the courtyard. Just on the other side of that wall. It looked like she had been pushed from the bell tower! A punishment for failing to do her part in your little conspiracy, I would guess."

"What was all this about? The barony?" Martha asked Anisa.

"Of course it is about the barony!" Anisa scoffed. "We must remove you if we are to make room for the rightful heir."

Rightful heir? Leah could not believe what she was hearing. Thomas was no more the rightful heir than she was. This woman could only be uttering such nonsense in order to get a rise out of Martha. Leah was incensed. "You are a fool if you think Thomas will honor any deal he made with you!"

Anisa's dark eyes swiveled to Leah. Leah tensed, clutching the club tighter, but the Saracen woman only threw her head back and laughed as though this were all part of some great joke. "Oh, this is too much! You are moments away from your grave, and you truly have no idea what is happening."

Leah felt herself flush, which made her even angrier. "Tell me, then," she snapped, "tell me what I have failed to comprehend."

"Do you think that we have worked for lo these ten years in order to replace one pathetically weak Dawning with another?"

Leah glanced uncertainly at Martha, but the matron was watching Anisa closely and gave no hint of what she might be thinking.

"You stupid girl! This is about the ascension of the Saracen Dawnings to their rightful place as the strongest, proudest members of the Dawning line. My brother, Amir, is the eldest son of Braden Dawning, and it is he that will inherit all that his father has, as is his right."

"You are mad!" Leah retorted, but neither woman was looking at her; they were staring intensely at each other.

They stood frozen for a moment until Martha suddenly slapped Anisa across the face. Anisa's hand came to her cheek in shock before she struck Martha in return.

Martha stumbled back, and Anisa used the moment of distraction to snatch the knife from her hand.

Leah jumped forward. Anisa spun to meet her, but the club was already in flight. The rough end of the board connected with Anisa's hand with a satisfying crunch, causing her to cry out in pain as the dagger went skittering away again.

Anisa hunched protectively over her broken hand, and Leah immediately brought the club around again.

The Saracen woman saw the blow coming and pivoted to absorb it with her back. The club struck her across the shoulder blades, and she fell to her knees with a gasp of pain.

Leah raised the club in both hands and looked down at Anisa, whose eyes were wide with fear and pain. All the menace that had been present only a moment ago fled, and in place of the murderous predator was now a helpless, cowering victim.

Leah hesitated. In that instant she was back at Henry's wedding, watching William ruthlessly murder a disarmed man begging for his life. She had not been able to forgive him for that, and if she now did the same thing, was she any better than him?

"Leah," Martha said, slowly circling the pair, her voice soft but extremely firm, "finish her now. Her actions have cost us countless lives, and even now she will kill us in an instant if we afford her the slightest opportunity."

Leah knew that was true, but she did not hate Anisa the way she hated William. Anisa had done those things, but she had not done them to Leah personally. She had only been doing what she thought was right. All Leah saw before her now was not a hated assassin but a terrified human being.

"She must not be allowed to roam free in these critical hours, when our very survival is at stake," Martha said, louder than before. "By her own admission, her hands are drenched in the blood of our people."

Our people? Leah thought with disgust. *The Dawnings? The lowly, traitorous Dawnings? I am no Dawning.* "I am better than that," she muttered and let the club fall to her side.

"Are you mad, girl?" Martha demanded, rushing forward to take the weapon from her. But Anisa saw her opportunity and lunged through the curtain.

For just a moment Martha directed a look of mingled disgust and complete incomprehension at Leah but then rushed after Anisa.

Leah dutifully followed her, but Anisa was already disappearing through the door at the back of the chapel. Leah knew that was a problem, but she was not sorry that she had spared the life of a fellow human being. She was better than William, and she would unflinchingly declare exactly that if Martha challenged her on it. But Martha did not even look back as she followed Anisa into the castle.

Leah stood looking after them, ignoring the surprised stares of the women in the room. She could not get Martha's expression out of her mind. It made her feel shame, which made Leah angry. Why should she feel bad for sparing another's life? She resented Martha for that. She resented all of this. She just wanted to leave now; to put all this behind her. *Where is Anthony now?* she thought bitterly.

But as overwrought as Leah was, she knew that Martha was running into harm's way, and Leah could not leave her to face it alone. She reluctantly ran after her.

Forty-three

Thomas hurried down the corridor after Sebastian. Finding Martha and Leah together with their only guard the ancient steward was fortune smiling on him at last. Martha was the last obstacle standing in the way of Thomas' rightful claim to the barony. He had counted on Amir killing her when Amir took control, but with three different armies now vying for the castle, it was not at all certain that Amir would take over. And if Aden or the Braddocks won the day, there was no guarantee that she would be killed.

If he were honest, he found the task of matricide distasteful, but he no longer cared—he could not afford to care. His plan—his life—was falling apart, and he was only going to salvage something from this disaster if he had the strength to do whatever was necessary. And at this particular moment, he was feeling strong after decimating those watchmen without even breaking a sweat. He had never felt so much his father's son as he did at this moment.

Thomas entered the stairwell after Sebastian's retreating back. A sneaking suspicion was growing in his mind. While he was close enough to catch glimpses of Sebastian, he had not caught a similar glimpse of the ladies in the past few minutes.

Thomas rushed out into the Hall of Arms. It was bustling with people, and he could see Sebastian cutting through them. The steward was making his way to the far stairwell, trying to throw off any pursuit. Taller than most people, Thomas had a clear view over the heads of those between him and his query. He could see that there was no one with him.

It is a trick! Clearly the ladies had ducked into some side room along the way, but where? He turned around to retrace his steps but stopped. He was standing in front of the Wall of Arms, the long wall of the room covered in the shields of those who were currently pledged to Dawning Court. Above the mantle, above all the pledges, stood the shields of the family in their preeminent position—where they belonged. There was the Dawning crest on the shield of Richard and Henry. Even John's shield had been restored—placed back on the wall with the others—but Thomas' own had been reversed—the sign of a disavowed knight.

Thomas could not believe that in the midst of a siege, someone had taken the time to turn his shield around. Had Martha, in her spite, formally disavowed him? The thought that they would have gone out of their way to do something like that when their very lives hung in the balance hurt Thomas. Could they not see that he was doing what he had to do? Didn't they understand that this was the only way to prove his greatness? And he had done just that! He had beaten them all. Richard, William, even Martha herself.

Someone bumped into Thomas, jostling him and reminding him that he was not alone. "Clear this room!" he roared above the din of voices, which had grown significantly as people began to recognize him. "This castle will fall within the hour; should you not be assisting in her defense?"

With obvious uncertainty, the room's occupants made their way out, and Thomas turned his attention back to the wall of shields. This seemed like a personal insult. *They wanted me to find this! They knew I would take the castle, and they wanted me to see that they still believe I am a lesser man than the rest!*

The pain of the moment was rapidly turning to rage. Thomas squeezed the shaft of his mace tighter, wanting to smash something or someone for this offense.

Martha rushed down the hall after Anisa. She could not keep up with the younger woman, but she was counting on the fact that Anisa stood out in a crowd—now that Martha knew what to look for—to keep the assassin from hiding from her.

Anisa pressed the wrong way into an unusually large crowd of people exiting the servants' stairwell and disappeared.

Martha caught a woman who was just coming off the stairs. "What is this? What has happened?"

"T—Thomas," the woman stammered in consternation.

"Thomas? My son?" Martha clarified but did not wait for an answer. "Where is he?"

"The chamber what's decorated with all them shields."

Martha's resolve hardened then. She was done running. She was unlikely to survive the fall of the castle regardless, and she was not going to do it cowering in some closet. She was going to face her treacherous sons and make them answer to her for what they had done.

It was dangerous, though, possibly even fatal. She glanced back toward the chapel, but Leah had not emerged. Her disappointment in Leah was compounded when Martha saw that she had not followed her, but she pushed that aside. If Leah was not with her, Martha would not have to fear for her safety. And given Leah's current weakness of mind, perhaps it was better that she not be present.

Anisa momentarily forgotten, Martha mounted the stairs to the Hall of Arms to confront her son.

Leah left the chapel just in time to catch a glimpse of Martha going up the stairs. She grudgingly continued after the old woman, who seemed determined to get herself killed.

Leah climbed the stairs, half-hoping that she would not be able to find her. She could then, in good conscience, leave the Dawnings to their own fate. She was disappointed, however, when she reached the third floor and saw Martha walking up behind Thomas, whose attention was fixed on the wall of shields.

Leave him be! Leah wanted to scream at her. *What is she doing?* Confronting Anisa was one thing, but Thomas was a brutal killer twice her size.

Leah did not want to see what was about to happen. Martha was brazenly taunting death, and it was going to end badly. Leah thought of running, of hiding, even of getting help, but there was no time. This was happening now!

She did not know what she could do to help, but Leah could not leave Martha to perish alone. She had no choice but to remain, if for no other reason than to witness her gruesome end.

She took a few tentative steps into the room, hoping not to be noticed.

"Thomas?"

Thomas whirled and found his mother striding toward him across the room. She looked haggard and older than she had when he had last seen her only a few weeks before.

Thomas gripped his mace tighter. He was angry, and if the object of that anger was stupid enough to arrive unescorted to confront him, then so be it.

He was just deciding how best to lead into the many things he wanted to say to her when Martha struck him across the face.

"How dare you, Thomas?"

He blinked in surprise.

"Your brothers," she struck him again, "your people," she struck him again, "and now this. You spoiled, impudent fool! I—" she cut off when Thomas answered her slaps with a backhand, sending her sprawling backward.

"How dare you treat me like a dog!" Thomas roared. "I have beaten you all! I have defeated your strongest son in combat, I have outmaneuvered your cleverest son, I have outthought your most intelligent son, and I have even made rubble of the mighty Dawning defenses. Me!" he screamed at her, jabbing his thumb into his mailed chest. "The son you thought to lure into complacency with your meager scraps!"

"Thomas, what have you done?"

Thomas looked up to see Leah running to Martha's aid. His surprise was replaced with pleasure at the sight. Here he was in an empty room with the very people he had sought presenting themselves to him. That was as it should be.

If Thomas had been struck by the changes in Martha in so short a time, he almost did not recognize Leah. She was dirty and disheveled, with her hair starting to pull free from the combs that held it in place. There were dark rings under her eyes, and she looked drawn and pale; but it was more than that. She just did not look as he remembered. She was darker now somehow.

When Thomas struck Martha, Leah had reacted without thinking, running into the room before she even realized what she was doing. Now that she was committed, she took the last few steps slowly, watching him carefully. She could not believe that she was watching this boy she had known since childhood prepare to kill his own mother. It seemed hard to believe this was the same person. He too had become the darkest version of himself, with all his charm, wit, and kindness stripped away, leaving only jealousy, fear, and hate in their wake.

Some part of her thought she should try to reclaim him, try to reach that sweet boy she had once known, but she knew it was too late. There was nothing she could do for him now. It was as if the world she had known had melted away and left only a dark shadow of itself and its occupants behind.

Is nobody truly good? she wanted to cry to Heaven, but of course she already knew the answer to that. Anyone good enough to withstand life's vicissitudes, as Eve had been, was killed by lesser beings surrendering to their vilest natures. That left only the naive and the survivors behind for the evil to prey upon.

That is what Martha was, Leah realized. She was a survivor. She was not evil like Thomas and William, nor good like Eve, neither was she naive and foolish like Leah herself. Martha was simply devious enough to survive. *Perhaps the dead are the lucky ones,* she thought. *What are the rest of us spared for except to watch us become the worst versions of ourselves?*

Leah knelt beside Martha and helped her into a sitting position while watching Thomas closely. But even as she did so, she realized that she should not be taking sides in this power struggle between these two. Her best chance for survival was in being able to appeal to either side. After all, wouldn't Martha be the first one to tell her that it was all about survival? *Hadn't she been inadvertently telling me that very thing when she sent Anthony to remove me from the castle before it fell?*

"You strike your own mother, Thomas?" Martha asked, wiping the blood from her cheek with the back of her hand.

"*Mother?*" Thomas cried. "You were never a mother to me!" He glanced at Leah, and mistaking her frown for disapproval, demanded, "Are you so blind that you do not see what is happening here?"

"Why not explain it to me?"

"You think Martha a heroine and me a villain for wresting power from her, but you do not understand!" Thomas was almost yelling in his passion. "She," he said, jabbing his mace at Martha, "has been systematically disposing of each of her sons—my brothers—in order to retain power. Think about it! She disavowed John. She withdrew support for Richard's campaign when he was in deepest Persia surrounded by enemies, trusting that he would never return! She forced Edward into a military campaign that would have been certain doom for one as weak as he was. She encouraged Henry to take command of an army, knowing that his command would lead only to folly. She even opened the door for William to flee in disgrace, trusting that he would never show his face here again. And what happened when he did return with news of Richard? She attempted to send all her remaining sons on a mad quest to recover him—a quest that was sure to fail and rid her of all of us in one fell swoop!"

Leah let that wash over her. A week ago, she would not have even entertained the notion that Martha was some insidious mastermind bent on retaining power at any cost, but now that she understood how scheming and wicked all of the Dawnings were, did she have anything apart from her own naive beliefs with which to discount this version of events? What if it was not actually from Braden that the sons inherited their vile, devious temperaments, but from Martha?

Leah looked at the matron. She looked feeble now, but Leah well knew that that appearance of frailty only belied her hard, even ruthless, temperament. Though Martha had always been kind to her, what if that too was an act? What if it all was a gambit to win favor with the locals so that if any of the rightful heirs did challenge her for the barony, the locals would support her?

"But what of you, Thomas?" Leah's voice was almost a whisper as she struggled against the overwhelming current of evidence that now seemed impossibly obvious. "Martha has always supported you."

Thomas' lopsided smile twisted into a sneer. "That is what she wanted us to believe. But just as she used all my brothers' own weaknesses to trap them, so too was my cage custom-built for me. She used comfort and complacency to keep me in line. Each time my better nature threatened to stir me into action, she heaped upon me more of the trappings of wealth in order to keep me complacent and blind me to what she was withholding. She made a great show of looking after my best interests so that any thought to the contrary would seem ludicrous."

Leah found herself involuntarily recoiling from the matron, and Thomas saw it. "Now you see why it had to be this way, Leah. Martha is an infection that goes right to the bone; we had to cut deep to save the patient."

Leah pushed herself away from both of them. "Diabolical," she whispered to no one in particular. "Your whole family is ... wicked."

"Come now, Leah," Martha said, still trying to shake off the effects of Thomas' backhand. "You have known me all your life; surely you do not put any stock in this nonsense. I wanted nothing more than for each of my sons to step into their birthright, but each one," she flicked a glance at Thomas, "disappointed me in turn. When at last Richard did repent, I willingly relinquished the barony to him, and Dawning Court was on her way back to prominence until Thomas betrayed us all!"

Thomas stepped past Martha as Leah got her feet under her in a crouch, preparing to run. "Leah, look at me," he said, forcing her to meet his eyes. "The castle is falling, the Dawnings' numerous enemies are howling for their destruction. But you are innocent," he said with sudden softness. "You never deserved any of this." He held out his hand to her. "Come with me and let me see you to safety."

"All these years I thought I was nursing a wounded fledgling," Martha spoke from behind him, "when I was unwittingly raising a viper."

"Shut your mouth, devil-woman," Thomas shot over his shoulder with intense ferocity, "or I will dash out your brains this instant!" He then turned back to Leah and resumed his former soft tone, his hand still extended to her. "Leah, you have known *me* all your life! Can you truly say that you were not shocked to hear that I had betrayed my people? Of course you were shocked because that is not who I am. Would I have committed such a despicable act had there been any other way? Now please, allow me to assist you, my beloved friend!" His voice was gentle and pleading, a shocking contrast to the anger and menace displayed only a moment before.

Leah inched back farther for every step he took toward her. "What of William? Is he working with you?"

Thomas' face clouded for a moment before resuming its soft cast. "You should know better than anyone that William follows none but his own inner demons, and his allegiances change by the moment. He cannot be trusted. Now please, Leah, you cannot tell me that you do not wish to leave all this behind—the death, the heartache, the fear? Let me take you from this now, while there is still time!"

Leah did not trust Thomas, but much of what he said did resonate with her. How could she even be considering this when only an hour before she had run from Anthony, who had been trying to force her to leave with him? But so much had changed. The world she thought she knew then did not even exist anymore. She was not even sure who she should be fighting for now. And with the west wall gone and the enemies in the gates, there was no victory to be had.

Leah squeezed her eyes shut. All of her grief, fear, and heartache were tied to this castle—this prison in whose walls she had unfathomably fought to remain. She was suddenly desperate to be free of them. She wanted no more of the lies, deceit, blood, death, and horror. She was through trying to decipher which of these villains was less evil. She was ready to take any exit, and Thomas was offering the most direct one.

She slowly reached out her hand toward his. It felt wrong, but she did not need to stay with Thomas; she could simply take her leave of him the moment they were clear of this hell.

"Leah!" Martha's voice cut in on her thoughts when her hand was only inches from Thomas'. "You are overwrought; you are not thinking clearly."

"I said be still!" Thomas spun on Martha and smashed the head of his mace into the floor only inches from her.

Leah pulled her hand back at that, her mistrust of Thomas returning in an instant. But then she was reminded of the way that Martha had insisted that Leah finish off Anisa. Why had she been so determined to murder a helpless woman? Could it be because of the threat to her claim on the barony that the Saracens represented? And if Amir truly was the eldest son of Braden, didn't he deserve the barony? Wasn't it his right, regardless of his mother's bloodline? After all, everyone had overlooked the fact that Martha was a Saxon. Why should it matter that Amir was part Saracen? And if Thomas was really willing to give up his own claim in deference to Amir's, didn't that prove that he was not the completely vile, self-centered villain that Leah had believed?

"Come now, Leah," Thomas raised his hand again, this time with more urgency, "we must go now!"

Leah looked between the two Dawnings. It seemed to her in that moment, with Martha on the floor, helpless before Thomas, who seemed so strong and able by comparison, that she was looking at two different worlds. With Martha lay the crumbling remains of the old world, and in Thomas there was hope of ... something.

Leah was at last going to decouple her fate from that old world, whose evil she had been blind to her entire life. She swallowed hard and thrust her hand into Thomas', silently willing him not to let her down as every other person in her life had already done, though part of her recognized that she hardly cared any longer, so long as all the intrigue stopped. Maybe then she could finally feel safe again.

Forty-four

"Is this what they are fighting for?" Bertram chortled contemptuously. He and the Golden Sword had unknowingly stopped to assess the situation exactly where Aden and Martin had stopped on the road a short time before to do the same thing.

Dawning Court was a disaster. Aside from the churned up, burned, and destroyed fields and houses, the thousands of bodies littering the landscape, and the Swiss-cheese outer wall and crumbling battlements, the whole area looked to be overrun in a massive free-for-all, without order or even clearly delineated sides. It looked more like a massive riot in which thousands of peasants were looting and burning everything they could get their hands on.

Half of the west wall had been destroyed, and thousands of soldiers, the allegiance of whom Bertram could not distinguish, nor did he care to, fought in hand-to-hand combat. Meanwhile people ran and rode at will through the break in the wall.

"Is this hovel even worth fighting for?" he scoffed.

"Your orders, Lord?" Marsden asked without any particular interest.

Bertram knew that after being away for so long, his men really wanted to be back at home with their families. They did not have the personal attachment to Collin that Bertram himself had due to their being friends since childhood. But he also knew that his knights were exquisitely well-trained and would follow orders.

"The larder has been overrun with rats," Bertram said ominously, sliding his helmet over his head. "We will drown every last one of them."

"We've got them now!" Aden exulted to Martin. They had trapped the Mayfields' mercenary army and the remnants of the Saracens against the castle wall. With nowhere to run combined with the helpful, if not consistent, barrage from the battlements, the enemy force was being ground down. It had gotten ugly, and for a time Aden was not certain they were winning; but now victory seemed certain. "They will have surrendered or been destroyed within the hour. And we will be able to take the castle back! In another hour, it will not matter if Collin arrives with his army, as we will be safely inside the castle."

Martin grinned back at Aden in his usual understated way, but both men understood the significance of what was happening. They had defied the odds, taken a chance, and won the day.

He was not at all happy about the west wall, but as no new enemies had appeared, it had not meaningfully changed the battle with the Mayfield-Saracen army. If Collin were to arrive before they had a chance to build some makeshift fortification in its place, they would simply have to use the castle as their primary defense. It was not ideal, but it could be done, provided they had some time to prepare before Collin arrived.

"Sir Aden!" someone shrieked. Aden looked at the panicky soldier and saw where he was pointing, and his own heart stopped.

There, from the very road that Aden's army had ridden in on that morning, the Braddock cavalry was riding down the slope toward the outer gate.

"This cannot be happening," he exclaimed, "not when we are so close!" Another hour, perhaps two, and they would have been ready; but as things stood now, his army was totally exposed, trapped between two enemy forces in the worst possible scenario. *Was this the Braddock plan all along? Perhaps their army purposely delayed until most of the enemy force was depleted, allowing them to now step in for an easy victory.*

Martin was concentrating on the approaching force that was stopping just inside the outer gate to form a proper line, a luxury that had been denied Aden during his attack, he noted resentfully. "I count at least one-hundred score, with more still on the road."

Aden's exhausted force, which must have dwindled to somewhere near fifteen hundred during the morning's battle, now stood against two thousand mounted knights and the remainder of the mercenary-Saracen army, which had been whittled down significantly but was still substantial.

"We cannot withstand that many," Martin said, as if reading Aden's thoughts, "not without fortifications."

"Somehow," Aden said, bracing himself as the first wave of cavalry started toward them, "I do not think it is up to us!"

Aden started to scream over the field, "To me, men! To me!"

Forty-five

Thomas helped Leah to her feet as the pair inspected each other, Leah with cautious optimism and Thomas with satisfaction.

Martha took advantage of Thomas' distraction and ran.

She was still woozy from Thomas' punch, but she ran as fast as she dared, hoping to make it to a lower level, where the crowds of people would make it more difficult for Thomas to catch her.

Ignoring Thomas' vulgar exclamations of dismay, she plunged into the stairwell, her eyes tearing up from a pain that had nothing to do with her bleeding face. This had all cost her too much, but to lose William and Leah in the same hour was more than she could bear. And how had it come to this? How had Leah, whom she loved like her own daughter, been manipulated into accepting Thomas' twisted version of reality? Martha could not believe that this girl, who was practically family, would even entertain the ideas that Thomas had espoused.

Why should that surprise you? The rational voice in her head asked frankly. *Hasn't all of your actual family turned on you? Why should Leah be any different?*

Martha knew she was letting her emotions get the best of her, something she had striven for decades to control. She had trained herself to make her emotions subservient to her logic. Reason had to govern passion, and that was never truer than it was right now, when she was so close to giving over to despair.

No! she insisted. *That woman who joined her hand with Thomas' is not Leah. The pure, innocent creature who grew up in the castle alongside my own children would never have been persuaded to believe Thomas' horrible lies.* The woman in the Hall of Arms was only a shell of her former self, broken by suffering and not in her right mind.

The woman standing with Thomas *needed* to believe in something other than the dismal reality that awaited all those who were still in the castle, particularly the nobility. And though it made Martha sick to think about what it was going to cost Leah, if Thomas would do what Anthony had failed to and get her to safety, then maybe it was for the best that she went with him.

Martha rounded the bend in the stairs and slammed into Amir. Even in the dim stairwell, there was no mistaking that giant physique.

Amir cringed at the contact, clenching his teeth to smother a cry of pain and recoiling from her.

Martha gasped. Even in this low light, she could see the burns. Much of his hair was melted to stubble, and all the exposed skin on his left side was bubbling in angry red and white patches.

The twisted grimace of anger and pain on his face broke into a smile a moment later. "Lady Dawning," his gravelly voice almost purred. "How good of you to find me in the very moment I was seeking an audience."

He reached out to take hold of her, but Martha scraped her nails across his burned flesh, and he recoiled again, roaring at her in visceral rage.

Martha did not wait for him to recover; she turned and rushed back up the stairs. Bypassing the third floor, where Thomas had mercifully not appeared in the stairwell yet, she continued upward, where she could cross over to the main stairs to descend to the Great Hall.

She rounded the first bend in the stairs and almost ran straight into Anisa, who was coming down from the other direction.

What miserable luck! Seeing no other option, Martha turned and ran back into the Hall of Arms she had only just left.

Anisa lunged off the stairs after her and seized her roughly by the arm. The Saracen woman spun Martha to face her and drew back to strike her.

Martha threw her arms up to protect her face, so she did not see the new figure explode from the stairs behind Anisa until he was hitting Anisa so hard across the chin that the assassin was thrown to the floor and slid several feet before coming to rest in an unmoving heap.

"William!" Martha gasped in shock. Though she had been forced to accept that he was alive, she did not realize until this moment that she had not really believed it; yet here he was, standing before her right when she needed him the most.

"Hello, Mother," he grinned at her. His boyish charm was unchanged, but his countenance was altered considerably. He looked pale despite the layer of filth that covered his face; his once regal armor hung in tatters, with missing plates and holes in it that exposed his sweat and blood-stained tunic beneath. And instead of projecting the raw energy of coiled springs as he always had in the past, he now stood like a scarecrow, as if every movement required effort.

"William, behind you!" Martha cried suddenly.

Without looking behind him, William shoved her back and leapt to the side just as Amir charged from the stairwell, ramming his sword through the air where William had been a moment before.

The giant regained his balance and Anisa got to her feet, shaking off the daze.

"That is my sword!" William exclaimed indignantly. "That is twice you have tried to kill me with my own sword!"

Thomas, too, who had stopped partway to the stairs, evidently undecided about chasing Martha or staying with Leah, now pushed Leah protectively back and came forward to meet William with his mace at the ready. No one spoke as the three formed a semi-circle around William, who stepped in front of his mother, placing himself between her and the trio, but trapping her between him and hearth in the process. Leah retreated toward the opposite wall, her eyes intent upon the scene before her.

"I need a weapon!" Anisa hissed at the other two.

Without looking at her, Thomas drew his dagger and tossed it over, which gave William the opportunity to snatch a spear from a nearby display. He noticed also that Anisa caught Thomas' dagger with her left hand before gingerly taking it in a light grip with her right.

Amir, Anisa, and Thomas spread out in front of William, blocking both exits. Anisa was on his left, Thomas on his right, and Amir directly before him. He noted Amir's burns, the woman's injured hand, and Thomas' bruised face from where William had beaten him...when? Was it really only a day ago? He could use that to his advantage, he thought. but then he took a mental inventory of his own physical condition and was not reassured. Over the past week, he had been beaten, stabbed, sliced, and fevered. He had eaten little, slept less, and worked his muscles to failure on multiple occasions. His ribs still ached from his joust with Collin, he was certain he had at least cracked them, if not broken them outright, as even mild pressure on that side sent a shot of pain through him. His left arm also ached, but at least it was responding to his commands again. He was not in any condition to be fighting even a single opponent, let alone three.

To make matters worse, one of his adversaries was none other than the Saracen giant, Amir, his oldest, most feared enemy, the man who had beaten him in his first battle and taken such a toll upon his psyche that William had switched from using his sword—which, in a twist of irony, Amir now held—as his weapon of choice to primarily using a spear because of the extra reach it afforded him.

"Well," Amir rumbled, "this is indeed a happy reunion. I feared that we would never have this opportunity."

"Yes," William replied without enthusiasm. "Any chance we could reconvene after some food and rest? I have had a terrible week... although," he added, looking at Amir's burns, "perhaps not as bad as yours."

"You are going to die now," Amir snarled.

"Could be," William sighed, "but I can probably take you with me ... and your handmaid too," he said, nodding toward the unfamiliar woman lined up beside the giant.

Anisa scowled, which made William smile. "I am Anisa of the Nizari," she hissed.

"She is Amir's sister," Martha supplied from behind William. "There is as much Dawning blood on her hands as there is on his."

"I would not have seen the resemblance," William said, as the three slowly closed in on him, "but now, with Amir's burns—"

"We are going to finish what we began with John here and now!" Amir growled.

"That may be the first true statement you have ever uttered." It was not that William was in a particularly jovial frame of mind, nor was he feeling his old, flippant, devil-may-care defiance of death; he simply recognized the inevitability of it. He had known that salvation for the barony would likely cost him his life, and now, standing before the three people who most wanted him dead in the world, there was no sense denying the certainty of his fate. Had it been only one of these three, he might have held out hope. But meeting all three at once could only be Heaven's doing.

For the first time, William's eyes fell upon the figure behind Thomas, and his heart skipped a beat, as it always did upon seeing her. She was there, dirty, disheveled, flushed, and beautiful. But why was she here? And why did she not run while all the attention was fixed upon him? Perhaps she too was shocked by his presence, as she was also staring, wide-eyed, across the room at him.

"There is no need for the women to see this," William suggested casually, as though it did not matter to him. "Release them so that we may conduct our business unfettered."

"I am not going anywhere!" Anisa hissed.

William blinked in surprise. "Forgive me, I meant the ladies."

Anisa snarled something at him in Arabic, which made William smirk, but that passed as quickly as it had come. "Thomas," he appealed to his brother, "surely you do not wish them to be here? Whatever the outcome?"

"Leah," Thomas called over his shoulder, without taking his eyes off of William. "What do you wish to do?"

Leah stared at William with all the bitterness and resentment for every misery he had brought down upon her: for Eve's death, for being trapped here, for her unrequited love, for all of it. Now here he was, about to get his comeuppance for everything. She would never get this chance again, and she would not miss it.

"Kill him." She meant it to be a declaration of conviction, but it came out as a barely audible murmur.

Quiet though it was, everyone in the room heard it, and William rocked back on his heels as though he had been slapped in the face. He looked past the villains and the lopsided smirk that had appeared on Thomas' face to the love of his life. But instead of the anxious gaze of a woman fearing for his safety, an expression, he was sorry to admit, that he had seen on her face too many times, he now recognized the unfamiliar look for what it was—an emotion he had never seen on Leah's face—hatred.

He was not sure what reception he had expected when she discovered that he was alive. He had known that she might blame him for all this, and he could not deny that such a feeling was warranted for all the suffering he had caused; but he had hoped against hope that Leah, of all people, would be able to look past that and forgive his mistakes. But he realized now that it had obviously been too much to hope for.

All his efforts to right his wrongs, to save the castle, to undo what he had done, all that he had endured, he had done with Leah as the light leading him on, his hope that pulled him through the hopeless times. But it had all been a mirage. He had lost her, and to whom? The most vile, despicable people he had ever known.

"Much has changed, brother," Thomas grinned. "All of Dawning Court has seen you for what you really are. They know that it is your actions that led to their destruction."

William felt Thomas' words twisting in him like a knife. Leah hated him for what he had done, but what hurt even worse was realizing that she had embraced the vilest enemies of the barony, the people who had murdered John and Richard and were trying to do the same to him and his mother at this very moment. And Leah had sided with them!

William felt his heavy limbs catching fire as a fresh wave of fury surged through him. Though he did not realize it, the plaintive expression on his face twisted into a snarl as the pain of Leah's betrayal turned to rage.

The familiar feeling coursed through him, but instead of trying to relax out of it, to let it go as he had been struggling to do for so long, he welcomed it as he stared through the men toward the woman who had just driven a dagger straight into his heart.

William's knees coiled beneath him, and his hands twisted on the shaft of the spear. He was dimly aware of Thomas' smug smirk abruptly falling as he saw the change come over his brother.

"Do you remember what I told you, Leah, when Vincent Braddock challenged me on the lists?" he asked in a voice just loud enough to carry across the room to her. "When you insisted that I could not win because he was a trained knight?"

Leah too recognized the look she knew all too well. She saw the rage that was taking hold of him and took another step back until she came up against a support column.

"And what is that?" Amir asked lightly when Leah did not answer, as though he were listening to some cute story.

"He started this, and I will finish it!"

William launched forward, thrusting the spear in one hand to drive Amir back before spinning it toward Thomas, also forcing him back a step; but William did not stop rotating, catching Anisa by surprise when she jumped toward William's unprotected back and sweeping her legs from beneath her. She hit the floor, and the wind exploded from her lungs.

Before William could capitalize on her mistake, though, Amir was cutting at him. William only just managed to bring his spear up to protect his head. He stopped the blade, but a large chunk of wood peeled off the shaft from the force of the blow.

Then Thomas was coming around with his mace, which William ducked just in time, causing Amir to pull up to avoid being clipped by Thomas' weapon.

William used the opportunity to crack the butt of his spear across Amir's burned left side, causing him to scream in pain. William then rammed the spearhead at Thomas' chest.

Thomas deflected the blow with his shield and took another ferocious but slow swing at William, who spun aside and leveled a side kick at Anisa, who was just pushing herself into a crouching position.

Anisa was ready for him this time and ducked beneath the kick, delivering a slice to his inner thigh, one of the few areas not protected by his armor.

William jumped back and stopped. The cut burned, but he did not dare inspect it for fear of taking his eyes off his enemies. Other than the intense pain, however, he did not notice any impaired mobility, so he guessed that it was not too deep. Nevertheless, the clock was now ticking, as he was leaking blood from his already depleted body. There was no denying the fact that, angry or not, he was tired. He knew he could not keep this up for long against all three opponents.

Then they were upon him again.

Amir marveled at the superb weapon in his hand as he swung blow after effortless blow. The exquisitely honed steel did not seem to dull at all, even as he continued to slice away at the wooden shaft of William's spear.

He could see that William was nearly spent. If the boy had looked beaten when Amir faced him at the siege towers, he looked positively brutalized now. He was still fast, but his reactions were just a bit dulled and his movements just a bit sloppier than in the past. He was obviously hurting, and yet he continued to trace a circumspect path around his mother, trying to stay out of harm's way while not exposing her to danger, still naively believing that he could protect her *and* survive this battle.

William had been a thorn in Amir's side since they first met during the peasant revolt Amir had fomented against the Dawnings so many years ago. It was there that Amir had crossed swords with the boy, and though William had been no match for him, William had managed to occupy his attention long enough that the tide of the battle turned against Amir's peasant force.

William had then orchestrated Richard's kidnapping from the Nizari after Amir had expended so much time and countless resources to capture Richard. William had continued to defy Amir at every turn since then. It was he and Richard who had stopped Amir's army, forcing Amir to make a pact with that idiot Braddock. William had then undermined his efforts to take the castle and had even come very close to spoiling Amir's deal with the Mayfields by revealing it to the others. Why, if they had not caught him on the siege towers that night, he would have even—

Amir stopped, suddenly putting it together for the first time. William had been in the siege towers. What had he been doing if not soaking them with oil? That was why the tower Amir had been riding in had gone up in flames so unexpectedly! *William* was the reason that Amir was only half the man he had been just hours before. It was William who had done this to him! William was the cause of this unbearable pain!

The hatred that Amir felt for William and the Dawnings blossomed into a feeling heretofore unknown to Amir. Even Braden Dawning himself did not command the level of hatred that he now felt for William. It was no longer enough to simply kill this man.

At this moment, Amir's life-long struggle to take the barony was secondary to his lust for vengeance. William was trapped, depleted, outnumbered, and forced to defend himself with only a poorly made infantryman's spear. No, Amir was not simply going to kill William. He was going to break down his defenses, hurt him, and bring out the fear in him until he begged for his life in front of the women. Amir wanted to take William's soul, strip away his façade, and bring out the animal terror in him; and only then would he allow him to die.

Leah watched the fight with bated breath. Though Thomas had convinced her that he was on the side of right, her emotions were not a candle that she could simply snuff out in an instant. Her lifetime of loyalty to the Dawnings, and Martha specifically, did not simply wither because of an intellectual decision.

As she had watched these three...brigands—she could not kid herself that they were noble warriors—gang up on William, she could not entirely bring herself to root for them. Ganging up on one opponent did not seem right, but if there was one thing she was being forced to learn over and over, it was that in the face of a deadly enemy, one did what one had to do. And she could not deny that there were none more dangerous than William.

But William looked so small compared to Thomas and Amir. *William,* she cried silently, *how could you have let it come to this? How could you have murdered Eve?*

In her wrath, she had ordered his death, but what if she was wrong to do so?

After all, if William was here defending Martha, didn't that mean that he had not been the one in the castle trying to kill Martha? But Leah had seen him with her own eyes! *Was this also a ploy?*

She covered her eyes. She didn't want to think about any of it anymore, but she nevertheless found herself getting more and more agitated. She could still see him, robed and hooded, leaping down on that platform to break it loose. He had looked exactly as he had when he had come into the chapel—

Leah felt ill. *What if it was not William on the platform? What if it was Anisa!* Seeing them together now, it was impossible to mistake one for the other. Though they were about the same height, William was much broader; but on that night, she had not seen them side by side.

It was not him, she realized with sickening certainty. *But she had seen him in the chapel! Why would William and Anisa have been in the same place at the same moment if they weren't working together?*

Because, you fool! a voice screamed in her head, *he was doing exactly what he is doing now! He was protecting his mother!*

"No! No!" Leah cried aloud, recoiling at the implications of that thought. It *had* to be William's fault!

Tears momentarily blinded her. If William was still true to her, if he was still *her* William, then that meant *she* was the villain! "I—I cannot watch this!" She buried her face in her hands.

William continued to block, parry, and evade, but no matter how he figured it, time was short. Aside from his diminishing strength, the shaft of his spear was being carved away with each deflection of Amir's sword—his sword. It was starting to look like a log, rotting and pitted on a forest floor. At this rate, it would only take minutes before it would inevitably fail. One way or another, this would not be a lengthy battle.

"Spread out!" Thomas ordered. "If we all attack at once, he cannot stop us all."

The three spread out in a 'Y' formation around William.

William had a problem. He well knew that the first step in any group attack was to get every opponent on one side of you, where you could see them all. But if he moved at all, he would be exposing his mother to one or more potential attacks. He could not afford to do that, not only for her safety but because there was no question that any of these three would willingly exploit such a vulnerability, and he would be stuck.

So he let them surround him, orienting himself toward Amir and Thomas so he could see them both in his peripheral vision while listening intently for sounds of Anisa coming from behind.

For a moment time froze as each of them waited for the others to act; then with a snap, all three charged.

William dropped his spear and stepped into Thomas' swing, letting Thomas' own momentum, along with a helpful shove from William, send him careening into Amir, who tumbled over Thomas with a curse and landed on all fours. But much to William's dismay, Amir did not drop his sword.

William could not hear Anisa in the scuffle, but he was certain she was descending upon him at that moment. Remembering a hard-learned lesson from Jurou when William had first decided to take up the spear, he did not stop to look for her; instead he ran straight ahead toward Amir. But instead of attacking Amir, he put a foot on his side and used him as a launchpad to bring his leg around in a flying spin kick.

He was not disappointed. As he came around, he found Anisa only a pace behind him. At a disadvantage with the short range of her dagger, she was forced to get closer to William, which exposed her. Once again, she was totally unprepared for his surprise attack and took the full force of his armored shin in the head.

She crumpled to the ground, and William kicked the dagger from her limp hand toward Martha, even as Thomas kicked William's spear out of reach.

William found himself panting from the exertion. Though he had eliminated one of the threats, it had come at too high a cost. Not only had he lost control of his primary weapon, but he was also now spent. His limbs felt heavy.

Nevertheless, he drew his dagger; it was not much against two armed warriors, but it was all he had.

Recognizing that they had the advantage, Thomas leapt toward William with a brutal downward swing of his mace.

William dove aside to avoid it, but the sudden motion did not allow him to protect his ribs properly, and the roll caused his side to explode in pain. William barely made it back to his feet, but he could not hide the agony he was in as he hunched over his wounded left side. He knew he was in big trouble.

"He is done!" Thomas gloated to Amir. "He is injured and exhausted." Thomas raised his mace again. William bent his knees, preparing to respond, but his legs were trembling with fatigue and pain now.

But just then, from the side of his eye, a sudden movement. Thinking it was Anisa, he shifted his gaze from Thomas just in time to see Martha dart from the hearth and ram the knife William had kicked to her into Amir's shoulder.

Amir roared in pain, and Martha staggered back out of shock and fear, leaving the dagger protruding from his arm, even as he turned his fury on her.

William was amazed. He realized that his mother must have also recognized that he was beaten, and so instead of using the dagger as a last line of defense, as William had intended, she tried to help him.

Amir's face twisted with hatred such as William had never seen, making him appear that much more menacing.

William was suddenly terrified for his mother. Amir was incensed, and all his rage was now focused on Martha. But William was trapped. Thomas stood in front of him, and Amir was between William and his mother.

The giant ripped the knife from his shoulder, glanced at William to make sure he was watching, and then turned his vengeful eyes toward Martha.

"No!" William cried as he darted forward, heedless of the danger from Thomas, his own pain forgotten; but there was no way he could reach her in time.

Martha's eyes went wide as Amir closed the distance to her in two long strides and rammed the knife he had just removed from his arm into her chest above her right breast.

He lunged forward with such force that he slammed her body back into the wall and held it there until her limbs went slack before stepping back with a smug grin to allow William to see the full extent of what he had done.

Martha gripped the blade in both hands as she slid to the floor.

William felt like he was moving in slow motion as he watched the unthinkable happen right before his eyes. Maybe she could still be saved if he could only get to her—

Stars exploded in front of him as his head felt like it was split in two by Thomas' mace. His legs gave out beneath him, and he crashed to the floor.

Thomas stood over William, watching him struggle to crawl to Martha despite the pain. Thomas had struck reflexively when William had panicked and rushed toward Martha. It was not a clean blow, but he could rectify that now without difficulty. Yet he hesitated.

It was not the sight of William's pain that stopped him but the sight of Martha bleeding against the wall. While Thomas had known it would come to this, there was something about seeing it now that shocked him.

"What have you done, Thomas?" William cried weakly. "Our mother!"

Thomas' gaze bounced between William and Martha, who was still awake and staring at him. Under her scrutiny, shame overcame him, and he slowly lowered his weapon.

What is wrong with you? he demanded. *Do not stop now, when you are this close!* He was about to finish off his last brother, proving once and for all that he was the ultimate

Dawning; his mother no longer stood in his way; and the two women he had most dreamed of possessing were here in this room with him now. It was almost as though this was some horrible nightmare, where he was getting everything he had always wanted, but it had somehow been stripped of all the promised pleasure.

Maybe this wasn't what he wanted. Perhaps what he really wanted was to rule Dawning Court *with* his family. He just wanted them to stop treating him like the jester and treat him like an equal. "It did not have to come to this!" he cried in a voice of anguished regret. "Why did you force my hand?"

Thomas was angry now. He needed to vent it on someone, and who better than the miserable heathen that had dared to lay his hands on Thomas' mother?

Thomas gripped his mace tighter and turned to find Amir when a sudden, intense pain in the back of his right leg caused his knee to give out. He fell backward, landing beside William on the floor.

Amir leered in satisfaction at the three dying Dawnings after having used Thomas' moment of doubt to sneak up behind him and hamstring him. This was better than he could have hoped for! Not only were the last three Dawnings all dying within feet of each other, but they had all lived long enough to see it. The brothers had seen Amir murder their mother while they stood by, and she had watched one son kill the other as he tried to help her. This was sweeter than any vengeance Amir could have dreamt up.

Amir vividly remembered how helpless he had been as a boy when Braden Dawning had murdered his own mother in front of him for her defiance. He still wore the scar on his cheek Braden's gauntlet had given him when he had tried to stand up to him.

Now, as he watched Braden's last "mighty" son use his final moments to crawl in desperation across the floor toward Braden's dying lady, he was delighted. Sweeter still was the fact that it was Braden's own legitimate sons who were killing each other.

Amir smirked as the shocked expression on Thomas' face slowly turned to realization and then fear as he recognized that Amir had bested him.

"After everything," Amir rumbled smugly, "you never really expected that a 'simple Moor' would get the better of you." Amir stabbed Thomas through the other thigh, and Thomas twisted in pain, his mace crashing to the floor as he hunched over his wounded legs.

Amir bent down close to him, much as he had done to John in his final moments. "Now, not only do I have the pleasure of watching you die but also of seeing your mother watch as the last of her family is exterminated right before her eyes!"

Thomas opened his mouth to say something, but Amir kicked him in the face, cutting off whatever he had been about to say.

Leah gasped out a strangled cry as she watched Martha get stabbed and William be struck down. In that instant she realized that she would never have the chance to make amends, to explain herself, to beg forgiveness. Both of these people that she had loved like her own family would go to their graves believing her to be a traitor.

Was this how the adversary worked? Did he keep blinders on you until you reached your lowest ebb and then rip them off in time for you to watch with perfect clarity as all your worst fears came to pass and you ran your life straight off a cliff?

It was too horrible to contemplate, but it was not over. William was still moving, struggling to get to this mother. Maybe there was still time to do...something.

She searched around for something to throw. It was rash. She knew the smart thing to do was run while she still had a chance, but she didn't care. She could not stand by while this travesty continued. Her eyes came to rest on a candelabra on a nearby sideboard.

Amir stepped past Thomas' writhing form and stood gloating over William as he continued to drag himself toward his mother. That was it. Leah could stand it no longer. She snatched up the candlestick and, without stopping to consider, hurled it at the side of Amir's head.

Though the candelabra was heavy and capable of inflicting a devastating injury to an unprotected skull, most of the weight was in its base, which caused it to spin unpredictably and whip past Amir's head, several inches to the right.

It did have some effect, however, as one of the arms of the candlestick struck a glancing blow across Amir's temple and tore a strip of his red, burned flesh away.

He screamed and spun toward Leah. In that moment she saw all the twisted hatred that William had seen, all of this monster's single-minded obsession with their destruction, and she immediately regretted putting herself in his path. Nothing save death itself was going to stop this man, and Leah was now the object of his fury. And she was unarmed and alone.

William struggled toward his mother. He was dimly aware that Amir had stepped away from him but was not interested in why. It did not matter why. His life no longer mattered, as the only things he had fought for were all lost to him now.

He saw his mother was gasping something inaudible and gesturing behind him, but he could not make it out until he was a few feet from her. "Leah!" she was saying. "Save Leah!"

William turned to look behind him. His head hurt, and it took him a moment to focus on the object of his mother's distress. Amir was at that moment closing in on Leah.

William turned a plaintive look at his mother. In agony, drawing what could only be close to her last breath, she was only concerned with everyone else.

He squeezed his eyes shut against the pounding in his head. "I cannot help her," he said through gritted teeth.

"Save her, William," Martha's voice was barely audible, "for me. Save her."

"But Mother," *you're dying!* He could not bring himself to finish his protest.

"Now, William!" She managed her commanding tone one last time.

William roared in frustrated fury, the sound reverberating through his skull and turning to red daggers of pain. No matter what he did, he was always wrong. Even now, in his mother's last moments, he could not simply take the time to reconcile with her—to ensure she knew that he had not abandoned her. *Very well, if her last wish was that he rid the world of this scourge, then so be it!* William struck the floor with his fist and got unsteadily to his feet.

He stepped over to Thomas, who lay on his back with blood pooling around him. William paused for a moment and looked at his brother. Thomas looked helpless and pathetic, like an injured animal. There was so much that William wanted to say to him, to scream at him, so much pain he would like to inflict on Thomas to make him feel what he had done to everyone else; but he didn't do any of that. Instead, he just stooped down and picked up Thomas' mace.

Amir rushed after Leah in agony-fueled rage, but even as he did so, he realized that her timing could not have been better. He had been on the brink of killing William, but that would have been premature. He could not kill the boy when there was one more stake left to pierce his heart. Leah's betrayal of William must have hurt him terribly, but how much more exquisite to now watch her die right before his eyes, even while holding his dying mother in his arms?

Leah's back was against a support column; she was trapped. Amir heard William cry out behind him and knew that he had won. Perhaps he had not accomplished his ultimate objective yet, but he had beaten the Dawnings once and for all.

He stopped in front of her to savor the look of terror in her wide eyes and the feeling of helpless horror that William was undoubtedly feeling. Amir smiled as he raised William's sword to her chest, thinking that even the fact that it was William's own weapon stealing her life away was delicious. Allah was smiling upon him after all.

He pressed the point against her chest. He would drive it in slowly so she would feel every bit of the agony and would scream until he pierced her lungs.

The blade punctured her skin, and he twisted it, rolling his elbow upward in the process.

She gasped in pain, and Amir held her pinned there with the blade while he turned back to ensure that William was watching, but his heart suddenly stopped in shock.

William was not across the room looking helplessly on as Amir had expected, but was instead only a few feet from him, flying through the air, Thomas' mace in his hands, already descending on him.

Amir lurched back, but his hand was still on the hilt of the sword. The heavy metal head of the mace missed his forearm, but the shaft of the mace crashed over it with so much force that it exploded over his arm, crushing his vambrace and shattering the bones beneath it.

Amir roared in pain and staggered sideways to try to get clear of William, but William stayed on him, smashing at every exposed part, blinding Amir with pain.

He needed a moment to collect himself, to do a damage assessment and regroup, but the Dawning was everywhere at once, knees, fists, feet, elbows flying from every direction, pummeling, crushing, and scraping on his raw flesh. All Amir could think to do was to keep backing away, waving his intact left arm wildly before him while trying to protect his crushed right one.

But William was relentless. He bludgeoned Amir's burned left side over and over, forcing the giant to pivot protectively, but that then exposed his shattered right arm to the whirlwind attacks.

Amir let out a roar, a visceral sound of pain, hatred, and frustration. He knew that he could match this boy in combat, for he had done it before; but the shock of the sudden attack and the intense pain of his burns and shattered limb were overwhelming even the massive dose of his herbal mixture and fogging his mind until he could not think clearly.

In desperation, Amir kicked out with his right leg at William, the only one of his four appendages not seriously injured. But he was off balance, and the movement was clumsy and slow. William easily dodged it, causing Amir to overextend his leg to try to catch his balance.

William stomped down on the exposed joint.

Amir felt his knee pop and knew it had just suffered catastrophic damage, not because of the pain but rather because of the lack of feeling that came from the joint. He dropped onto his other knee in a genuflecting position, which brought him eye to eye with the boy for the first time in years.

William grabbed a fist full of Amir's hair and reared back to strike him with every bit of force his hate and fury could muster, but Amir only smiled up at him, causing him to pause.

"I win," Amir rasped smugly. "Your home is fallen, another will rule the barony before the day is out, your brothers are all dead, your woman has turned on you, and your mother's life is spilling out onto the floor as we speak. Kill me, William, and set me free while you watch helplessly as your world burns."

Amir started to laugh a hoarse, guttural cackle until William silenced him with a brutal right cross. But that did little to quench his anger, so William hit him again. And again. And again. Amir could offer no resistance, and William bludgeoned him until his face was a bloody pulp. William reared back for a final throat strike, to finish him once and for all, but stopped.

He could feel the eyes of his mother and Leah upon him and suddenly could see, clearly reflected back at him in the man before him, all his own demons. He recognized the intense, focused hatred that Amir used to push aside all the pain. He could see that Amir's desire for vengeance was the only thing that had carried him through all the years of failure, defeat, and setbacks; it was the only thing that kept him even now, in his final moments, trying to hurt the Dawnings.

Was it not William's own rage that had kept him also pushing through all the pain and fatigue? Was that not, even in this moment, the very thing that was fueling him? What was Amir if not a shadow of William in the future?

William released the giant and let him slump back over his heels. He stared down at the broken body on the floor at his feet. "It is finished," he muttered.

Leah did not dare move as she watched William relentlessly pummel Amir; she remained exactly where she had been pinned, when Amir had come within an inch of taking her life, while William dispensed justice with that same terrible brutality that had once so sickened her.

Only now she could not bring herself to be appalled by it. With every awful blow, she felt a pang of relief at seeing that viciousness unleashed upon the author of all their terror. With every strike to that face, she thought of Eve, she thought of the hundreds of dead and maimed who had come through the doors of the Great Hall, she thought of the perpetual dread in which they lived, she thought of Thomas and his pernicious lies. It was not without some shame that she exulted in the giant's downfall, but exult she did.

Amir collapsed, and Leah let herself breathe again. William would dispatch him, and it would finally be over. But William did not kill the hated assassin. Instead, he stepped back from the beaten man and turned away from him. Leah expected to see the murder that was in her heart reflected in his eyes, but that is not what she saw. His expression was grim, to be sure, but it did not look as it had that day at the wedding, when he had slaughtered the Nizari assassin begging for his life. In this moment, Leah thought she saw...peace.

But it was a peace that she did not share. Leah was horrified when, instead of finishing off this vile man, William turned and ran back to Martha.

Leah wanted to cry out, to scream at him that his job was not yet finished! These people had murdered Eve! For once, she actually *wanted* him to use that murderous streak in him, and he was failing her!

Some detached part of her whispered of the irony that William was finally putting his concern for another above his own desires, and it was she who wanted blood; but she did not care. The debt had not yet been paid. The three people that William had fought in this room were responsible for all the death and misery the entire barony had suffered. They had taken her sister in her prime and robbed Leah of her innocence, and not one of these villains had yet paid with their life!

Leah picked up William's sword from where Amir had dropped it only inches from her. She looked down the length of it and tried to comprehend the attributes of a metal that had ended hundreds, if not thousands, of lives. Did it have a will of its own? Or did it somehow attract like-minded individuals with murder in their hearts as it had attracted her? Perhaps it called the Angel of Death to it, for he was surely nearby.

Leah almost felt as though she were in a dream as she walked toward the giant form on the floor. Everything else fell away except Amir. She no longer saw the room or even William and Martha. Her vision narrowed to the object of her hate and what she had to do.

She stopped beside him, staring down at the quivering mass. Upright he had seemed a terrifying spectacle, but now, broken and powerless, Amir's larger-than-life size made him seem all the more pathetic, like an overgrown child who had the appearance of an adult but who was in reality helpless.

She was surprised to see that his eyes were open, and he seemed to be conscious. She stepped closer to where she was sure she would be in his field of vision. She wanted him to see her, to know who it was that was stealing his life from him as he had done to countless others. It was not some great warrior but an innocent, just as Eve had been.

"P—p—pleash," Amir managed the slurred words from his misaligned jaw, though his voice was barely a croak, "help me."

Leah sneered at him, "I will return to you all the sympathy that you showed my loved ones and me when you stole our lives from us without remorse. Now," she hissed, "reap what you have sown!"

Martha managed a weak smile when William again knelt beside her. A stream of blood was running from her mouth, and she had both hands clutched against her chest in a vain attempt to relieve the pain from the wound. "My son," she said in a whisper, pausing to draw a shallow, breath. "I—I am so glad to see you." Her words were inadequate to convey all that she was feeling about seeing him here now, with all her doubts and fears about his character put to rest once and for all.

"Mother," he said in a voice thick with emotion, "forgive me for failing to protect you."

Her face contorted into a grimace of pain. "Hold me, William. It has been too long since I have been held."

William slid an arm under her shoulders and gently lowered her down until she was lying across his lap. He used his sleeve to wipe the blood from her face. "Mother, you cannot leave me behind. What will I do without you?"

She managed another weak smile. "You are not alone, William. That is what I have been trying to make you understand since you returned; your isolation is self-imposed."

"Mother," his voice broke off as he was overcome by emotion.

"Death is nothing to fear; it is merely waking from a dream," she whispered, wiping his tears with a blood-drenched hand that left streaks wherever she touched him.

"And truth be told, William, I welcome it. I have earned the rest."

"Forgive me, Mother, my selfishness," he said and looked away, unable to stem the flow of tears. "Forgive me...."

It took him some time to regain control of himself, and when he did, he spoke through the emotion. "I understand now ... all that you tried to teach me. You, Richard, Jurou, even Leah. But I have lost all of them. I cannot lose you, too."

"You...have not...lost everyone...yet. But you are about to." Martha flicked her eyes across the room.

William followed her gaze and saw Leah standing over Amir, holding his sword.

"Stop her," Martha gasped, "or she will never forgive herself."

William laid her carefully down and started to rise but was restrained by her weak grasp on his arm. "I am proud of you, my son," she gasped.

William smiled at her and wiped the tears from his face. "Thank you for never giving up on me, for always believing in me, even when no one else did."

"Hurry," she rasped.

William glanced over at Leah. "I will be back in a moment," he assured her and ran.

Leah held the sword over Amir. Her face was racked with emotion. She knew that killing this man while he was totally helpless might make her no different than he was, but she didn't care. She wanted to do it. She wanted him to feel all the anguish he had inflicted on so many others, wanted him to know what it was like to see that his life was forfeit and that he was helpless to prevent it.

Leah spit on him and rose up on her toes to drive the blade down with as much force as she could muster.

She was suddenly grabbed from behind, not violently but firmly, one arm wrapped around her waist and the other taking hold of her wrist.

She started in surprise and tried to jerk free, but she was held fast. "Do not do this," a soft voice said in her ear.

"Leave me be!" she cried, struggling to regain control of the sword. "He deserves this!"

"And will you soil your own soul in order to punish this fiend?" William demanded gruffly. "It is done," he said sternly. "Let it go and leave it to God."

"No!" she cried, resuming her struggle until she broke free from his grasp. "God has forsaken us! He will not punish these monsters as they deserve!"

An angry expression crossed William's face, but Leah was already turning back toward Amir. "I must finish this devil before it is too late!"

Then William was upon her again, more roughly than before. He snatched the blade from her hand. "You would trade your purity for him—for this?" he demanded. "Has he not stained enough souls? Must he have yours, too?"

"He murdered Eve!" she screamed.

William froze at that. "Eve is—" he broke off, and his shoulders visibly slumped as though he could not take one more thing.

Somehow, seeing William heartbroken over Eve made it hurt even more. *Why doesn't he love me like that?* This thought, too, flashed into her mind unbidden; but she pushed it away, angrier than before.

"Stay out of my way, William!" she cried. "That is something you are good at." She gave up on getting the sword from him and looked for other weapons within reach.

Her dig at William seemed to snap him out of his shock. "You want him dead?" he demanded suddenly, shouldering her aside to stand over Amir. "Will that make you feel better?" He raised his sword in both hands over Amir's chest. "Will this bring you peace, Leah? Just say the word!

My hands are so bloody, the life of one more miserable wretch will matter but little."

Leah stared at him. *Was that what she wanted?* She thought it was, but it seemed different somehow to order someone else to do it.

"Give the command, Leah!"

Leah looked at Amir, bloody and helpless, barely even able to writhe in pain. The sight that would have evoked pity in her a week ago gave her some grim satisfaction now. She liked that this despicable man was suffering. But she wanted him dead, wanted to know that he could not hurt them anymore.

She opened her mouth to give the order, but then her eyes met William's. They were still the same soft, brown eyes of the boy she loved, only they looked so tired and hopeless now.

What has he suffered over these past weeks? She had not given it a thought since learning that he was alive, but now she could not escape it; it all flooded in on her, and the scab was torn from her raw heart. William had been alone through it all. Not William the murderer—the unfeeling villain she had conjured up in her mind—but *her William,* the sweet, uncertain, scared boy that she had loved since she was old enough to understand her own feelings.

Her William was by himself when Thomas betrayed him, killed Richard, and left him facing Amir and his army alone. *Her William* had been beaten and wounded while working to protect her. He must have been alone and terrified, perhaps sustained by the thought that she was somewhere worrying over him, praying for him; but instead, she had been plotting his death! And yet, somehow, he still saw her as pure; he did not see the rot that lay beneath the surface.

Leah did not want to feel it; she was not strong enough to take on any more guilt or pain, but it crashed in upon her all the same. She covered her face to hide his eyes from her view, to hide her face from him, before dropping to her knees as shame-filled sobs of anguish and regret burst from her.

William looked urgently between her and his mother, dying across the room, but he finally stooped and pulled her to him.

"No, William, please," she sobbed, "do not comfort me of all people, I beg you!"

"Do you not see, Leah?" he said softly, refusing to release her. "We are all wounded. It is what we do after that that matters." He held her for another minute until the great wracking cries had passed and then whispered in her ear, "I will return shortly."

William let Leah go and started to hurry back to his mother, but he knew before he had made it three steps that she was gone. Her unnaturally motionless body that should be writhing in discomfort and her wide, staring eyes that appeared to be watching him and Leah told him all he needed to know.

His steps involuntarily slowed. He didn't want to see, did not want to face it, but of course he had to.

Then movement at his side caught his attention. Thomas!

Thomas, who had caused all this pain; Thomas, who was responsible for all the death, still lived! He was trying to crawl away from William, leaving a trail of his own blood as he did so.

William stared down at his pathetic brother and was surprised that it was not rage he felt but sadness.

Suddenly he understood Richard's injunction not to kill Thomas. At the time Richard had said it, the idea was unfathomable to William. Richard knew that he was going to die, that he would never get to meet his only child, and he had known that it was Thomas' fault. William could not comprehend it then, but as he watched Thomas writhe on the floor, the broken shell of the man he could have been, he finally understood.

William remembered a time more than a decade earlier when he and his brothers, by the light of the setting sun, had all covenanted to be a united force for good. And what a force they could have been! This must have been what Richard was feeling in that moment on the battlefield, when he had allowed Thomas to live even after Thomas had attacked him. Richard was seeing what could have been, lamenting what never would be, and perhaps holding out hope that at least some of the Dawnings would make good on their promise.

William knew that he too had let Richard, as well as the rest of those who loved him, down. But he could at least honor this one promise.

William turned away from Thomas, and all the anger and hate he engendered, and returned to his mother.

Forty-six

Leah hugged herself as William walked away, both grateful that he was leaving and desperately wishing that he would never let her go. She watched him stop over Thomas and wondered if he would kill his brother even while sparing Amir's life. She wondered if he would torture Thomas before finally cutting his throat.

William stood peering down at Thomas, who was looking fearfully back at the brother whose retribution he so richly deserved, even as he struggled to drag his wounded body to safety. Leah was no longer sure of what she wanted. Unlike her view of Amir, a being who had brought nothing but sadness into her world, she was of two minds about Thomas. Though he was loathsome and despicable, she had also known the witty, charming man he had been, and she could not entirely wish for him to suffer. Maybe William would have mercy and kill him quickly.

But then William turned away from Thomas without so much as a word and returned to his mother. He perfunctorily checked her for breath before slowly hunching over her still body.

Guilt stabbed Leah's heart like a knife. She realized with horror that the last thing Martha ever saw Leah do was betray her. *I am the most selfish, stupid, weak creature who has ever lived! I am the meanest of hypocrites! After yearning for his death, I allowed William to comfort* me *instead of his dying mother!*

Before she realized what she was doing, Leah started to rise. She could not be here; she had to run, to flee, to escape the tidal wave of guilt and shame that threatened to consume her.

No! The command came so loudly that Leah could not be sure if she had heard it audibly or if it was only in her head; but she froze in place. *You will watch this! Look at them and know that you do not deserve a place with them!*

Leah watched, awash in emotions that she could not possibly process in the moment as the object of both her most tender and her most vile feelings sobbed over the body of the woman who had most believed in Leah—the woman that Leah had most bitterly disappointed. Martha had been raising Leah up to be a leader to these people, but instead of stepping into that role, Leah had betrayed her—betrayed them all.

She was so caught up in the drama unfolding both inside and out that she did not notice Anisa across the room sitting up and taking in the sight of Thomas and Amir, who appeared to be dead, and of William kneeling over his mother with his back to her.

Leah did not see Anisa retrieve the dagger from where William had dropped it after being hit from behind by Thomas. It was only the sound of the sudden footsteps that alerted her. Anisa was charging across the room, dagger raised, intent upon plunging it into William's exposed back.

With no time to consider, Leah snatched up William's sword and jumped in front of Anisa, driving the sword straight out in front of her.

Anisa was so intent upon William that she did not notice Leah until she was right in front of her, when it was too late to stop herself, and ran headlong into Leah's extended blade. Anisa's momentum slammed her into the sharp steel sword with such force that the point ran straight through her and out her back.

The feeling of the weapon sliding through flesh deeply disturbed Leah, though not as much as the spray of hot blood that showered her hands as she stood face to face with the woman she had just killed.

Leah watched in intimate proximity as the look of shock on Anisa's face turned to rage, then pain, then fear, all in the space of a breath. Leah could not bring herself to move as the light faded in the eyes of the woman who was so close that Leah could feel her last breath on her own face.

In that instant, several heavy truths struck Leah with perfect clarity. She realized that she had just taken a life with her own hands and done it of her own free will and choice. But she also understood something else. She knew now that it was not her strength that had granted Anisa her life down in the chapel but her weakness. Leah was sickened by what she had just done, but at last she understood why William had granted no mercy to the man begging for his life at the wedding: because to do so was to hold the life of that murderer more sacred than the lives of the victims—more sacred than the lives of her loved ones. She had released Anisa, telling herself that it was proof that she was better than William; but in reality it was a way of excusing herself from doing the hard but necessary unpleasant business of protecting those she loved.

All this was as clear as day to her in that moment, but it did not make the act any less horrible. Anisa's limp body slid off the blade and collapsed in a heap.

Leah looked down at her bloody hands and then back over her shoulder at William, who had not stirred from his mourning.

I am not better than William, she thought. *It is I who was too weak to do what he has done; it is I who am not worthy of him!*

Well, no more. With one last regretful look over her shoulder at the Dawnings and her beloved mentor, who could no longer benefit from Leah's healing arts, she left the room. There was work to be done, and she would see that it was done. William would not have to carry this burden alone any longer.

Forty-seven

What now, lads?" Anthony's swarthy rescuer asked in the aftermath of the west wall crashing into rubble. The three had stopped on the north wall, where they had landed after their narrow escape, and watched the resulting madness.

Anthony took a deep breath and sighed as he watched the peasants running frantically to and fro in the escalating panic.

"Do they not see that there is nowhere for them to run?" Rylan asked, more to break the silence than out of any desire for an answer.

"Lord, should we not see about restoring order?" the dark soldier prodded a minute later.

Anthony sighed again. How did he explain that he had nothing left to give these people? There was no hope for them, so what was the point of fighting any longer?

"What is your name, soldier?"

"Silas, Lord."

"Silas, Rylan, you two did well." Anthony continued to stare out over the courtyard, giving no indication that he intended to move from that spot.

"You do not—er—are you unwell, Lord?" Rylan asked nervously.

"When is the last time you slept?" Silas asked directly.

Anthony turned his hollow eyes on him. "Who's to say? A day, a week, a fortnight? I do not recollect."

Silas, who had not taken his eyes from Anthony, continued, "Our mind begins to play tricks on us when it is deprived of sleep. Our ability to make wise decisions and act on them is compromised."

"We cannot win now, Silas. Surely you must see that."

Silas shrugged. "It may be that victory is out of the question, but should we not do what we can to orchestrate an organized surrender? Those people are tearing each other apart down there."

"You are welcome to try," Anthony said but then dropped his eyes. "I have tried and failed. I put everything I had to offer on the altar of sacrifice: my strength, my love, even my faith; but God did not respond."

"As a common soldier, I am not even permitted to speculate on the mind of the nobility, so fathoming the mind of God is well beyond me. Instead, I think in terms of what I can and cannot do when it comes to a task before me, and if God chooses to put his thumb on the scale in my behalf, I am certainly not going to turn my nose up at him."

Anthony snorted. "God has not come to our rescue up to this point. Do you really expect that he will do so now?"

"I do not expect anything!" Silas was intense. "But those people are terrified. They need someone to rally them, someone they recognize! They will not listen to me."

Anthony did not respond. He only continued to stare into the distance. He knew Silas was right, but what was the point?

Silas drew his sword. "Rylan and I are going to join them. Do what you must." With that, Silas led the younger man down the battlements to descend into the maelstrom.

Watching the two soldiers running into the heart of the chaos, one of them not even old enough to shave, persuaded Anthony that he could not ignore his duty any longer. With an effort, he climbed to his feet and started to run after Silas.

417

Forty-eight

Sebastian!" Leah was pleased to find the aging servant near the postern.

"Lady Leah?" Sebastian said with obvious relief at seeing her alive. "I lost Thomas. I was just gathering a squad to search for you and Lady Dawning."

Comprised only of those men unfit for combat duty, Leah looked over the frail faces of the watchmen and pictured the slaughter that would have ensued had it been them instead of William who found Thomas and Amir. She had to suppress a shiver.

"Very good," she nodded, not bothering to explain. "Send several of these men to the Hall of Arms. Lord William is there and could use your assistance."

"Er-yes, Lady. But what of Lady Dawning? Shall we not look for her?"

"Lady Dawning is..." Leah hesitated, unable to say the words, "with William."

Sebastian perked up at hearing that. "Then I shall lead the men myself!"

"No!" Leah said, an idea forming in her mind. "On second thought, William will see to Martha; I have a different task for you. Take the rest of the men and gather up every weapon—or anything that can be used as a weapon—from the armory and meet me in the eastern courtyard."

"Lady?" He looked confused. "I do not understand."

"I intend to take back our grounds!"

"But, Lady, the Mayfields...."

"Are invaders!" she snapped. "Invaders that we outnumber a hundred to one. The only thing our people lack to defend themselves is a leader."

"And you intend that to be you?"

Leah whirled on him and stopped, seeing the aged face of the man who had been looking after the affairs of the castle since long before she was born, and softened the sharp retort she had intended. "Sebastian, there is no one else."

"Is not Lord William—"

"He has done enough!" she said too loudly but then forced her voice to soften again. "William is injured. Now please, do as I ask."

"Forgive me, Milady, but will the people follow you— what I mean is that you are not a knight or even a soldier."

"I do not see anyone else stepping up. If you would like the position, you are welcome to it." She held his gaze until he dropped his eyes. "'Tis madness to continue to treat the wounded when no one is doing anything to stop the destruction," she pointed out. "These people need a leader, and if no one else will do it, then I will!" Her voice filled with passion. "Not one more innocent person will die if I can prevent it!"

Leah pushed her way to the exit. "Open this door at once."

The watchmen looked to Sebastian for confirmation, and he reluctantly nodded.

"Sebastian, Richard himself could do nothing with an army that has no weapons," she said, reminding him of the urgency of her request.

"There is not much left in the armory, mostly armaments in need of repair."

"It does not matter. This is our last stand. Let us not send our people into battle with empty hands."

The stairway down to the courtyard was clear now that the people had given up trying to gain entrance to the castle, but the chaos in the courtyard was no better than it had been when Leah was there just a short time ago—though it felt like a lifetime ago. She could see the Mayfield soldiers holding a line around the doors to the Great Hall as they chopped at it with their axes.

Leah set her jaw. That was where she would begin, and she did not have much time. She descended the stairs and pushed her way around the side of the castle to the east, where her actions would be hidden from the view of the Dawnings' enemies.

"People of Dawning Court," she called, "you must listen to me!" But it was hopeless. No one even seemed to notice that she was speaking.

Undeterred, Leah snatched up a cooking pot beside an overturned wagon and then climbed up onto the side of the wagon, using it as a platform from which she could be seen and, hopefully, heard by everyone in the vicinity. She used William's sword to bang on the pot over and over until silence began to spread outward from her like ripples in a pond. The crowd calmed down, at least as much as a panicked crowd is likely to calm down, and turned to Leah expectantly.

"Cease this madness at once!" she commanded, tossing the pot aside. "Do you not know that even now, Sir Aden is battling our enemies beyond the gates! Can we not hold this courtyard against a small number of men when our liberation is at hand?"

"We are no match for armed soldiers!" someone yelled.

"They will cut us down like wheat," someone else added.

"Is this the end, then?" Leah countered hotly. "Are we to fall, after all we have endured, when salvation is at our gates?" She looked around at the anxious faces. "Very well! And when our enemies come for us, when we can no longer hide back here, what will we show them? Will they find our cowering backs, or will they have to look us in the eye and know that though they may slay our bodies, they will never conquer our spirits! We are greater than this!" She gestured around at the yard and castle. "Death will come for us all, perhaps this very day." She shrugged indifferently. "So be it. But when we again meet each other at the gates of Saint Peter, we will have to give an accounting of our lives, and what will your account show? Did you die cowering and whimpering, or did you fall defending your families and your people, having given your life to prevent an enemy blade from taking one of your brothers or sisters? Will you die grasping and clinging to your little life above all else, or will you die defending your home?"

Leah looked over the uncertain faces in the crowd. She was failing to rouse them. Was it because they were too scared? Or was it something else? She did not have to wait long to get her answer.

"What do you know about leading an army?"

And there it was, the reason she could not rile them up was because, though many undoubtedly knew her, she simply had no credibility as a military leader.

"I will follow you!" A man's voice came from behind her.

Every eye turned to see Neil astride a war horse, slumped in the saddle, but otherwise looking for all the world like a knight ready for battle.

Leah's eyes went wide with shock, but before she could respond, Neil raised his voice over the crowd. "You know me. I have fought alongside you from the beginning. And so long as there is breath in my lungs, I will continue to fight for Dawning Court. Lead the way, Lady Leah, and I will follow."

An excited murmur went through the crowd, and Leah's heart swelled with gratitude for her surly old friend. She had to resist the urge to run over and hug him, but the crowd had one more objection to raise.

"We have no weapons!"

"You do now!" Sebastian's timing was perfect, as at that moment he led his group of watchmen into the crowd and began distributing armfuls of scavenged weapons.

The assembly grew silent as they looked upon the armaments, many broken and cankered with rust, and pondered on the ramifications of carrying them into a fight against armed and trained soldiers.

Leah knew they were scared. So instead of pretending otherwise, she simply addressed it. "No one will call you a coward for simply giving up," she said with no accusation in her voice. "It is only you who will have the rest of eternity to deliberate on your inaction—to contemplate on the difference you might have made had you only been willing to act in this one crucial moment when it mattered the most.

"For at the end of the day, my friends, we had every excuse to fail. We were outnumbered, the enemy was better trained and better equipped. But justified or not, failure is still failure, and it brings with it all the same horrific consequences. I have seen your better nature, and I do not believe that when I go to meet our enemies, I will do so alone." She looked over the silent peasantry. "I go to drive away the intruders who even now are breaking down the doors of the castle. I do not believe you English—you Dawnings—will leave me to meet my fate alone. But if you choose to do so, I do not judge you. I only say that when we meet again in the next life, I will be the one holding my head high, for I gave my life for a cause greater than myself! I gave my life for my people! For you!" Her voice swelled and she thrust her sword in the air before jumping down from the wagon and starting toward the front of the castle.

Anthony's attention was riveted on the angel atop the overturned wagon. He could not believe what he was seeing. When he had last seen Leah, she had seemed every bit as defeated as he felt; but now, only an hour later, where he had all but given up on the cause, she had been transformed into some mythical goddess and now stood over the courtyard, calling the crowd to action.

He had not known—would not have believed—that Leah had it in her. He was enamored with the spectacle. Maybe God had sent him an angel after all, it was only that she had not descended from the clouds but had been someone he had known—or thought he had known—all along.

When the moment of awe passed, it brought with it a devastating sense of shame. Here was Leah—his betrothed—stepping into the leadership vacancy he himself had left. And if that were not enough of an indictment, here was Neil back from the dead, barely able to stay in the saddle, but still offering his all to defend the barony.

Anthony felt as though he had failed. Failed these people, failed Leah. But as the crowd cheered and began to take up weapons to follow Leah and Neil around the castle, he also knew that it was not over. The struggle continued, and there may still be time to redeem himself.

Forty-nine

We are too late!" Captain Serge echoed Henry's initial thought as they looked upon the devastation that was Dawning Court. Henry and Serge, with a small force, had let themselves up onto the outer wall. From this vantage point, they could see the collapsed west wall and the three armies fighting before the castle, with the Braddock cavalry dominating the field.

On the journey from France, Henry had told Serge and his men of their purpose, though they still believed they were there with Lord Ambroise's blessing. But now Henry worried that they might become too disillusioned with the odds of success to engage when he needed them. After all he had done to get them here, he could not stomach that thought, so he tried to sound more optimistic than he felt. "There is hope yet."

"Hope?" Serge looked at the battle dubiously.

"Do you not see? They are still fighting. That means Dawning Castle still stands."

Just then, one of the scouts Henry had sent forward to get the lay of the battle returned. "Sir Henry, I can make out at least two banners aside from the Dawnings'," he said, nodding toward Henry's own crest of white and blue, "but I am not familiar enough with the English nobility to know them by sight."

"Describe them to me."

The scout described the Braddock banner, which Henry identified instantly. "And the other?"

"'Tis a white cross of spear heads upon a red field."

"Why, that sounds like ... the Mayfields," Henry paused in thought.

"You know these 'Mayfields'?" Serge asked.

"Indeed I do."

"Are they friends?"

"I ... am not certain." As much as he wanted to believe that they had heard of Dawning Court's distress and ridden to the rescue, that just did not seem like behavior he had come to expect from Mary and her family. But surely they were not so opportunistic as to attempt to take Dawning Court by force while it was fighting for survival. Mary was his wife! She was loyal to him. "That must be it!" he concluded. "Mary—my wife—sent to her family for support in our most desperate hour!"

"Er ..." the scout shot a nervous glance at Serge.

"What is it?" Henry demanded, his ire instantly piqued that he would dare suggest that his wife was anything but the faithful creature he wanted to believe.

"I do not mean to contradict you, Lord, but the soldiers fighting under the banner I have described ... these Mayfields?"

"What of them?"

"It is only that, well, they appear to be fighting against the Dawning soldiers."

Henry stiffened. He wanted to lash out at the lad for his impertinence, but he caught himself. It was not the soldier's fault that Henry was embarrassed; he had embarrassed himself by revealing that his wife was a Mayfield, only to be told that she was the enemy. *Once again*, he thought, *I am proving that I am unfit to command; I cannot even command the respect and loyalty of my most intimate companion.*

But maybe that was not it at all. Perhaps this was just some giant misunderstanding. He wanted to believe that. A misunderstanding could be corrected with diplomacy instead of blood. But then he remembered the reality check he had received at Edward's hands and sighed.

"Sir Henry," Serge prodded him, "your orders?"

"Instruct the army to ready themselves. We attack at once.... Anyone on the field not wearing a Dawning Crest is an enemy," he added darkly.

"But how can we know that we will not be treated as merely another enemy by the Dawnings?"

"Fly the Dawning crest beneath the Ambroise banner."

Fifty

illiam's tears were spent. He rolled from his knees to a sitting position beside his mother's prone body and found himself looking out over the Hall of Arms. In his grief, he had all but forgotten that he was not alone in the room.

He noticed with some disappointment that Leah had left. She was no longer beside Amir, who was still lying in a heap where William had left him.

William was glad to realize that Amir's presence no longer caused that fearful tightening in his chest. He had conquered that fear, but had he really been victorious?

He could not help thinking about what Amir had said in that final exchange about William's world burning down around him. He was not wrong. Everything William had fought to protect and everyone he cared about was lost to him. William's body might be in slightly better shape than Amir's, but did he have anything more to show for his life than did Amir?

Amir had been wronged by William's father and had spent his life attempting to exact retribution for those wrongs. All his anger, hate, and fear had led him to this brutal, ignominious end at the feet of his enemy, without a friend in the world to mourn him.

Had William's life, driven by the same anger, yielded any better results for him? Instead of the happy, comfortable life he might have had with Leah, she had been unwilling to even stay with him through his darkest moment. How that hurt! Of all the times he had yearned for her presence, he wished for it now more than ever. But he had burned that bridge, and she was gone.

Everyone was gone, everything destroyed. William may have killed those who challenged him, but like the mythical hydra, each time he cut off one head of fear, two more sprang up. Killing Vincent Braddock had made an enemy of Daniel Braddock and cost him his association with Jurou. His anger then drove him to reassign David, and he lost both David and Neil as a result. He fought Daniel Braddock and ended up across the lines from Hans and Amir, which had cost him everything else.

This was exactly the outcome that Jurou had predicted all those years ago if William did not learn to control his demons. He had not, so they had controlled him; and it had cost him everything. William had tried to exploit the very weakness that had created the problems in his attempt to solve them, and it had only made things worse and worse until everything—everyone—was gone.

It was too little too late, but William was done with it. He was done being controlled by his rage, hate, and fear, done keeping his worst fears so close that they prevented those he loved from getting near him. No more chasing death. No more exacting revenge for every perceived slight, no more would he exchange the precious moments he had with loved ones for time with despicable people like this. He was going to spend whatever time might be left to him focused on those things that mattered.

Amir was not dead, but William no longer cared what happened to him. His fate no longer mattered. William could see clearly that it was not Amir who had ruined his life but William himself; he was his own worst demon. Amir had simply been the outward personification of all the darkness that William was holding inside.

William turned his eyes from the tortured figure on the floor and found them resting upon someone else. It struck him suddenly that the body that lay unmoving between him and Amir should not have been there.

"Leah!" he cried and scrambled on his hands and knees over to the prone body. He gasped in relief when he saw that it was not her but Anisa. The Nizari assassin that he had left unconscious now had a hole clean through her sternum.

What is going on? It was only now that he noticed that Thomas also was nowhere to be found.

William hurried over to Amir to look for his sword, but it too was gone. That is not what caught his attention, though. Amir was still lying prostrate, having fallen back over his heels; but his face had been caved in with the head of Thomas' mace, the one William had used to shatter Amir's arm. The bloody head of the mace lay beside Amir's body, left behind as a useless weight without its shaft.

"Was I asleep?" William demanded of the air. "What happened here?"

He took a long breath. It was clear that his work was not yet finished. Dawning Court was not yet safe, so whatever meager strength he had left had to be employed in her defense.

He sighed deeply. He honestly did not know how much more he could endure, but he had to try.

He covered his mother's body and then picked her up to carry her to a nearby sitting room, where she could rest undisturbed until she could be buried properly. But he was troubled at how heavy she felt.

His head swam as soon as he stood up straight. He realized that he did not have much time and hurried for the door but was already staggering by the time he reached it.

He was spent. Though he was on his feet, he had used every last ounce of energy he still had, and now the blow to the head was making it impossible for him to even see straight.

His skull ached, the room was spinning, and his mother's body in his arms felt like it weighed a ton!

"Don't you drop her!" he commanded himself through clenched teeth.

He crashed through the door of an adjacent sitting room, staggered to the divan, and half-dropped his mother on it before falling to his knees and retching on the floor. Then everything went black.

Fifty-one

F all back, men!" Aden roared over the battlefield, dismayed by the bedlam. The Braddock cavalry had decimated his line. His men likely would have been routed completely had the Braddocks not also been forced to contend with the mercenary army on the other side.

Aden, for his part, had managed to unseat one of the Golden knights, but it had then taken him more than a quarter of an hour of sparring with the man before Aden was able to drive his sword through the knight's visor and put him down.

Now that he was freed up again to oversee the battle, he was not pleased with what he saw. His soldiers were scattered across no man's land. Some were chasing Braddocks, and many were being chased, but their only chance to withstand the mounted knights was to hold their line. As things sat currently, they would be ridden down and cut to pieces one by one.

"Fall back," he shouted again, though his voice faltered as the futility of his plight settled on him. Nobody seemed to respond to the command.

"We have lost too many men!"

Aden turned to see Martin, covered in mud, with blood streaming down the side of his face from a gash on his head, in the process of dispatching a Braddock knight. "We will not last another hour on the open field!" he panted.

"We've nowhere else to go!" Aden said through gritted teeth as he caught the blade of another knight on his own and riposted. "With the wall compromised and enemies already inside, we have no choice but to face them here on the open field."

Martin spun beneath a new attacker and smashed his mace into the head of the knight attacking Aden, dropping him; then both men turned on the new arrival.

"It has not been an hour, and as near as I can judge, a third of our men are down. This is a catastrophe!"

Both men charged the man before them with their shields together, bowling him over and smashing his helpless body until he stopped moving.

Aden scanned the field as a light rain started to fall, which only added to the dismal scene before him. Everywhere he looked his men were dropping, but he felt absolutely powerless to do anything about it. *This is the end,* he realized but did not dare voice it. *We are finished.*

"Who is that?"

Aden turned to look where Martin was pointing, wondering what more could possibly go wrong.

Charging in from the west rode a new group of mounted men, hundreds and hundreds of them, lances poised, an unfamiliar pennant flapping from the tip.

"This cannot be happening." Aden's incredulity replaced his despair as he watched the column of mounted men swing around the trees and descend onto no man's land.

The newcomers hit the Braddock column as the Braddocks were galloping toward Aden's men for another pass. The new army's attack was timed perfectly to take advantage of the Braddock charge that was already underway, rendering the Braddocks unable to respond to a hit from the flank.

The new army obliterated the first column of Braddock knights, including many of the Golden Sword.

Martin looked at Aden in disbelief, but Aden had begun running down the field, shouting with renewed vigor. "To me, men! Fall back to me!"

Aden snatched a horn from the body of a nearby soldier and began blowing it furiously to call his men to regroup.

Martin, still uncertain what he was seeing, continued to watch the new cavalry sweep from west to east across no man's land and then turn for another pass. Finally, he saw what Aden must have seen: beneath the unfamiliar pennant, the new arrivals were flying the Dawning crest.

Martin did not know what to make of it. Was it a trick? Was it another pseudo-ally, like the Mayfields, hoping to capitalize on the Dawnings' moment of weakness?

He did not know, but it was unquestionably a chance for them to regroup and perhaps survive the day.

Henry was nervous. Their surprise attack had hit the unsuspecting Braddocks exactly as he had hoped. The first pass must have unhorsed more than a hundred Braddock knights without the loss of a single man. But the second pass was harder, as the Braddocks had had time to regroup, and Henry's charge was not half so successful this time. And now, as they set up for the third pass, the Braddocks were lining up to meet them. This is where the knights' superior training was going to show itself over his soldiers.

"Charge!" he called, not wanting to allow the knights time to fully form up, even though it meant starting his own men forward before they were completely ready. Henry set his lance for the center-most Golden Knight, who did the same for him. The two rode out ahead of their respective forces and met with a mighty impact just seconds before the armies collided with each other.

Henry's steel-tipped lance hit Bertram's shield with devastating force, but Henry too was rocked back in his saddle so hard that he barely managed to keep his seat.

Then the armies were crashing into each other. Men shouted in pain, horses whinnied, and steel clashed against steel in a horrific cacophony.

Henry, righting himself in his saddle, was disturbed to see that many of the saddles of his soldiers emerging from the charge were empty. He could not estimate how many of the Braddocks had gone down, but regardless of the numbers, he had no choice but to see this through.

The Braddocks swept around for another pass, but Henry's men were not that well-coordinated. They had to stop and turn their horses back and reset their line, which cost them the advantage; the Golden Sword was already descending upon them, with the rest of the chivalry in tow by the time they were ready.

Henry again took his aim for the central figure, though with decidedly less enthusiasm than before. The blow he had sustained had been brutal. It had punctured his shield and sent a shockwave through his body that made him worry about whether he could sustain another blow like that. But as Bertram zeroed in on him, Henry noticed that Bertram's shield was hanging at his side.

His arm is broken! Henry exulted. *The advantage is mine!*

They collided again, but this time Henry hunkered down behind his damaged shield and drove his lance into Bertram's sizeable chest, trusting that he could weather one more strike.

Henry struck Bertram above his heart with tremendous force, spinning the big knight from his saddle and sending him rolling shoulder over shoulder to the ground, where he lay with his arms splayed in an unnatural position.

Unfortunately, Bertram's aim was also flawless, and as Henry took no evasive maneuvers, he took the full force of the strike in the center of his shield, which smashed his arm into his body and rolled him off the back of his horse.

Henry landed in the mud on his face just as the armies were colliding again. But this time it was not a clean pass. As lances broke and horses stumbled, the two armies ground to a halt, causing the men to discard their lances and draw swords.

Henry shook his head to clear it. He was unsteady but did not seem to be seriously hurt. Bertram had not moved. *I won!* Henry could not believe it. He had beaten one of the best knights in Braddock Court in the joust!

That briefly made him wonder where Collin had gotten to. But he pushed that thought aside, for now he had a bigger problem. The battle had devolved into hand-to-hand combat much sooner than he had hoped. That was a big problem because with man-to-man combat, the advantage continued to skew in favor of the Braddocks and their superior numbers.

But Henry had just beaten Bertram! With renewed confidence, he pushed himself up and drew his sword. He may not be Richard or William, but he could certainly give any ordinary knight a run for his money in hand-to-hand combat.

Just as Henry started forward, a huge line of Aden's infantry plowed into the side of the Braddocks.

Fifty-two

Mary could sense something was not right as her guard detail, under the direction of her father, continued to hack their way through the gates of Dawning Castle. She tried not to look at the red carpet of dead peasants that paved their path from the barbican. But it was not even that grisly sight that was bothering her; the problem was that they had not met any real resistance. The peasants, panicked, fleeing, and mostly unarmed, had been easy kills. But where were the soldiers? Why was no one standing up to them? Amir had said that the castle was down to a meager peasant army, but where were they? Surely not every soldier was dead. Why were they not here now?

She tried to bring her concern to her father's attention, but it was too chaotic, and he was too excited about taking the castle. Nevertheless, she could not shake the feeling and tried again to warn him. "Father! Something is not right!"

"Not now, Mary!" George snapped.

"If we get through the door, are you prepared to withstand the people inside? What if they have planned to ambush us? Should we not fetch more men?"

"Enlisting soldiers from outside the walls will bring Aden's men with them," George groused impatiently. "Besides," he scoffed, "there is nothing but more peasants inside, and you see how little resistance they offer. Remain steady, and we will control the castle inside the hour."

Mary chewed her lip nervously. What her father said did make sense, and as much as she was the dominant one in the relationship, she had to defer to him on matters of combat. Perhaps they would be all right. After all, her soldiers were almost through the door, and maybe the fact that they had not met any real resistance was simply a blessing for which she should just be grateful. Maybe it was only her inexperience that was allowing it to unnerve her.

Mary heard the danger before she saw it. Over the tumult in the courtyard, a great wall of sound drew her attention. She tried to call George's attention to it, to ask him if it was anything to be concerned about, but it was too late.

From around the eastern wing of the castle came a great rush of hundreds of armed peasants. Some ran down to the lower ward and the main gate, but most of them set their sights upon Mary's company as the closest, most obvious target. They were a motley assortment of women, youth, and elderly, but they were all armed and all evidently in a battle frenzy; and they massively outnumbered her troops.

"Father." She meant to scream, but her terror stole the sound from her throat.

"Father!" This time she found her voice, but it was not necessary. George had already spotted the incoming tide, and his eyes grew wide with fear. "F—form a defensive line!" he stammered to his soldiers.

The Mayfields' mercenaries, who were just as shocked as the Mayfields, made some show of obeying the order, but George was not watching them; he was wheeling his horse. "Get through the breach in the wall!" he hissed at Mary, hoping not to be overheard by the soldiers he was intending to sacrifice so that he and Mary could escape with their lives.

Mary tried to do as George instructed, but she soon found that galloping in the courtyard was impossible with the detritus of rubble, people, animals, and dead bodies stuck in the ankle-deep mud everywhere she looked. Their horses offered little advantage over the pursuing peasants, who could sidestep or jump obstacles much more easily than they could.

Mary shot a nervous glance over her shoulder just in time to see the defensive line of her soldiers dissolve before the peasant army, which was now within twenty feet of them. Most of her mercenary soldiers turned and fled in the face of such overwhelming odds, and the few who tried to stand their ground fell in an instant.

"Get out of here! Go!" George called as he let his mount fall back a step behind Mary's and started swinging his blade at the first peasants to reach him.

Mary's entire focus was required as her horse leapt over the trench of filth running the length of the courtyard. But she turned back just in time to see George dragged backward out of his saddle. She screamed as he disappeared into a group of raving peasants that consumed him like a pack of wild dogs taking down a deer.

Mary remained frozen in shock for only a moment before realizing that she was losing precious time. She drove her heels into the horse's flanks and charged toward the gap in the west wall, galloping on the very edge of calamity.

Fifty-three

Hildebrant watched the great wall of peasants overwhelm the Mayfields at the castle gates and knew that their fight was over. The meager remnants of his army might have been able to affect the outcome of the fight against a similar-sized group of mercenary or Saracen soldiers, but watching the peasants sweep across the courtyard, eating up every enemy in their path, he knew that if they did not flee right then, all would be lost.

"Fall back, men!" he cried into the commotion. Most of the men, who like him had been unconvinced about the wisdom of this attack, had not yet fully engaged anyone in combat, choosing to hold a defensive line near the breach instead. They responded to his call to retreat instantly, turning and exiting the courtyard the way they had entered only minutes before.

It was only Hans, who had jumped in with relish and had begun riding down everything in his path, that did not seem to hear Hildebrant's call to retreat. Instead, he stopped in place, watching the retreating Mayfields race down the slope toward him as though he were waiting to greet them.

Hildebrant continued to urge his men back out of the courtyard, casting one last glance over his shoulder at Hans' back as they made their escape. For a brief moment he considered going back for Hans but decided that this was the best way for this to end. Hans could die the glorious death he sought, and he would not be able to inflict any more harm on his own people.

"God speed, you mad bastard," Hildebrant muttered before following the last men out. "Circle around behind the castle and get back to our wounded," he ordered. "We will ride out this storm as a unit!"

Hans waited as Mary raced down the hill toward the lower ward, the breach, and ultimately toward him. He sat mounted, ready to face the woman who had shattered his plans for the barony. She was galloping at full speed, unable to stop. All Hans had to do was lower his lance, and she would impale herself—a fitting end for this treacherous consort of mercenary scum.

Yet she was not uncomely, Hans admitted to himself. Her dark hair streamed behind her, and her figure was undeniably appealing. And she was desperate. It clung to her like a shroud. Perhaps there was a use for her beyond leaving her body to rot in the mud. After all, hadn't Salena been in a similar position when she came to him? That had worked to his advantage. Why not this too?

Hans just needed a moment to think, but there was no time. As much as he wanted this woman, larger concerns loomed. *Just kill her and be done with it!* his father's gruff voice commanded in his mind.

It was the logical course. She was, after all, the enemy who had led the charge that dashed his hopes of victory over the Dawnings. But his father had never understood Hans'...proclivities. And Hans was not thinking of taking Mary in *exchange* for victory; he just wanted to salvage something for himself.

Mary barreled toward him on the verge of losing control. Hans beckoned to her as if offering her safety, and for a moment it seemed to work. But at the last second, she veered past him.

Cursing, Hans turned his horse and gave chase. But by the time he coaxed his mount into a gallop, Mary had already leapt over the rubble where the wall once stood.

Hans dropped his head low over his horse's neck and charged, determined to catch her before she could make her escape. He lowered his lance, preparing to kill her if necessary, and bore down on her.

He was so focused on Mary that he almost didn't notice the mounted figure charging at his flank. He twisted just in time to avoid a blow that could have been fatal.

Momentarily forgetting Mary, Hans turned to face the rider who had tried to ambush him. He lifted his visor to get a clearer look. The man wore no helmet and was using a spear as a lance, but he carried himself like a knight, not a peasant.

"Identify yourself!" Hans called.

"I am Sir Anthony, brother to Grace Dawning, baroness of Dawning Court. And I challenge you, Hans Braddock, to a duel for your dishonorable deeds!"

Hans felt a thrill. "So, you are the force behind the Dawnings' peasant-army, the one keeping me from my rightful claim."

"You allied with heathens and traitors against your own countrymen! I am here to deliver justice!" Anthony spat.

Hans glanced wistfully toward the breach where Mary had disappeared. This man truly intended to take everything from him. He set his jaw, knocked down his visor, and charged.

The two riders thundered toward each other. Anthony had the advantage of the high ground, but Hans' lance was longer and would hit first.

His aim was true, striking Anthony square in the chest, directly on the Dawning crest. But Hans' triumph was short-lived—his lance shattered into splinters, barely moving Anthony from his saddle.

Meanwhile, Anthony's spear struck home, and Hans was thrown from his horse, crashing into the mud. His head slammed against the ground, and his left arm twisted painfully beneath his body. Dazed and hurt, Hans realized he was in serious trouble. His arm throbbed, and even the slightest movement sent pain shooting through him.

Anthony was circling back for another pass. Hans knew he had seconds to act or he was as good as dead. Gritting his teeth against the pain, he forced himself onto his knees.

Get to your feet! his father's voice barked in his mind. *Die on your feet like a man, not in the mud like a dog!*

Shaking, Hans rose though his legs felt weak. He pulled his sword from its sheath, the motion making his vision blur. He barely had time to raise it before Anthony bore down on him again, spear aimed at his chest.

In desperation, Hans swung blindly—and to his astonishment, his blade deflected the spear. Anthony galloped past harmlessly.

Hans couldn't believe his luck. He turned to face Anthony, expecting him to wheel around for another charge; but instead, Anthony was heading for the breach, where Saracen soldiers were now pouring through.

Hans saw what was happening and knew that he did not want to be caught in this chaos. He scrambled toward the fallen rubble, finding a small opening in the collapsed wall. Crawling beneath the precariously balanced stones, he squeezed into the narrow space, hoping to escape unnoticed.

Fifty-four

As soon as Mary was clear of the debris, she stopped, looking back into the courtyard. There was no one in immediate pursuit. She looked for her father, for some hope that he yet lived, but there was no sign of him. It made her sick to think of the grisly death he had likely suffered at the hands of these ... peasants! And not just any peasants, but the very people she had just saved from being subjugated by Hans Braddock. And not only had they failed to welcome her as their savior, or even as one of their own, but they had treated her like an enemy!

The terror Mary had been feeling only a moment before was all but forgotten now as she considered all that had happened. These people had been in no danger from her, had they simply complied with her wishes. And now they had murdered her father in a most horrific way and very nearly done the same to her! This was no longer simply about establishing herself in a new barony; this was about answering a personal challenge. These serfs had thrown the gauntlet down, and she was not going to flee with her tail between her legs!

She just needed reinforcements. Her army was fighting Aden's, but perhaps she could peel some of them off and lead them back into the courtyard. Mary turned her horse to the south but had not even gotten up to speed when Rafiq came riding around the corner with hundreds of bedraggled Saracen soldiers in tow.

"What is all this? What has happened?" she demanded, as if she had been waiting there for their report. "Are we defeated?"

"Collin Braddock has arrived," Rafiq said simply. "It has forced all sides to regroup and reassess."

"Regroup?" Mary repeated caustically, referring to the fact that they were very clearly running away.

Rafiq gave an embarrassed shrug. "We are outnumbered; the defenses we were counting on to shield us from Collin's superior force are in ruins; it seemed an opportune time to take our leave."

Mary considered that. If Collin was now in the fight, then her window for action was rapidly closing. She could understand why Rafiq was leading his men away, but that was an option she did not have. Mayfield Court was no more. George had sold most of it off in pieces over the years, and they had traded what little remained to finance the mercenary army. If she failed here, Mary had nowhere to go!

"We have only one possibility left to us. Nothing but poorly armed peasants stand between us and the castle. If we take it before the battle with Aden and Collin is decided, we can still control the barony."

"Forgive me, Lady, but I believe we would be better served using this opportunity to make our escape."

"If we run now, we will be scattered and hunted, and what have we gained?" Mary looked hard at Rafiq and added, "and how many years of your life have been wasted?"

Rafiq glanced through the breach at the peasants running pell-mell over the last of the enemies, looked back at the beleaguered soldiers still making their way around the wall from the south, and finally shrugged.

"Perhaps you are correct, Lady."

Mary smiled. This had not worked out the way she had planned at all, but if she were the only one left to take the barony, then so be it! "Into the courtyard, men!" she shouted, turning her horse and using her sword to point dramatically toward the castle. "We do not stop until we take the castle! The castle is safety!"

Perhaps it was the prospect of the protection of the castle walls, or maybe it was simply that they would rather fight armed serfs than trained soldiers, but the Saracens reluctantly began to stream around Mary's horse and push into the courtyard.

Mary watched with satisfaction as they pushed the confused rabble back and took over the lower ward.

She spurred her horse into the fight sooner than she might otherwise have done so she could see the faces of those impudent serfs who dared to attack her and her father. She wanted to see their surprise and fear as they watched the tide turn against them and saw that they were now going to pay for their insolence.

But something was wrong. While her army had quickly taken the lower ward, they had advanced no farther.

Mary continued to move through her troops until she emerged at the front and found that she was looking up the slope to the upper ward, which was packed with an army of armed peasants lining the donjon wall and barring the way to the castle on every front. Though numerous, the army seemed to be comprised of women, children, the elderly, and even some wounded. *Was this the force that killed my father and sent me fleeing in fear?* She was embarrassed that she had so overreacted but was glad none of her men had seen it...at least none that were left alive.

She turned back to the soldiers. "This is what has stopped you? A bunch of dirty peasant women? Gather your courage and follow me!"

She raised her sword to signal the charge, but just then a flushed and disheveled woman with a sword in hand pushed her way to the forefront of the peasants until she was staring down the slope at Mary. Mary did a double and triple take.

"Leah?" Mary almost did not recognize her. "Leah, do you not know me? It is me, Mary. Your sister! I am here to rescue you from all this. Why do you stand in my way?"

Leah was unmoved. "We have had enough *rescuing,*" she spat. "For any affection we once shared, I will grant you one last opportunity to do the honorable thing—take this heathen army and leave Dawning Court—leave *my home*—forever!"

Mary puffed up indignantly. "How dare you, a lowly franklin, presume to dictate to me, the wife of the heir of Dawning Court, whether I may come or go? My father died protecting this miserable patch of swamp for the Dawnings. Do you think that I will simply turn from it now because the consort of the disgraced youngest brother commands it?"

Leah's face flushed with anger at everything implied in Mary's words: Her dig at Leah's unrequited love; her insult to William, who was even at that moment mourning his mother, whose death came as a result of Mary's alliance with the Nizari; but mostly because Mary actually had the audacity to pretend she was there out of kindness, as their savior, rather than acknowledge her presence there for what it really was—a self-serving attempt to capitalize on the Dawnings' misfortunes and take over the barony. "I will not argue what you know to be vain assertions of rights to which you have no claim or altruism that was never intended. But given the numbers," Leah glanced at the lines of peasants standing between Mary's army and the castle, "I should think that you *do* need our permission."

"You would sacrifice your serfs to my trained soldiers in a futile attempt to keep me from my right?" Mary snorted.

"My people and I are Dawnings," she said loudly enough for a murmur of agreement to pass through the people around her, who suddenly stood just a bit taller. "And we will defend to the last against any low opportunists who think us too weak to resist them."

Mary's eyes narrowed. "Oh, I see what this is. You seek power for yourself. You want to rule."

Leah would have laughed had she not been too tired. "I will give you a second and final chance, Mary, for the sake of your late husband. There will not be a third. Withdraw this instant, and your life will be spared."

"*You* would kill me?" Mary cocked a quizzical eyebrow at Leah. "I seriously doubt that. Forgive me, Leah, but you are not a killer."

"You had best be certain of that before you take one more step."

The tension was electric as the two stared each other down. A snapping twig could have set them off.

It was at this moment that Mary noticed the blood on Leah's sword and realized that Leah was not simply playing a part; she had used that weapon. It was unnerving to Mary, who had never had any real combat training aside from some rudimentary fencing that George had insisted upon but which she had never taken seriously. After all, she had never imagined a scenario in which she would actually be swinging a sword in a fight. She was a lady!

But Mary did know enough to recognize that she had the advantage in a duel with Leah. Leah had the high ground, but Mary was mounted and armored, while Leah was on foot and wearing only a filthy, tattered dress, torn in a hundred places and covered in brown stains that Mary now recognized as dried blood.

But more than that, even were she inclined to retreat, Mary simply did not have a choice. She was not about to back down in front of her own army, which she would be unable to pay without the Dawning coffers; nor was she willing to let her father's death go unrequited. George had been wronged by Braden Dawning decades ago, and if she were to run now, then it would be tantamount to admitting that the Mayfields were less than the Dawnings; she would be disgracing his memory.

Without taking her eyes from Leah, Mary raised her sword, kicked her heels into her horse's flanks, and charged up the slope.

Leah descended to meet her, her own mostly-female army flowing down the causeway around her, not hesitating to cross swords with the trained, battle-hardened mercenaries.

"We are Dawnings!" Leah shouted into the air and was answered with a roar of ascent from the crowd.

For Mary's part, though she felt brutish to be personally involved in combat, there was something in her that reveled in it. She was no longer trying to manipulate some weak man from behind the scenes; she was taking her destiny into her own hands. *She* would win her barony, and *she* would rule unashamedly, as Martha had done.

Mary swung first, but her horse's unpredictable movements made it hard to aim. Leah, who was on foot, easily side-stepped Mary's clumsy swing and slashed Mary's horse across the neck, causing the animal to rear back in pain and toss Mary from the saddle.

The horse bolted into the fray but created enough of a barrier between her and Leah that Mary was able to recover her feet just in time to find herself standing face to face with Leah. Without the advantage of horseback, she felt decidedly less sure of herself. Leah was taller than Mary was, and the grim expression Leah wore did not look inclined to pity.

In her anxiety, Mary took her sword in both hands and swung a cross-hand swing at Leah as though she were trying to cut her completely in half. Leah jumped clear and then immediately lunged forward, with her curved blade extended out before her just as Mary reversed her swing.

Leah's blade pierced Mary's armor and sunk into her chest just beneath the breast, which caused her to stumble backward, but not before her swinging blade raked Leah's right side, slicing into her arm and across her ribs and hip.

Leah pulled reflexively back as Mary staggered and fell into the maelstrom of the battling armies all around them and was lost from view.

Leah looked down at her blade and saw that there was at least an inch-and-a-half of Mary's blood on the tip. That was not guaranteed to be fatal, but it was certainly going to put an end to Mary's warrior pretensions.

Fifty-five

Leah did not try to follow Mary into the crowd. She instead withdrew a step to check her own wounds. She could not see the three slices very well, but judging by the amount of blood dripping onto the ground, she guessed she would probably need to be sewn up.

When Leah let herself think about what could happen—bleeding out, fainting, infection, etc.—panic started to rise in her. She had seen firsthand all those things, and the thought of it happening to her caused her to feel lightheaded.

Stop that at once! she commanded herself. *You are in no immediate danger, and these people are looking to you! You will not let them down!*

"Drive them back to the mainland!" she found herself shouting as her peasant army surged down upon the enemy, overwhelming them with their sheer number. Leah felt a tremendous pride in these people—her people—doing the grisly business that she herself had spent too long wringing her hands over. "We are Dawnings! Show them what that means!"

Unlike herself, when these people had been called to fight for themselves, their families, and their loved ones, they had answered the call, and as a result they were saving not just themselves but all of Dawning Court.

But Leah pushed those self-defeating thoughts from her mind and ran into the fight, cutting and stabbing at any part of a Saracen soldier that presented itself.

Like a receding tide, the overwhelmed enemy was driven back toward the breach. But they were being pinned there because they could not retreat fast enough, forcing them into a desperate fight for their lives, which was like sending her people into a meat grinder.

"Open the gate!" she cried. "Open the gate!" But nobody could hear her. She searched around for someone to convey the message and found a barefoot, redheaded girl of about twelve, who was carrying a club as a weapon.

"You there!"

"Freya, Lady."

"Freya, can you get word up the battlements to open the gates? We need to allow the Mayfields to escape."

Freya's expression said that she did not entirely understand, but she nodded and disappeared across the courtyard, dodging in and out of people and obstacles like a fleet-footed fox, barely even breaking stride as she did so.

Rafiq had misgivings about entering the courtyard after Mary. While he had seen the necessity of it, he could also see that if the tide turned against them, the remnants of the army would be trapped, and escape the way they were entering would be problematic. So he had stepped aside and let Mary and the mercenaries enter first, preferring to direct the remaining soldiers instead.

"This is madness!" Khalid rasped from where he had sidled up behind Rafiq. Khalid enjoyed frightening people that way. It was a subtle reminder that at any time he could appear unnoticed and drive a dagger through your back, and you would never see it coming. But Rafiq had grown used to such antics and did not let himself show his surprise.

"When did you return, brother?" he asked without bothering to turn around.

"I arrived before Collin's army in order to warn you, but there was no one to hear my message."

"Yes," Rafiq admitted glumly, "events have not unfolded as we might have wished."

"And yet you wait upon the woman and her soldiers? I say again, that is madness!"

"I do not think so. The Mayfield woman is correct; our only hope of salvaging this doomed endeavor is from the safety of the castle."

"Have you not seen what is happening only a furlong to the south?" Khalid demanded. "The Mayfields will be obliterated."

Rafiq shrugged. "I do not intend to put myself into the lion's den until I am certain that it is safe."

"And if it is never safe?"

"Then we will return to Mount Alamut to report our defeat."

"And Amir?"

"Amir will not survive this."

"And if you are wrong? If we report him dead, and Hassan learns that he still lives, he will think us complicit in some subterfuge."

Rafiq considered that. Khalid was right, of course. The brotherhood had already issued the succeed or die order for Amir. If he failed to take the barony with this attempt, the Nizari had been ordered to dispose of him before returning to Alamut. Amir's head was the others' guarantee of safety after more than a decade of taking Nizari time and resources with virtually nothing to show for it. *But how to be sure that Amir is actually dead?* Rafiq stroked his beard thoughtfully.

As if in response to his question, a figure rolled clumsily through the break in the wall and landed in a heap not fifty feet from where Rafiq and Khalid now stood. He leaned against the wall, and his eyes darted around like a frightened animal. He was obviously injured.

"Is that …?"

Rafiq's face broke into a grin. "Allah is smiling upon us." He turned to look at Khalid for the first time. The tall, lean man was standing in front of one of the horse-drawn carts used to pull down the wall, which he had evidently commandeered as an escape vehicle. "I have a plan, but you must hide in the trees; he does not trust you."

Khalid looked uncertain but started to lead the cart deeper into the trees before Rafiq stopped him. "No, leave it!"

Khalid quickly wrapped the reins around a branch and moved off to conceal himself while Rafiq made his way farther down the wall.

Fifty-six

Thomas hobbled out the postern door near the kitchens, where he had first entered. To his surprise and relief, the alcove was empty. But he did not dwell on it. His focus was on the pain and urgency of his situation. He had a strip of cloth, torn from one of the castle's displays, pressed against one wounded leg, with another makeshift bandage wrapped around his hamstring on the other leg.

He looked down at the flight of stairs that he had climbed so easily just an hour ago but that now seemed like a descent into hell. Each step would be torture, but with no other option, he leaned against the wall and started down, gritting his teeth with every step.

The almost deserted state of this portion of the courtyard was a small relief, though it made him wonder where everyone had gone. The cacophony coming from the south, however, quickly answered his question—a massive battle was underway. *Dawning Court's last stand*, he thought grimly and quickened his pace.

As he reached the last few stairs, his leg finally gave out. Whether it was from bending it too much or the repetitive jarring motion, his sliced quadricep muscle buckled, sending him crashing down the stone steps. He tumbled to the bottom and lay there, moaning in agony.

As he struggled to control his breathing and wiped tears from his eyes, he had to admit to himself that these were not just tears of pain; he was scared. He had never felt so weak and vulnerable, a stark reminder of his complete isolation. "I was so close!" he moaned, his bloody hand smearing across his eyes. Leah had chosen him; Martha was within his grasp; but then William and Amir had ruined everything!

Realizing that he needed to move before someone found him in such a helpless state, Thomas pulled himself up against the castle wall. Clenching his teeth against the pain, he started to hobble forward. Although the extra distance to the stables was daunting in his condition, he avoided the most direct route to the exit and instead circled around to the north of the castle, where there would be fewer people and no fighting.

The eerie emptiness of the castle grounds as he made his way around was unsettling, but he was grateful for the chance to escape unnoticed. By the time he reached a line of wagons beside the castle wall, he was exhausted. The stable was only about a hundred yards away, but crossing the open courtyard would leave him exposed and unable to rest.

"This is not going to work," he muttered to himself, trying to focus through the pain. "I cannot ride in this condition." He needed a wagon or carriage, like the one he had given to Neil, but getting one out of the courtyard amid the battling armies would be impossible. "Change of plans," he said aloud, as if giving orders to troops. "Forget the stable; head to the breach, get clear of the castle, and find transportation in the village."

Taking a deep breath to steady himself, he prepared to move. From here to the breach, he would be fully exposed and unable to pause for a rest. He could only hope he would not be recognized.

As he pushed himself upright, he glanced into the wagons he was using for support and started violently.

They were not empty but filled with bodies laid side by side for identification before burial.

Thomas tried to look away, but he could not help but be horrified by the grisly sight—deaths from catapult fire were never pretty—and a terrible fear gnawed at him that some of these might be people he knew. *Look away!* he commanded himself. *This does not matter now. Escape is all that matters.* Yet, he couldn't stop his eyes from flicking back to the wagons as he slipped past them. So many dead, including women and children not so different from his own family. He hoped that Annie had followed his instructions to take the children to visit her family, but he could not be sure. *What if your family is among these bodies?*

Pushing the thought aside, he forced himself to focus on the immediate need for escape. He began limping across the courtyard as quickly as his aching legs allowed. The movement was painful and awkward but not enough to keep him from reflecting on the dead he had just seen.

Those people are all dead because of you!

"No!" he shouted aloud. "The Nizari were coming for them anyway. I tried to direct the attack to my advantage, so I could protect these people and minimize casualties.

And if your family is among those bodies?

Thomas could not bear the thought of his children being among the dead. He quickened his pace, welcoming the increased pain to distract him while he made his way along the ruins of the west wall toward the breach.

"This is not my fault! This is not my fault! This is not my fault!" he repeated over and over, desperately trying to silence the incriminating voice in his head.

Anthony had been in the middle of the Saracen army in the lower courtyard, hacking and slashing from his saddle as they surged in through the gap in the wall, driving everyone before them. Forced to retreat with the peasants to the upper courtyard to make a stand, he once more witnessed Leah, at the head of the resistance, turn the tide of battle in their favor.

As Leah faced off against Mary, Anthony again watched from the sidelines. But this time he *chose* not to intervene. It didn't feel right; Leah was the leader of this army, having earned their trust and respect. For Anthony to assert his dominance now would not only seem presumptuous but would also leave him feeling like an imposter, akin to Hans Braddock taking control of an army that wasn't his.

Instead, Anthony seized the opportunity presented by the disorganized retreat of the Moors and cut down another dozen men before the main gate began to open. As he turned away from the fleeing Saracens and rode toward the gate to confront the next threat, a sense of dread gripped him.

To his surprise, however, no new enemy entered the gate. Instead, the retreating Saracens began to pour out, escaping through the gate much faster than the narrow breach allowed. The men Anthony had been fighting only moments before now forgot about him, pushing and shoving their way to safety. He noticed that the peasant army made no effort to stop them.

Was that Leah's doing? he wondered in awe. Had she opened the gates to allow the Moors to flee instead of stacking up at the breach and fighting for their lives, where they would undoubtedly kill many of the peasants in their desperation? How could the same broken woman he had led up the battlements just two hours earlier have transformed so drastically? Was this some hidden strength in the mild-mannered woman that had been there all along? Was this what Martha had seen in Leah that prompted her to include Leah in all the planning? *Or is this what I forced her to become when I failed to step up?*

The thought that he had failed his betrothed so completely filled him with deep shame. He needed to do something grand to prove his worth to her. But what could he do now that Leah had vanquished the immediate foe?

His reflection was abruptly interrupted by the sight of a familiar figure limping toward the now partially cleared breach, half-climbing and half-falling over it.

No! Anthony thought. This might not be the grand gesture he needed, but he couldn't let this stand. He spurred his horse into a gallop, determined to chase down the figure, but was soon obstructed by a new wave of Saracen soldiers that had not yet been able to make their escape.

Thomas swore under his breath as he stumbled over the wreckage of the wall's foundation, landing awkwardly on the other side. Despite managing to get his feet beneath him, he leaned back against the wall stone for support, wincing as he waited for the pain to ease.

Gasping for breath, he took a moment to appreciate his narrow escape. Yet at the same time, he couldn't shake his frustration with his brother. What good was it to be alive if he was stripped of all means of remaining that way?

"Lord Thomas?" a whisper came from his right, causing him to jump. He reached for the mace that he no longer had, muttered another curse at William, and tensed, preparing for whatever was to come.

"Lord Thomas, is that you?" Rafiq's form emerged from the shadows, crouched low to avoid detection.

"Rafiq?"

"Yes. Things are not going well, are they?" Rafiq's voice carried a faint sycophantic edge as he settled beside Thomas.

"Disappointing that your betrayal has not worked out for you," Thomas muttered.

"Not my betrayal," Rafiq hastened to correct him. "This was entirely Amir's doing."

"I know you are lying, Rafiq," Thomas said, shutting his eyes against the pain, "but I am in too much pain to care."

"Lord, you have been hurt!" Rafiq exclaimed with seemingly genuine concern.

"That can happen in a war," Thomas replied sarcastically. He refrained from mentioning Amir's role in his injuries, fearing Rafiq might decide to finish the job his master had started.

"Lord Thomas, we need to get you to safety so I can tend to your wounds."

"Would it not be simpler to let me die here?"

"Let you die?" Rafiq's shock sounded authentic.

Thomas had to admit that despite his mistrust of the Saracen, Rafiq's concern seemed real. It had been a long time since anyone had shown any worry for him, even if it was insincere.

"Lord, Amir is missing, and I fear the worst. We need your leadership to navigate this confusion."

Thomas studied Rafiq's anxious expression. "Amir is dead," he said flatly, "along with Anisa. William killed them."

"Is that so?" Rafiq's disappointment was fleeting. "Then you are our leader now. Will you allow me to minister to you?"

Thomas sighed, reluctantly agreeing. If Rafiq wanted him dead, there wasn't much he could do about it anyway.

"We must get away from here," he said. "It is too dangerous."

"I cannot ride."

Rafiq looked thoughtful for a moment and then led him by the arm. "I saw a wagon just inside the trees. You can ride in that."

True to his word, there was indeed a wagon hidden at the edge of the grove, hitched and waiting. Thomas was too pained to question how Rafiq knew about it.

"Gently now," he pleaded as Rafiq helped him into the wagon.

Without waiting for permission, Rafiq began removing the armor from Thomas' legs.

"Is this safe?" Thomas asked uneasily, "So close to the enemy?"

"You are badly wounded, Milord. Preliminary treatment is necessary before we move you."

"We?"

Suddenly the wagon shook as someone jumped into it and yanked Thomas' arms behind him. He looked up to see Khalid's grinning face.

"Did I not promise you that it would come to this?" Khalid taunted, binding Thomas' arms.

Thomas' first reaction was confusion rather than anger. "If this was your plan, why not just let me die here?"

"We have no intention of letting you die," Rafiq assured him as he tied off his ankles. "We need you healthy for the journey to Mount Alamut."

A chill ran down Thomas' spine. Well did he remember the gruesome tales of Richard's torture at the hands of the Nizari. Thomas knew he couldn't endure that. He needed to escape while he still had a chance. So, he did the only thing he could think to do; he started to scream for help.

Khalid's hard slap stunned him into silence.

"Someone is approaching," Rafiq hissed. "Gag him and get him out of here. I will catch you up once I am sure we are not being followed."

Thomas curled up on the rough wagon floor as Khalid stuffed a rag into his mouth and secured it with a strip of cloth.

"Relax now," he said, throwing a blanket over Thomas' body. "It is a long journey."

He then jumped into the driver's seat and whipped the horses into motion.

Rafiq stepped from the trees, signaling a rider on horseback to stop, pretending to be the one who had called for help.

He thought the man on horseback with sword in hand looked familiar, but he could not quite place—

By the time Anthony cleared the breach, Thomas was nowhere to be seen. Anthony shouted his frustration at Heaven. Why were the enemies of his peace continually being placed tantalizingly close, only to then be allowed to slip from him before he could exact retribution for their crimes, before he could purchase his redemption with the heads of these vile men?

Desperate to find Thomas, Anthony was just putting his spikes to his horse when a voice rang out from the nearby trees—a man's voice, calling for help. Anthony directed his horse toward the sound, his mind racing with the possibility that Thomas might be preying on some soldier, perhaps trying to steal a horse. He had to get there before Thomas could mount and disappear as Hans had done only minutes before.

His horse started into a gallop, and he flew toward the trees and the source of the sound. To his surprise, however, someone stepped out into his path that was not Thomas, or even a wounded soldier fleeing from Thomas; it was the Braddocks' Saracen confederate, Rafiq. Anthony was surprised, but in his fevered state, he did not even slow as the steward raised his hands to get Anthony's attention. It did not matter what he wanted. Anthony was tired of their schemes, their constant ploys; he was done listening to them. He did not take time to deliberate before galloping by and removing the head of the Saracen as he plunged into the trees after Thomas.

Anthony did not glance back as the Nizari's head spun into the air. He hardly even gave it a thought as he crashed around the glade looking for any sign of the traitor. In his frenzied state, he had difficulty sitting still long enough to look for blood trails or indications that Thomas had been through, so desperate was he to find the villain, punish him, and return to Leah with proof that he was not a failure and that God had not forsaken him.

But what if that was the problem? What if he really had been forsaken by Heaven? Everyone always said that William had divine protection. If that was the case, then wasn't it possible that Anthony had done something to incite divine wrath? The thought would have seemed preposterous to him only a week ago, but how else did one explain his every effort being foiled? Maybe that was the missing piece of this puzzle that he had not been able to make sense of. Maybe it was not that he was fighting for the wrong side; maybe it was simply him. Could the reason Dawning Court did not prevail under his leadership be that *he* was unworthy?

Anthony looked up suddenly, barely aware of where he was. It was eerily quiet. Though distant noises continued, the immediate vicinity was silent, with no sign of Thomas or anyone else. How long had he been sitting there? He did not know. He had not even noticed that he had come to a stop. It could have been minutes or hours; it was long enough that his horse had begun grazing. But one thing was certain—Thomas was gone.

Of course he is, Anthony thought. It was all so clear to him now. Heaven was never going to let him succeed; he was not going to be able to redeem himself, and he was never going to be worthy of Leah. So what was left for him?

Is this insanity? The thought sprang into his head. *Am I mad?*

No, No! He tried to reassure himself. *I am simply exhausted and overwrought. I must get back to the courtyard and find Leah; show her that I am still fighting for Dawning Court!*

He wheeled his horse and started back for the courtyard. But how would he ever explain to Leah that he had both Hans and Thomas dead to rights, and he let them both get away?

Fifty-seven

Leah commanded her peasant army to hold the line but not pursue the fleeing Saracens as they rushed out of the gate. She felt a grim satisfaction watching the trained soldiers retreat from her peasants.

The moment was short-lived, however, because as the Saracens surged out of the gate, they collided with their comrades trying desperately to get inside. Though she could not decipher the frantic shouts and cries in the mercenaries' foreign languages, Leah soon grasped the gravity of the situation. Calvary from an army she didn't recognize—neither her father's nor the Braddocks'—ripped through the Mayfield and Saracen foot soldiers, scattering bodies and slaughtering those who couldn't escape in time.

Leah was stunned by the sudden appearance of this new potential threat, barely processing that she had inadvertently opened the gates to an even greater danger. While they could have entered through the breach, that was a bottleneck which would limit entry, whereas she had just allowed a flood of mounted, fresh soldiers to pour in.

The cavalry tore through the remaining Mayfield-Saracen troops before eventually halting, causing the courtyard to drop into an expectant silence. Leah's force awaited her command to attack, but for the first time since leaving the Hall of Arms, she was paralyzed with indecision. The newcomers wore peculiar, angular helmets she didn't recognize, and when they stopped and put up their weapons before her army, she was doubly confused. Was this some sort of power play?

Determined to get a better view, Leah climbed back to the upper bailey, ignoring the cold, blood-stained side of her dress. Unsure of whom to address, she called out to the group, "Who speaks for you?" But there was no immediate response.

Then, from the back, a new rider approached. The soldiers parted to make way for him. As he rode through the gate, Leah's heart skipped a beat in disbelief. For the first time since she'd been trapped in the castle, she felt a surge of real joy, though she quickly suppressed it, not daring to believe it.

"Who is in charge here?" the newcomer demanded.

All eyes turned to Leah. "Father?" she whispered, still not daring to believe.

Aden's frowned deepened as he looked up at his bloodied daughter with a sword in her hand. But then he broke into a wide grin. "Leah?"

She raced down the slope, and Aden dismounted to embrace her. Leah couldn't hold back her tears.

"You are safe now," Aden assured her, holding her until she calmed down.

Leah stepped back, wiping her face. "I am very pleased to see you," she said, laughing through her tears.

"You are leading these people?" Aden's voice was a mix of incredulity and pride.

Leah gestured at the decimated courtyard littered with bodies. "There were not many contenders for the job."

"Where is Eve?"

Leah only shook her head and dropped her eyes.

"How?" Aden asked sharply.

"I will tell you all, father, but there is much to do first. Is it over? Are we safe again?"

Just then a new soldier, one from the recently arrived army, rode in and stopped right in front of Leah before removing his helmet.

"Bind those men!" Henry ordered his soldiers. "If they resist, kill them!" Both the Mayfield-Saracen army and now the Braddocks had finally surrendered. The battle had been fierce, but Henry's arrival—rarely perfect in timing—had this time struck just when it was needed. His surprise attack had knocked the Braddocks back on their heels, and they had never managed to recover. With more than half their force decimated, they had been compelled to capitulate. Now Henry's task was to ensure they were properly restrained before any pockets of resistance could form. Henry's cavalry had formed a perimeter around the captives while Aden's men began binding them.

"Lord Henry!" Serge's voice cut through the chaos.

Henry turned to see Dawning Court's gates creaking open. Uncertain of what to expect but unwilling to be caught off guard so close to victory, he called out, "Form up around me, men!"

But many of the mercenary soldiers who had not yet been restrained saw this as their opportunity to escape and darted past Henry's men in a sprint for the gates, even as Saracen soldiers came rushing out.

The two groups crashed into each other in a panic that almost devolved into a battle of its own as they shoved and wrestled to get past each other,

"Take back the courtyard!" Henry roared. "Attack!"

The cavalry crashed into the mercenary-Saracen soldiers who were trying to scramble over one another, catching them totally unprepared and tearing through them with almost no resistance save for the sheer number of men that were packed into the barbican.

Those of the enemy who survived the initial charge quickly realized that the threat posed by those in the courtyard was less deadly than facing Henry's death mill and turned to rush back in, only to be blocked by those who were still streaming out.

"Push them back and grind them to dust!" Henry roared. He was determined to dispatch them quickly to prevent the surrendered men from rallying and resuming the fight.

As Henry drove the mercenaries into the barbican, something caught his eye. He pulled up sharply, though his men continued pressing forward. He dismounted and moved closer to be sure that his eyes were not deceiving him, but in fact there, lying among the dead and dying enemy soldiers, was a woman.

She had dark hair and wore chainmail and was lying near where the portcullis would fall. She was bleeding from her chest and appeared to have been trampled by the panicked soldiers.

"Mary?" Henry said in disbelief, grabbing her shoulders and pulling her to safety out of the main thoroughfare of fighting men.

He could see at once that she had at least a broken arm and leg, and her chest wound was severe. She was breathing shallowly, and her pale face was so bruised and bloodied that she was barely recognizable.

"Mary, what ...?" Henry started, but at a loss for words, he finally settled on, "Not you, too."

She opened her eyes and managed a weak smile. "Thought you...were dead," she whispered.

Henry's concern turned to indignation. "This was always your goal. If you could not coerce me into claiming the barony, you would try to take it from my family! Power was always your first love, not me."

"And...was I...your first love?"

Henry recalled Leah's rejections and realized she had a point. He would have married Leah if she had accepted. But he shook off the thought. "You are doing it again!

Manipulating me to cover your sins. You murdered innocent people, Mary. My people! What am I supposed to do with that?"

"It does not matter... now."

For the first time, Henry faced the reality that Mary was dying. Despite her despicable actions, berating her now seemed pointless. "Did you ever love me?" he asked before he even realized what he was saying.

"I loved the idea of what you could have become."

"Were I a different person," Henry filled in for her. Mary's lips twitched into a fleeting smile before her breath grew fainter and stopped altogether.

Henry stood there, grappling with his emotions. Mary had essentially admitted that she married him for his position, and when he failed to meet her expectations, she sought power elsewhere. She was a greedy, grasping opportunist, but part of him wondered if he was to blame. If he had been more like his father, would she have been content? Would she have loved him then?

"Lord Henry," Aden's voice broke through his reverie, "we must enter the courtyard before hostilities escalate." Then he noticed Mary's body at Henry's feet. "Forgive me, I...did not know."

"Nor did I," Henry admitted. "I suppose I should have— I just did not want to admit.... Let us finish this quickly, Aden. I intend to ride on Braddock Court the moment we have stabilized matters here."

"Lord, surely we must—"

"Their army is scattered, their chivalry defeated," Henry said, still staring at Mary's body. "They attempted to use our moment of weakness to seize our lands; they will rue the day they made enemies of the Dawnings."

Aden, seeing Henry's resolve, understood now was not the time for further debate. "If it is any consolation," he said, glancing at the battlefield behind them, "I reckon they already do."

Henry did not respond to that. "Go on ahead, Sir Aden. I will join you shortly."

"Of course. At your leisure, Lord," Aden spurred his horse through the barbican and into the courtyard.

Henry continued to gaze at Mary's lifeless body, mourning not just the loss of what could have been but also the realization of their mutual disillusionment. He had wanted to believe that Mary loved him for his ideals, but instead she had seen him as an easy mark whom she would be able to manipulate. Both were disappointed in the end.

"I am going to show you, Mary," he said to her still form, striking his chest with his fist, "that I am the man you never believed I could be, the kind of man you could not manipulate...but that you could have loved." The thought lingered, a poignant reflection on his need for acceptance and love.

A loud cheer went up from the courtyard, snapping him back to reality. "I must go now, Mary. I am sorry that you will not be there to witness my triumph."

William came to on the floor beside the divan where his mother's body rested. He felt so weak that it was an effort to rise and so groggy that he barely remembered how he had gotten there. But seeing his mother lying there was a stark reminder that the war was still going on, and he did not know what had become of Leah.

He pushed himself up and staggered toward the door. He needed to get outside, needed to see what was happening. Maybe there was still something he could do to help.

"Henry?" Leah's voice was full of astonishment as he rode up behind Aden.

"Lord Henry was our salvation this day," Aden told her. "Had he not arrived when he did, we would have been overrun by Collin Braddock."

Henry stopped to take in his surroundings, and a wave of realization washed over him. This was it—his moment, the one he had always dreamed of. His triumphal entry. He was being welcomed as a hero, with none other than Leah standing at the forefront while her father proclaimed his deeds.

Was he dreaming? His heart still ached from the revelations that had come with Mary's death, but here he was, with the woman of his dreams standing before him, recognizing him as a hero. Was this the life he had long desired?

He looked at Leah—the woman who had been the object of his desires and the source of his torment for most of his adult life. She was filthy, covered in blood, disheveled; yet her beauty remained undeniable. But something had changed. She no longer stirred his heart the way she once had.

She had twice rejected his proposals, but Henry could no longer blame her for that. He could see now how naive and self-deluded he had been. No woman as strong and self-possessed as Leah would have seen him as a suitable partner.

But what about now? Henry was no longer that uncertain boy, and Leah no longer seemed the sheltered woman she once was. What's more, Henry was about to claim Braddock Court as his own. With a barony, she would be a fool to reject him again. But was that what he wanted? He was surprised to realize that it was not.

Leah, as remarkable as she was, represented his past—just like Mary. He was no longer the man who had proposed to her, and he didn't want a permanent reminder of the mistakes he had made. He wanted a fresh start with someone who knew nothing of the man he used to be. He wanted Katriane.

Still lost in thought, Henry dismounted and embraced Leah absently.

"I am troubled by the fact that Collin Braddock has yet to appear," Aden said, his voice laced with unease. "Why was he not here?"

"If you mean to deter me from my purpose, Sir Aden," Henry replied, not caring who overheard, "then you had best reflect upon the fact that we are about to face shortages of every kind, given the siege and the destruction of the crops. The Braddock stores could help to ease that burden."

"We cannot risk it while Collin's whereabouts remain unknown!"

"Collin Braddock is not a threat!" a voice called. Every eye turned to see Neil hobbling toward them.

Henry's expression brightened while Aden's narrowed. "How do you know that?" Aden asked.

"Because he is dead."

Aden's brow furrowed further. "Who killed him?"

"William," Neil replied.

"Impossible!" Aden protested.

Henry turned to Leah and quipped, "My brother and that family really do not get along."

But Leah was focused on Neil. "What do you mean, Sir Neil?" she asked.

"'Tis true," Neil assured her. "I saw it with my own eyes. William challenged Collin and bested him in a joust."

"William does not know how to joust," Henry pointed out.

Neil wiped a hand across his flushed face. "I have not the strength to give details right now. Suffice it to say, if you are going to exploit Braddock Court's weakness, now would be an excellent time."

Henry glanced hopefully at Aden, but Aden remained skeptical, still focused on Neil. "Was it not you who swore to me not one day since that William was a traitor?"

Henry laughed, but as he noticed the tension, he quieted. "William a traitor?"

The others ignored him. "William is no traitor, Father. Of that I can assure you," Leah stated resolutely.

"But you have feelings for him. How can I trust that your judgement is not clouded?"

It still stung Henry, hearing Aden openly acknowledge Leah's feelings for his brother, but he had moved past that. He couldn't let old jealousies influence his new life. So, for the first time, he defended William. "My brother may be many things, but he is no traitor."

"Sir Aden," Neil took a deep breath, "when last we spoke, I believed him so to be. In fact, I spent most of the night attempting to prove it to prevent you from marching into a trap."

"And?" Aden demanded, irritation clear in his tone.

Neil looked embarrassed. "I proved just the opposite. I believe William may have been this barony's greatest ally in recent days."

Leah suddenly slumped, exhaustion overtaking her. Henry rushed to catch her, his hand coming away bloody.

"Leah, you are hurt!" he exclaimed.

"It is nothing serious," she said, though she was pale.

"We will have you seen to at once!" Aden said, offering his horse, but she waved him off.

"I should think it will be less painful to walk to the Great Hall."

They began moving in that direction, Aden issuing orders for the troops and Henry assisting Neil, who looked even worse than Leah.

As they moved, Henry turned to the onlookers. "You are safe now! We have triumphed! Begin gathering your belongings and prepare to return to your homes. You will receive instructions shortly."

Anthony raced back into the courtyard, cutting and stabbing at anyone who stood in his way, not caring whether it was a Saracen or mercenary body. He was so angry at losing Thomas and so desperate to keep the dark cloud that was building in his mind at bay that he was like a wild man.

Without even realizing he had done it, Anthony had cut all the way through the enemy ranks and emerged on the upper bailey amidst his own people. He could not even remember the dozens of men he must have cut down and ridden over to get here.

He reined in his horse to get his bearings, just as he had done in the forest minutes before—or was it hours? He felt strangely disconnected from all this, as though it was not him but someone else, somewhere else doing all these things, and Anthony was simply watching.

From this vantage point, Anthony could see over most of the courtyard. He could see the main gates where Leah had stopped the enemy force, and to his horror, they appeared to be surrendering! The site struck him like a knife to the heart. It was all true. He was the reason they had not prevailed! Even while he was denied any chance of restitution, Leah had been ordained to do in a matter of hours what he had been unable to do in weeks. The only explanation was that heaven was raising her up in order to show to the world that he was unworthy!

He could not believe what he was seeing. He circled around for a better view and stopped dead. There, slipping out of the castle at that very moment, was William! His job complete—he had sabotaged and murdered his own people—he was now slinking away, hoping no one would know the part he had played in all this.

This was the ultimate indignity. Anthony could not let it stand! In one fell swoop, he would exact retribution, keep his oath to Leah, and prove that he was not a lost soul; and nothing save God striking him down was going to stop him! He gripped his spear tighter and kicked his heels into his horse's flanks.

William skulked out onto the landing before the Great Hall and found Leah with an escort arriving at the same time, as though he had come out to meet her. William's eyes locked with hers. She stepped out in front of her escort, her eyes on the traitor and seemingly oblivious to everyone else around her.

Anthony felt ill. Was this all part of it? Was Leah going to him? Hadn't she always loved William? Was she going to be with him now? An image of her rushing to William, kissing him, giving herself to him flashed through his mind, and he drove his horse harder, pushing the animal faster and faster until it was nearly impossible to control on the muddy, uneven surface.

Anthony's rage boiled into a fury greater than he had ever known. His vision narrowed on William. He trained his spear like a lance and hunched down for maximum impact.

The peasants around Leah laughed and cheered as she made her way up to the Great Hall. They reveled in their well-deserved victory, and Leah smiled and thanked them as she went.

The truth of the moment was starting to settle upon all of them, including her. The threat was vanquished. They were safe again. Though it was cold outside, the sun was shining for the first time in recent memory, causing Leah to feel warm all over. This was a new day!

Then Leah saw him on the landing. Their eyes met, and the old, familiar electricity shot through her whole body. Now her victory was complete. He was here, alive and safe and true as ever. And now she did not feel so unworthy of him. The blood running down her side—blood spilt in defense of Dawning Court—was her atonement for failing so miserably. While it would not bring back his mother or undo the damage she had done, maybe it at least entitled her to face him and tell him all that had happened; and maybe one day she could even reveal what was in her heart.

William looked like he was barely on his feet, but his face lit up when he saw her. He came down off the landing to meet her.

Even in her weakened state, she could not resist rushing out ahead of her father, Henry, and Neil. She did not notice Anthony galloping toward them until he broke from the crowd only thirty feet away.

In a flash, Leah realized what was happening. Anthony still believed William to be a traitor because *she* had convinced him of it and had made him swear an oath to avenge Eve.

Leah looked frantically at William, but his eyes were still fixed upon her, blissfully unaware that he was seconds away from doom!

Everything seemed to happen in slow motion. She screamed an inarticulate warning and rushed toward William as Anthony closed the last few yards.

William followed her gaze in time to see Anthony bearing down on him, but it was too late to react. William's eyes opened wide as Anthony drove his lance home.

In that last instant, Leah, who was still several paces away, hurled herself between Anthony and William.

Anthony saw Leah run ahead, but it was too late to change course. In the instant he had to act, his first instinct was to yank back on the reins, but the horse's hooves only slid on the muddy surface.

The lance took her in the side rather than hitting William in the chest, but the force of the charge was too much to be stopped.

The spear sliced through Leah's side an instant before the horse's shoulder slammed into her, hurling her like a ragdoll several feet away. The weight of her body, however, had dragged the head of the spear down, causing it to strike William in the stomach rather than the chest, even as he was reaching out to catch her. Weapon and animal collided with him and threw him backward as well, leaving him in a crumpled heap on the ground, ten feet from where Leah lay.

Anthony skidded to a halt and leapt from the saddle. He was horrified that Leah had intervened and been injured. But some part of his over-taxed mind whispered that he should have expected this. If Anthony was going to be permitted to kill William, then of course he was going to lose his betrothed in the process.

He was horrified at what he had just done, and his anger toward William turned to rage. It was his fault that Leah had been in the way! It was time to see this villain finally receive justice. Anthony could not be deterred, could not rest until he was certain that William was dead. He was aware of the screams and commotion all around him as he drew his sword and went for William, but he did not care. He was going to finish this!

As one, Neil and Henry bowled into Anthony, tackling him and wresting the sword from his hand. "What are you doing?" one of them screamed at Anthony, but he was howling that they had to let him loose.

"I will finish this!" he shouted as he fought savagely to get free from the men who were attempting to pin him down. "Release me!"

Henry hit him then, but that only added to Anthony's wild fury; so he hit him again and again until Anthony finally lost consciousness.

William lay on his back in agony. The world swam before him, and there was commotion all around him. His stomach screamed at him, and every little movement sent fits of pain through him. He pressed a trembling hand to his stomach and felt where the spear had pierced his overstressed armor and cut deep into his flesh. He raised his hand and was not at all surprised to see it was covered in blood.

He was not thinking clearly. His head was spinning, he was in shock, and he was scared—terrified even—but it was not only because of his own wound. Despite the pain, he was not thinking about the fact that it was likely a mortal wound. It did not occur to him that he should not move or even that he needed help. He was only thinking about one thing.

The scene of Leah jumping in front of him and her body being flung aside like a toy was playing itself on repeat in his mind. Was she dead? He had to get to her, had to see to her. He rolled onto his side, but bolts of agony shot threw him, seizing up his muscles. He tried to call out to her, but no sound came.

A few feet away, he was dimly aware of shouts and people running, but he did not care about that. Leah might be dead. And if she was not, she needed him!

William pulled himself onto all fours, found a position that did not engage his traumatized core muscles, and began crawling toward her crumpled body lying in an unnatural heap on the ground.

He kept his movements very small to prevent his wounded muscles from seizing, which made him feel like he was barely moving. But he kept on, despite the fact that he was on the verge of passing out. He simply could not let that happen before he got to her.

In his periphery, he detected a great commotion around Anthony, wrestling and fighting, but that seemed like something distant and disconnected from him.

At last he reached her. He crawled up to her and rolled her onto her back. Her breathing was ragged. There was a large gash in her side where the spear had sliced her open, and blood was everywhere. He started to panic, but he felt his vision narrow even more as he did so.

He tried to tear a strip of cloth from the hem of her dress, but the strain was too much, and his vision went dark, oblivion threatening to overwhelm him. Instead, he pulled the hem up and pressed it into the gaping hole in her torso.

His vision was blurring, and William knew that he did not have much time. He gently straightened her limbs so she would be as comfortable as possible and lay down beside her. He could sense people starting to gather round, but it did not even occur to him that they might be there to help. It was simply something that was occurring unrelated to him, like clouds passing in the sky, so he kept on. He placed Leah's hand over her wound, and draped his own numb fingers over hers, hoping that their combined weight might provide enough pressure to at least slow the bleeding.

With the last of his strength, he reached out and took her other hand in his. He was not certain if he imagined it, but he thought he felt the faintest of squeezes from her, and as the darkness closed in on him, they were kids again, once more lying side by side on the bank of the river on a spring day, thrilling at the first indications that the love each felt for the other was reciprocated.

Then all went black.

Fifty-eight

Salena had intended to flee Dawning Court as Neil had instructed, but she found herself unable to leave. The thought of never returning to her home made her want to see it one last time. Instead of heading straight for the highway and freedom, she circled the outer wall until she found a breach large enough to drive through.

She could not believe the change that had come over Dawning Court. The sheer devastation was shocking. The fields, so lush and ripe for harvest when she had left to enlist Hans in her revenge, were now barren and stripped. The roads, once neatly maintained, had been churned into mud under the weight of thousands of boots, hooves, and wagon wheels. Smoke billowed from the camps overrun by the Mayfields, where the glut of tents, paddocks, pavilions, horses, wagons, and huts were left in ruins. The animals were either dead or roaming aimlessly.

The castle had fared no better. The once-majestic battlements lay in ruins, jagged chunks missing as if a celestial blade had cleaved into them repeatedly. The west wall lay in a long heap of debris, scattered a hundred feet from where it had originally stood. And the bodies! So many bodies. They were everywhere she looked, across the camp, along the roads, and among the trees. The sheer number was overwhelming.

The devastation mirrored Salena's inner turmoil. Consumed by rage against William, she had felt he had taken everything from her. Yet she hadn't realized how much more she had to lose until Hans had prevented her from leaving Braddock Castle that night.

She shuddered at the memory of Hans' touch. "That could not be me," she whispered to the shadow of her past, hoping it would vanish. "That must be someone else!" But it *was* her. She had become something unrecognizable, a figure so degraded there was no place left for her. Stripped of self-respect and cut off from loved ones, she felt as though she were a ghost, haunting the remnants of her past, living the nightmare that Neil had described, tormented by what was lost and powerless to change it.

She tried to silence the thought that echoed in her mind: *Am I responsible for all this misery and death?* The question was too heavy to bear. The idea that her quest for vengeance had, in turn, brought suffering to countless others was unbearable. She forced out any further thoughts of guilt by repeating the phrase she had recited a hundred times. *This destruction is William's fault, not mine. I was the only one courageous enough to do what was necessary to stop him.* But this rationalization did little to ease her conscience.

Even if that were true, hadn't she seen for herself that William was trying to make amends? Hadn't he granted her a pardon when she did not deserve one?

Almost unconsciously she followed the inside of Dawning Court's outer wall, driven by a need to find something good amid the devastation—something that could offer a reprieve from the overwhelming sense of death and doom. What she truly longed for was to see her daughter, Rachael, but that was impossible. Rachael had been sent away with David's mother before Salena had gone to meet Hans and reveal the castle's weakness. But the little cottage where she had lived with David and

Rachael would still be there. Maybe she could just see it again.

Though she had once resented the modest home, she would now give anything to return to it with her little family. *I would not waste a single moment on resentment or complaints if I could just go back there now.*

Tears streamed down her face as she approached the small cottage by the roadside. Long stalks of untended grasses reached her knees, but otherwise it was much as she remembered. The little fence still stood, though the gate dangled from one hinge. The house was too remote and humble to warrant a second look from any soldiers, and whatever looting had taken place was long over.

The fields around the house lay fallow as David had not been there to see them planted, and she did not have the means to hire help. The neglected dirt, sprouting weeds and a few lingering seedlings, gave the cottage an even more desolate feel. As Salena stood gazing at the small house, a part of her screamed that she should flee, that she should escape while she still could. But she remained rooted in place, knowing that she could never return. Even if Dawning Court did somehow survive, she could never face these people again. She just wanted one last look at the little house that had been home to the happiest times of her life, though she hadn't realized it then.

She drove the carriage behind the house, out of sight of the road, and tied it there. Before entering, she paused and looked across the fields toward where David's mother, Bronia, had lived. It took all her strength to resist running there, throwing open the door, and calling for her daughter. But she knew no one would answer.

With a sigh, Salena opened the back door of her tiny three-room home. It took a moment for her eyes to adjust to the dim light inside. The bare remnants of her once tidy house greeted her. Her table lay overturned with a broken leg, and anything of value was long gone.

As she stepped inside, the improperly hung door swung shut behind her. The sparse, looted remains of the cottage felt jarringly out of place against the flood of memories rushing through her mind. Her eyes registered an abandoned shack, ruined by thoughtless hands. Yet it didn't feel empty—it felt as though David was still there, just in the other room, putting Rachael to bed. It felt like coming home.

Salena pressed her hand to her eyes as the tears flowed unchecked. "Please, Lord," she whispered aloud, "forgive my blindness. If thou wilt return me to my family, I shall never breathe a word of complaint again."

"Salena?" a familiar male voice asked with delighted incredulity.

She wiped her eyes, struggling to focus on the figure emerging from the back bedroom. She could not believe it. "D—David," she said, and a fresh gout of water poured from her eyes.

He stepped closer, and she could hear the creak of his armor, smell the sweat and blood. But something didn't feel right. "H—how can this be?"

Suddenly, the figure grabbed her roughly by the neck, pulling her into a savage kiss. The illusion shattered in an instant. Salena knew the taste of that kiss—and it wasn't the taste of love; it was the taste of vile, revolting cruelty. She shoved him away violently, but he still gripped her hair.

"How fortuitous that you would seek me out in my time of need," Hans sneered, pulling her closer as she struggled to get free.

"No, please," Salena screamed, though she knew it was futile to beg Hans for mercy. Her cries were instead directed Heavenward, pleading with God to spare her from this nightmare. *Why didn't I run when I had the chance?*

"I was beginning to think that I had no friends left," Hans said, tightening his grip. "But then you came looking for me.

And why wouldn't you? Once a woman has been had by a Braddock man, what is left for her among other men?"

"You disgusting pig!" Salena shrieked, her hand trying to loosen his grip on her hair.

"You have a carriage, yes?"

He must have seen me through the window, she thought as she desperately fought against his hold. The idea of being under his control again was unbearable. "Take it and leave me here to die in peace," she pleaded.

"Our bargain is not yet concluded," Hans growled, forcing her to bend at the waist, his hand still painfully tangled in her hair.

"What bargain?" she cried, frantically searching for a way to break free. His armor protected all the vulnerable spots she might have struck, and although he wasn't wearing a helmet, hitting him in the face would only enrage him further.

Hans' voice rose sharply as he slipped behind her, still holding her bent over. "What bargain?" he snarled. "I avenged you of the Dawnings! And it cost me everything— my army, my honor, even my place among the Braddock nobility!"

Suddenly, he released her hair and yanked her upright, his right arm locking around her chest as he pulled her back against him. He whispered into her ear, his breath hot and foul. "You must perform one last service for me, and after that, you may do as you wish."

"Wh—what service?" Salena asked, not daring to hope he would actually let her go.

"My arm," he murmured, his lips brushing her ear. "It needs tending. You must wrap it for me."

For the first time, Salena realized his left arm hung uselessly at his side; he had been doing everything with his right hand. "That is all you ask?" she asked dubiously.

Hans exhaled heavily into her ear in a gesture that may have been intended as erotic, but his fetid breath only made her want to wretch. "That is all," he said, his voice softening, though he still held her firmly. "Then you drive me out of Dawning Court concealed in the back of your carriage. Take me to the hostel, and from there, we will part ways."

He slowly eased his grip, clearly wary of her bolting the moment she was free. But before she could act, Hans drew a dagger and held it up as a warning, letting her know he wouldn't hesitate to use it at the slightest sign of resistance.

Realizing she had no choice, Salena decided to play along—for now. She might have been willing to do as he asked if she believed he would keep his word, but she knew better. He would likely kill her once she was done or change the terms as it suited him. That's when an idea sparked in her mind.

"Sit here," she said, righting a rickety chair. Between his armor and his injured arm, he would not be able to run quickly. Furthermore, he was clearly bent on not being seen, so if she could find an opportunity to make a run for it, especially toward the armies, he would be reluctant to follow. "I need to find some cloth to wrap your arm." She was slowly edging away from him, hoping to buy herself a few precious seconds.

"This will do!" Hans declared, producing a torn length of cloth likely ripped from someone's clothing.

Salena hesitated, contemplating a desperate dash for the door. But she wasn't even a step away, and he could easily catch her—or worse, throw his knife. She might have risked it had it not been for the smug, knowing look on his face, as though he knew exactly what she was thinking and was one step ahead of her.

Seething with hatred, she snatched the cloth from him. He sat down, and she began to wrap his left arm against his chest. She could feel his lecherous gaze crawling over her as she bent over him, and it took every ounce of self-control not to shudder.

When she finished tying the knot, Salena stepped back, making it clear she was done and ready to leave. But just as she feared, Hans had other plans. He pointed the blade at her and then at his lap.

Salena shuddered but complied, lowering herself onto his lap, her stomach churning.

"What is your hurry?" he purred, wrapping the arm holding the dagger around her. "We cannot leave until nightfall. And I think a proper farewell is in order for two who shared so much passion."

That was more than Salena could bear. She began to struggle against his hold, and Hans' demeanor shifted in an instant. "Do not make me cut your throat!" he barked, tightening his hold.

But Salena no longer cared. She had nothing left to lose. She twisted and fought, and Hans was forced to drop the knife to secure his grip on her. The blade clattered to the floor. With renewed determination, Salena redoubled her effort to get loose. But Hans was too strong. His arm felt as unyielding as an iron shackle.

"There is that fire," he hissed, his voice twisted with perverse excitement. "I knew you still had some fight left."

Desperation surged through Salena. Planting her feet on the floor, she threw her weight back against him. Without a way to brace himself, she, Hans and the chair toppled backward. He hit the ground first, and she landed on top of him.

The impact broke his grip, and in a flash, Salena rolled free. Her eyes locked on the fallen knife, and she snatched it up. Without a moment's hesitation, she drove it through the exposed flesh of his neck, just above the breastplate.

Salena stepped back, staring in shock as blood spurted around the blade still lodged in his throat. Hans raised a trembling hand toward the wound, as if to pull the knife out, but his strength failed him—or perhaps he realized it was too late.

All the fear, hatred, and sadness that weighed on her evaporated, pouring out like the blood pooling at her feet. The more of his life that bled out, the safer she became.

As that reality settled in, Salena felt strangely detached, watching him writhe in agony. She did not feel triumphant, nor did she regret her actions. She simply stood there, observing, as Hans' expression shifted from shock to agony to terror, as the awareness of his imminent death dawned upon him.

In one last desperate plea, Hans reached out toward her, but Salena only tilted her head, watching his outstretched hand with a mixture of curiosity and disdain.

"I have a friend," she said calmly, her voice eerily steady, "who believes that when the wicked die, they are condemned to wander the earth, burdened by all the misery they created but powerless to rectify it. Such a fate would truly be hell, and I cannot think of a more fitting end for you, Hans."

Hans gurgled something incomprehensible, his body writhing as the last traces of life ebbed away. Salena remained still, standing just close enough for his fingertips to brush the edge of her shoes, watching until the pathetic creature finally stopped moving.

Fifty-nine

William opened his eyes to a flood of vague, mostly violent images flashing through his mind before they started to fade. Soft light streamed in through the open veranda doors, carrying with it a gentle breeze. A chair sat empty by his bedside.

He pulled the blankets tighter and nestled deeper into the warmth. He was in the castle, in what appeared to be the baron's chambers, though he had no recollection of how he had gotten there. Lying in the big, comfortable bed, safe and warm, William could almost convince himself he was a child again—that the horrors haunting his thoughts were just dreams. He might have even believed it if not for the sharp pain slicing through his torso.

And if those images were not part of a dream, then the two images that pierced his heart the most must also be real. His mother wasn't going to walk through that door to sit by him, as she had done when he was a boy, and Leah ...

Tears filled his eyes. Leah had given her life to save him. *Why?* It had been his duty to protect her, not the other way around. Surely she knew that he would much rather that he died than her. Now he was the one left behind, forced to live in a world without her—a reality he had never imagined and didn't want to face.

Warm air wafted in, carrying with it the sounds of a busy courtyard. The voices were no longer panicked or frantic; they belonged to people going about their normal routines.

From the adjacent chamber, he could hear what he took to be the sounds of the castle coming back to life. Curiosity stirred in him, causing him to wonder how things had turned out; but for now, he relished the quiet, the momentary freedom from the grim reality that he knew awaited him.

William didn't yet know all that had happened, but he knew the consequences of the past few weeks would follow him for the rest of his life. For now, he wanted to stay suspended in this bittersweet limbo, where nothing was confirmed. Perhaps Leah and Eve would walk through the door at any moment, laughing and teasing him for lying in bed. His brothers might arrive after, boasting about their exploits, downplaying his injuries, and telling him he was just playing them up for sympathy.

Reality would intrude soon enough, and once it did, there would be no coming back to this moment. He would be thrust into a world where everything was final, where Leah was truly gone. It reminded him of the fever dream he'd had, where Leah from the past called him to join her on a perfect spring day, but the window between them wouldn't open.

One could never go back. The only path forward was to accept what was. But William wasn't ready for that just yet.

He couldn't say how long he remained in his delicate limbo before the door inevitably opened, and reality intruded. His visitor was a tall, beautiful blonde woman, her belly bulging in the late stages of pregnancy.

Blinking in surprise, William instinctively tried to sit up, but pain shot through his torso, forcing him back onto the pillow with a groan.

"Here, let me help you," Grace said, stepping forward. She expertly propped a pillow behind him, half-dragging him into a sitting position with a strength that belied her condition. "Drink this," she ordered, handing him a cup from the bedside table. Her no-nonsense manner reminded him that she was trained in the medical arts and had plenty of experience with difficult patients, which must have come in handy when she had been nursing Richard back to health.

"Truth be told, I am relieved to see you awake and coherent."

"I take it that has not been the case for the past..." He let the question hang in the air as he cautiously sipped the water.

"Twenty-one years?" she teased, a sly smile playing on her lips.

William managed a weak grin, but his anxiety kept him from more. "How long?"

"Ten days," she answered more seriously.

"Ten?" William coughed, nearly choking as he spat the water over his blanket.

Grace chuckled, pulling a cloth from the table to dab at the mess. "Yes, ten. In truth, we were not sure if you would pull through for the first week. But a few days ago, you turned a corner. You have been improving steadily ever since."

She pulled the chair closer to his bed. "Do you mind if I sit for a bit?"

William glanced at her, then gestured around the room. "Considering that I am in your bed, how can I refuse?"

Grace lowered herself into the chair, though she did not look like she could really get comfortable.

"Very well," she said, "let us talk. First things first—your wound. Do you remember who gave it to you?"

"I ... do," William's voice faltered. Until this moment, he'd been consumed by thoughts of Leah's and his mother's deaths. Now the memory of the attack resurfaced, and with it, a deeper shock. Was Anthony a traitor? Had he been acting on Grace's orders? Panic welled inside him at the possibility.

Sensing his distress, Grace gently laid a hand on his shoulder. "You are in no danger, William," she reassured him, her soft blue eyes filled with sadness as she coaxed him back against the pillow. There was such tenderness in her gaze that he found himself trusting her despite the questions swirling in his mind. "Your loyalty is beyond question. In fact, it may interest you to know that my late husband's final missive proclaimed your unfailing loyalty and his wishes for your future." She paused. "We will come to that in time. But for now—while your loyalty may be beyond question, your judgement is another matter. Do you know why Anthony attacked you?"

William ran through the possibilities, but none seemed clear. He shook his head, unwilling to guess, given the circumstances.

Grace sighed deeply. "Anthony believed that you too were a traitor working with Thomas—sneaking around the castle, sabotaging their armaments and food supplies, and even murdering people. Are you aware that Leah saw you that night in the chapel and thought you were there to kill Martha?"

"My own mother?" William asked, stunned.

"Yes," Grace nodded. "Leah thought you were trying to remove Martha from power so you and Thomas could seize control. And when Eve was killed during the subsequent chaos, Leah assumed you were responsible for that as well."

The news of Eve's death struck William with renewed force now that he had a moment to process it. "Eve... is dead," he said the words out loud for the first time.

Grace's frown deepened. "You did not know? But of course, how could you have known? I am so sorry to tell you in this way, but yes, Eve has passed."

William didn't mention that Leah had screamed it at him while he was trying to keep her from murdering Amir. It did not seem worth discussing now. The pain of hearing it again felt like discovering it anew. Tears welled in his eyes, and he tried to hide them by placing a hand over his face. He had truly cared for Eve. Though she didn't hold the same place in his heart as Leah, she had been a bright light in his life when he felt utterly alone.

"Shall we continue this later?" Grace asked gently after a moment.

"No," William sniffed and lowered his arm. "'It was a brutal war, but I need to know all that happened."

"Very well," Grace said, though her voice was tinged with doubt. "It was for those reasons that my brother believed you a villain. He is absolutely devastated," she added when William made no reply.

William dropped his head back against the headboard. "It is not for *me* that I mourn his actions."

"Of course," Grace said, seeming to understand the reference to Leah. "Despite my protests, Anthony is withdrawing from Dawning Court in disgrace. He will return to our homeland."

"He does not need to do that on my account," William said to the ceiling.

"It is his decision," Grace replied. "He feels that he has let down the barony with the fall of the wall, disgraced himself, and broken his vow to Richard. He can no longer serve the Dawnings with a clear conscience. I have released him from his vow," she added, her voice heavy with sadness.

William struggled to find a response. Anthony had been a loyal friend to the barony, but he was also the man who had killed Leah—even if it was accidental. Forgiveness seemed impossible. "The toll of this conflict cannot be measured by lives alone," he finally said.

"Well said," Grace agreed. Then she leaned forward in her chair, her eyes intense and pleading. "William, please, tell me of how my husband died."

William hesitated, reluctant to revisit the painful memory. He wanted to argue that he still had countless unanswered questions, but he realized she had been waiting weeks for a firsthand account of Richard's fall, and he was the only one who could provide it. "I will tell you," he grudgingly agreed, "but are you sure you wish to hear? It will be painful."

Grace's face tightened, "I am confident that he did nothing that would cast a shadow over his reputation!"

"Quite the contrary!" William hastened to reassure her. "He was the strongest, bravest, and most selfless person I have ever known. And he fought like a pack of wolves. I just mean are you sure you want to hear of his death rather than remembering him the way he was."

Grace's expression softened with a mixture of grief and resolve. "Painful or not, I must know. My child," she glanced down at her rounded stomach, "will need to know."

William closed his eyes, drawing a slow, deep breath, forcing himself to go back to that awful day. He had tried so hard to push it from his mind, but now, for Grace's sake, he needed to relive it.

So, he told her. He told her of their encounter with Thomas and Amir's army, how they had almost overcome them when the Braddocks had appeared and shifted the balance. He told her of Richard's plan to remain behind while the remainder of the army retreated in the night to fortify Dawning Castle. He described the battle between Richard and Thomas, where Richard had let Thomas live and made William promise to do the same. "A promise I made good on, though it took everything in me not to kill the man who had destroyed our home, had Richard killed, and helped to murder my mother." William expected Grace to object, but she only nodded her understanding, so he continued.

As Grace absorbed all that he shared, her eyes shimmered with unshed tears, but she remained composed, her lips pressed tightly together. William told her of the two of them being the last ones alive and withstanding wave after wave of enemy soldiers. He told her how Richard had fought like a lion until the very end. Finally, he explained his encounter with Amir and hitting his head. He wanted her to know that he had not abandoned Richard, even in death.

The tears Grace had been holding back finally spilled over. She lowered her head, letting them fall silently onto her lap. William averted his eyes, giving her a moment of privacy while trying to control his own emotions.

"Thank you, William!" Grace embraced him suddenly. "Thank you for not leaving my husband in his final moments."

"Forgive me for not being able to save him," he whispered back. "Forgive me for not treating him better when he was here. I was afraid to believe in him."

"I'm sorry for pressing you so soon after your own ordeal," Grace said softly. "But I had to know."

"I understand," William replied. "Richard was... a great man."

Grace smiled slightly. "He admired you greatly. You should know that."

After a brief pause as both pondered these things, Grace asked, "So what happened then?"

William shrugged and swallowed the lump in his throat. "When I woke up, I was in the Braddock encampment. They had found me and assumed I was one of their own. I did not know what else to do but try to make the most of it by, ironically, doing there exactly what Anthony thought I was doing here in the castle."

"I feel like there is much that you are leaving out," Grace smiled.

"Nothing significant."

"I have heard tell of some very wild escapades. I should like to hear the truth of it from you."

"Forgive me, Grace, but *I* still have no answers. What happened after I ... died? What became of the Braddocks and the Mayfields? Why are you here now, and why am I in the baron's chambers?"

"Very well," Grace sighed, brushing a tear from her cheek. "You have been out for ten days, William. Much has happened in that time."

She settled herself back in the chair, her hands resting protectively over her belly. "The Braddocks surrendered soon after you were struck down. Without a leader, their forces crumbled quickly. The Mayfields also surrendered or fled, but for now, Dawning Castle is safe.

"I returned shortly after the victory—I had not gone so far away as Lady Dawning had wished," she confided in him slyly. "I do not know if she truly understood that in my heart, I am a Dawning now. This is my home. I could not abandon it; I would not have left it at all had I not been bearing the only heir."

William nodded slowly, but her words didn't fully explain why he was in the baron's chambers—her chambers. "And the castle? What of the people?"

"There was damage, of course. Many were lost. But the worst is over. The people are resilient, and they've begun rebuilding. The barony will recover, though it will take time."

"But why am I here?" he finally asked, gesturing around the room.

"You were placed here in the baron's chambers because it was being used for storage during the siege and was therefore about the only room that was not completely destroyed. When I returned, you were obviously still convalescing, and I had no interest in occupying these chambers that I shared with my late husband, so I chose not to disturb you."

There was a soft knock at the door, and Henry poked his head in. "Is he awake?" he asked Grace.

"See for yourself."

Henry stepped into the room and came over to the bed.

"William?" he said cautiously, noting his brother's shocked look. Like everyone else, William had just assumed that Henry was either dead or a traitor.

"You are alive!" William exclaimed in disbelief.

"Oh, that is right!" Grace interjected. "You were not present for the denouement. It was Henry that proved our salvation. The Braddock army attacked unexpectedly and had nearly overwhelmed Aden's force when Henry arrived with an army he had recruited in France. That shifted the balance."

William turned to Henry, his face filled with questions.

"Thomas and I were both ambushed by the Nizari," Henry began. "I, of course, had no idea that Thomas had orchestrated the whole trap. I believed that he had been killed, right up until I arrived here with reinforcements."

William blinked in confusion. "Was it the blow to my head, or did that explanation make no sense?"

Henry chuckled, looking a little embarrassed. "I was captured," he confessed, glancing at Grace. "Those of us who were not killed by the Saracens were taken prisoner. We were held in a makeshift cell while you were fighting the Braddock-Saracen forces. When I managed to escape, I realized that my lone sword would do little to offset the overwhelming odds against us. I needed an army. So, I left to gather reinforcements. As it turns out," he shrugged with a faint smile, "I was correct."

William groaned. "Oh, this is going to be unbearable. Did he really save the barony?" He turned to Grace, who nodded. "Great. He is going to be insufferable for the next decade! You know that, right?"

Grace smiled but turned to Henry. "Tell me, Sir Henry, how were you able to recruit such a large, well-trained army so quickly?"

Henry hesitated. "I knew we would need more men to face the Saracen army, so I went to the mainland and..." he paused, "I enlisted Edward's help."

William's eyes widened. "Edward?!? He was willing to help our family?"

"Er...yes," Henry replied, noncommittally.

"I must have misjudged him," William said, shaking his head in surprise.

"Not exactly," Henry muttered.

Grace furrowed her brow. "Then he did not help?"

Henry sighed. "Well, let us just say that none of us would be here if not for Edward."

"Do you know of our estranged brother?" William asked Grace.

"Richard told me of him, yes. It is astonishing that he would be so magnanimous after so many years with no contact."

Henry's expression darkened. "While it is true that his aid saved us, he is not as generous as you might think.

Believe me when I tell you that we are all that remain of the Dawnings."

Grace's brow furrowed further. "Is Edward dead then?"

"To us, I should think so." Henry answered quietly.

William caught the meaning. "He was not what you thought, was he?"

Henry shook his head. "It seems, little brother, that I am a very poor judge of character."

William's face softened. "He was your brother. There is no shame in wanting to see good in him, even when nobody else could. I regret not giving Richard that same chance."

"It is not only Edward of whom I speak," Henry's voice was heavy with regret.

William, completely lost, looked to Grace for help.

"Mary," she said so softly it was almost a whisper.

"Then it was Mary beneath the Mayfield banner?"

Henry nodded, the sadness evident on his face. "I found her dead amongst the Mayfield mercenaries."

"Among the mercenaries?" William asked, surprised. "She was fighting?"

Grace interjected, sensing Henry's discomfort. "It seems she had no choice. Mayfield Court is no more. They used what little money George had left to hire the remnants of King John's mercenary army. If they were not victorious, she would have been not only disgraced but completely destitute."

"That is ... unbelievable. I am sorry, Henry."

Henry shrugged, though he couldn't hide his sorrow. "I cannot say that there were no warning signs, though I must admit that I could never have foreseen this."

Trying to shift the mood, William asked, "So, what is next for the Dawnings?"

As if on cue, there came a soft rap at the door, and Sebastian entered.

"Sebastian," William greeted him with a smile, "I am glad at least one fixture of Dawning Castle remains."

The old steward bowed. "It is good to see you awake, Master William." He turned to Henry. "Baron, the caravan has been unloaded and is awaiting your orders."

"I will be right there," Henry replied with a nod.

Sebastian bowed again and left the room.

"Baron?" William was shocked. The thought of Henry assuming the title hadn't even crossed his mind in the wake of Richard and Martha's deaths. He wasn't sure how to feel about it.

Henry grinned. "You did not see that coming?"

"What? No...." William stammered, trying to recover. He glanced over at Grace, who was smiling knowingly. "I just had not considered it before. But I think you will make a great baron."

"Well, for Braddock Court's sake, I hope you are correct."

"Yes," William agreed before thinking about that statement. "Wait, what?"

"I am not baron of Dawning Court; she already has a leader," he gestured toward Grace. "After defeating the Braddock army here, it seemed a shame to let their castle go unprotected."

William nodded, a smile playing at his lips. "Of course, the honorable thing to do was to take your army and ensure their safety."

Henry grinned back. "Exactly. And if the people chose to pledge their loyalty to me for defending them, well, who was I to deny them?"

"You were duty-bound to accept their allegiance."

"I could not leave them without leadership," Henry agreed. "That would have been irresponsible."

William chuckled but then paused as Henry's expression turned more serious.

"In truth, they offered no resistance. It seems that Collin Braddock had only lately been killed in a duel, just a short time after winning his castle back from his own men."

Henry waited for a response, but when none came, he continued. "That's a story I'd very much like to hear."

"As would I," Grace added.

William glanced between their expectant faces. "Why do you both assume I had anything to do with it?"

Henry smirked. "Sir Neil was present when Sir Anthony—when you were struck down. We had to restrain him from tearing Anthony apart even though Neil could barely stand. He told a very interesting tale once he had settled down."

William grimaced. "I am afraid I remember very little of that night," he lied. He didn't really feel up to rehashing the events, nor was he particularly proud of the outcome. Though Collin had forced his hand, killing a man who sought only to avenge his family left a bitter aftertaste. Worse still, innocent people had died because of the ruse he had perpetrated on Braddock Court.

"Another time, perhaps," Henry said, getting to his feet. "I have much to tend to at present. I only came to deliver some much-needed supplies from Braddock Court, but I daren't leave my newly won fiefdom for long lest the natives become restless. William, I truly am grateful that you are alright."

"And I you."

Henry hesitated and then said, "Do you happen to remember that oath we made with our brothers all those years ago?"

"In the yard?" William nodded. "I remember."

"That is the one."

"That has not gone as we had imagined, has it?"

"No," Henry admitted. "It has not. But I wonder... could the two of us still honor it?"

"You want us to become the unstoppable force for good?" William raised an eyebrow.

Henry gave an embarrassed shrug. "Maybe we will not be quite what we imagined, but could we not at least try?"

William smiled. "I would like that. But as the youngest son of a barony hanging by a thread, I am not certain how much help I will be."

Henry glanced at Grace, who had mostly remained silent throughout the exchange. "You have not told him?"

"I have not had the opportunity."

Henry turned back to William, a grin spreading across his face.

"Tell me what?" William asked, feeling a knot of anxiety form in his stomach. Then a sudden, dreadful thought crossed his mind. "Lady Dawning, surely you are not abdicating?"

Grace smiled sadly. "Your mother was a strong and wise woman. But whether she intended it or not, one of the main lessons she imparted to me is that I have no wish to lead. 'Tis a worrisome, dangerous, thankless task."

"But your child?" William asked, his frown deepening. "The birthright will fall to him, surely."

"Oh, I intend baby Richard to take over in time," Grace replied, "but I have no interest in holding the seat until then."

"Hmm." William's concern grew. "Interim leaders often find it difficult to relinquish power when the rightful heir comes of age."

"I am aware," she said calmly.

"Wait ... surely you do not mean ..."

"What about you, William?" Grace asked, her gaze steady.

"What about me?"

"Will you act as regent until my child comes of age?"

William blinked, then shook his head. "Forgive me, Lady, but that is quite possibly the worst idea anyone has had at any time in all of history."

"Nonsense!" Henry cut in. "What about King John?"

That stopped William. "Very well, the *second* worst idea—"

It was not my idea, William," Grace said calmly, "it was Richard's."

William froze mid-protest.

"It was in the letter I alluded to before. For some reason he believed you would survive to see this through. It would seem he was rather prescient; would you not agree?"

"About me surviving, perhaps, but I am no leader, Grace. I am impulsive, selfish, and not to be trusted. Tell her, Henry!"

Henry, still grinning, only shrugged.

"Wipe that stupid grin off your face and tell her."

Henry dutifully repeated, "My brother is impulsive, selfish, stupid, and not be trusted."

"Thank you," William groused. "I noticed you added *stupid* in there."

"Do you want to convince her or not?"

Grace, unfazed, said, "Many said similar things about my late husband, but I believe he would have been the greatest leader Dawning Court had ever known."

"I agree, but I am not he."

Grace shrugged. "After Richard returned from the Nizari—after you rescued him," she nodded in acknowledgement, "he developed a keen insight into people. I never quite understood it, but it guided him in many decisions, including this one. If that same insight told him to trust you, I will not argue."

"Is that what changed him?" William asked.

Grace shook her head. "I think mostly it was his deciding to change ... and, of course, the right woman," she added, smiling.

William felt like he had been punched in his wounded stomach. "Yes, well that last part might be a problem."

Grace's smile faltered. "Of course. How insensitive of me." There was a brief silence before she continued. "Eve will be greatly missed. If it helps, Leah told me she is planning a memorial service to honor her."

William froze. "What did you say?"

Grace looked at him in confusion. "Leah is planning—"

"Leah is *alive*?" William almost screamed.

Grace blinked in surprise. "Well, yes," she said, glancing at Henry. "She has been recovering in her home. I believe my brother is with her now."

William was on his feet before she had finished speaking, searching frantically for clothes. He grabbed a tunic and trousers from the nearest wardrobe—Richard's wardrobe—and found himself drowning in the clothing of his much larger brother.

"I am sorry, Lady Grace, Henry. I must go."

"William!" Grace called after him. "The regency. Think about it!"

"Yes, yes. I will," he said over his shoulder as he rolled up his cuffs enough to walk without tripping and hurried from the room as fast as his wound would let him.

"What was that about?" Grace asked in shock as the door slammed behind William.

Henry looked after William with a knowing smile. Though there was still a pang of sadness in his heart over Leah, especially after Mary's betrayal, he no longer felt jealousy. For the first time, the thought of Leah and William being together not only did not bother him, it actually pleased him.

"Lady Dawning," Henry said, turning to Grace. "There is a piece of Dawning lore of which you should probably know... though it is a delicate matter under the circumstances.

Sixty

"Milady, I am pleased to find you looking so well," Anthony said with a formal stiffness as he approached Leah, who was seated in her garden. It was an unseasonably pleasant day, and she rested on a white bench, still unable to stand or walk for longer than a few minutes.

"You as well, Milord," Leah responded. This was the first conversation they'd had since the incident apart from that brief, agonizing moment when she had regained consciousness just long enough to see William's body being carried away as Anthony pled tearfully for her forgiveness. Now he stood before her, stiff and formal, neither of them quite able to meet the other's gaze. "Will you sit?"

Anthony hesitated before awkwardly lowering himself onto the bench beside her.

Leah had known this moment had been coming, but she had not let herself think about it. She stared at the ground, her heart thudding nervously in her chest, waiting for him to speak. But he was silent for a long time.

Anthony's gaze remained fixed on the barren fields. The sun shone, but a cool spring breeze chilled the air, dampening any sense of hope such a day might otherwise bring. Leah wrapped her shawl tighter about her shoulders, but even as she did so, she feared that the gesture would cause Anthony to offer his cloak to her as he surely would have done in the past; but he did not comment on it.

"Leah," he finally spoke, though it seemed like he struggled to find the right words. "Grace—Lady Dawning, my sister—has returned, as I am sure you are aware. She wishes to send an account of what has happened here to our family in the kingdom of Sicily."

Leah nodded silently.

"I have decided to deliver that message personally."

Another silent nod.

"I..." he paused, as if the words were difficult to utter, "I shall not return to Dawning Court."

Leah looked up sharply, but Anthony was not looking at her; he still stared straight ahead.

"Given all that has happened, Grace has released me from my pledge to this people. Now I—" he paused again, his voice unsteady, "I must beg of you to release me from my vow to you. I know this will bring shame upon you—"

He stopped short when Leah reached for his hand.

"Oh, Anthony," her voice cracked with emotion, "you have been so dreadfully wounded, and I know much of that was my doing." Saying it aloud tore at Leah's heart. She had hurt this man deeply—accepted his proposal when she couldn't give him her heart, leaned on him when it was convenient, and in the end, used him as a pawn in her bitter pursuit of revenge.

"Much has happened that I would not have chosen," he conceded delicately.

"I do not deserve you, Sir Knight," she whispered, her voice trembling. "And for that reason, I release you—with all my heart."

As soon as the words were spoken, Leah let go of his hand, and they sat in heavy silence. Both knew this was the right decision, but neither could have envisioned things turning out this way when they had first committed to one another. In this quiet moment, they both felt diminished, like shadows of their former selves.

"What will you do?" Anthony finally asked, his voice barely more than a whisper.

"I do not know," she admitted. "I am not certain where I fit in this new world." But it was not just that the world was new; she had changed as well. All her dreams were shattered. There was no version of her life that she had ever imagined which encompassed this dystopia.

And now, with Dawning Court's recent war and corresponding drop in status, and Leah now in her early twenties and abandoned by her fiancé, it was unlikely that anymore noble suitors would come seeking her hand. That thought might have been a relief had it not also meant the loss of any possibility of a family or children of her own—a lonely prospect indeed.

Anthony turned to face her, looking even more worn from their encounter, which tugged at Leah's heart. "You are a lovely woman," he said softly. "I pray that you will find happiness."

"Oh, Anthony," she said, taking his hands and pressing them to her chest, "I beg of you—" she hesitated, not willing to ask anything of him. "Please. I cannot bear the thought that you are worse because of our association. You must know that you are the best man I have ever known."

In that moment a memory suddenly surfaced. She was standing in the stable with William, who was pleading for her to stay away from him, claiming that a person as good as she was would only be brought down if she were to associate with him. She had not understood at the time what sounded to her like the rantings of a slightly deranged man. But suddenly she saw exactly what he had meant. Anthony, once pure and innocent, was now wounded and disillusioned. He was worse for having known her.

If Leah had had the courage to refuse Anthony's proposal despite the immense pressure, he might have returned to his homeland before any of this had ever happened. He would still be brightening the world with his unrestrained faith and kindness.

They sat in silence, each lost in their own thoughts as they stared across the Dawning lands. "Can it ever be like it was?" Anthony asked softly.

Leah felt his pain echoing her own inner turmoil. She wanted to offer reassurance, but she could not shake the feeling that this dismal state might be their permanent reality.

"Father Garand says that we may never be the same but that our better feelings are not dead; they have merely gone dormant for a season, like crops struck by an early frost. He says it is the result of war."

After another minute Anthony stood, and Leah followed suit, despite the discomfort it caused. What more was there to say? They both felt they had failed the other, and no amount of conversation was going to change that.

He gazed at her with sad eyes, then gently pulled her forward and kissed her forehead. "May God keep you, Leah."

"And you, too, Sir Knight." Leah lowered her gaze.

As Anthony turned to leave, Leah called him back. Stepping close, she cupped his face in her hands. "You are a wonderful, kind, God-fearing man. *I* have failed *you* and do not deserve you. Nothing would bring me greater satisfaction than to know that you have found a maiden worthy of you, one who is equal to you in both heart and temper."

Anthony's eyes grew moist, but he did not try to hide it from her; he held her gaze, so full of unspoken regret, until, after a long moment, he gave a small bow, turned, and was gone.

Sixty-one

Villiam dismounted from the carriage he had commandeered and hurried up the walk toward Leah's house, his urgency perhaps imprudent given his condition; but he was driven by a singular focus: she was alive. The thought of seeing her, maybe even holding her again, was overwhelming. Would that be inappropriate? Did she still feel the same about him?

Before he could think too much about it, however, a familiar figure appeared from around the side of the house, walking with his head bowed. He did not see William until they were almost face to face.

The two men stopped and stared at each other, neither quite knowing what to say. Anthony spoke first. "William, I am glad to see you up and about."

William hesitated. It wasn't just the fact that Anthony had very nearly killed both him and Leah that made him reticent but also the feeling of being caught by the very man whose woman he had come to steal. "I am doing better, Sir Anthony," he replied, the formal title making the conversation even more uncomfortable. "I hope this day finds you in fair health as well."

"William..." Anthony hesitated, struggling to control his emotions, "can you forgive me for..." he trailed off, unable to find the right the words.

William felt a surge of empathy for Anthony, who had given so much to the Dawnings and received nothing in return, save for the woman of his dreams. In that moment, William knew he couldn't take Leah from him. He could not cause Anthony any more pain.

Instead, he placed a reassuring hand on Anthony's shoulder. "If there is one thing I know about you, Anthony, it is that you have never put yourself before anyone else. To act as you did, you must have believed me to be a threat. The fault lies with me for not making my intentions clear."

Anthony's gaze dropped. "I will, of course, remove myself from Dawning Court."

"Anthony, this is not right. You served this people valiantly. It is because of you that there *is* a Dawning Court! You must not punish yourself for what happened in the final moments. You are a hero!"

"'Twould that I could believe that, William. But there is much that you do not know, much I have learned about myself that I would rather not know."

"Anthony," William chuckled in an attempt to lighten the mood but immediately felt that it was inappropriate. "Anthony," he continued more seriously, "you are my friend, and I am forever in your debt for being there for my family when I could not be."

Anthony managed a weak smile. "My thanks, William." He started to move past him but then paused. "I hope you have come to visit Leah. She needs a friend now. She is in the garden."

William watched as Anthony walked back to the road and mounted his horse, never looking back. He felt a pang of sorrow seeing the man so burdened and broken. William wished he knew how to ease his pain, but he understood all too well the weight of carrying such a burden. There was nothing anyone could say or do to relieve it; Anthony would have to find his own way through.

William continued up the walk, moving more slowly than before. Moments ago, he had been certain of his intentions: he would find Leah, sweep her up in his arms, and pour out his heart to her. And she, he told himself, would respond in kind. But now, he didn't think he could bring himself to do it. He could not hurt Anthony any further or force Leah to choose between her betrothed and her childhood love. He wasn't willing to cause more pain just to fulfill his own desires. He was no longer that person.

By the time William stepped into the garden, uncertainty weighed heavily on him, making him question whether he should even be there. He pushed open the gate and saw her sitting on a white bench—her hair pulled back, wearing a simple pink gown that was undoubtedly hiding bandages beneath it. When she looked up and their eyes met, the familiar jolt of electricity surged through him as it always did after an absence. He started to smile, but his expression faltered when he saw her frown deepen.

"Lovely day, Lady," he said, trying to sound casual, but it came across as awkward.

"It is indeed, Milord," she replied softly, turning her gaze again toward the landscape.

William was unaccustomed to Leah acting distant with him, and it pained him deeply, especially now when he was so relieved to see her alive. "Are you well?"

"I am very well, thank you," she answered in the same quiet tone.

"I am pleased to hear that. I was... so relieved to learn that you had survived."

"I regret any grief I may have caused you, Milord."

Unable to tolerate the formality any longer, William broke first. "Leah, what is happening? Why are you behaving this way?"

She refused to meet his gaze.

"I know your heart was shattered by the loss of Eve," he said, his voice unexpectedly cracking with emotion. "I know I played a part in that. I should have been there for you. But Leah, we are both so wounded. We need each other now more than ever. I need your listening ear and your understanding heart.... There is so much I would confide in you," he added plaintively, revealing more than he had intended.

That caught her attention, and she finally turned to look at him. "William, please do not do this," she pleaded.

"What have I done to cause my closest friend to avoid me?"

"William," her voice broke, "this cannot be."

"What? What cannot be?"

"*We* can never be," she blurted and turned away.

The weight of her words hit him like a tidal wave. He felt dizzy, as if the world were spinning beneath him. Leah had seen through him instantly and struck him down before he had had a chance to utter even a hint of what he was feeling.

I was fooling myself, he realized. *I was fooling myself that she would simply overlook all the hurt I caused and want to be with me over Anthony. Perhaps her harshness is a mercy that will spare me from any further embarrassment.*

"I under—" his voice cracked, and he cleared his throat, trying to regain his composure. "I understand," he managed, though the pain of her rejection was strong enough to cause him to forget his physical wounds for the moment. "Forgive me, Lady, for imposing on you. It was inappropriate of me to come here unannounced."

Feeling utterly hollow, he turned to leave. His heart felt the way his arm had after Collin's lance had ripped the shield from it, shocked and numb, and only time would reveal the true extent of the damage.

Before he reached the gate, he turned back. Leah was still refusing to look at him. "I am pleased that you will marry Anthony," he said, the words hurting him more than he had expected. Yet he found a part of him truly meant them. "He is a great man, perhaps the only man I know who is worthy of you, and he will treat you as you deserve."

With that, William pushed through the gate and made his way back to the carriage, feeling so drained that he doubted his ability to make it home under his own strength. The window of hope that had been opened when he had learned that Leah was alive had abruptly closed, with the shutters slammed and nailed shut. While he was relieved that she had survived, it no longer felt like divine confirmation of their bond. Instead, she would forever be a reminder of what might have been had he not been so blind.

In stark contrast to the burst of energy that had almost made him run from the room earlier, William barely managed to return to his bed, each step feeling like a struggle. He had to lean on Sebastian for support up the many stairs to the baron's chambers.

"That was rather foolish, Master William, running out like that so soon after a major injury," the old steward chided as he settled William into bed. "Can you imagine what your mother would have said?"

"I think I can," William replied, the reminder of Martha's absence cutting deeper now. At this moment, he would have sought her company above all others. Instead, he was left to the darkness, the light he thought he had seen turning out to be nothing but a mirage. He truly was alone now.

Sixty-two

Neil sat at a small table in his modest homestead, listlessly stirring a cold bowl of porridge, when a knock came at the door. But he ignored it.

Father Garand had re-dressed his wounds after the war ended, and despite the cleric's objections, Neil had insisted on returning home. He just needed rest and thought that he would get more in the comfort of his own home, forgetting that his domestic servants had fled and his home had been ransacked. But rather than return to the recovery ward, he made do with what remained.

To his dismay, however, Neil found that the solitude he had sought only deepened his melancholy. Despite his naturally reclusive nature, he felt intensely lonely. The weeks of meaningful work to save Dawning Court had left him craving the shared purpose he once had with Anthony and the others.

It also stung a little, if he was honest with himself, that no one beyond the orderly assigned to check on him each day—almost certainly the one knocking at the door now—had even taken the time to look in on him.

He knew his hurt feelings were irrational. Who was left to worry over him? William and Leah were fighting for their lives, Henry was overwhelmed with his new barony, and Anthony had been so horrified when he learned what he had done that he had scarcely shown his face in public since. So who did that leave that might spare a thought for Neil?

"You know," he muttered aloud while stirring the unappetizing sludge in front of him, "it is you who drove them all away. If you were not so surly, you might have friends and a wife to look after you."

The knock came again, and Neil reluctantly got up to answer it. His stomach wound was much improved, but he still felt tired and achy.

He swung the door open, already halfway through dismissing the orderly, when he froze.

Standing before him, freshly washed and wearing a clean gray dress, was Salena. The transformation from the filthy, beaten urchin he had ridden with to a poised lady was striking. He had forgotten how pretty she was.

"Milady," he nodded lamely.

"Sir Neil, how fare ye?"

He shrugged slightly. "I think that I shall yet remain in the realm of the living."

"I am pleased to hear it," she said, and glanced around nervously. "May I come in?"

Neil glanced back at the state of his house and considered refusing her on the grounds that it was not proper but then, with a resigned shrug, moved aside.

She stepped in after him and looked around at the overturned sitting room. "It is cold in here," she said, hugging herself, "colder than outside I think."

"Come with me to the kitchen. There is a fire in the stove."

She followed him to the kitchen, where he returned to his seat at the table while she moved to the small woodstove to warm herself.

"My domestics have not returned," Neil said by way of explanation.

"Then who has been looking after you?" Salena asked, eyeing the mess with skepticism.

"I need no looking after."

"Everyone needs looking after sometimes, Neil. Even you."

"Is this why you came? To chide me about my housekeeping?"

"And so I might have done," she snapped, "if you had done any housekeeping. I was merely concerned for my friend."

"Are we friends?" Neil grunted.

"I think we must be," she replied, then hesitated. "Why did you—" she stopped and started again in a softer tone. "You said nothing of my ... indiscretions."

It wasn't really a question, but she left it hanging in the air, waiting for his response. "Why do you assume that?" Neil asked, his natural perverseness getting the better of him.

"Because had it been otherwise, I would have surely been drawn and quartered by now."

"William pardoned you," Neil said simply, as if that settled everything.

"But you and everyone at Dawning Court suffered because of my selfish actions. William's pardon would mean little if you had spoken out."

"There has been enough damage done to our people. What would it profit them to know that one of our own caused so much of their suffering?"

Salena's eyes found the floor. "I deserve to be punished. I am prepared to accept my fate."

"Have you not suffered enough?"

Salena considered and finally nodded. "You will keep my secret, then?"

"I have no intention of telling anyone. And William is not talking at all in his condition, so if anyone learns of it, it will have to come from you or Hans Braddock himself."

Salena's face hardened. "Hans Braddock," she repeated slowly.

Neil scowled. "That slippery coward escaped."

"He did not," she said tersely.

Neil could see that there was a story here, but from her expression it was clear she was not interested in sharing; so he dismissed it with another shrug. "Anyway, I doubt it is an offense you are likely to repeat."

Salena looked at him hopefully. "Are we—are you still my friend, despite knowing my shame?"

"Salena, I do not think either of us has friends enough to discard any over a grudge."

"You grant me more honor than I deserve."

Neil sighed and slumped back in his chair. "Many of us have learned through this ordeal that we are not the people we believed ourselves to be."

"I thank you," she said and turned to go, but then hesitated.

"Was there something else?"

"I fear to impose any further," she admitted.

Neil grimaced. "Speak your piece."

"I—I must go fetch Rachael. She is with David's mother near London. I—I would prefer not to travel alone."

"Nor should a lady travel unescorted," Neil agreed.

"Would you be available—that is to say, are you well enough ..." she trailed off, unable to ask him directly.

Neil paused to consider the offer. Wasn't she just a female version of himself—damaged, trying to rebuild from the ruins of her life? She had obviously come to him because she had no one else to turn to, and really, who else did Neil have?

"I should be glad to escort you, Lady," he said finally with unexpected warmth. "Provided we travel by carriage. I am not yet fit to ride a horse."

"Of course," she said with visible relief. "We would need a carriage anyway—Rachael is too small to ride. I will make all the arrangements. Is two days sufficient time for you?"

"Ample, Lady," he smiled at her.

She turned to leave but suddenly ran back and kissed him impulsively, a brief, light peck, before rushing out with a furious blush and a bright smile.

Neil watched her go from his chair, surprised to find himself grinning. He felt a warmth spreading through him, as though the sun had just come out and was shining down upon him.... Perhaps it had at that....

Sixty-three

"Lady Dawning!" Aden stammered, betraying a rare moment of awkwardness as the widow was shown into their drawing room. "To what do we owe the honor?"

When the steward had announced her, Aden had not really believed it could be her. No baron or baroness had visited their homestead since Braden was alive, and even that was exceedingly rare. It was not that Aden was particularly flustered around nobility; it was just that her unannounced visit caught him off guard, and in his own private space, he was suddenly uncertain how to behave.

He had quickly summoned Anne, his wife, and asked her to bring Leah from her bedchamber, where she was still recovering from her injury. He was relieved to see that despite her condition, Leah was well-presented. Though Grace likely would have been understanding, he was sure that both Leah and Anne would have been mortified to greet the baroness in a dressing gown.

Leah sat on the sofa, her back erect and poised to meet her guest. Though she looked pale, she showed no sign of discomfort.

"Please," Aden said formally, gesturing to the opposite end of the sofa, "Won't you sit?"

Grace leaned awkwardly over her bulging stomach to give Leah a gentle, somewhat awkward hug, touching her cheek to Leah's head. She then took the seat across from

Leah, and Aden settled into his own chair. "To what do we owe this honor?" he asked.

"You must forgive my intrusion," Grace began.

"A visit from your grace could never be considered an intrusion," Leah responded formally.

Grace waved off the sentiment. "It was most unseemly of me to arrive in this manner. It is only that I have just been to look in on Sir Neil and was passing by here on the way home. I could not pass up the opportunity to stop in and check on Leah's progress and personally express my gratitude to your family for all you did to save our little barony."

"Lady Dawning, you should not have troubled yourself. But please tell me, how is Sir Neil?" Leah asked.

"Sir Neil was … somewhat surly."

Leah smiled at that. "I am pleased that he is doing well."

"His wound still needs more time to heal, but I required his assistance on another matter, so I could not wait."

"Oh, what matter was that?" Anne asked, her interest instantly piqued at the gossip.

"Mother!" Leah exclaimed. "Lady Dawning's affairs are her own business."

"Surely there is no harm in asking," Anne said defensively. "She need not tell me if she does not wish to."

"The restoration of the barony must be keeping you very busy," Leah said to change the subject.

"Indeed," Grace said, smiling appreciatively at Leah and turned back to Anne. "But I have been reliably informed that without the heroic actions of your husband and daughter, there may not have been a barony to restore. I understand that it was Leah who personally led the people to hold the castle until the army could subdue our enemies outside the gates."

Anne swelled with pride at the recognition, but Grace noted that Leah deflated. "I wonder," Grace said to Anne and Aden, "if I might trouble you for a little something to take away the evening chill?"

"Of course, Lady," Aden responded, catching the hint. He pushed himself up and gripped his wife's arm as he passed by. "Perhaps you could assist me in the cellar?"

"What?" She looked up at him in surprise. "Oh, very well," she said, reluctantly rising and following him.

Once they were alone, Grace turned back to Leah and spoke softy. "Surely I have not been misinformed about your role in the castle's defense?"

"My father and Henry deserve most of the credit," Leah said quietly. "To say nothing of Sir Anthony's gallantry. As there are so many more deserving than myself, I would be grateful if you would not mention it."

"But do you not see, Leah? The difference between your contribution and theirs is not in the magnitude but in the singularity of it. They are all knights, sworn to protect our people. What you did was extraordinary!"

Leah winced, a reaction that had nothing to do with her injuries. "There was much that precipitated that desperate gambit that I would prefer not to remember."

Grace sat in respectful silence for a bit before continuing. "I am certain that you saw and endured much that no one would ever wish to experience. I regret that I did not insist that you leave Dawning Court with me. Of course, I never imagined that you would stay behind," Grace chided her mildly. "But by the sounds of it, it is fortunate that you were here looking after things."

Leah lowered her gaze.

"Did you know," Grace asked suddenly, "that Martha Dawning used to speak about you?"

"I did not know," Leah replied, her eyes still downcast.

"Oh yes, she was very fond of you. She saw in you a great woman that you, yourself, were not yet aware existed. She believed only adversity would bring that person out. It seems she was correct."

"I fear if you knew all that transpired, you would realize that I fell very much beneath Lady Dawning's expectations."

Grace placed her hand over Leah's. "You must not reproach yourself for what might have been. You did what you could, and in the end, the barony is better for it, regardless of any missteps made along the way."

"I once thought the path of virtue so simple. It was easy, so I believed, to remain aloof from the snares of wickedness in which so many are caught." Leah's voice broke. "I so often judged others for their choices when I could not begin to understand the depth of the conflicts that were playing out in their hearts and minds at those critical moments."

Grace squeezed her hand. "But you are wiser now. You will not be so quick to judge in the future."

"That wisdom was purchased at a terrible price, Lady. I was brought to the precipice again and again, forced to confront my own weaknesses; and each time I failed."

"Failed? Who have you failed?"

"I failed my people; I failed Anthony; I failed myself."

"But in the end, you saved us all! Leah, listen to me," Grace gently lifted Leah's chin, forcing her to meet her eyes. "I am saddened that your marriage to my brother is not to be, but I will not presume to understand all that has led to this. You are both worthy individuals, and I trust your judgement.

"But as for failing people, my late husband would have understood your feelings better than anyone. He had more blood on his hands than you or I can even comprehend. But after he saw the error of his ways, he did not let his past mistakes define him. He became the great man we knew because he chose to move forward. Is that not the same decision you need to make right now? You have learned things about yourself and others that are painful to know. You have discovered that you have a breaking point, as do we all. But now you have a choice; you can shrink into yourself and hide your light from the world, unable to forgive yourself or learn from your failures; or you can use your newfound empathy to reach out to others and perhaps administer relief that would have been beyond you in simpler times."

"I do not understand, Lady. Who am I supposed to help?"

Grace smiled. "Would the Leah from before this ordeal have asked such a question? You used to find opportunities to serve everywhere you looked. Whether it was feeding the poor, comforting widows, or tending to the sick, you never waited to be asked. You were always the first to volunteer."

Leah dropped her eyes. "I do not know if I am that person any longer."

"You are deeply troubled in mind and spirit," Grace said, moving closer and putting a comforting arm around Leah. "It is too much to expect that anyone can simply return to their old ways so soon after the horrors of war. Start small. Begin with one person at a time."

"Did you have someone in mind?" Leah asked absently, already dreading the prospect of social engagement.

"As a matter of fact, I did," Grace said, releasing Leah and turning to face her again. Leah was instantly nervous. "I need help, Leah. I cannot manage the barony in my condition. My energy flags quickly, and time grows short until I am due."

"Of course, Lady, but you must understand that Sir Anth—"

"I need William!" Grace cut her off.

Leah stopped, a shocked expression on her face as Grace's words sank in. "Pardon?"

"I need *William's* help."

"Surely, Lord William would not deny you—"

"He has scarcely left his room in the past week."

"His injuries—"

"Were indeed severe," Grace acknowledged. "I am trained in the medical arts, and I well understand his physical condition. Yet I believe there is more to it than that. Like you, I believe he too is suffering from an injured spirit."

"I … am not certain how I can help with that."

"Leah, may I speak candidly?" Grace asked, holding Leah's eyes with her intense gaze.

Leah nodded, though she braced herself for what was to come.

"My first choice for you and my brother would have been for you to marry. Is there any chance of that happening?"

"I fear not, Lady."

"Exactly. So, let us dispense with that matter and speak freely. I was at William's bedside when he awoke lucid for the first time. He was in a great deal of pain."

Leah nodded. "Of course."

"Yet when he learned that you were alive, he jumped out of bed as though he had been launched from a catapult."

A smile briefly touched Leah's lips before she was able to suppress it.

"Ignoring all medical advice, rules of decorum, or proper standards of grooming, he rushed to see you without a moment's hesitation. I presume he succeeded?" Grace raised her eyebrows inquisitively.

"Yes, Lady." Leah looked away again.

"What transpired between you two is not my concern, and I will not pry. But whatever it was, William did not return in the same spirit in which he left. Sebastian had to help him into bed, and as I say, he has scarcely left it since."

"I am grieved, Lady. Truly."

"Will you not see him?" Grace pleaded. "I am not asking you to marry him," she added quickly. "Only talk to him. Reassure him that he has something to live for. He has said little since that first night, but I sense that he feels much as you do—that he has failed; that he has lost those he loves most and let everyone down."

"Lady, I am really not the person—"

"Are you not his friend?" Grace asked pointedly. "I understood that you two have been the closest of friends since childhood. Is that not true?"

"Our friendship has been strained since his return to Dawning Court. Things...are not as they once were."

"Then I fear I am at a loss," Grace said, turning her palms up before her. "With Braddock Court consuming all of Henry's time, William was my last hope.... Unless..."

"Lady?"

"Were you aware that Martha believed you would one day lead these people? Surely, you noticed her grooming you for that role?"

"I did notice her unusual interest," Leah replied, "but I was never certain of her reasons. But I could never lead," she quickly added. "Perhaps I could write William a letter if you believe it will help, but that is all I can do."

Grace considered this. "A visit would be better."

"Forgive me, Lady, but I am afraid that is quite out of the question. The way we left things makes such a visit...impossible."

"Very well," Grace said, obviously disappointed. "If a letter is all that you can manage, then I will have to accept that. My only concern is that with a message of such importance, I would hate for your intent to be misconstrued in the text...." She trailed off before adding, "But I am sure it will be fine."

Leah felt as though she had been slapped. Did Grace know about William's letter that had pushed Leah over the edge after Eve's death?

Just then Aden and Anne returned with a cup of brandy, and Anne carefully handed it to the baroness. Grace dutifully took a sip and sighed with satisfaction, as if it were just what she had needed.

"Thank you, all," Grace said standing. "I have troubled you enough for one evening, and I really must be going."

"No, Lady," Anne protested. "Please stay. We would like to hear of matters around the barony. Is it true that William Dawning will act as regent?"

"It is true that I have asked it of him, but I fear his injuries make it uncertain whether he can serve in that capacity," Grace said, pulling her gloves back on her hands and deliberately not looking at Leah as she spoke.

"Is that wise, Lady?" Anne asked before realizing that she might seem to be questioning the baroness' judgement. "What I mean is that he is so young."

"I believe the boy will make a fine leader," Aden said, causing every eye in the room to turn toward him.

"Father?" Leah gasped in astonishment.

"Good leaders do not use their positions to enrich themselves, they use them to serve their people. From what I have seen of William during this war, I believe he cares nothing for wealth or power." Aden shrugged, a hint of embarrassment in his voice. "Perhaps he will make a good leader," he said less definitively.

"But he is so young," Anne repeated, as if that were truly her only concern.

"The boy will make mistakes," Aden agreed, "but it is easier to teach someone how to manage a barony than it is to instill in them altruism, compassion, or charity."

"Father..." Leah almost whispered, her eyes brimming with emotion that Grace couldn't quite grasp.

Aden met her eyes, and Grace watched as something she did not understand passed between them.

"Quite right," Grace said suddenly, using the opportunity to extricate herself from the situation. "Well said, Sir Aden." She turned to leave but stopped at the door. "That reminds me; there will be a celebration soon—after Dawning Court has been restored to some semblance of order. Your family is to be honored, so dress appropriately."

"Lady, no!" Leah cried. "You mustn't!" Aden's frown deepened, and only Anne looked pleased at the news.

"I did not mention it to give rise to argument but to give you time to prepare. Like it or not, Leah, you are a heroine to our people, and you must accept this honor with the grace and aplomb for which you are known. You are an inspiration, and we need that now more than ever."

Sixty-four

It had been a week since William's ill-fated visit to confess his love to Leah. Despite the initial surge of energy he'd felt upon learning she was alive, he had barely had the strength to stir from his bed since. It was only the daily walks enforced by Sebastian or Father Garand that pulled him from his solitude. Otherwise, he remained locked away, struggling to contemplate a future bereft of Leah, Martha, David, Eve, and Richard. He had never expected to live this long, nor had he envisioned what his life would be like if ever he did return home to stay. In the moments when he did allow himself to daydream about it, it was always with Leah at his side. Now that he was here, the reality was a bleak, colorless landscape, like a painting faded by years of sunlight.

It was day seven or perhaps eight when a light knock came at the door. William groaned and forced himself to sit up as Sebastian entered. "It is time for your walk, Master William."

William wanted to refuse, but he had learned it was simpler to comply than to argue. He placed a hand on Sebastian's shoulder and slowly stood, allowing the aging steward to guide him out of the room and through the castle.

William felt a bit foolish relying on Sebastian, whose shoulder felt more like a dried twig than it did muscle and sinew. It forced William to walk on his own wherever he felt safe to do so, despite still feeling very weak.

"I thought we might pass through the garden today," Sebastian announced, leading them toward the exit.

"Is there even a garden left?"

"Much of it was destroyed in the siege," Sebastian admitted, "but some seeds survived and are beginning to bloom. Lady Dawning thought it might lift your spirits."

"Ever the optimist, that one," William grumbled, but he didn't protest as Sebastian led him toward what remained of the hedge that had once created a private sanctuary in the courtyard—a place where William and Leah had often sought refuge from the ever-jealous Eve.

They had only made it a few steps, however, when a familiar figure appeared. Tall and lean as ever, Neil used a cane for support but otherwise looked relatively healthy.

William froze. He had not seen Neil since the siege, and though their shared ordeal on the road from Braddock Court had rekindled some semblance of their old friendship, he wasn't sure where they stood now.

He was somewhat relieved when Neil greeted him with a friendly, "How are you feeling?"

"Like a skewered pig," William muttered.

"I know the feeling," Neil replied, glancing down at his own stomach, though the bandages were concealed by his tunic.

"I suppose you do at that," William conceded, feeling a bit embarrassed.

"Where are you headed?" Neil asked Sebastian.

"We were going to pass through the garden before returning to the baron's chambers."

"Fine," Neil said. "I will see that his lordship makes it back in one piece," he assured Sebastian, stepping between William and the steward.

Sebastian flicked a glance at William, but seeing no objection, stepped aside with a slight bow. "Very good, Sir."

"I do not think Sebastian trusts me to catch you if you fall," Neil said, watching the Steward disappear back into the castle. "And in truth, I doubt that I could, so try not to trip."

"Why am I always in more danger when you are around?" William complained.

"Because we are both so disagreeable that you can never be certain if I am here to help or hinder," Neil replied, resuming their slow pace through the yard.

"'Tis a terrible state to be in," William muttered.

"Am I correct in assuming that it is not entirely your wound keeping you locked away?"

"My limbs are heavy, and I am perpetually weary. What matter the cause?"

Neil sighed. "That feeling, too, I know very well." They walked in silence for a minute before he added, "For a long time, I felt as though nobody cared if I lived or died. What reason did I have to rise each morning?"

It again struck William that Neil understood his place better than he realized. He shuddered inwardly at the thought. *Oh, Heaven forbid, I am becoming Neil!* But he kept that to himself. "Perhaps," he grudgingly admitted, "that thought has crossed my mind."

"Do you think that is in fact the case? That nobody cares, I mean."

William sighed. "I suppose I do not really know." What he didn't say was that he wasn't sure if anyone he wanted to care actually did.

"What of Leah?" Neil asked, as if reading his thoughts. "She always proved more than adequate motivation to get you moving before. You know Anthony has left for Sicily? She released him from his vow."

"I heard that from Grace," William nodded. "Neil ..." He hesitated. He wanted to confide in someone, but was Neil a safe place for something so sensitive? On the other hand, did he have anyone else? "Leah rejected even the possibility of a friendship with me," he finally admitted. "I doubt that has changed with Anthony's departure."

"Is that so?"

"Why the surprise?"

Neil shrugged. "I wonder if she would be open to a suit from a surly, misanthropic noble?" he said with a sly smile.

"I just told you that she rejected me."

"Not you; me! I am told that I am some sort of hero now."

"Some hero you are; you actually brought an assassin to murder me while I was trying to rescue the army from itself!"

"I apologized for that."

"No, you did not."

"Oh … well, sorry about Salena trying to murder you."

"My thanks, Sir Knight," William said sarcastically but then turned serious and stopped to look at his friend. "In truth, though, Neil, you have always been a good friend to me and our people. Not only have I not shown you the respect and appreciation you deserve, but I have treated you like the enemy—an outward manifestation of my own guilt and pain. I wronged you. Will you forgive me for that?"

Neil looked suddenly awkward and stared at the ground as he spoke. "Well, I have not been without my faults in our relationship. I blamed you for David's death because I too needed someone to blame. I was so despondent that I needed somewhere to place those feelings. But William," he looked up earnestly, "it was not your fault. None of us could have stopped David from doing what he did. He chose to sacrifice himself to protect you, and he would have done so regardless of his position."

"Thank you, Neil," William said, his voice trembling with emotion. "I needed to hear that."

"And take heart," Neil said, brightening, "if Leah does not want you, there will be others. I promise you that. But I wonder if you should not at least talk to her again before moving on?"

"She was quite definitive in our last encounter. I do not think I can handle another rejection like that."

"I am not suggesting that she will change her mind and fall into your arms. But clearly, she has hurt you; would it not be worth a conversation to avoid regrets and misunderstandings?"

William sighed and shrugged. "I will consider it," he said noncommittally, but the pain and embarrassment he was still feeling made him reluctant even to think about seeing her again.

"Well," Neil said cheerfully, "as I have often said, I know less about women than any man alive. But there is one thing in which I'm an expert."

"Damascus steel?" William smirked.

"Wootz!" Neil corrected automatically. "But no, not that. Well, yes, that too. But what I mean is that I might be the world's foremost authority on feeling sorry for oneself."

"Um...what?"

"Ellen left me, William, because I am irascible."

William looked at him, unsure of how to respond. "All right...."

"Thank you for arguing," Neil said sarcastically but then continued. "She too realized she could do better than me and acted upon that realization, leaving me alone and distraught."

"That is harsh."

"The problem with being a misanthropic curmudgeon is that there are not many people to whom you may turn when you do need someone."

"You had David." William pointed out.

"Yes, I did," Neil nodded. "But when you do not care for people, you start to expect that they feel the same about you. You begin to feel that you do not *deserve* companionship and empathy. Can you understand that?"

"Better than I can say."

"So, when Ellen—the one person in the world who pledged to love me, come what may—took my only child and fled, what reason did I have to even exist? Nobody wanted me; I did not even want to keep my own company."

"So what did you do?"

"First, I wasted a lot of time sulking and doing nothing. But then the war started, and a new sense of purpose was thrust upon me. I did not seek it—did not even want it—but there it was, and duty demanded that I take up the cross to look after these people."

"And what happened?"

"I think you know."

William looked down, suddenly feeling guilty for how he was behaving and somewhat embarrassed at how transparent his motives were. "You forgot about yourself."

"I forgot about myself, and the world changed for me. It is time to grow up, William."

"You are still a misanthropic curmudgeon!" William retorted, though Neil's grin made the comment seem almost affectionate.

"And you are still a brash, arrogant noble. But there is still good that we both can do. And there is a very pregnant matron who sorely needs help overseeing the restoration of this disaster." He gestured at the battered courtyard, still in disarray despite the cleanup efforts.

"I do not know if I can do it," William told him frankly.

"You will not be alone. You will have me, and Henry, and a hundred others to help you."

"I appreciate that, truly I do, but that is not exactly what I meant."

"Ah. Well, even if Leah has come to her senses and realized that she could do better than you, trust me when I tell you that when you stop thinking about yourself, you will not be alone for long."

William didn't want to admit that he couldn't imagine being with anyone other than Leah, so he only smiled. "So, you will help me?"

"Well, about that," Neil said, suddenly looking uncomfortable. "I am going away for a few weeks."

"You *are* a big help!"

"It is a personal matter, but I wanted to ask you...about Salena...."

"What about her?"

"Do you recall the exchange you had with her on the road after Collin's death?"

"I believe so. Why?"

"She confessed some rather grievous sins to you. But you pardoned her," he hastened to add. "Does that pardon still stand?"

William had barely even thought on it since that night, with all that had happened, but he did not have any particular inclination to rescind his forgiveness. "It does."

"Is she...still welcome in Dawning Court?"

"Do you believe her to be a danger to me or our people?"

"Goodness, no!" Neil said quickly. "She is most repentant for her part in all this. She is even considering self-exile."

"It might be better for her to make a fresh start, leave all this behind," William suggested. "But I do not require it of her."

"I..." Neil coughed uncomfortably, "would prefer that she remain close."

"Oh, so it is like that, is it?" William's eyebrows shot up.

"I see in her a kindred spirit. Quite apart from our shared history, she has seen the worst in me and I in her, and we..." he hesitated, trying to articulate his feelings.

"Are at peace with each other?" William offered.

Neil smiled. "That might be a good way to say it."

"Well, I am pleased for you both."

"Oh, it is nothing yet," Neil hastened to reassure him, "but there is a feeling."

William was in much better spirits when Neil left him back at the door of the baron's chamber. He had intended to return to bed but instead turned and went looking for Grace. He found her alone in a small sitting room, pensively sipping a drink by the fire, the chair beside her empty.

"William!" Grace said, her expression brightening as she saw him. "Do come in."

"I hope I am not interrupting," William said, standing awkwardly at the door.

"Not at all," she insisted a little too quickly. "Please, have a seat."

He hesitated before sitting down across from her. "You looked … thoughtful," he remarked, noting the distant look in her eyes.

"This is the first quiet evening I have had since returning, and I was just reflecting that the last time I sat here, Richard was sitting across from me."

The mention of Richard caught William off-guard, adding to his feeling of intrusion. Grace, however, continued smoothly, denying him any excuse to retreat.

"Have you given any more thought to my proposal?" she asked.

"I have thought of little else." He rubbed his sweaty palms on his trousers. "How did Richard know that he would make a good leader?" he asked abruptly. Grace raised her eyebrows. "He did not know. He was reluctant to accept the barony because he so feared his inadequacies."

William grimaced. "That is where I struggle as well. I am full of inadequacies and shortcomings, but I am not certain that I share any of Richard's strengths."

Grace considered this. "Richard's self-doubt kept him humble. It may have made him a better leader, helping him lead with empathy and caution."

William sighed. "The Richard I knew was not introspective, nor was he wont to reflect upon past mistakes."

"That is a man I know only from the stories. Why do you bring this up now, William?"

"Because I need to understand how he did it. How did he change?"

"Have you not been changed through your ordeal?"

"I do not know," William admitted. "I wanted to believe I had, but..." he left off with a shrug. Grace waited, and William realized he needed to say more. "When I was out there," William gestured around as if to indicate the barony at large, "attempting desperately to put right all that was wrong, much of which was my own doing, I realized that all my biggest regrets—leaving Leah behind, reassigning David, hating Richard—all came because I was thinking only of myself. I resolved then that if I lived long enough to see the other side of this conflict, I would no longer be governed by my own selfishness. If I again found myself in a dark place, I was going to try to forget myself and serve someone else. But when the first opportunity came, when you asked me to step up and serve, I could not see beyond my own sorrow."

"You have lost so much, William. Do you not deserve some time to grieve?"

He shrugged again.

"You have been injured," she nodded at his stomach.

William grimaced. "Is that so? I had almost forgotten about it."

Grace gave him a look that made it clear she was holding back a retort through sheer force of will. "What I mean is that you have an expectation that you will one day heal and be as active and strong as before, do you not?"

"I *hope* I will return to full strength," William acknowledged. "But I suppose that only time will tell."

"Why do men—especially warriors—assume that their emotions should be any different? You would not expect a soldier to ride into battle in your condition; he would not be strong enough. But neither is he forever useless as a soldier because he was once injured. Why then do you not extend the same grace to yourself over your unseen wounds? You very recently lost your mother, Eve, and two of your brothers; can you not be as patient with your mental wounds as you would be with the physical ones?"

Grace studied him with a thoughtful gaze as she placed her cup on the end table.

"To answer your question, Richard changed when he was finally able to look at himself honestly, without evasion or pretense. Richard the general refused to face his own flaws. As you said, he never allowed himself to consider that he might be wrong. He was entirely selfish, driven only by his own desires, and quick to blame others for his failures.

"Richard the baron, on the other hand, my husband, confronted his most profound character flaws. He was painfully aware of them and worked hard to avoid falling back into his old ways, fearing a resurgence of his darker nature. He even feared going into battle with you."

William was taken aback. "Richard was afraid to fight?"

"Yes," Grace nodded. "But it was not his enemies he feared but himself. He knew he was stronger than any man on the field and exceptional at killing, and he had once reveled in it. He was terrified of what he might unleash within himself by riding into battle again. If I may be so bold, William, it seems that God has granted you a similar opportunity to become someone new. He has humbled you. You could either view this as a loss of everything or as a chance to rebuild from the ground up, to make yourself into the man you choose to be.

"I do not care for this gift," William joked, but it felt misplaced.

Grace's gaze was steady. "Some people in your position simply give up. Under the crushing weight of despair, they stop living." William shifted uncomfortably, recognizing that this was what he had been doing since Leah's rejection. She continued. "Others simply pretend none of it happened and continue on as before, just happy to have survived the ordeal." She shrugged. "I do not judge. That is familiar. It is comfortable. But some few," she said, leaning forward intently, "some few will do as Richard did. They will accept that their character was fragile and that, under pressure, it collapsed like a house of cards. And then they will rebuild."

William felt a surge of emotion as he looked at Grace, feeling a newfound respect for her. She was beautiful, and it was clear she had to be strong to have nursed Richard back to health. But she was also much wiser than he had realized.

"It is easy to see why Richard loved you," he said, standing. "Thank you for your wisdom, thank you for not abandoning this people, and thank you for making my brother's last year the happiest in his life." He paused a moment before adding, "I will do it. I will accept the regency. It is how I can honor my brother. I can serve his wife, his child, and his people since he cannot be here to do it himself."

Sixty-five

onald," William said, trying to keep his exasperation in check with the foreman in charge of rebuilding the west wall. "I am not an expert on fortifications, but I am almost certain that all of the walls should connect." William was pointing at the line where the masons had begun rebuilding the wall as though it were a self-contained structure, without joining it to the existing north and south walls. The new wall was standing waist-high, with perfect vertical gaps between it and the adjacent walls.

"To do that, we would have to tear out part of the walls that are still standing!" Ronald protested.

"One moment." William turned to a steward who had hurried up beside him and stood awkwardly, hoping to be noticed.

"Er, forgive me, Milord," the steward began hesitantly. "Sebastian reports that the remaining stores have been distributed, but we still do not have enough seed to plant the spring crops."

"I have already sent a request to Henry for more," William replied, turning back to Ronald. "The wall is not strong enough like this; it will not hold."

"You couldn't knock it over," Ronald countered. "'Ere, push on this," he said, pressing his hand against the stones to show that they would not budge.

William squeezed the bridge of his nose. "See this?" he said, lifting his tunic to reveal the bandages still covering his torso. "This is where a spear ran me through."

"Looks painful," Ronald said, nonplussed.

"It is," William snapped, "but it is only half as painful as the headache that you are giving me!"

"But Sebastian says the fields must be planted immediately," the steward protested.

"Lord William," a runner raced up with a report. "Here is the update you requested on the remaining chivalry," the boy said, shoving a page into William's hand. "Lord Martin requests your instructions."

"It will take twice as long and be twice as difficult to do what you are asking," Ronald continued to argue. William had questioned his own suitability for the role of regent when he accepted the charge, and this obstinate stonemason was only confirming his doubts. He longed for the simplicity of war, where there was one way to resolve disputes, and he was usually better at it than everyone else.

William closed his eyes as two more people spotted him across the courtyard and started toward him. His health was improving, but he could only manage about four hours on his feet before exhaustion set in and he had to return to bed. Now, eight hours into the day, in pain and at his wit's end, he was seriously considering challenging the stonemason to a duel when a new voice interrupted.

"Perhaps I may be of assistance here, Lord William?"

William turned to see a large, bearded knight standing there, towering formidably over everyone around him, with a blonde squire by his side who looked even younger than his fifteen years.

William's face broke into a grin. "Oh, thank the great merciful Heaven. Please tell me you are here to kill me?"

"I reckon I can do you a might better than that," the bearded knight rumbled.

"Sir Hildebrant, I should gladly make you baron if you would explain to this stonemason why his time-saving strategy is problematic. Or, failing that, lock him in the dungeon.... Do we have a dungeon?"

"Master craftsman," Hildebrant snapped, causing Ronald, who barely reached Hildebrant's chest, to shrink back nervously. "Are you an imbecile?" William nodded in response to the question, but Hildebrant ignored him. "Did you fight to preserve Dawning Court, only to leave it vulnerable to the first enemy with an ox cart? *Lord* Dawning has given you a direct order, and you see fit to argue with him? You will tear down this travesty of a fortification and you will rebuild it properly. And you will do it now! Is that understood?"

Ronald, shrinking beneath Hildebrant's anger, barely managed to squeak his consent.

"You will then report to the stocks to be lashed for your disrespect. You do not disobey orders from your benefactors! Is thirty lashes sufficient, Lord?" Hildebrant turned to William, his fierce demeanor softened by a glint of mischief in his eye.

"Er—I think we can forgo the lashing, provided it does not happen again."

"I assure you, with thirty lashes on his back, it will not happen again," Hildebrant insisted.

William pretended to think about it long enough to let the stonemason squirm before declaring magnanimously, "I will overlook the indiscretion this one time."

"Very well!" Hildebrant turned to Ronald. "You heard Lord Dawning! See to it! And count yourself fortunate for his mercy, which you do not deserve!"

When Ronald had scurried off, Hildebrant turned to the steward, who had gone pale. "I believe Lord Dawning already responded to your query. Was there something else?"

"Er, quite right, your Lordship. Very good." He bowed and quickly hurried away.

They all then turned to the runner boy, and William said, "Tell Sir Martin that I need time to review his report and will respond to him on the morrow."

When they were alone, William turned to Hildebrant and Finn, who both now wore grins to match his own. He started forward to embrace them but stopped. "I am new to this diplomacy thing. What do we do, do I hug you or challenge you to a duel, or what?"

Hildebrant snorted and pulled William toward him in his beefy arms. "William, you are either the most likable enemy or the worst friend a man could have. But either way, you do grow on a person."

"Like mold," Finn added.

William grinned at him. "But seriously, why are you here? You are not here to kill me, are you?" he asked, only half-joking. "Though you might be doing me a favor if you were."

"When we heard the news that some fool had made you regent, we had to come and see for ourselves if it was true."

William glanced around to make sure they were not overheard before confiding, "It is a disaster! I have no idea what I am doing, and every worker seems to need direction for even the smallest detail. I do not know what to tell any of them about anything! I am just making it up on the spot."

"It does not matter," Hildebrant waved dismissively.

"What do you mean, it does not matter? How do I know what I say is correct?"

"It is correct because you are the acting baron and you said it."

William searched his face for some trace of irony, but finding none, asked, "But if I am certain that I am correct, and I happen to be incompetent, does that not make me Hans Braddock?"

"Not if you recognize your limitations and surround yourself with competent people."

"Alright, but where do I find such helpers?"

"Right here!" Finn interjected, impetuous as ever.

"What?"

"'Tis so," Hildebrant grudgingly acknowledged. "Perhaps you heard that Braddock Court is in a bit of disarray since new leadership took over? Finn and I figured if we must be subject to one miserable Dawning, it may as well be one we know."

"Are you in earnest?"

"If you will have us?"

William impulsively embraced them both at the same time. "This has not been my finest hour. I welcome your assistance." He stepped back and asked, "So what do we do now? Do I just give you a list of the tradesmen I want killed, or what?"

"Perhaps we can postpone the swearing-in ceremony," Hildebrant said, handing his pack to Finn. "And let me see if I can help deal with the tradesmen before we jump right to executions. Perhaps your Lordship will grant us chambers to stow our gear so we may get to work?"

"Of course! Forgive me, I've only been dignified a few days; it takes some getting used to. Stable your horses, and I will arrange accommodations."

The two turned to go when William called after them, "It is good to see you both," he said, genuinely feeling like he had friends for the first time since Leah had turned him away and Neil had left with Salena. "Truly."

Sixty-six

"ord William?"

William had just finished giving Sebastian instructions regarding the accommodations for Hildebrant and Finn when yet another person was calling out with yet another demand. He turned, ready to deliver a sharp retort for whatever trivial matter they asked about, but the words caught in his throat.

Leah stood before him, her gaze cast slightly downward. She wore a gray dress with a red panel sewn into the bodice and looked effortlessly stunning. *How does she always manage that?*

"Forgive me," she said softly. "I see that you are very busy." A smile spread across her face.

"Is something amusing?" William asked, trying to mask his irritation.

"It is only, seeing you in charge here," Leah said in a teasing manner. "I remember a boy that told me he dreaded this very thing most of all."

William recalled confessing to her that he had no desire for the burdens of leadership. But he was not in the mood to reminisce with the girl who had broken his heart. What purpose could that serve?

Still, he recognized that she was attempting to lighten the mood and didn't want to seem rude, so he kept silent.

"Perhaps this is not a good time?" Leah suggested when he didn't respond.

"It is not," William agreed, "but I do not expect things to improve anytime soon. What can I do for you, Leah?"

"I do not wish to take too much of your time," she said, glancing around the busy great room filled with servants and workers. "Is there somewhere more private where we might talk?"

"Private?" William mused. "The library, I suppose." When Leah didn't object, he led the way through the castle and up the stairs until they reached the familiar oak doors. He pushed them open, revealing a room restored to how Leah remembered it from countless visits with Martha before it had been turned into a war room during the siege.

Leah stood in the entry, letting the memories wash over her.

"Are you alright?"

"It is just this room," Leah said softly. "I almost expected to see your mother sitting at that table waiting for me.... I love this room."

"Of course," William nodded. "I had forgotten that you had as many memories with my mother here as I do. Only now the table stacked with the endless business of the barony is my responsibility. Will you sit?" He gestured to the sofa across from the table.

Leah hesitated only a moment before sitting on the edge of the sofa.

"May I offer you some refreshment?"

"Nothing for me."

"That is just as well, as I am not certain there is anyone to answer the bell, even if I were to ring."

William resisted the urge to sit beside her as he would have in days past. Instead, he turned a chair from the table around and sat to face her. "I find that I still cannot stand for long," he explained.

"I never would have guessed," she said. "You are looking very fit."

"Me? What of you?" William protested before he could restrain himself. "You carry yourself as though nothing had happened."

A brief smile flickered across Leah's face before vanishing, leaving an awkward silence. William hated the tension but understood there was no way around it. Their past intimacy had been sweet but was now a relic of a relationship she no longer wanted. What choice was there but to try to force any social interactions into the proper form of a young lady and a young noble, even if it was like trying to drive a wagon in ruts on the road where the wheels did not quite fit.

"What can I do for you, Leah? I do not mean to rush you, but it turns out that rebuilding a barony is far more work than destroying one, and it appears that part of my penance involves overseeing every last detail personally."

"Yes. Forgive me for imposing," Leah said, her voice trembling slightly. "It is only that, well, I have not been able to rest since I was so beastly to you at our last meeting. I have written and discarded at least a dozen letters trying to explain myself, but that seemed, well, cravenly. The very least I could do is face you and explain my actions in person."

"Lady," William said, raising a hand to stop her, "I assure you that is not necessary. The arrogance and impropriety with which I descended upon you before—to say nothing of the strain I put upon you while you were convalescing from wounds you received protecting me—is inexcusable. The fact that you did not have me thrown off your land only speaks to your grace and refinement. You are a lady, Leah, to the very core. I—"

"No, please do not do that!" Leah protested with such vehemence that William abruptly stopped talking. "William, do you not see? This is exactly why I had to come." Her voice was thick with emotion. "I left you feeling rejected, as though you were unworthy of *me*. William, I could not face you that day in the garden because I could not bear to see you after failing you and your family so catastrophically. After all that you did to rescue me—rescue all of us—I could not endure seeing you barely able to stand as a result of the wounds inflicted upon you because of me, and I absolutely could not tolerate any professions of affection. That was more than I could bear."

"Leah, what are you saying?" William asked, bewildered. "How could you think yourself unworthy of anyone, especially me? The only reason I am here now is because you sacrificed yourself to save me!"

She tried to meet his gaze but could not and dropped her eyes. "William, I am not the noble woman you believe me to be. During the siege, I learned much about myself that I would rather not have known; but the memory I am least able to bear is what I did to the man who sacrificed almost everything to save us."

"Leah?" William's confusion was almost comical, but this was not a moment for levity. She was carrying something heavy, and he was going to have to hear it, even if he did not want to.

Tears were streaming down her face now, but she still did not look up. "William, please do not interrupt me until I have said what I have come to say. I will willingly submit to whatever rebuttal you deem appropriate after that."

William nodded, bracing himself for what was to come while trying not to let his imagination run away with him.

"William," Leah's voice trembled as she spoke, "*I am responsible for your mother's death.* Anisa, Amir's sister, found Martha and me hiding in the chapel that day before you found us. She tried to kill us, but we managed to overpower her. Martha ordered me to kill her, as I was the only one with a weapon, but I refused. I allowed Anisa to escape. Martha was chasing after her to do what I was too weak to do when she ran into Thomas and the Nizari."

William was stunned. He opened his mouth to respond, but Leah held up a hand to stop him from saying anything.

"No, please," she said, wiping her eyes, "I am not finished. You see, I *hated* you, William. You hurt me so deeply when time and time again, you left me languishing here while you kept running away. I finally accepted Anthony's proposal because I believed that you did not want me. But when you took up with my sister, it cut me more deeply than I can express. Every insecurity I harbored about why you did not want me was confirmed in that moment. Eve was more beautiful, more charming, more spellbinding than I was. It reinforced my deepest fears that the reason you never came back for me was because you knew there were better, more desirable women than me."

"Leah," William interrupted gently, "why are you telling me this?"

"Because I need you to understand why I acted as I did," Leah said, producing a small cloth to wipe her face, only to have her cheeks instantly wet again. "It does not make it right, but I need you to understand why, even if you hate me for it."

William lapsed back into silence, and Leah continued, her voice breaking. "In my anguish, the love I cherished for you all those years turned to bitterness. I do not know if I ever said it aloud before," she managed a small chuckle and wiped her nose, "but I loved you since we were children. So when you rejected me after all the waiting and hoping for your return, it hurt more than I can say. I was angry and devastated, and that anger turned to hatred. I needed you to be the villain. And when I saw you in the chapel that day we went to rescue Martha, I wanted to believe that you were a traitor. I *needed* to believe that you were a wicked murderer. And if you had killed Eve, then I was justified in hating you. I know it does not make any sense!" She almost screamed at him when he opened his mouth to protest. "But I needed it to be true! Because if you were a vile, despicable traitor, then the fault wasn't with me for being rejected—it was with you!"

"That is why, William..." Leah trailed off, visibly gathering the courage to continue. "That is why I aligned with Thomas against you. I wanted to see you punished for what you did to Eve... for what you did to me. And that is why Anthony attacked you; because I made him swear to kill you if given the chance. He did not believe that you had betrayed us, but I convinced him it was so and exacted his vow of vengeance.

She paused, drawing in a shaky breath. "But then, in the Hall of Arms, I finally grasped the truth. I was forced to confront the fact that it was you who had remained faithful, while *I* had betrayed *you*.

"In my desperation to prove to myself that I was something more than I had shown, I went in search of a way to redeem myself. And to be honest, I forgot all about Anthony and his vow until he burst from the crowd, charging toward you. I knew at once what was happening and threw myself in his way to protect you from what I had done—to protect you from me."

William was stunned into silence. Leah's rejection in the garden had been painful, but this new revelation was overwhelming. To hear her admit that she had loved him, only to follow it with an admission of deep-seated hatred that led her to order his execution, was more than he could process. And what was he supposed to do with the revelation that his mother was dead because of her?

"Do you see now, William," Leah said, rising from her seat, "why I could not allow you to believe that I had rejected you because of something you had done? I was thrown into the refiner's fire and watched as layer after layer of my character melted away, revealing nothing but dross. There was no pure sterling beneath, as I had always wanted to believe. That is why I released Anthony from his vow of marriage and why I cannot bear the thought that you might believe yourself unworthy when the fault lies entirely with me."

She stood a moment, waiting for a response, but William was so shocked and horrified that words utterly failed him. What could he say? How could he reconcile the love he felt with the pain she had caused?

Leah walked to the door and paused with her hand on the latch. "Please know, William," she said without turning back, "that I would give anything to undo what I have done. I will not be so presumptuous as to ask for your forgiveness—that is too much for anyone—but please know how truly sorry I am."

With that, she was gone, leaving William sitting in stunned disbelief. The world he had been trying to piece back together had once again shattered, taking with it any semblance of understanding that he thought he had.

William remained where he was, staring out the window until long after the sun had gone down. How had the woman and the relationship that had once represented his ideal of happiness and safety turned so bitter?

It was hard not to view his current life as some grotesque mockery of what could have been—a beautiful possibility turned tragic.

One question echoed relentlessly in his mind: *What now?*

Sixty-seven

How are you settling into your new role, Baron?" Henry asked with a grin, having come with the latest caravan from Braddock Court to check on Dawning Court's progress.

"This is awful!" William exclaimed without hesitation. "Why would anyone fight to do this? I would happily go to war just to avoid being a baron."

Henry's grin widened, and William groaned. "Ugh, do not tell me you are actually enjoying this?"

"What is not to enjoy? We give orders, and people follow them. I get to focus on planning, building, and solving problems rather than clashing swords with brutes."

"Well, I suppose you are naturally suited to this," William begrudgingly conceded.

"It will grow on you," Henry assured him.

"I doubt it," William replied. "In fact, I think I now understand why Braden was always at war—it was his excuse to avoid all this."

"Well, you may want to wait until the barony is a bit stronger before you start a war."

"I was thinking of attacking Braddock Court," William grumbled, "I heard only a dozen men took Braddock castle recently."

Much to William's surprise, Henry laughed rather than getting defensive. "But then the war would be over in a week, and you would have two baronies to manage."

William shuddered, and Henry chuckled again before turning serious. "William, I have a delicate matter to discuss with you."

"I am nothing if not diplomatic," William replied dryly, sinking into a chair and draping his leg over one arm.

"Yes, I have often heard that said of you."

"I am, after all, the noble ruler of Dawning Court. Now tell me, what is on your mind, Henry?"

"I wish to marry again," Henry said.

William's mind immediately went to Leah, and a knot tightened in his stomach. Henry had long pined for her. Though he'd tried to hide it, even a deaf and blind dog could not miss the change in his demeanor around her. "Oh?" William responded noncommittally.

"Well, as you know, Mary is...no more. I am seeking your counsel because I have not always proven the best judge in these matters."

"Henry, I am happy to help, but you may have noticed that I am not exactly surrounded by young maidens myself. I might not be the best advisor on this topic."

"I do not need courting advice; I need objectivity."

"Very well. Is this someone I know?" William asked, still feeling the knot in his stomach.

"No."

"Then she's perfect."

"She's a peasant, William," Henry blurted suddenly.

William paused. "A serf?"

"No. But she is a woman without station or means."

William raised an eyebrow. "That will not do much to strengthen our family, which, if you have not noticed, is not exactly at its Zenith."

"Does it help if she is currently in the employ of an enemy?"

William stared at him for a moment. "Er, yes."

Henry looked down. "It is an impulsive flight of fancy. I am mortified that I even gave voice to such foolishness."

"Now hold on there; before you fall on your sword, tell me about her."

Henry briefly described Katriane's efforts to support her family, omitting the more sordid details and the fact that Edward was her employer.

"You clearly must care for—what was her name? Katriane?—if you are even contemplating such a thing."

"It is difficult to explain. She is the first woman with whom I ever felt that I could truly be myself. Is that nonsense?"

William shrugged. "Probably, but it is nonsense that I understand. And does she care for you?"

"I believe she does, yes," Henry said after a brief hesitation.

"Well, it is not a difficult problem to solve," William said with a shrug.

"How so? Lord Ambroise despises me!"

"So? Just offer him money."

"No, you do not understand. He really and truly hates me. He would likely retain her services simply to spite me."

"Oh, come now. Over a servant? How could you possibly have engendered that much rage in someone...who is not related to you?"

"That army I used to rescue the barony?" Henry said, looking away in embarrassment.

"Yes?"

"It belonged to Lord Ambroise," Henry confessed.

"So?"

"So, he may not have exactly given his consent to the endeavor, and my taking them may have left him vulnerable to rivals."

"I see; well, if you send them back with—"

"And I may have burnt his vineyards when I left ... which may have burnt his house with it."

"Are you in earnest?" William asked, though he saw the truth in Henry's averted gaze. "No, you cannot negotiate with him."

"No, I rather thought not."

"However, I think you are missing the obvious solution."

"And that would be?"

"Simply provide for her family on condition that Katriane leave Ambroise's employ. She is free to leave, I presume?"

"Of course!" Henry snapped his fingers. "Then Ambroise never even need know that I was involved."

"And she is free to seek you out."

"I will send her a gilded wagon train! What? You do not think that wise?" Henry asked when William shook his head.

Again, William shrugged. "It is your decision. But if you swoop in with gold from the Braddock coffers to rescue her and her family, then usher her back here to propose, that is a tremendous obligation on her. Whether she loves you or not, how will that feel any different than working in Ambroise's household? She is obviously a very dutiful woman; will she not feel like she is moving from one overlord to another?"

"I had not considered that."

"Do not fret," William laughed. "Ensure that she has the means to pay for her passage and that she knows that she is welcome here; but leave the decision to her. If she chooses to make the journey, then I would say that that is a very positive sign; if she does not, well, you just avoided another disastrous marriage."

"Surprisingly wise…"

"For one so foolish?" William finished for him.

"For one so *young* is what I was going to say."

"Of course."

"And the fact that she is a peasant?"

"The way I figure it, we brothers have done about all we could to destroy this family. If we could not do it, this probably won't either."

Henry stood up, smiling. "Thank you, William. I will act on your advice at once."

"I will walk you out," William said, also rising. "I need to make the rounds through Dawning Court and see where work is stalled. If I lose track for even an hour, not only do they stop working, but I think they actively work to undo everything they had accomplished."

"Very well, William," Henry said as they walked the halls of the castle. "You have helped me with my romantic troubles; allow me to help you with yours."

"Henry, there has to be the prospect of a romance for there to be a romantic problem," William pointed out.

Henry stopped and looked at him seriously. "What about Leah?" he asked. "She has always loved you—" He grabbed William's arm and pulled him back when he started to walk away. "She has always loved you, and you have been in love with her since you were fifteen! I know that Anthony left. Do not continue making the same mistake you have been making for years!"

"Henry, I appreciate your concern, but you must believe me when I tell you that the situation with Leah is far more complicated than you can imagine. Impossibly complex."

"From the outside, it appears the same as it has always been. She has turned yet another suitor away, and my brother is too stubborn or too stupid to swoop in and snatch up the most eligible lady in the kingdom."

"I understand how it may appear," William could not hide the emotion in his voice as he spoke, "but believe me when I tell you that it is not what it appears."

Henry gazed at him for a moment before saying, "Forgive me, William. I did not mean to cause you pain."

"Pain? What pain?" William tried to sound casual, though he discreetly brushed away a tear, hoping his brother wouldn't notice.

"I know you cared—care—deeply for her. I am sorry that it did not work out."

"Well," William said as they resumed walking, "there are plenty of fish in the sea for the regent of a ruined barony.

"You jest, but there are plenty of noblewomen who would be interested in a handsome, unattached baron."

"Thank you," William said.

"Oh," Henry sounded surprised. "I was talking about me. But, yes, I am sure there is some woman with low enough standards who does not yet know you, whom we could con into—" He was cut off when William lunged at him. Henry laughed and fled from the castle, with William shouting threats and chasing him into the courtyard.

Sixty-eight

A week later, the courtyard—now restored, with only the west wall still under construction—was filled with people once more. This time, however, the atmosphere was festive rather than fraught with fear and anxiety. Tables were set up for the hundreds of guests in attendance.

Dawning Court's serfs, villeins, returning nobles, and a few newly pledged knights had been invited to the celebration. Entertainment abounded, with an abundance of food provided by Henry and Braddock Court. The lively atmosphere almost made it possible to forget the recent siege and the toll it had taken on everyone present.

At the head table, situated on the steps leading into the Great Hall as a makeshift dais, Grace sat with a smiling Henry on her left and a frowning William on her right. William knew he needed to be here, but he still found himself looking longingly at the waist-high west wall, wishing he could jump over it and escape from all this.

He sighed, hunched lower in his seat, and hid behind his wine glass, hoping that no more people would approach him to tell him what a hero he was or try to engage him in conversation. He had never liked crowds and pageantry, but this was his reality now. This was what he had agreed to when he took the responsibility of the barony from Grace. He was now the face of Dawning Court, so there would be no more slinking off with Eve into the night.

He sighed again. He missed Eve all the more during moments like this because she had shared his disdain for such events. Even if they could not have slipped away, she would have been someone to laugh with about the fact that he was a prisoner.

As he scanned the crowd, his gaze landed on Leah, who was seated at a nearby table with her family. He had been avoiding looking in her direction all evening because each glance felt like a painful stab in his heart. This time, however, he did not look away. Leah was not looking at him but making conversation with a stream of well-wishers who wanted a moment of her time. Unlike William, however, she was not shutting down the conversation as quickly as possible; she engaged with each person, displaying genuine interest, regardless of their status.

You could learn from her, Martha's voice sounded in William's head.

Stop that! He ordered himself but found himself arguing as though he were speaking to his mother. *She is the reason you are dead!*

Do not be silly," came Martha's response in the exasperated tone she used when he failed to see the obvious. *Leah is not the reason I was killed any more than you were.*

But you would not have been there if she had not forced you to chase after Anisa.

And I would not be dead if you had protected me. Does that make my death your fault? Or does it simply mean that you are human and cannot do everything? Leah did not force me to do anything. I well knew the risks when I went after that assassin. But my blundering into Thomas and the others slowed them down enough to allow you to catch up to them.

She betrayed us! William almost shouted, determined to hang on to his pain.

She was hurt, confused, and exhausted. And wasn't clinging to her resentment, as you are doing now, exactly what caused her to behave as she did?

William continued to watch Leah. He repeatedly caught himself admiring her beauty, charm, and kindness. When she laughed at something, he felt a pang of jealousy. He longed to be the one making her laugh, to feel her affection again. But he quickly shut down those thoughts. *Too much has happened! That bridge between us is too damaged to ever cross again!*

Do you think that is what I want?

But you were endlessly forgiving, William protested. *I am not like you.*

"She is going to move on."

William almost jumped out of his skin when he realized that not only was someone actually speaking to him, but that someone seemed to have been reading his mind.

"What?"

"Leah," a significantly reduced-in-size Grace said, leaning over to him in a way that would have been impossible a few days before.

"Er ... what makes you think—"

"You have been staring at her long enough to constitute a threat," Grace smiled. "She will have other suitors, and she will move on soon."

"She is very beautiful," William reluctantly acknowledged.

"Is that what you think? That it is her beauty drawing people to her?"

William looked at Grace's incredulous face and suddenly felt uncomfortable. "Uh, well, not just that; she is also very charming."

"William," Grace said as though she were speaking to a dull child, "it is her *light* that attracts people to her. She radiates goodness and kindness. That is what makes her pleasant features seem extraordinary. Have you—her oldest friend—really never noticed that?"

William looked back at Leah and saw the truth of Grace's words. Leah was pretty, but what made her so irresistible was the way her features radiated goodness and love. "She does not shine so brightly as she once did," he muttered belligerently.

"She has had a rough time, as have we all. But do you think her light is extinguished forever?"

"I do not know," William grumped, feeling defensive. "I am the oblivious friend who does not really understand her, remember?"

"You are oblivious, at that," Grace retorted, though she said it kindly. "So, I am going to make this simple for you. Her light will return and will continue to grow until it exceeds even its former glory; but if you are still sitting on your hands by then, it will be too late."

"You know not of what you speak." William was getting worked up.

"I know enough."

She does not know all that has passed between us, William thought. *She does not know our history, or she would not be so quick to judge.* He turned to suggest as much, but Grace was already greeting a noblewoman who had made her way up to the main table.

"You look like you are about ready to murder someone."

William was relieved to finally see a face he actually wanted to see. "Silas? Where have you been?"

"I did not know if a simple soldier was welcome at the grand table."

"Anything goes under this administration; *I* even managed to procure a seat here."

"It is going to be anarchy."

William pulled him in and embraced him. "Why are you only now finding time to visit?"

"Forgive me, Lord, but you may have heard that there was recently a war here, and it left our homes and fields in a bit of a shambles. Took some work to set them right."

"You know, now that you mention it, I believe I did hear something about that. I heard that a great hero saved the day, despite his incompetent sidekick."

"'Tis true," Silas shrugged, "only it is a bit harsh to call you incompetent."

William laughed at him. "It is good to see you. In earnest, though, I could use your help here, managing the affairs of the barony. If you find that the quiet life of a farmer no longer suits you."

Silas smiled a lopsided smirk at him. "As I'm getting older, I've come to appreciate a quieter life. I've not had to climb any battlements or had anyone try to kill me in weeks."

"Sounds pretty boring to me."

"I will consider your offer." Silas smiled and retreated as Grace stood and called the crowd's attention.

"Good people of Dawning Court," she began, "thank you for gathering to celebrate the birth of the new baron of Dawning Court!" A cheer rose from the crowd, and she waited for it to subside before continuing, a more somber note in her voice now. "It is difficult to believe that it has been only a year since we were last assembled to celebrate the inauguration of my late husband as baron. As you are well aware, he was taken from us all too soon. We lost a great man, a great leader. But all of us lost loved ones in this conflict. We shall remember them with honor by living in such a way that their sacrifices will not have been in vain."

"Long live Baron Dawning!" someone yelled, and a great cheer rose from the crowd. Grace raised her cup to that, and everyone drank a toast.

"But it is not to mourn that we have gathered," she said, setting her cup down again after the modest sip she had taken. "It is rather to celebrate! On this occasion we mark the resurgence of Dawning Court and her people! With the vanquishing of our foes and the birth of my son, Richard, we are ushering in a new era of peace, prosperity, and strength."

She waited for the crowd to cheer and drink again before continuing. "Through this terrible ordeal, we lost many, but we also saw many rise up to lead and defend us in our darkest hour. Every man and woman in this company played some part in that, and each one of you should feel a great swell of pride for your valor. You, the people of Dawning Court, met the finest trained warriors that our enemies could produce and withstood them all!"

The crowd erupted at that, and it took a full five minutes before they settled down enough for her to continue. "It would be impossible to list by name all those who distinguished themselves in this conflict, so I will not attempt to do so. We would be remiss, however, if we did not take a moment to honor a few individuals whose bravery, sacrifice, and wisdom, are the reason we are still here today.

"Ordinarily this would be the baron's responsibility, but since he is currently asleep in his cradle, I will delegate this to our regent, who has graciously agreed to act as leader of the barony until young Richard comes of age. William?"

William reluctantly stood, and the crowd again erupted in wild cheers, the stories of William's exploits having circulated thoroughly through the people thanks to Silas, Finn, and many others telling their stories at every opportunity.

William did not like the attention. While he understood that he had contributed a lot to their victory, all that was on his mind was all the people he could not save and all the ways he had inadvertently made the situation worse. He did not feel like a hero and did not want to be treated as such.

"William, will you do the honors?" Grace took her seat again, leaving him standing awkwardly in front of the entire barony.

"You all understand, I trust," he said when he could again be heard, "that I am about the least noble nobleman in the realm?"

Another round of cheers.

"But Richard taught me something in the short time we were graced with his leadership. Leadership is not about decorum—of which I have none—it is about serving your people. I want to assure you that my priority is to see that my people thrive." More cheering.

"As Lady Dawning indicated, there are a few individuals that we need to recognize here. Henry, will you stand?"

It took much longer than William had hoped to work down the list of contributors that needed to be named. But it was the list of those they had lost that really proved difficult to get through. He got choked up speaking of his mother, which emotion carried over when talking about Timothy being killed by Amir while standing up for her, and even more so when he recounted Eve's sacrifice, such that he had to pause to compose himself before continuing.

"And finally, I would be ungrateful indeed if I did not mention Sir Anthony," William concluded. This caused a lot of whispered conversations throughout the audience, word of William's own life-threatening injury having spread. "Anthony's sacrifice in blood and sweat to preserve this barony was exceeded only by those who gave their lives for it. Nobody else worked so valiantly or fought harder than he did to preserve our freedom. I only wish he understood what a hero he is to us."

William turned to yield the floor back to Grace but seeing that she had gotten emotional and was in no condition to stand in front of everyone, instead he said, "Now, please enjoy yourselves! You have earned it!"

The crowd cheered and drank; the minstrels started to play, people began to dance, and the festive atmosphere returned as quickly as it had left. But William could not seem to shake the heaviness that had settled upon him while he spoke. Instead of joining in the celebration, he used the moment to slip off the dais and out through the partially constructed wall. He had used up the little energy he had to spare for social occasions and wanted some time to be alone.

The sun had nearly set, the evening was warm, and there was something strangely comforting about all the barony being engaged in celebration. Though the world was not as he would have chosen it, in a flash of clarity, he realized that this was a rare moment of peace to be cherished. Though there was sadness, the people were resilient. They were rebuilding, and for the moment, at least, they were safe.

William walked up by the river to the footpath that wound in and out of the trees, a path he had walked a million times, usually with Leah.

"May I walk with you?"

William turned, an excuse for wanting to be left alone halfway to his lips, but he stopped. Leah stood there looking slightly embarrassed, not quite able to meet his eyes, evidently unsure of what reception she might receive.

William did not know what to say. The jolt of excitement he always felt at seeing her was quickly replaced by the warring voices in his head: one reminding him of the mistakes she had made, and the other telling him that his stubborn refusal to allow her to be human was making him even more miserable.

"I could use a break from the crowd," Leah half-laughed to try to break the tension.

"I was...just walking the footpath."

"Up to the lookout?"

"I—uh—had not really thought about it."

"I have not been to the lookout in...I do not know how long. I was probably last there with you."

"Please, join me," William said politely, though in truth he was thinking that he really would have preferred she not be there. He just wanted some time to clear his head, but with her present, his mind would be running at a frenzied pace, analyzing every word, every action for the smallest nuance, trying to interpret its meaning. It was exhausting.

"How are you settling into your new role as regent?"

"As well as can be expected, I suppose."

"In earnest, I was surprised to hear that you had accepted the responsibility."

"Why surprised?" he asked, feeling his defenses go up.

"I remember you referring to leadership as something like a prison."

William grimaced. "And so it is. But what my younger self never quite grasped is that when duty calls, it does not ask about your preference. Were it just about that, I assure you that I would not be doing this!" He could not keep the bitterness he felt about having to shoulder such a heavy responsibility alone out of his voice.

"Well, I am proud of you, William. Few know as well as I how contrary a role like this is to your nature."

"My nature," William repeated. He had not meant it to sound defensive, but it came out that way anyway. In that moment, all of the overwhelm, worry, and loneliness William had tried to keep below the surface for weeks now suddenly came spilling out. In the face of his own insecurities, Leah's words felt like criticism and mockery. "You think me unaware of how unfit for this role I am? I never wanted this, but there was no one else!"

"William, I did not mean—"

"John is dead! Richard is gone! My mother is dead! Who else was there, Leah?"

Leah did not turn away from his formidable anger. She saw in him all the anguish that was feeding it, and it no longer frightened her as it had in the past. Now she could see the little boy behind the eyes, the one who was trying his best but felt completely overwhelmed and utterly alone. Instead of responding to his ire with ire, she reached up and touched his cheek.

"William," she almost whispered, "I never realized—I never considered how lonely this must be for you. I have thought only of my own loss. Yet I still have people. I should have recognized that you are staggering under the weight of this responsibility with no one to lean on."

William looked away to hide his eyes from her; she always saw too much. "*You* were my people, Leah. Don't you understand that? You were the only person that I ever felt truly safe with."

Leah abruptly dropped her hand. "That is not true. You chose—you had Eve.

"Why would you say that? I started spending time with Eve because she was the only person who was even willing to be around me. You had agreed to marry Anthony, and I was alone. Eve was a ray of light in the darkness when I so desperately needed someone—anyone. And I will always love her for that."

That statement twisted in Leah like a sudden stab to the heart, and her own pain surged up in response. "I wanted to be that person!" she almost screamed. "I wanted you to come to me, come after me, need me, but you never did!"

Now it was William's turn to bite back the angry retort and pause to consider what she had been through. "I—I never wanted you to be alone, Leah. It pierced my heart to think about my Leah, running out her life here alone, waiting for someone as worthless as me. But I wanted to be with you, in your arms, more than anything in the world!"

"Then why didn't you let me in?" she demanded in tearful exasperation. "How much pain could have been avoided?"

"Leah, if I had it to do over again, I would have swept you off your feet the moment I had the opportunity. But I was hurt, confused, and so scared. I knew that I was not worthy of you and believed that the selfless thing to do was to let you find someone better, more deserving."

"Why did you never ask me what *I* wanted?"

"Because I was terrified of what you would say. I was scared that you would be settling by choosing me, but so much more worried that you would not want me."

Both of them were silent as they thought back over all that had happened between them. "Oh, William, if only we could start over." She covered her eyes with her hand, heartbroken at the realization of all that had been lost.

William looked up and saw the sun had very nearly set, and an idea occurred to him. "Come with me," he said, taking Leah's hand and pulling her after him.

"William, where are we going?" she asked but let herself be led up the path until they crested the peak of the lookout.

"Here," he said, gesturing out over the trees and walls of Dawning Court to the horizon that was exploding with fire. "It is just like the night I left."

He heard Leah's breath catch, and he turned to her with unexpected emotion. Taking both her hands in his, he looked into her hazel eyes that were wide with expectation.

"Leah, there is so much that I would go back and change if I could. That is impossible now, but we could still have a bright future if we are brave enough not to continue the mistakes of the past. Leah, you are my good angel. I have loved you since I was fifteen. Do you..." he trailed off, afraid to ask the question, but then continued. "Do you feel the same about me, even after all this mess?"

"I do." Her words were barely a whisper.

"Then do you think we might still pretend we were those same naïve children, with hearts so full we could not contain it? Do you remember when we were on this same hill, with the same sun setting on us? It seems a lifetime ago now. And I cannot speak for you, but my heart was overflowing with love for the angel who stood before me ... who stands before me now. And my heart would burst again with that same love, if I would allow it to—if I felt safe to allow it to. Do you think, in this moment, we could let go of all the death and darkness and pain? And this time, instead of running away, we could do it right, the way we should have from the beginning—together.

Leah stared into his eyes. Oh, how she wanted to believe they could do this! But how could she just let it all go? How could she just forget all the heartache and pain and trust that he could do the same? She couldn't stand to be hurt again; could she trust this man with what was left of her wounded soul?

"I love you, Leah. I have always loved you, and I will never stop loving you. I want you in my arms, where I may know that you are safe and I, in turn, am whole."

And with that, the last of Leah's resistance melted away. "Oh, William," she choked out. All the heartache, the loss, the longing, all of it came gushing out as she threw herself exultantly into his arms. "I love you, William, desperately!"

They clung to each other in a passionate embrace, as though they might be ripped apart at any moment.

"Marry me, Leah?" he said to the top of her head, unwilling to relinquish the closeness with her that he had longed for his entire life.

"Yes, William!" she cried, tears streaming down her face as she looked up into his eyes.

William kissed her then, passionately, urgently; and she returned it with all that was inside her.

"It took you long enough!" she muttered when they finally separated. William grinned as he wiped away the tears coating her cheeks.

"But Leah, are you certain you are willing to take the name of the regent of a disgraced barony?" he asked, only half in jest.

"We can work through it," she chuckled, "provided you do as you are told for once."

He kissed her again then and held her close till long after the sun had disappeared, neither wanting to let go of the other.

"I suppose," he said after a while as the two sat together, William leaning back against a tree with Leah leaning back against him, enfolded in his arms, "that I am going to have to ask for your father's blessing."

She nodded.

"You are aware that he hates me, maybe even more than Amir hated me?"

She nuzzled into him with a sigh. "I think you might find him more agreeable to the idea than you imagine."

"Why is that? Did he get hit in the head?"

"You know," she said coyly, "my father is at the celebration. You could ask him tonight."

William's eyes bulged. "Why would you want to ruin the sweetest evening of my life?"

"Would you rather wait and agonize over this, or get it over with?" She was already standing up and pulling him to his feet.

William's stomach tied in a knot at the thought, but he realized that she was right. So much better to get the unpleasant deed over with; the problem was, he genuinely did not know what to do if Aden refused. Where did that leave them? Their engagement would be over before it had even begun.

Nevertheless, he let himself be led back down the path toward Dawning Castle and the celebration.

When they arrived, Leah did not hesitate. She did not even pause long enough for William to collect his thoughts. She led him straight over to the table where Aden and Anne were seated.

"Father," she said, "Lord William wishes to speak with you privately."

Aden looked up at his daughter's beaming face and then at William, and his frown deepened.

"Er—if it is convenient," William added lamely.

Leah released William's hand and pulled Aden out of his chair. "Listen to what he has to say, father, and be nice to him!"

Anne looked between their faces, and her hands went to her mouth in surprise. Aden, after a moment of stunned silence, grunted. "Oh, very well." He walked with William a short distance away from the crowd before turning and glowering down at William expectantly.

"Er, yes, well," William began awkwardly. He really had no idea what he might say. Though he recognized that this may be one of the most crucial conversations he would ever have, second only to the one he had just had with Leah, he knew that Aden hated him. In fact, the last time they had met, in Aden's camp, they were exchanging death threats. How did one go from that to asking for the man's only remaining daughter's hand in marriage? "I suppose that I should begin by asking your pardon for the things I said in your camp that night I arrived seeking your help. That was not my finest hour."

Aden closed his eyes and held up his hand to cut William off. But what he said next surprised William. "That was neither of our finest hours. I let my own feelings cloud my objectivity at a very critical time, and it nearly cost me everything.... I am given to understand that you are the reason it did not."

He left it there, halfway to an apology; but William took that as the best opening he was likely to receive and plunged in. "About those personal feelings..." he almost lost his nerve, when Aden visibly tensed. "I ... have been in love with your daughter for as long as I can remember." Aden's frown deepened, so William increased his rate of speech in hopes of getting out a barrage of persuasion before Aden had a chance to respond. "I have sensed that you never particularly cared for me, and I would not blame a father for not being thrilled with me as a suitor. The disgraced youngest son of a baron, who was constantly putting himself and those around him in harm's way—I would not want such a person coming near my daughter."

Aden's eyes narrowed, and William realized that not only was he not making his case, he was doing just the opposite. "But," he added quickly, "my circumstances have changed; I have changed. I have done what I could to mend my reputation and right my many wrongs; and my situation now will allow me to provide for your daughter. She will not want for anything."

"And will she want for her husband, a confidant, a safe place to call home?"

Those questions caused William to flinch because they struck at the heart of his character. Would he be there for

Leah through the hard times, or was he still that boy who would lash out at and run from every problem?

He paused a moment before responding. "I understand your concern, and in truth I do not blame you. But I beg of you to consider that recent events have changed me, have humbled me. Indeed, it would be hard for any man to not be changed by all that has happened of late.

"I know there is still so much for me to learn, a lifetime of lessons. But it is clear to me that I will learn those lessons better and faster with Leah by my side. I know I am not worthy of her. But I love her, and if you will grant your blessing for me to marry Leah, I will show you my gratitude for the rest of my days by doing everything I can to ensure her happiness. And with her at my side, I will no doubt become a more prosperous, wiser, better leader than I could ever hope to be without her.

"I know I am asking a lot—I am asking you to have faith in me when I have given you little reason to do so. But if you could see into my soul, you would see that I am in earnest and that your faith in me will not be misplaced." Having poured his heart out to Aden with all the sincerity he could muster, William finally lapsed into silence and nervously awaited his response.

Aden continued to glare unflinchingly at William while he stroked his chin thoughtfully. "You pose a problem for me, William. You are flippant, crass, and wild, the sort of man I would not trust with the transportation of a bushel of wheat, let alone with the future happiness of my daughter."

"Er...um...sorry," he responded awkwardly, not knowing what else to say.

"But then I also saw something else in you during the war. I saw a boy who gave every last bit he had to try to save his people—even to save me from myself. It would have been easy for you to give up after all that you had been through. But you kept going, kept trying, though it almost cost you your life. I did not expect that of you."

Hearing the not totally negative tone, William did not dare speak again for fear of ruining the moment.

"But the bigger problem is Leah." Aden nodded back at the table where Leah and Anne were watching intently, only turning away and pretending to be engrossed in conversation when both men looked their way. "She is my light. Since she was born, she has brightened my world and the lives of all those with whom she has interacted. I would never want her to be with anyone who would dim that light."

"It is a gift to the world," William agreed.

"That light has been gradually getting dimmer for months. Her mother and I have despaired of what to do for her."

He left that hanging in the air, as though William were supposed to address it, to reassure him that William could fix it and all would be well; but he had no idea what to say. "Er ... well—" he started, but, mercifully, Aden cut him off.

"That right there," he said, nodding at Leah, "Is the happiest I have seen her in recent memory. It may gall me, but I have no choice but to honor my own rule; I cannot do anything to dim her light."

William was so excited that he thought he might burst. "Do you mean—are you saying—" He couldn't bring himself to say it in case he was wrong.

"Yes, William. I give you my blessing to marry my daughter."

William was so giddy that he impulsively hugged Aden before quickly withdrawing in embarrassment.

"Perhaps we should return?" Aden suggested to end the awkwardness they were both feeling as a result of William's impulsive gesture.

William wanted nothing more than to race back to Leah, but he forced himself to remain with Aden as they walked back toward the table. "Remember, William," Aden added just before reaching the waiting women, "I live right down the road. I will hear if you do not treat her right, and I will come calling."

"Er... yessir."

Leah was on her feet in anticipation before they had reached the table. Aden still looked severe, and William tried to look solemn as well to keep her guessing as long as possible, but he could not hide his grin as he got near her.

She ran to him and threw her arms around him, and he held her close despite how self-conscious he felt under Aden's scrutiny.

Tears started in Anne's eyes as Leah released William long enough to hug her father. "Thank you," she said, and he squeezed her tight.

"Is this going to make you happy?" he asked her softly.

"More than I can ever say."

"Then perhaps something good came out of this war after all."

"Good?" She pulled back to look up at her father. "How could any good come from something so terrible?"

"Because had I not seen what I did of your husband-to-be during that time, I would have gone to my grave determined to prevent this union."

She stared at him, trying to wrap her head around all the implications of that statement. Could something so horrible as war, that had wounded them all so deeply and taken so much from them, actually produce something good?

"You two must announce this at once," Anne said excitedly, "while all the barony is present."

William looked over at Leah with his crooked smile. "Well, shall we make it official? Last chance to back out."

"Are you getting cold feet already?" she asked as she linked her arm in his to walk to the dais.

"No, not at all. But maybe just one more trip to the Holy Land before—ouch!" William jumped at the pinch on his arm and turned to look at Leah, whose face had not changed a bit. "Wow, you really are a stateswoman."

They reached the dais, and Leah banged on a glass to get the revelers' attention. "Forgive the interruption," she said, "but Lord William has one last announcement to make."

"Yes, well," he said, suddenly awkward with every eye upon him, "many of you have noticed the problems with the reconstruction of the west wall. I have decided to imprison the stone-mason—ouch!" William jumped again. "Oh, and I have asked Leah to marry me, and she has consented."

William felt a little foolish taking everyone's time for something that was so intensely personal. He, of course, was excited beyond words, but why should they care? But when a thunderous cheer went up in response to his announcement that was so loud, they might have heard it in Braddock Court, he began to think that perhaps the people had more of an interest in the two of them than he had realized.

"And of course, you are all invited to celebrate with us!" Leah added, which prompted a second round of cheers and toasts.

"Oh!" Leah suddenly exclaimed. "What of Grace?"

They both turned toward the baroness, and Leah let go of William long enough to face Grace, who was just approaching them. "Lady, I fear this is the very soul of impropriety, with Anthony having so recently departed."

Grace just smiled. "I could not be happier if I had orchestrated this myself." William's eyes narrowed then, but Grace was already moving on. "I am pleased beyond words for the happiness of two people I love dearly."

Leah put her hand on Grace's shoulder and kissed her cheek. "And I could not be happier to have you as my sister."

Grace hugged them both and then made her apologies and retired.

"Are you at peace with that?" William asked Leah as they watched her walk away.

"Anthony is a good man," she admitted frankly. "But I could not in good conscience marry him when my heart has always belonged to another."

Relief flooded William. Of course, he had hoped that was the case, but to hear her admit to feeling exactly as he did filled him with such indescribable joy that he thought he might burst. All he could do was pull her close again. "I hope this man you love is worthy of you," he said with mock severity.

"Oh, he is a scoundrel," Leah returned without missing a beat, "a no-good brigand...and he is perfect for me."

William sighed in contentment, "I cannot imagine what you ever saw in me, Leah. I truly am a scoundrel, but I love you more than words can ever express, and I cannot imagine living in a world without you by my side. I love you," William whispered to her.

"It is about time you figured that out," she said, and they kissed again, gently but warm and lingering, reveling in each other, with nothing between them at last.

"That knucklehead is going to be your son-in-law," Aden grumped to Anne, taking her arm in his as they watched the pair up on the dais. "Are you resigned to that?"

"She could do a lot worse."

"Is that so? How?"

"She could marry someone she does not love."

Aden did not respond, but there was no question as he watched the pair that they adored each other with their whole hearts. Maybe Anne was right. Maybe they would be okay after all.

Sixty-nine

William stepped out onto the balcony of the baron's suite late at night, long after the wedding festivities had died down and he and Leah had been allowed to slip away. He breathed in the crisp night air. Leah *Dawning,* his wife—he still loved the pleasure that came each time he thought of that designation—was asleep in their bed behind him. His heart was filled to overflowing with love for that woman. He thrilled that she was finally his, and he hers.

The night was silent, and a nearly full moon bathed everything in a cool glow. The manor houses stood silhouetted beyond the wall, but now, instead of a collapsing castle and barony, he saw clearly the signs of new life. Somehow, this duty that had begun as a monotonous drudgery, with the promise of nothing but a lifetime of interminable obligation, had turned into something beautiful and exciting. What had seemed once to be prison walls now looked to be the beginning of a great adventure with the woman of his dreams by his side. He felt safe. He felt complete.

Gone was the intense melancholy of the past few weeks. Gone was his hopeless despair, as though it had never existed. All he could see now was hope and joy. For the first time, he started to believe that he could handle his calling. He *could* lead Dawning Court through this precarious period of regrowth, now that Leah was with him.

For just a moment, William thought of his mother, David, and Richard, and wished that they could have been here to celebrate with them today.

Suddenly, William's eyes were brimming with tears, but they were not tears of sadness. Rather he was filled with overwhelming gratitude. Gratitude not just for his beautiful wife nestled into bed behind him, but for all the people who had crossed his path and helped him along the way. It now seemed almost like God had planted each one of them to be present at his weakest moments.

From Jurou's discipline in putting William on a path, to David's selfless act even in the face of his humiliation, to Neal and Anthony and countless others being willing to sacrifice everything to defend his people. In fact, the more he thought about it, the more people he identified that had given him something he would never be able to repay. Not just major influences like his mother, who had carried the barony all alone for so long, and Richard, who even in his last hours, when he was so weighed down with thoughts of his wife and unborn child, still spared a thought for his wayward youngest brother; there was also Hildebrant, who had protected him from being murdered by Amir, even when Hildebrant no doubt felt betrayed by William. Finn, with his endless optimism, had spurred William to keep trying even when all seemed lost. Aden had allowed his last precious daughter to marry William despite his many flaws. Grace, rather than harboring a grudge, had supported and even encouraged their marriage. And finally, all the people of the barony, his people, had chosen to move forward and get to work despite their own personal losses.

After only a few months as regent, William had been ready to quit and flee the responsibility. Only with Leah, the most amazing woman he had ever known, working with him did the task now seem manageable. That his mother had shouldered the burden of the barony alone all those years, even as her own sons schemed and plotted against her, was rather remarkable...Perhaps Leah was the second most amazing woman he knew.

William sank to his knees, humbled beneath the realization of how blessed he had been throughout his life. He turned his face up to Heaven to express his gratitude for everything and everyone who had been put in his path to help him along the way. He cried his thanks that he was born of one angel and passed off to another. He realized now that even at his lowest ebb, when he had believed himself to be a lone wanderer in the world, without a single soul who cared for him, he was never really alone. As much as he had told himself otherwise, he had never been forsaken.

When William had emptied his heart of all that was in it, he was again filled with an excitement like he had never known, enthusiasm for what the next day would bring, and so much gratitude for the fact that he would be spending it with Leah.

He got to his feet and returned to bed, leaving the balcony doors open so he could feel the contrast of the chill air against his skin while he was tucked up safe and warm with his wife. He slid beneath the duvet and pulled his wife to him, reveling in her closeness and all that feeling entailed. All the years of loneliness and desperate longing were finally at an end for both of them.

She stirred slightly and snuggled into his chest while he wrapped her in his arms and squeezed her in a protective embrace. He was overflowing with a love that words could not express. He was safe. He was home.

Epilogue

Near Mount Alamut

Khalid awoke suddenly. Something was wrong. He snatched up the dagger he always kept nearby. One could not be too careful when transporting a prisoner alone.

It was still dark, but his eyes darted to the tree near the fire where he had left Thomas tied for the night. He was gone! He had escaped.

Khalid jumped to his feet. He could not afford to lose him now, not when they were so close to Alamut. Thomas was Khalid's bargaining chip with the brotherhood. Thomas could prove that the others were dead and possibly even be used to make another attempt on the Dawnings if Hassan still had an appetite for that. But without him, Khalid's own life may just be forfeit.

Khalid stole silently around the wagon, dagger held at the ready, but Thomas was not there. He again turned in a circle to verify that his immediate perimeter was clear before he knelt down by the tree where he had tied his prisoner. Both Thomas and the rope with which he had been bound were missing, but as Khalid had hoped, the fine, dry sand of the desert had left clear tracks.

Khalid started into the sparse trees, slowly, carefully. There was no rush. Though Thomas was dangerous, his wounds had not been healing well on the road, and he would be both slow and weak. As long as Khalid could find his tracks, Thomas would not get away; and without a weapon, he would not be able to prevent Khalid from bringing him back.

He moved farther in. Thomas had not been trying to hide his tracks; was he just in a hurry, or was he trying to lure Khalid into some sort of trap?

Khalid bent down to see if he could learn anything else from the prints. Perhaps Thomas had help?

Then he heard something up ahead. The trees were sparse enough that had it been daylight, Khalid could have seen well enough to identify the source of the sound; but as it was, he had to hurry. If a desert animal had gotten Thomas...

Khalid ran into the trees and stopped. There were no more tracks. He listened, bent in a crouch, knife held at the ready.

When someone touched his shoulder, he almost jumped out of his skin, spinning and swiping his blade before he realized what he was looking at.

Thomas' feet had touched Khalid's shoulder from where he was swinging by the neck from a tree branch. He had used the rope that had bound him to hang himself.

The End

About the Author

James Batchelor was born in San Jose, California, the ninth of ten children. He was raised in California, Utah, and Arizona. He received a BA in History and a BA in Political Science from the University of Utah.

A bit of a nomad, James has lived all over Japan and the United States. He currently resides with his wife, Elizabeth, and their six children near Salt Lake City, Utah.

www.ingramcontent.com/pod-product-compliance
Lightning Source LLC
Chambersburg PA
CBHW071332020726

47502CB00001B/66